AFTER THE FINALE

ZHOU DAXIN

Translated by

WU JIAMEI

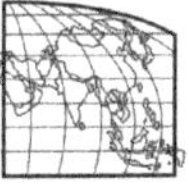

Paperback published by
ACA Publishing Ltd

eBook published by
Sinoist Books (an imprint of ACA Publishing Ltd)

University House
11-13 Lower Grosvenor Place
London SW1W 0EX, UK
Tel: +44 (0) 20 3289 3885
E-mail: info@alaincharlesasia.com
Web: www.alaincharlesasia.com

Beijing Office
Tel: +86(0)10 8472 1250

Author: Zhou Daxin
Translator: Wu Jiamei

Published by ACA Publishing Ltd in association with the People's Literature Publishing House

Paperback ISBN: 978-1-910760-83-3
eBook ISBN: 978-1-910760-84-0

A catalogue record for *After the Finale* is available from the National Bibliographic Service of the British Library.

AFTER THE FINALE

ZHOU DAXIN

Translated by

WU JIAMEI

ACA PUBLISHING LTD

To my cyberfriends,

Darlings! A few days ago, I was entrusted by a mother and a daughter to write a biography of a deceased governor. At present, material collection phase has ended, the biography is still being written, and it is estimated that the work will be completed in two months. At that time, I would be very grateful if you guys could put this biography on your WeChat platform and make it available for more people to read. Right now, if any of you who happen to work in a publishing house read the following materials I have collected, believe in my ability to write a biography, and feel this biography is worth being published and has the potential to make money, please contact me. My requirements are 50,000 initial prints with hardback binding and 12% royalty. My mailbox is 666666666@163.com and my mobile phone number is 1999999999.

Yours sincerely,

Zhou Daxin

MATERIAL DIRECTORY

DEATH NOTICE

GOVERNOR OUYANG WANTONG

Comrade Ouyang Wantong, former governor of Qinghe province and deputy secretary of the Party Committee, passed away at 11.28pm on 10 February 2015 in Chengzhou at the age of 66. A farewell ceremony is to be held at the Lan Hall of Yinshan Funeral Parlour at 9.00am on 17 February 2015, followed by cremation.

Ouyang Wantong Funeral Committee

11 February 2015

1

CHANG XIAOWEN

THE WIFE

MR ZHOU, I'm very grateful to you for accepting the responsibility of writing Ouyang Wantong's biography. My daughter and I have read your previous books, and we both believe you'll do a good job. We would like to be the first readers once you've completed the first draft. The second remuneration will be transferred to you upon our authorisation of the book. We entrust you with the task of letting the world know him through your words and giving future generations the knowledge that a governor like Ouyang Wantong lived in this world.

Shall we begin now? Let me tell you what I know about him first, and then you can go to interview others who are familiar with him. You're free to choose anyone you want to interview – we won't interfere.

Where should I begin? Well, let's begin with the night he died.

That night, a folk band from Beijing came to perform in Qinghe. I knew he liked listening to folk music, so I asked Secretary Zheng to book two tickets in advance. When he found the last item on the programme was the suona performance of *A Hundred Birds Worshipping the Phoenix*, he agreed to go. He was especially fond of this one, and whenever he came home from work, he would ask the nanny to play this music for him. His chauffeur knew his preference too and always played the CD with this music in the car, and he never got bored with it. I was very happy that night as I accompanied him to the concert, hoping it would help him relax and get out of his post-retirement discomfort quickly.

I noticed he listened very attentively when the concert began, with smiles all over his face. When he was still in office, he was occupied with so much work that seldom did we have the chance to go to a concert together. During the interval, I went to buy him a cup of hot tea. He took a few sips and told me the concert was great. I laughed and said: "It's good you like it!" At that time, I never expected it would be our last night together. The second half of the concert began, and he enjoyed that as well, beaming all the time. When *A Hundred Birds Worshipping the Phoenix* on the suona began, I noticed he became very excited, clapping his hands several times during the performance. He even stood up suddenly when the suona player was finishing the last note, perhaps paying his tribute to that musician. As I was about to stand up with him, he sat down and covered his chest with his hand. I asked him what was going on, and he said he just felt a little bit uncomfortable. I kept asking whether he needed to go to the hospital, but he shook his head and declined. His driver came over and helped him walk out of the theatre. When we arrived home, he looked quite pale. I urged him to wash his hands in the bathroom and asked the nanny to bring a glass of milk which he drank every night before he went to sleep.

When the milk and a small plate of snacks were set on the table, Wantong finished washing his hands and came over to sit down. However, I noticed that he didn't drink the milk as usual but sat there still, holding the glass in his hand. Only when I reminded him of this did he come back and take a small sip.

He remained silent while drinking the milk and he didn't respond to me when I spoke about the concert. I went to the bathroom to wash and then went to the bedroom to change into my pyjamas.

When I returned, I heard him talking to himself: "My mother told me not to walk away with any stranger – I don't know you."

At the time, I thought this was funny, and I interrupted him: "What are you talking about?"

He turned around and looked at me blankly: "Did I speak?"

I smiled and went into the bathroom again to prepare the tub for him, not realising that it was actually a symptom.

After I made up the bed, he came out of the bathroom with his pyjamas on. I reminded him to dry his hair in case he should catch a cold, but he did not answer. I felt this was strange, so I turned around to look at him and was surprised by what I saw – he was sitting on the sofa beside the bed, staring straight at the corner. I followed his sight and looked at the corner, thinking the nanny had placed something there that she shouldn't, but there was nothing – it was as clean as a shining mirror. When I looked at him again, he was talking to the corner: "Who has sent you here? I'm going to sleep. What on earth are you doing here?"

Hearing that, I froze and asked him: "What are you talking about? Who are you talking to?"

He continued with a serious look: "You should make an appointment with my secretary Xiao Zheng in advance. You can't break in without permission. I haven't been sleeping well recently!"

I was still amused by his solemnity, not realising that it was indeed another symptom. I said loudly to him: "Hey, Wantong, who are you talking to?"

He raised his head and looked at me, a trace of bewilderment and confusion flashing in his eyes. A few seconds later, he turned to look at the corner again, shook his head and resumed his normal appearance. He sighed: "Did I really see something there? I thought someone had come to me for help and was sitting in the corner right there."

"Even if someone wanted to do that, how could he enter our bedroom?" I was still laughing at him.

"You're right," he smiled a little, as if taking a joke on himself, and went to lie in bed, silent again.

When I switched off the bedside lamp, he suddenly reached out his hand and grabbed mine, which surprised me. It was something he used to do when he wanted to make love with me. But after he turned sixty-two, he seldom did that – probably because of physical impotence, for which he sometimes would apologise to me: "I'm really sorry! I couldn't make you happy!" Whenever he said this I would always smile and comfort him, saying I was not young anymore, and my lust was gone as well, and the most important thing for both of us was to take care of ourselves.

That night when he repeated that action, I mistook it as a sign that he felt good enough to do that with me, so I moved closer and snuggled up to him. He held me in his arms and whispered to my ear: "Xiaowen, it's a little cold here! Have you switched on the air conditioner? Don't you think the temperature is too low in the room?"

I told him I hadn't. The heater was still on and why would I turn the air conditioner on? I remembered he had complained about pains in his ears and teeth a few days ago, so I started to worry that he might have a fever caused by the inflammation of his ears and gums. I touched his forehead with my hand, but there was no fever. Then I pressed my forehead against his to double-check, and it seemed everything was all right. I remembered once reading a book that said people had physical and psychological feelings about temperature – he probably felt cold in his mind. I pulled out my arms and hugged him, whispering in his ears: "Go to sleep. You'll feel warmer after you fall asleep. We might go to the hospital tomorrow."

I fell asleep first that night. Perhaps it was because I was younger than him. I released his arms unconsciously and lay on my back as usual. In my dream, I seemed to hear him utter a cry, but I was too exhausted after a whole day of gym exercise to wake up and check what had happened to him until I was dragged out of my sound dream by a continuous touch. As I opened my eyes, I felt his hand clutching my pyjamas and poking my side feebly, which drove my sleepiness away at once. I turned to him immediately and asked what was the matter with him. He didn't answer. I was so scared that I sat up and turned on the lamp to check what had happened. There he was with a painful look on his face, clenching one hand on his chest, while the other was holding something towards me. I knew immediately he was suffering from a heart attack. With my first-aid knowledge from books, I fumbled for the quick-acting heart reliever pills under the pillow, put them under his tongue and grabbed the phone to call the ambulance.

But it was too late.

When the doctors came, his eyes had already closed. They tried their best to save his life for quite a long time, but finally they announced that his heart had suffered from a massive infarction and there was nothing they could do. Crumpled up under the shocking news, I began fixing his pyjamas on his body and found that there was a key held tightly in his hand, which reminded me that he tried to hold his hand towards me when I was woken up by the noise. I then realised that he had wanted to give this to me before he died. With tearful eyes, I looked at the key, wondering why he kept it to himself since it was me who usually kept all the keys to the house.

His body turned cold little by little, while I went blank little by little. You know, since he was older than me, I would sometimes think about the day when we would be parted, but never had I expected that day would come so quickly! Wantong, how could you leave me alone in the world like this?

The doctors later told me that the pains in his ears and teeth were, in fact, a kind of symptom of a heart attack, and his discomfort in the concert hall that night was indeed a sign too. What if I had taken him to the hospital at that time? I'm so stupid. I'm not a good wife, and I'm such a fool!

After his death, I remembered he might have already had a hunch about the coming of this day. It was a couple of weeks earlier when I took a walk with him along the Yulin river, together with his secretary Xiao Zheng. He spoke to Xiao Zheng about the news that a will depository centre had been established in the city. He wanted him to enquire about the registration process and specific formalities because he wanted to write a will and save it there. I stopped him and said we both could live up to eighty or ninety years old at least. The thought of being an old widow was ominous.

He must have felt something wrong with his body – otherwise, he wouldn't have talked about his will. What a thoughtless blockhead I am! Why hadn't I taken this into consideration?

I first knew about him when he was the mayor of Tianquan. You want me to tell you the whole story? Well, it'll definitely involve some private details. Do you think it's proper to make it open to the public? I'm afraid you'll need to be sure about what you can and can't write before you start the biography. All right, I trust you. At that time, I was fresh out of university and assigned to work in the Tianquan Public Security Bureau. I saw him almost every day on *Tianquan Daily* and news programmes of Tianquan Television Station. He always had an imposing appearance and walked very energetically. In my eyes, he was a political celebrity in Tianquan, an awe-inspiring official, and I had never thought there could be any story between him and me – an ordinary and unimportant police officer – and I could never have expected there was a silk thread wrapped randomly around our hands by an unknown force.

It was on 18 January 1988. China Southwest Airlines Number 222 Ilyushin IL-18 crashed on its way from Beijing to Chongqing, and 108 people died, including 10 crew members and 98 passengers. Only six days later on 24 January, Number 80 Express Train from Kunming to Shanghai derailed, leaving 90 people dead and 66 seriously injured. In response to the two accidents, the State Council issued an urgent announcement calling for an inspection on any potential problems of poor management, loose regulations and slack labour discipline in all regions. This document about public security was sent to our Public Security Bureau too. It was in an afternoon when my colleagues and I were listening to this announcement that a comrade in the office walked in and waved me out. I thought he just wanted me to fetch some office supplies as usual. I went out with him but surprisingly found a minivan with curtains in front of the building. He pulled the door open for me and asked me to get in. I was very surprised and asked where we were going.

"Get in the van!" a man's voice came from the van. I looked inside and recognised a deputy director of the Provincial Public Security Bureau dressed in plain clothes. Beside him was a deputy chief procurator at the provincial level. I had seen both of them in the newspapers. I understood immediately that this was a special task. I was right. When I got into the van, I was informed that we were going to arrest an important person and my task was to knock at the door. The action group gave me some ordinary clothes that city girls usually wore, and I put them over the top of my uniform while sitting in the van.

I was very nervous because it was the first time I had taken part in such a mission, and with the provincial leaders!

The van was driven directly into the city government's residential area. I felt that the person we wanted might be living in this place. It was the first time I had walked into this courtyard, and I had little knowledge of the residents living there. The van stopped in front of a three-storey apartment building, and the deputy director handed me an envelope and said: "Go to the third floor, knock at room 302. If someone asks who you are, tell them you're delivering a document from the Municipal Government Office. When the door is open, your task is complete. Someone else will take care of the rest." I nodded, took the envelope and got out of the van, followed by two plainclothes officers – a man and a woman keeping a distance of about two or three metres away from me. Seeing them walking hand in hand, I could see they were disguised as a couple. The van drove to the other end of the building after the three of us got out.

It was about noon. The people who walked up or down the staircase didn't ask us who we were, believing we were relatives of someone living in the building. I walked to room 302 and rang the doorbell. There was a mirror in the door, so the people inside could see me. I thought about the reason why I had been chosen to do this. The people inside the room didn't know me. Fresh from university, new in the bureau and a non-native here, few people knew me. I rang the doorbell twice, but no one came to open the door, which made me a little nervous. I wondered whether it was my dress that had caused suspicion in the house. To my relief, the sounds of footsteps and a voice came when I rang the doorbell for a third time. "Who is it?" I answered immediately as the deputy director had told me. The door opened with a click, and a girl, about eighteen or nineteen years old, stood in front of me – she looked like she might be the nanny. Behind the girl stood an elegantly dressed middle-aged woman, who asked why she hadn't been notified and why she didn't know me. There was no need for me to answer because the two plainclothes hiding nearby had already rushed into the room and grabbed the two arms of the woman. Then I realised this woman was the person we needed.

My mission was complete, but to cover their action, I slid into the room and closed the door quickly. The middle-aged woman didn't resist but snapped at us: "Are you going to do this in broad daylight? Don't you know whose home it is?"

The male plainclothes said to her as he handcuffed her: "Yes, we know. You're Lin Qiangwei, the director of the Tianquan Land Bureau. We're from the Provincial Procuratorate, and this is the arrest warrant." When the woman heard this, she was stunned.

As we were about to leave with Lin Qiangwei, something unexpected happened. A person outside was opening the door with a key. It was obviously the resident of this house who had just returned. The two plainclothes and I exchanged surprised looks. The door opened, and the man standing outside was Ouyang Wantong, the mayor! My goodness! How could it be the mayor? The moment the door opened, I saw the look of shock on Ouyang Wantong's face. He looked straight at the male plainclothes, who on the contrary didn't look surprised at all, indicating that he had known in advance who they came to arrest. He took out the warrant and said: "Mr Mayor, we're acting on instructions, please excuse us."

I was shocked. I noticed that Mayor Wantong had put on a serious expression. Without looking at the warrant, he waved towards the door, signalling us to leave. When we went out with Lin Qiangwei, she uttered a cry: "Wantong, save me!"

That was the most panic-stricken shout of a woman I ever heard.

When we came out of the building, the minivan was already parked in front of the unit. We got in and left quickly.

A few days later, I learned that the mayor's wife had been taken away. Ouyang Qianzi, the mayor's son, who was studying in the United States, had been arrested at Capital Airport. They were being held on suspicion of bribery. Someone reported to the Provincial Commission for Discipline Inspection that the mother and son had taken bribes totalling 900,000 yuan – a shockingly huge amount at that time. They presented photos and recordings of the mayor's wife asking for the money.

After a secret inspection, the Provincial Commission for Discipline Inspection confirmed the report and transferred the case to the judicial departments. Honestly speaking, what happened that day was a big shock for me. It was the first time I had witnessed the ebbs and flows in the political arena so closely and the awkwardness of municipal-level officials.

A week later, about clock-off time in the evening, news came that Mayor Wantong had been dismissed from his office. The Public Security Bureau is governed by the municipal government, so we had always been respectful and cautious when we talked about Mayor Wantong, but after hearing that his wife and son had been arrested and he had been dismissed, people's attitudes changed immediately. Some made fun of him, some commented ironically, some spouted bitter words and some even insulted him with abuse, which shocked me quite a lot. How surprisingly fast people's respect and reverence for political celebrities would disappear!

It was probably the tenth day after that morning that I went out in casual clothes after supper, ready to meet my best friend for a chat. Walking along, I suddenly caught sight of a man strolling not far in front of me under a dimly lit street lamp. I discovered that it was the dismissed Mayor Ouyang Wantong! Yes, I was quite certain it was him because a few days ago I had a very close look at him. Where was he going? For a walk? To visit a friend? Out of curiosity, I changed my plan and tailed him slowly.

I could tell he was in a miserable psychological state from looking at his back. He was hunching forward, shoulders sagging and stumbling along, which was miles away from the person I usually saw on television.

He walked along the street until he stopped beside the Kuan river, where there were no street lights and no sign of any living creatures. Following him plodding along the riverbank in the darkness to the distance, I came to the conclusion that he was probably looking for the right spot to jump into the river and end his life. I was scared and asked myself what I should do. How to stop him? As a girl, did I have the strength to hold him back? You know, I didn't have a mobile phone at that time, and there was no way for me to call for help. I had to go on following him and racking my brains about how to stop him from jumping into the river.

Finally, he stopped and stood facing the river. It was a place far from the urban area and was surrounded by nothing except the darkness of the night and the sound of the wind stroking the river. He lit a cigarette and, in my estimation, he was struggling. I was afraid he would jump into the river after he finished the cigarette, and it was at that moment I made a decision to knock him down first. Though I was not strong enough to pull him back, my combat training at the Public Security Academy made it totally possible for me to attack him and throw him down on the ground. Yes, knock him down first and then reason with him!

With this idea, I approached him stealthily, and in a big stride I dashed towards him and kicked the back of his legs when he was unawares. As he flopped onto the ground, I shouted: "Ouyang Wantong!" My voice was so loud that I myself was shocked. Ouyang Wantong was clearly frightened and didn't say a word for quite a while.

"You can't simply jump into the river and kill yourself like this! The case of your wife and son hasn't yet entered the trial process. What's more, you have your parents to think about! It's so irresponsible of you – a man – to do this!" I went on shouting at him, grabbing one of his hands at the same time.

About two minutes later, his voice came to my ears, not very loud but clear enough: "Who told you I want to kill myself?"

"Why did you come here then?" I asked.

"I was dismissed, but no one ever said they would restrict my freedom – or tell me that I'm not allowed to take a walk along the riverbank."

"Are you telling the truth?"

"If I did want to kill myself, don't you think it would be easier to hang myself at home? What's the point of coming all the way down here and jumping into the river, especially for someone like me who can swim?"

"Oh!" I was sort of tongue-tied when I heard this.

"You're from the Public Security Bureau?" he asked.

"Yes."

"Responsible for watching me?"

That was not true. I shook my head hurriedly. "I saw you by chance in the street. I was curious at first. Then I thought you were going to kill yourself, so I followed you here."

At that time, I let go of his hand.

"Well, thanks for your concern. Now everyone except you is afraid of my bad luck and stays away from me. I'm very grateful for what you just did. Could you tell me your name?"

Now he was sitting upright on the ground.

"My name is Chang Xiaowen."

"Have we met before?"

"No. The first time I saw you was in your house when your wife was arrested on that day."

"Oh, I see. Yes, you're the youngest one among them."

"Sorry, I shouldn't have kicked you down just now."

"No, no, what you did has warmed me quite a lot and let me know there are still some people who care about me. You know, a moment ago before supper today, my secretary, who has been working with me for many years and who I've been treating as a family member, refused to take my call for fear that he might get involved."

"Don't take it so hard." I tried to comfort him.

"Thank you. It's rather difficult to let it go all at once."

"You should look at the respect and reverence you have received as being for your title as a mayor rather than for you as a person. When you're not a mayor anymore, it's quite understandable for people to withdraw their respect and reverence. Try this and perhaps you'll feel better."

"You're right!"

"Nowadays, people are very resentful of those who extort and take bribes. Some of your family members have been arrested for taking bribes, so it's quite normal for people to make irresponsible comments and sarcastic remarks. You should be mentally prepared for this. Suppose you were one of them – wouldn't you feel angry if you heard that someone had resold government land approvals and taken public funds as their own or asked for bribes from others?"

"Yes, you're right. Whoever receives bribes and breaks the law should be punished."

"It's good for you to think like this. I have to go." With those words, I turned around and left.

That was our second encounter.

About a month later, I heard he got divorced from his wife Lin Qiangwei, who was subsequently formally charged with taking bribes. His son was released. Two weeks later, he was miraculously reinstated in his former post, appearing in television programmes and on the front page of *Tianquan Daily*, which nobody really expected. People in the bureau gossiped about how he could come back so fast – they spoke very carefully and quietly of course. As for me, although I was a bit surprised at his comeback, I quickly put him and his family issues behind me. You know, I hadn't had any other contact with him – the difference of rank between us was huge, and our lives barely overlapped.

One day, six months later, he came to inspect our work with his subordinates. After the inspection, he said to our director that he wanted to have a word with me. Our director was startled at first, and then he said: "Xiao Chang is a good comrade. It was me who told her to go to your house on that day. It had nothing to do with her."

When I was asked to meet him in the office, he was sitting there alone, having resumed the confident look he used to have. He said: "Xiao Chang, my family has experienced some misfortunes. Some people kicked me when I was down and rubbed salt into my wounds, some scolded and made insulting remarks, some gave me the cold shoulder, and some chose to stay away from me. All of this gave me a taste of this cold world. It was you, a stranger to me, who cared about my life and death sincerely. I'll never forget that. If you have no objection, I want to invite you to have lunch with me tomorrow at noon to express my gratitude."

I was very surprised by what he said. I didn't think he would still remember that small incident, and never did I expect he would invite me to lunch so formally. I had no idea what to do. Decline him? Would it be an offence to him, the mayor? Accept the invitation? Would there be rumours that I was playing up to him? Sitting there quietly, he looked at me with a little smile, waiting for my reply. It was probably his sincerity that moved me, so I said: "All right. Thank you for the invitation. Where shall I meet you?"

"Juxiang Restaurant in Qingfeng Street. See you there then."

That was our third encounter.

The next day, I put on some light make-up, dressed in casual clothes and went to Juxiang Restaurant. You know, it was totally out of politeness that I accepted the invitation – no other reason at all. But it turned out that I, a freshly graduated student, had to pay a price for meeting with such a public figure in this small and underdeveloped city.

He booked a small compartment and sat there waiting for me quite ahead of schedule. When I arrived at the restaurant and entered the room, he asked what I liked to eat, and I answered that I had no preference – whatever he chose would be fine. That was my first time to sit face to face with a man who I knew so little, let alone a man who was a mayor. I felt ill at ease. He ordered a lot of food and a bottle of white wine. I told him that I didn't drink wine, so hc ordered a glass of freshly squeezed watermelon juice. He then reached out his wine glass and touched gently with mine, saying: "Xiao Chang, here are the words from the bottom of my heart – thank you very much! You don't know this, but you did save my life that night. You're my benefactor!"

I stared at him wide-eyed, having no idea of what he meant.

"The truth is, when I went to the Kuan river that night, I did think of ending my life."

"Oh!" I was shocked by his words.

"I was beaten, although not heavily, during the Cultural Revolution because of the issues related to my father-in-law and also because of my low rank in the government. My life, though full of ups and downs, generally speaking, went on smoothly. Facing such a disaster in my life for the first time, I was struck so heavily that I didn't know what to do. You know, my wife and son were both arrested. I was removed from office. All my efforts in the first half of my life proved futile, all on the charge of bribery, a crime inexcusable in any dynasty. I was ashamed, I was bitterly humiliated, and I had no way out but to think of ending my life. On that day after supper, I was heartbroken when my secretary had turned his back on me too. I suddenly felt it was meaningless to go on living in this world. I made my way towards the river thinking about jumping into it. I didn't tell you the truth that night. You know, I don't know how to swim, so if I had jumped into the water, I would have died at once. Fortunately, you followed me and knocked me down on the ground at that critical moment. What's more, your words awakened me. I suddenly realised I had my parents to take care of and my family members in custody were waiting for me to find them a lawyer. I couldn't commit suicide like this. I couldn't. If I had done that, I would be seen as the one who had taken bribes and then committed suicide for fear of punishment."

Looking at him, I secretly congratulated myself for being there that night. It had been right for me to follow him out of curiosity.

He was very sincere in expressing his gratitude to me. He said many words of thanks and stated clearly that he would always be available whenever I should need his help.

I was glad because this kind of connection would definitely benefit me in the future. Whenever I should encounter problems in this city, I could turn to him for help. However, I didn't realise it would never be that simple to make friends with a person like him.

Just a couple of weeks after the lunch invitation, my best friend, who had just introduced a boyfriend to me, asked me very seriously: "Don't tell me you're willing to be that man's mistress if you can't marry him?"

Feeling as if I'd been hit by a stick, I grabbed her hand and said: "You're talking nonsense! Whose mistress am I willing to be?"

She said nothing, but took out a few photos and handed them to me. Good heavens! All the photos were from my lunch with Mayor Ouyang Wantong! In the photos, he was fetching me dishes, he was serving me juice, and he was chatting with me!

I was shocked and questioned her angrily: "Who did this?"

She told me she didn't know, and she simply was shown them by a friend who worked in the Commission for Discipline of Inspection. She took the photos secretly and came to me for verification. Also, her friend in the commission kindly asked her to send me a message – be very careful when meeting with the mayor.

Outraged by the rumour, I told the whole story to my girlfriend, but I could tell she was taking my words with a pinch of salt, which hurt me deeper. Nowadays, too many government officials had mistresses, and even my best friend found it hard to believe in my innocence.

The guy to whom my girlfriend introduced me didn't contact me any more after the photo incident. I knew it had something to do with those photos! I ground my teeth and cursed under my breath: "What a jerk! A few photos could steal your trust in me! Obviously, you have a lack of discernment! It's better not to date such a man."

Some days later, I noticed something in my colleagues' eyes when they looked at me – full of ridicule, contempt and flattery. I knew they probably heard about the photos. I felt wronged, and I felt indignant, but I was unable to explain it, which choked me quite a lot, and I wanted to have a quarrel with someone. Then the chance came.

One morning, a section chief asked me to come with him to deliver a subvention report to the municipal government. I was surprised and asked him why, since it had no connection with my work duty. He cast me a significant smile and said: "Aren't you familiar with the municipal leaders?"

Hearing this, I understood what he meant. Exploding with rage, I swore at him: "You animal! Why don't you go back home and ask your younger sister to go with you instead? Are other girls the same as your sister?"

That was the first time I had ever cursed someone like that. And in public! I had been driven crazy by what he said and behaved like a bitch without thinking about the consequences, totally abandoning the manners that a lady should have.

The very afternoon after I threw my tantrum at that section chief, I walked my bike straight up the bank of the Kuan river alone after finishing work, not in the mood to eat anything. I sat on the bank for quite a long time, staring at the rolling waves of water and thinking about what I should do. My fit of crying and swearing simply made the whole matter open in the bureau. Yes, people would not talk about it to my face from now on, but behind my back it was impossible for most of them to believe my innocence. Would I have to endure their looks forever? Could there be any man who was willing to be in a relationship with me after I made such a spectacle of myself? Why did all this have to happen to me?

It was almost twilight when I stood up and got ready to go home. Turning around, I found Mayor Ouyang Wantong was standing a few feet behind me. Startled, I asked him why he was here. He grinned at me bitterly and said: "I'm worried you might be taking things too hard."

Hearing this, I burst into tears and then cried out with my hands covering my face. He stood there still and then said in a muffled voice: "I'm sorry. Never did I expect that it would bring you so much trouble. I shouldn't have invited you to dinner. Now I understand that when a man is in politics, he might bring blessings to his friends – riding on one's coat-tails as we say – but meanwhile he might cause endless troubles or even disasters. I apologise to you again for getting you into trouble! Tonight, I came to see you simply because I want to help you out. We have two choices. First, job transfer – I can find you a new working environment. Second, I can transfer you to another city. What do you think?"

I stopped crying, looked at him and then shook my head. I didn't want to have more contact with him, and either a job transfer or moving to another city would eventually indicate that he had helped me, which would be impossible for me to explain. People would gossip about how the mayor could help a young woman for no reason, and I would definitely be regarded as his mistress. Nowadays, people would always presume that when a young woman had certain connections with a government official, she must be either a potential mistress or a mistress already.

At the end of that year, Ouyang Wantong's family case came to an end. Lin Qiangwei's second trial verdict was announced, and she was sentenced to 15 years' imprisonment. His son, Ouyang Qianzi, received a demerit punishment. And it was also at the end of that year that somebody introduced me to a man who worked in the university where I used to study in the provincial capital. His name was Zhu Tuo. He had been a teacher but later volunteered to work in the Office of Academic Affairs in the university. He was seven years older than me, plain looking and had a modest family background. Anxious to leave Tianquan quickly, I didn't want to wait for someone better. I agreed to marry him with only one requirement – transfer me to the provincial capital as soon as possible.

After I got married to Zhu Tuo, I was transferred to the provincial capital as he had promised, but I had to work in a suburban police station because it was very difficult to enter the Provincial Public Security Bureau at that time. My husband and my new workplace were far from my expectations, but I was at peace because I came to understand that there would always be some distance between what you really want and what you could get, and we should cherish what we have at present.

Six months later after we got married, Zhu Tuo came back from work one day and told me that there was a vacancy for the role of dean at the Office of Academic Affairs and he wanted to apply in order to advance in the political arena, since he had already given up his dream to be a professor. I supported him of course. He then said there were so many people who also wanted the position and the competition would be quite fierce, so he needed to work out some other ways. When I asked him about his plan, he told me it definitely wouldn't work to approach a school leader because the other candidates would do the same thing – the best way was to find a municipal leader to put in a good word for him. I sighed and asked him whether he knew any of them. He smiled and shook his head, saying: "I don't know any of them, but you do." I was very surprised and asked how could I, such an unimportant police officer who had just been transferred to Tianquan. Smiles prevailed on his face, and he said: "Don't you know Ouyang Wantong, the ex-mayor of Tianquan? He was appointed the mayor of the municipal city yesterday. A friend in the Provincial Public Security Department, who consulted the people in Tianquan Public Security Bureau, told me that you and Mayor Ouyang Wantong knew each other very well."

"What?" I stared at him. I was shocked by the news and wondered how it could be so coincidental. I married and moved to the provincial capital, and then he was transferred here. Had Zhu Tuo heard about those rumours from those people in the Tianquan Public Security Bureau?

"I'm an unimportant civilian police officer. How could I have a word with the mayor?" I wanted him to give up this idea.

"You'll never know if you don't give it a try," he insisted.

"How?" I was a bit annoyed.

"I'll ask a friend to arrange an opportunity for you to meet him. Having been in the provincial capital for so many years, I have the ability to make it happen. When you see him, ask him to do you a favour. Just have a try. It's all or nothing!"

I hated to do this. You know, I had wanted to stay away from Ouyang Wantong, but now I was required to find an opportunity to get close to him, and it was none other than my own husband who asked me to do it. I knew he thought highly of this opportunity and my refusal would definitely do harm to our relationship. Turning it over in my mind for quite a long time, I felt unable to turn him down and promised to give it a try.

It happened that there was a meeting held by some municipal universities, and Zhu Tuo knew in advance that Ouyang Wantong would attend. He asked me to change my clothes and go to the meeting with him, which made me feel very awkward, but I had to go. The meeting was held in the lecture hall on the second floor of Tianyuan Hotel. Zhu Tuo asked me to wait in the lobby, and when Ouyang Wantong should finish his talk and go downstairs, he would signal me at the second floor so I could wait at the entrance of the elevator pretending to go up. When the mayor came out of the elevator, I could come over and greet him. The whole plan made me very uncomfortable, but I had to abide by his wishes.

Things went as Zhu Tuo had planned. I stood in front of the elevator waiting for the mayor. When the door opened, he saw me first, and before I had a chance to say hello to him, he unexpectedly started the conversation by asking me: "Hey, Xiao Chang, what a big surprise! What are you doing here?"

I replied with a flushed face: "I married a man and have moved here. I heard you would be here for the meeting, so I came to see you."

Those who followed him all stepped aside when they saw him speaking with me. I knew he was busy and it was not the right place to have a talk, so I handed him the letter written by Zhu Tuo and his resume and said: "I'm asking a small favour of you."

He took the materials, looked through them and nodded. "Wait for my reply," he said.

Three days later, I received a phone call from him. He told me he had done some research, and Zhu Tuo was the only candidate who truly understood education and was competent for this position. He had recommended him to the relevant department. About ten days later, Zhu Tuo received his commission as the dean, and he was so happy at the news that he hugged me tightly and turned round and round in the room. That evening, he invited a lot of people to celebrate at home, but I was in low spirits. You know, I had worked in the political and legal system and had witnessed so many cases of the arrest and imprisonment of government officials. I knew that being an official was a high-risk profession. When he noticed that I was not as happy as he was, he said to me: "A dean is equivalent to a county Party secretary and a county magistrate. In the past, it was a prestigious county lord, a post of the seventh rank. Now you're the wife of a county lord, you have no reason to be so unhappy!"

I didn't want to let him down, so I squeezed a smile, refraining myself from telling him that Lin Qiangwei, the director of the Land Property

Bureau, had been sentenced to 15 years of imprisonment. She was a director at division-head level, the wife of a county lord!

In the following two years, I was busy with my work and my daughter. I didn't contact Ouyang Wantong again. It was Zhu Tuo who told me that Wantong had been promoted to become secretary of Municipal Party Committee, a deputy provincial cadre. I said to him the promotion of the mayor had nothing to do with us, but Zhu Tuo grinned and said: "It means a lot to us. You know, the vice dean of our college is going to retire, and when I compete for this position, he's the one we can turn to for help. The higher his rank is, the easier it is for him to help us."

"Why should he do that for you again?" I looked at him square in the eyes, figuring that he wanted me to go to see him again for help.

"Why? For the feelings he has for you!" He smiled playfully.

"What feelings?" I retorted coldly. My eyebrows must have been raised. I guessed he had heard some rumours from the Tianquan Public Security Bureau.

"You're a beauty, and he's a divorced man. Wouldn't it be quite natural for him to have some feelings for you?"

"You bastard!" I threw the teacup in my hand at him. It was the first time I had been mad at him since we got married.

Zhu Tuo moved aside and evaded the cup. He didn't get mad at me, but continued: "Relax! I'm not suggesting you have a crush on him. But it's very possible he has a crush on you, and we should take advantage of this."

"You make me sick!" I shouted out the words that had been hidden in my heart for quite a long time. You know, shortly after we got married, I discovered that he was a man who was particularly addicted to official titles. It's understandable for a man to dream about becoming an official. As the old saying goes – man struggles upwards, water flows downwards. It is indeed part of our human nature. Also, China has been a society where status is important, and people are usually measured according to their rank. That's why it's quite normal for a man to think about becoming an official. But I did look down upon a man like him, whose sole purpose in life was to be an official. Every day, he calculated who was going to be promoted and who wasn't, who belonged to whose clique, whose connection could reach who, which method could knock who down and which relationship could guarantee a position. I didn't know he could be such an official addict until I became his wife. What could I do? I could only blame myself for making such a wrong choice and follow the man I married.

"No matter how much you loathe me, I'm your husband! We're in the same boat. If I get promoted, you and our daughter can enjoy an easy life."

"I don't want to. I can live on my own salary."

I took out my anger on him that day, thinking he would never bother me with this again. But unexpectedly, when the vice dean of the college was reaching the retiring age, he again stuffed a package of gifts and his letter and resume to me and asked me to go to Ouyang Wantong. Without looking at those things, I threw them aside and asked him to do it himself.

He was neither angry nor impatient, but instead kept saying sweet words to me. "My dear wife, I'm sorry to bother you but please help me this time for the sake of our marriage. A vice dean is a deputy prefecture-level cadre, equal to the prefectural government officials in the past. If I could get this position, it would be an honour to the Zhu family. They all say you're the one who brings good luck to your husband. If you do me this favour, I'll always remember your kindness and be good to you for the rest of my life."

It was pretty funny and annoying of him to say it like this.

Under his repeated pleading, my heart softened, and I decided to swallow my pride and go to look for Ouyang Wantong once again.

It was the first time I had visited the municipal residential courtyard, and it was not easy at all for me, a plainclothed police officer, to enter the courtyard.

Luckily, Zhu Tuo had made preparations in advance. He borrowed a police car, drove me directly into the courtyard and stopped the car right in front of the building where Secretary Wantong lived. He then pointed to the lighted room on the second floor and said: "Go and knock at the door. Take your time – there's no need to come out quickly." With those words, he gave me a handbag and drove away.

It was indeed too much to ask for help again after you had already been given a favour. I hesitated, unwilling to move a step forward. The night was pitch-black, which made me feel a little bit better as nobody would notice my embarrassment. I managed to summon up my courage, climbed to the second floor and knocked at the door twice, but no one came to answer. This frustrated me at first but then I felt happy instead. Great! Since the secretary was not at home, I could simply go back without feeling so embarrassed. To my surprise, when I turned around and moved one step away, the door behind me squeaked open. I saw a young man standing in the doorway, asking me in a low voice: "Who are you looking for?"

"Secretary Ouyang Wantong," I replied hurriedly.

"I'm his driver Xiao Tang. If you tell me what you want, I promise to leave him a message." He was quite friendly.

"I… I'm from Tianquan Public Security Bureau, and I… I want to have a word with the secretary about a small matter." I faltered, thinking that if I wasn't asking for help, I couldn't be so humble in front of such a young man.

I didn't expect that the moment I finished my introduction, Secretary Wantong would appear in the doorway, saying to me with obvious pleasure: "Xiao Chang, what a surprise! Come on in. Xiao Tang, serve tea please."

He didn't shut the door on me! I sighed with relief.

I knew he was very busy, so I explained the purpose of my visit briefly after an exchange of greetings. He listened quietly. When I finished, he said without assuming any bureaucratic airs: "Well, I'll handle this and get some information first, but as for the appointment of a vice dean, very formal examination by the Ministry of Organisation is usually required before we submit a list of candidates. If your husband has performed well in the university and is an excellent division-level cadre, I believe he'll succeed. But if he should fail the assessment, there's nothing I can do."

I nodded to agree with him and expressed my gratitude. Then I stood up and said goodbye to him. As I was about to step out of the door, Secretary Wantong returned the bag to me and said: "I appreciate your kindness, but I can't accept the gifts. You know what happened to my family because of taking bribes. I hope you understand." Hearing this, I did as he asked. I took the bag and left his house.

When I arrived home that night, I told Zhu Tuo what had happened, thinking he would be happy with the result. But unexpectedly he complained instead: "Why were you in such a hurry to come back? Wouldn't it be better if you had stayed with him longer and got a definite reply?"

I was a bit surprised and questioned him: "How could my staying longer have solved the problem? Isn't it necessary to pass the department assessment? How could I be so capable?"

He curled his mouth: "Assessment? It's all excuses. The secretary has the unquestionable decision on the appointment of his subordinates. As long as he has a crush on you and touches you, he'll settle this for sure."

"What did you say?" His words shocked me. "What do you mean by having a crush on me? And touching me?"

He hesitated a moment and then remained silent.

"Tell me!" I said. "You should make it clear!" My face darkened, and I felt I sort of understood his implication.

"It's not a big deal to say it plainly. Didn't he have a crush on you in the past? If you had stayed with him a bit longer, he might have thought about his feelings for you. Then things would go very easily." As he said this, his face turned to the corner of the room.

I immediately rushed towards him, swearing: "You bastard!" I reached out my hand to scratch his face. Good heavens! How could there be such a man in this world? How could a husband sacrifice his wife for an official position?

He didn't fight back, but instead dodged and said: "You did ask me to put it straight, and honest words are of course harsh to the ears. But you'll understand after thinking it over for a while. It was you who asked me to say it out loud. If he had done something to you, you could have left at once. Wouldn't it be all right if you lost nothing at all?"

"Bastard! I couldn't bear to live with you even for one more day. Let's get a divorce tomorrow." My tears came down when I said this. Just imagine what a life it would be when the man you had chosen to marry would exchange you for something he wanted! In his mind, the position of vice dean was more important than me! Divorce! I made up my mind at that moment. You know, indecisiveness leads to disasters. Of course, it was painful to make such a decision, which was another important turning point in my life. Who didn't want to live a happy and peaceful life? Although it truly hurt, I had no choice. I couldn't be an object he would use to exchange for an official position. It broke my heart and filled me with regrets that the marriage I had been devoted to was so short-lived, but it was my fate and a disaster I couldn't escape.

He was surprised and unwilling to divorce, but I had made up my mind. I said to him: "Let's do it peacefully and we can look after our own interests. If you dare to drag your feet on purpose, I'll expose all the dirty things you've done to seize the official positions, and then you can say goodbye to your dream of being promoted."

He probably took my threat seriously and gave up any ideas of bothering me again. He followed me obediently and completed all the divorce formalities. When we came out of the marriage registration office, he said to me with a tone of pleading: "We were husband and wife once. A day together as husband and wife means endless devotion for the rest of your life. I hope you won't stand in the way of my future promotion."

I smiled coldly and answered: "Don't worry. I'll let it rot in my stomach. You go your way and I'll go mine. From now on, we're strangers. There'll be no interference with any of your stuff."

After the divorce, I rented an apartment with two rooms and hired a nanny to look after my daughter, beginning a new life of my own. One afternoon, about two months later, I received a pager asking me to call a strange telephone number. I had thought it was something to do with my work, so I called back immediately. To my surprise, Secretary Wantong answered. He said: "If you're free now, please come to the secretary's office right now." I knew it was probably about Zhu Tuo's appointment and wanted to decline, but it was me who had asked for a favour from him after all, and my refusal to see him would be somewhat unreasonable. I had no choice but to go through with it.

When I arrived at his office, the other people had finished their work and gone. His secretary showed me into the office, made a cup of tea for me and left. Secretary Wantong smiled and said: "I'm sorry for keeping you waiting for so long. I just had the result." I was about to tell him that I had divorced Zhu Tuo and there was no need to do anything for him, but he continued quickly: "I'm sorry to break the bad news to you – not only is it impossible for Zhu Tuo to be promoted to the vice dean but also he'll probably go to prison."

"What?" I was shocked by the news and stood up automatically.

"Someone in his college accused him of embezzling public funds. I thought he might be framed by some of his rivals, so I arranged for the Disciplinary Committee to investigate. To my surprise, what they found proved he truly did this. He took 400,000 yuan that should have been used to buy teaching aids."

"He did?"

"Definitely! They never dare to be sloppy with what I've ordered them to do. They have found witnesses and physical evidence, which have been handed over to the Anti-Corruption Bureau. To be honest, I don't want to believe this. You know, it's you who helped me at my most difficult time, and I never want to hurt you or your family. But now I can do nothing about it. For some people, working as a public official is not necessarily a good thing – on either side of the road are flowers, but behind the flowers is an abyss."

I just stared at him, unwilling to accept the news. Though I looked down upon Zhu Tuo, he had after all been my husband, and I didn't want him to be in such big trouble."

"The Anti-Corruption Bureau has already taken enforcement measures on him. I have to tell you this so that you can be prepared. I don't want you to be crushed under everything like I was."

"We have divorced." I managed to speak out at last.

"Have you?" It was his turn to be shocked. "So did you see the possibility of this happening from the beginning?"

I shook my head and smiled bitterly. "How could I have any foresight? I was just tired of giving him a leg up in his endless jockeying for position. It was painful! Remember the first time I came to see you? He forced me to do that."

"Oh? That makes me feel better. If you hadn't got divorced, you would have gone through all the bitterness that I tasted! I'm pleased for you. You know, people usually want their family members to be government officials and they themselves to be relatives of officials, but what they don't know is that being an official is simply a kind of occupation, no different from being a coal miner with similar occupational risks. If something should happen, wails and whines follow. There are few people in this world like you who choose to stay away from officialdom and willingly say no to being a relative of an official."

I forced a bitter smile and stood up to say goodbye. I didn't know how to go on with the conversation. At the doorway, Secretary Wantong said to me again: "I'm really sorry. Never have I imagined that my help would turn out like this."

I shook my head: "How could it be your fault?"

That night, I went to the apartment where I once lived with Zhu Tuo. Standing in front of the door, my heart was frozen. The door was locked, the lights inside were out, the night wind flew round and round in front of the door.

At that moment, an old saying came to me: "Resentment at a low official rank may lead to fetters and a felon's shame."

Zhu Tuo, if you had not resented your low official rank, your corruption would not have been exposed to the public so early! You're on your own now!

Soon, Zhu Tuo's punishment was announced – four years' imprisonment was not a heavy one, but he lost his job, which meant no salary to afford his monthly maintenance of our daughter. With my fixed salary to support three people – my daughter, the nanny and me – I began to feel tremendous financial pressure.

One Sunday morning, my nanny took my daughter out to play with my neighbours' kids, and I was doing the housework, sweeping and cleaning. Suddenly, someone was knocking on the door. I had thought it might be the neighbour, but when I opened the door, I found it was Secretary Wantong in plain clothes. It was a surprise, and I was in shock for a while. He spoke first: "I'm not welcome here, am I?"

I came back to my senses and hurriedly showed him in. A cramped room, shabby furniture, a particularly messy bed left by my daughter – my poverty was obvious at first glance. I hated so much to let him see this. Also, I wore a pair of old pyjamas to do the housework, my hair was uncombed and my face smeared with dust. I would be embarrassed to present myself in such a manner in front of a male stranger, let alone a secretary of the Municipal Party Committee at deputy provincial level.

"I came to visit a friend nearby, so I dropped in on you for a chat," he said as he invited himself to sit down, and even took a paper cup for some boiled water. I put aside the mop, washed my hands and served him some apples I had bought for my daughter.

"It seems I should have visited you earlier," he said in a low voice as he patrolled the small apartment I rented. "I knew you might go through a hard time, but never could I have imagined that you would be living in such a condition."

It was the first time for me to hear such kind words from a leader. I felt warm at first, and then a sudden sour bitterness struck me, tears flowing down my face involuntarily. I hated myself at that time. Why did you cry in front of him? I lifted my hand immediately to wipe the tears for fear that he might see them, but he did see and handed me a tissue. How shameful! I was so embarrassed!

"I'm an honest person and prefer speaking directly. I want to tell you something which might sound bold and abrupt, but if you feel offended, please don't be mad at me," he said and stared at me.

"You're the secretary of the Municipal Party Committee. Nothing you're going to say will offend me." I was sort of curious about his serious manner, so I just looked at him, waiting for him to go on.

"I've been single since I got divorced. It's not because no women want to live with me, but I have my principles. When I choose a woman as a wife, she must be easy on the eye, kind and well educated. In addition to that, there's a special quality – she has no lust for power, and she can see through privileges. Many women who want to enter my life fail to meet the last requirement. I've been waiting for quite a long time, and recently I think I've found someone. That is you. You're the only one who meets all my requirements. Also, to be honest, I'm attracted to you. Since I've found you, I don't want to lose my chance. Today I'm here, boldly expressing my love to you the way a young man usually does."

"What?" I was taken aback by his words. The secretary of the Municipal Party Committee was courting me? That was something I never dreamed about.

He mistook my shock as fear, so he smiled and said: "Don't be afraid. Please regard me as an ordinary courtier. If you agree to date with me, nod your head. If not, shake your head. I know I don't have any advantage considering my age. I'm a lot older than you, and I confess that has made me feel inferior to you."

"No, no, no…" I waved my hands at him. I never thought about such a specific issue like age. I was simply shocked.

"I know you were not prepared for my sudden visit and my bold proposal. You need time to think about it. Look, how about this – you don't need to give me your answer at once. Whenever you make your decision, be it yes or no, just give me a phone call." With those words, he left a piece of paper on the table and stood up to walk towards the door. I forgot to say some conventional remark, nor did I show him to the door. I just stood in the middle of the room, lost in thought.

I did nothing during the rest of that morning. I stood there thinking about the words he said and kept asking myself how could a high-ranking official like him lack women in his life! How could it be possible for him to have a crush on me, a single mother? What had attracted him to me? Was he serious about this or was he just playing with me? I was restless and confused by these questions. If other men had thrown all those questions at me, I might have ignored them, but he was different. He was the secretary of the Municipal Party Committee, a deputy provincial official! His courtship made me feel a little proud without reason.

Everyone has vanity, and I was no exception. As an ordinary woman, it was hard for me to hide my joy when the most famous man in the province came to say he loved me. Standing in front of the mirror, I looked at myself carefully, wanting to know what I had that attracted him. Did I have a pretty face? Big breasts? Or wide hips? Perhaps his proposal made me feel confident. Looking at myself in the mirror, I thought I was kind of pretty.

Later, I reflected on my feelings about him. Before misfortune befell his family, I knew very little about him. I only had an impression from newspapers and TV programmes that he was quite capable. When he was involved in his wife's corruption scandal, I had sympathy for him. After he had been restored to his post, I admired him and was even attracted to him a little bit when I saw him pick up the pieces from where he left off. After he had been transferred to the provincial capital and helped Zhu Tuo at my request, I felt grateful to him, and my affection for him increased. But could it be love? Did I really want to live with him?

I couldn't help imagining what my life would be like if I should live with him. Would he love my daughter? Could he get on well with her? I didn't like socialising – would he force me to visit his friends in officialdom? Would he get tired of me after the honeymoon stage? Would he allow me to see my friends at the bottom of society as usual? People of different ages had different hobbies – could he accept this?

I thought about it for a few days until I had a headache. Saying yes to him made me a bit worried. It was after all a life-changing decision, and I couldn't afford to be too hasty. Besides, I had divorced once, and I didn't want to repeat that mistake. But I felt reluctant to turn him down. My intuition told me this man was good and reliable, and I shouldn't let the chance slip away. After much deliberation, I decided to start a relationship with him, and if I didn't feel comfortable, I would end it as soon as possible.

One evening after supper, I dialled the number he had left. He answered the phone after two rings. He knew it was me because my name slipped out of his mouth before I spoke.

"Xiaowen, what is your answer?"

"We need to know each other first," I said.

"Great! I'll be there right away. Go downstairs in thirty-five minutes. There'll be a Santana in front of your building, about ten metres away. Open the door and get into the car." His voice sounded anxious.

That night when we met, I only asked him one question: "What do you think is the most important thing when a man and a woman live together?"

He said: "First, mutual attraction and sexual pleasure. Second, mutual appreciation and spiritual consolation. Third, mutual protection and psychological security."

I was basically satisfied with his answer. Amid a peaceful and pleasant atmosphere, we had an in-depth discussion about his answers. To anyone who happened to see us there, we looked like two professors talking about philosophy. We sat at the riverbank in the city's outskirts, keeping a distance of about one metre between each other. He didn't try to reach out his hand to touch me. I wouldn't have allowed him to do that anyway. His driver parked the car in a shadow in the distance. There were no other people around, and it was quiet. We had an honest talk, and I could feel the sincerity in his words. I had told myself before I went to see him that if I should perceive the slightest intention by him to play me for a fool or cheat on me, I would leave at once. At the end of our conversation, I had a glimpse of my long-lost happiness. As I returned to the Santana, my slow walk became brisk, just like it was when I was in college.

After that night, we had many dates like this. Whenever he had no meetings and I was not on duty, that old Santana of his would arrive in front of my building and take us to a quiet place in the suburbs where we could chat undisturbed. Gradually, it became clear that he indeed wanted to marry me and settle down, and I began to understand that his life was actually full of annoyance, worry and danger. Since I was certain about the whole thing, I readily agreed to begin a relationship with him. It was also on that very night when I gave him my yes that he dared to reach out his hand, pull me into his arms and kiss me. That was our first kiss – nothing like the rumours that Zhu Tuo spread on the internet after he had been released from prison. Zhu Tuo was a bastard! He dared to claim that Ouyang Wantong had framed him and sent him to prison in order to have me, and I had been Ouyang Wantong's mistress for a long time. He was distorting the facts, and God knows he was lying. May Heaven punish him one more time!

On the day of our wedding, he held me in his arms and said: "There is one thing I need to emphasise once again. You know I'm much older than you. As for our sex life, perhaps I won't be able to satisfy you. I hope you can be ready for this and understand me."

I told him I was not a woman who had a strong desire for sex. For me, the most important thing was the feeling of intimacy and warmth.

We had a simple wedding. He wanted to keep it low-key, and I didn't want to make it widely known either. He had wanted to book a private room in a five-star hotel and only invite the mayor and the secretary-general of the Municipal Party Committee. I shook my head and said: "There's no need to disturb others. Your parents can't attend because of old age. My father died, and my mother can't make it because of sickness. What about counting my daughter and your driver in, then we can book a private room and have a wedding banquet in a quiet restaurant in the suburbs?"

Eventually, he agreed and asked his driver to book a table in a restaurant in the suburbs discretely. He didn't even inform his secretary.

When the owner of the restaurant served the dishes, he smiled and said to Ouyang Wantong: "Brother, you're so blessed! You look like someone."

"Who do I look like?" asked Wantong.

The manager replied: "Our secretary of the Municipal Party Committee! But you're not him – otherwise, I would take a photo with you and put it on the wall in my lobby! That would be the best advertisement!" We all laughed at his words.

We had a happy married life. With my nanny and daughter, I moved into his apartment allocated by the Municipal Party Committee. He regarded my daughter as his own and played with her after he came back from work. Later, I discovered that his son had cut ties with him, probably because he divorced his ex-wife, and he had been living alone in the years since then. I once asked him after we got married whether he wanted to have another child. If he did, I would prepare myself for pregnancy. He shook his head and said: "We have a son and a daughter – that is good enough."

After that, I tried several times to go to see his son and wanted to straighten out their strained relations. Unfortunately, though I met him many times, the boy always kept silent in front of me and refused to see his father. Wantong went to see him when he was in Tianquan, but the boy hid from him every time. He didn't even inform his father of his wedding. My friend in Tianquan told me about it, so I quickly prepared wedding presents and a cash gift, dragged Wantong along and hurried to Tianquan. Two young men came out to stop us when we arrived at the wedding. They said: "Uncle and Aunt, please excuse us. We've been asked to stop you from attending the wedding ceremony. The bridegroom said that if you enter the wedding hall, he'll run away and there'll be no wedding ceremony today!" Hearing this, Wantong froze there for a second. Then without saying a word, he turned around and got into his car. I knew it would spoil the wedding if we forced our way in, so I secretly entrusted the two young men with our gifts and asked them to write down any name they could think of on the gift list.

After we got married, the biggest problem I had to face was rejecting all sorts of gifts. Wantong told me: "A lot of people attempt to send money and gifts to us – not because they have a feeling of affection and gratitude, but because I have a lot of power. They want to utilise my power to gain more benefits."

He continued: "Our institutional structure gives top local leaders in China absolute power. The NPC and the CPPCC have no right to supervise top leaders, while the Disciplinary Committee of the same level dare not do this. The Higher Party Committee has the right to supervise top local leaders, but they can only carry out their supervision through the lower level of top leaders, which usually makes it very difficult for them to detect wrongdoing. That's why so many people come to flatter the top leaders. If we give a green light for this, you and I will become corrupt officials within a few months, and that will end with a prison sentence. In order to protect us and spare our daughter from having to visit us in prison, we should learn to shut the door on anyone who attempts to offer bribes."

I became more vigilant after hearing this. I told the nanny and my daughter to close the door immediately after they got home, no matter whether it was in the daytime or at night, and never open the door, whoever was knocking. Wantong and I had the keys anyway.

One day after supper, I opened the door to throw out the rubbish, and the moment the door was opened, I saw a delicate young lady standing in the doorway holding a paper bag in her hand. She greeted me loudly: "Good evening, Auntie. My mum asked me to visit you and my uncle before school starts." I gasped for a second. Why didn't Wantong tell me that his niece was coming to visit? But since she was there, and it was after all the first time for me as an aunt to meet a niece, I dare not show slackness.

Hurriedly, I showed her into the room, made a cup of tea and prepared some fruit. When I asked her which university she attended, she stood up and said she had to go back because there was an event in their normal university tonight and all students were required to be there – she would come to visit on Sunday instead. I saw her to the door.

Before she left, she pointed to the paper bag and said: "That is some local specialities my mum asked me to bring to you."

I didn't feel anything was wrong about this and said: "Send my thanks to your mum! I have some local specialities for you to bring back to her when you go home during the holiday."

After I saw her off and went back to the room, I took the bag to see what local speciality Wantong's younger sister had brought to him. The bag was heavy. I removed the wrapper, layer after layer, and I was greatly shocked by what appeared in front of my eyes – ten shining gold bars! What kind of local specialities these were!

Instinctively, I felt something was wrong and called Wantong at once. He sneered on the phone and said: "They are playing tricks on me! I'll be back in a minute – you just wait for me."

Half an hour later, Wantong came back with his secretary. He took a look at the gold bars, signalled his secretary to turn the recorder on in front of the telephone and then dialled a number. The moment the phone was answered, he said slowly: "Hello, Mrs Zhong. Your present is here in my place. I'll now ask my secretary to send it to my office. You must send someone to take it away before eleven tonight – if you don't, my secretary will transfer it to the secretary of the Municipal Commission for Discipline Inspection, and then the Anti-Corruption Bureau will come to your home and arrest you on the charge of bribery!"

An embarrassing laugh of a middle-aged woman came from the telephone: "Secretary Wantong, why did you take it so seriously? You work day and night for our city, and we just want to express our gratitude."

Wantong replied with a little note of laughter in his tone: "I have to! Your gratitude is apparently sending me to prison, isn't it?"

After his secretary left with the gold bars, Wantong explained to me: "This Mrs Zhong is the general manager of a real estate company. She has settled on a piece of land near the city government and wants to have my cooperation. She has called me several times suggesting a meeting, and I refused. Never did I expect she would offer bribes like this."

I was more vigilant about bribery after this gold bar incident, but there was no way of preventing it. One evening, when I arrived at the entrance of my residential area after work, a director of the General Office of the Municipal Party Committee stopped me and said: "Here's a document for Secretary Wantong. Could you give it to him?" With these words, he handed me a large, tightly sealed envelope.

I knew this director because he often came to my house to discuss work with Wantong. I took it without any doubts: "Okay, as long as it's not something confidential."

I gave the envelope to Wantong after he got back, and he immediately pulled a long face after opening it. Inside were a few pages of that director's resume, with two gift cards for the Huatang shopping mall taped in between them. Each card was worth 100,000 yuan. I was shocked when I saw this. Why would a director of the General Office offer bribes? Wantong sighed: "For the promotion. Recently, we've been working on promoting a batch of cadres, and he must have heard about it. You know, officials in China are not elected by common people, but are determined by high-level officials. That's why some people who want to climb the political ladder have to curry favour or even attempt to offer gifts. He's a good director and should be promoted even if he doesn't offer a gift. It's a pity that he didn't believe me."

Wantong called that director and said emotionally on the phone: "I received the money, but I can't believe that you, who works with me all day long, would still believe I can be bought. It's very likely that those who are not close to me would have the same idea. Please have some respect. Come and take this back."

The second year after we got married, Wantong was transferred to the province as the deputy secretary presiding over organisational work. His new position, though a lateral transfer within the organisation, was more important. On the morning before he left to report for duty, he said to me: "Xiaowen, the two of us must keep a clear head about this transfer. Yes, in the eyes of outsiders, we're fortunate and triumphant, but in fact we're in more danger. Those who want to elicit our weakness will spare no efforts to investigate and calculate."

I nodded to let him know I understood.

After he went to work in the provincial capital, a vice governor's wife called me several times, warmly inviting me to play poker in her home after supper. I was not interested in poker games, though I had played a few times with my classmates when I was a college student. I declined her invitation the first few times, saying I was unavailable, but she insisted on inviting me again and again, and I was desperate to find another excuse. I'm not in politics, but I read some books about politics after I married Wantong. I know finding an ally is important in political circles. I was afraid that if I continued saying no to the vice governor's wife, it might do harm to the relationship between the two families and the cooperation between her husband and Wantong. I told Wantong that I wanted to accept the invitation and play poker with them. He was very supportive and encouraged me to go, saying that playing poker would help relax the body and it was good for health.

One evening after supper, therefore, I went to her house, where the other two players she had invited were already seated at the table. After the introductions, I knew one was the wife of the director-general of the Department of Transportation and the other was the wife of the director-general of the Land and Resources Department. We sat at the table, and the wife of the vice governor said: "To have more fun, let's do a little gambling, shall we? Whoever loses pays the money." The other two players clapped their hands, applauding. Seeing that, I thought it might be improper to object, as it might spoil everyone's enjoyment. If I should lose, it simply amounted to losing the money to buy a new dress. But to my complete surprise, I actually won more than 2,000 yuan that night, and they all complimented me on my good luck, great skills and experience. I was carried away by their praise, and on my way home I even wanted to sing a song.

I was apparently more enthusiastic about playing poker with them the next time they invited me. That night, I won 9,000 yuan – that was too much! All three of them marvelled at my luck and exclaimed: "How unbelievable! Why do you always win? It seems your luck has hit its peak, not only bringing good luck to your husband but also bringing money home." I was a bit embarrassed by their words, but inwardly I rejoiced. The next day I bought a piece of clothing each for Wantong, my daughter and my nanny with the money I had won the night before, thinking proudly that I earned it by my good luck.

Once again, before a poker game, the wife of the vice governor proposed to increase the bet so that she could win back what she had lost in the previous two card games. She also put her palms together and prayed solemnly for her good luck that night. The other two agreed happily. As the winner in the previous two nights, I couldn't show any objection to this. The game began at a new level, and I didn't expect to win. But that night I won 17,000 yuan!

When the game was over and we were busy counting how much we had won or lost, I suddenly felt uneasy. With a guilty apology, I said: "I'm sorry."

They all retorted with smiles: "What are you talking about? You won this with your own skills and that was the reward of your labour."

When I played poker with them for a fourth time, I intended to lose, thinking that losing at least once would make them psychologically balanced. But the result was again beyond my expectation – that night, I won 31,000 yuan!

I was full of doubts and instinctively felt that something strange was happening. The joy of earning money was gone. When I arrived home, Wantong was sitting on the bed, reading a book. I couldn't help but tell him everything about the card parties. He listened with furrowed brows. After I finished, he said: "Don't you understand? They are offering bribes in a disguised form to flatter you and to make an investment. Sooner or later they'll ask for something in return. What could we give to them? A government post!"

I was scared by his words and had no idea what I should do. Turning it over in his mind for a while, he said: "You've played with them four times and won 59,000 yuan in total. Add one more thousand, and go to buy three presents with the 60,000 yuan – 20,000 each. Then invite them to our home and give them the presents, saying they are only souvenirs for having a good time playing poker together. They'll probably never invite you again."

Following his instruction, I bought three presents and invited them to have tea at my place. They all agreed and arrived in a light-hearted mood. After conventional greetings and chat, I took out the presents and said: "Sisters, I'm grateful for your playing cards with me and giving me the fun of winning money. Based on sticking together through thick and thin, I bought each of you a present with all of my winnings. They are small gifts to strengthen our sisterhood." They were all surprised but had to accept with thanks when I placed the presents in their hands and insisted that they take them away.

Wantong was right. After that day, they never invited me to play cards with them. It was indeed fortunate that I ended the relationship with them as a poker friend because just ten months later, the director-general of the Department of Transportation was imprisoned for receiving a huge amount of bribes, and that vice governor and the director-general of the Land and Resources Department were detained and interrogated for quite a long time. Later, the vice governor was demoted and the director-general of the Land and Resources Department was removed from office.

I got scared when I thought about it again. If I hadn't controlled myself and had continued playing with them and winning, things would have definitely gone wrong, wouldn't they?

There was a lot of gossiping about our marriage. Some said it was my strategy to climb high, trying every means to seduce him and eventually lure him into my embrace and live a life as the wife of a senior official. I laughed it off, feeling it wasn't worth making any comment. God knows I've never done that.

Another story was that I looked a bit like his ex-wife, and it was his nostalgia that led him to marry me. That didn't worry me at all. Anyone who was familiar with his ex-wife knew that she and I were totally different in terms of physical appearance, temperament and personality.

There was another rumour that he was a cradle robber and I was simply his latest conquest. To be honest, I was somewhat concerned about this one, and I had been observing him since we got married, wondering as time went by whether there would be any change in his attitude towards me after the period of feeling fresh and excited ended.

I must admit I had been feeling his deep love for me, and he continued to be like this even after the initial stage of intoxicating sex had ended. He would always come home to have dinner with us in the evening when he didn't have to work or go to an appointment.

Sometimes, after supper, he wanted me to watch a movie with him at a nearby cinema. He seemed to have a particular obsession for movies. He enjoyed watching any type, even some poorly made ones. I was curious about this and asked him about it once. He said there were probably two reasons. First, it might be the psychology of compensation because his desire to watch movies had never been satisfied when he was a teenager. He was brought up in the countryside and it was very difficult for young people in his village to watch movies. Sometimes they had to walk more than a dozen miles to watch an outdoor movie. That's why he would feel so satisfied and so happy when sitting in the cinema. Second, watching a movie made him relaxed. You know, he had to deal with a lot of social issues every day, which would inevitably exert pressure on him. Watching a movie helped him forget about the reality temporarily, forget about troubles and annoyances in his work, and enter an illusion of an easy life, in which his stress had been relieved.

On holidays whenever he was free, he liked me to drive the car and take him and my daughter to the suburbs for a walk along the riverbank, where we could enjoy the scenery in the fields and listen to the birds singing in the trees. He said he grew up in the countryside and always had deep feelings for the fields. Whenever he saw a field, a sense of intimacy would rise in his heart, and this often reminded him of his folks who still lived in the countryside. Then all the troubles he encountered in officialdom would be diluted.

The most memorable time of my life was those years when I lived with him, and I have never regretted my choice.

With him, I had to keep one thing in my mind – let him forget the age difference between us and prevent him from feeling inferior to me because of his age. This is probably something all the young wives have to pay attention to when dealing with their old husbands. When in public and in officialdom, Wantong was covered with a kind of aura that made him feel very powerful, but when he returned home, his power was left outside and he was restored to a common man. At home, the young me had an advantage over the old him. If I wanted him to stay with me for a long time doing sports and entertainment or making love, he would feel that was too much for him and therefore made apologies to me again and again, which would indeed give him a sense of inferiority. That's why I would always give him the opportunity to demonstrate his wisdom rather than his strength, his refinement rather than his physical appearance. I wanted him to maintain this confidence in front of me all the time. This not only benefitted his mental state but also improved his performance in our sex life.

A few years after we got married, he was promoted to the rank of governor.

That was certainly a happy event. On the day when the central leadership announced his appointment, he was bombarded with calls of congratulation from all directions, on both the home phone and his mobile phone. He asked me to answer all the home phone calls with three sentences – He's not at home! Thank you! Please call again later! His secretary dealt with his mobile phone similarly – Thank you! He's busy now! Please call again later! When he went to bed that evening, he sighed:

"If we fail to keep a cool head, we'll be carried away by those congratulations and flatteries and slip into an illusion that we're someone. In fact, I'm the same Ouyang Wantong. Everything remains unchanged – my height, my intelligence and my personality. The only change in my life is that I have a letter of appointment – a piece of paper that could be handed to you, taken back or declared null and void."

I said I understood.

"That piece of paper was called a commission in the Republic of China, an imperial edict when we had emperors. In every dynasty there are some people who've been carried away by this piece of paper," he continued.

"You're lecturing me, aren't you?" I laughed.

He laughed too and sighed again. "Remember He Shen in Qing dynasty? He thought his official position given by the emperor would belong to him forever, but he ended up in prison when another imperial edict to search his house and confiscate his property was declared."

Not long after he was promoted to governor, I felt he had more things to worry about. One night when we were sound asleep, the telephone rang suddenly. It was quite alarming as we usually didn't get calls at that time. I instinctively felt something serious must have happened. Sure enough, the moment I grabbed the receiver, the anxious voice of Wantong's secretary came from it: "Please tell the governor a big fire broke out in a karaoke bar in Tangchuan. Casualties might be heavy."

Wantong took the phone and said only one thing: "Get the car ready at once." He then reached for his clothes, and I got up to help him. After he put on his jacket, I noticed he had forgotten to change his shirt – he was still wearing his pyjama top. Before I could ask him to take it off, he rushed out of the door and said to me: "I shall be late."

When I turned on the TV early the next morning, the rescue scene of the Tangchuan fire appeared on the news programme of the provincial TV station. Twenty or more bodies covered with white cloth were placed on the ground. Many relatives of these dead people cried bitterly as they tried to hold each other. The firefighters were still there cleaning up the mess. With mud all over his body and deep grief on his face, Wantong was talking to a few crying people. The camera was then completely focused on him, and he said in a low and grave voice: "I, as the governor, have the inescapable responsibility for this disaster. Please accept my deepest apology. I assure all of you that we'll get to the bottom of the fire and severely punish those who have neglected their duties on behalf of the injured and those who have lost their lives. Meanwhile, we'll supervise and close security loopholes throughout the province to ensure similar accidents will never happen again."

He got back home very late that night, his face full of weariness. I was about to help him change his clothes when someone knocked on the door. From the door mirror, I could see the secretary-general standing outside with another cadre. I hurriedly opened the door and let them in. Wantong didn't invite them to sit down but asked with a long face: "Why did you come here?"

"Mayor Jiang of Tangchuan thinks that although he's responsible for the fire, he is after all indirectly responsible and it's unjust for him to be punished with a demerit. He insisted that I bring him here and make a statement to your face, in the hope that you could rescind the penalty," said the secretary-general.

Staring at Mayor Jiang behind the secretary-general, Wantong lost his temper and shouted: "You feel aggrieved? I held a meeting at the beginning of this month to emphasise the supervision of safety issues, especially the elimination of hidden dangers in entertainment venues. For what? This is a matter of life or death. I ordered all of the mayors and county magistrates to give safety issues their personal attention in their districts. And what did you do? You were busy participating in a company's opening ceremony and you failed to deal with the matter. You just handed the document over to the Municipal Government Office. More than twenty young lives are gone! All young girls and boys! Could it be easy for any household to raise a child? If you had followed my instructions and carried out an inspection, their lives would have been saved. How dare you complain that your punishment is heavy? You're the head of Tangchuan – why don't you care about matters of life and death? You're fucking…"

I hurried forward and slapped his arm to stop him from swearing at people.

"I'm sorry, I…" Mayor Jiang mumbled.

"You may go now! Reflect on what you have done! The decision of your disciplinary action will not be changed. When you do a good job in your post and achieve some good things, the provincial government will cite you for meritorious service."

Not long after they left, the telephone connected directly with Beijing rang. Wantong picked up the receiver. "Good evening, senior leader! Why haven't you gone to bed yet?"

The voice in the receiver was very loud, and it was impossible to ignore it. "Ouyang Wantong, it's not very long since you became the governor. You shouldn't be so quick to punish your subordinates. Remember – live and let live!"

Wantong smiled grimly: "Senior leader, why would I want to offend people? It was his negligence that led to the fire, which has cost the lives of more than twenty people – a heavy loss. It would be hardly justifiable if we didn't punish him. And suppose people knew of the relationship between him and you. It would do harm to your reputation."

That night, Wantong had a long conversation with that senior leader on the phone but he failed to persuade him in the end. I clearly heard that leader slam the phone down, leaving Wantong sat there holding the phone and staring blankly for a long time.

"What are you going to do?" I asked worriedly as I sat beside him. He didn't say anything but gave a long sigh and lay back on the couch, staring straight at the ceiling. I urged him to wash and go to bed, but he simply lay on the sofa until midnight, as if he hadn't heard me at all. Then he made a phone call to the provincial secretary. "Do as we agreed! No one is an exception, no matter whose nephew he is!"

The next day, the administrative disciplinary measure from the provincial government for Mayor Jiang and the others who were responsible for the fire appeared on the front page of the provincial newspaper.

I was seized with fear for him.

After Wantong became the governor, many relatives came to ask for favours, but we rejected most of them. To my surprise, my younger brother would join them. He was a staff member of the County Department of Agriculture in my hometown. One day, he came to visit me with a large bottle of sesame oil. When I asked him why, since it was not the New Year or a festival, he smiled and said: "It's nothing special! I just miss you and my niece." I thought he might be telling the truth. You know, since I was transferred to work in the provincial capital, I went back home a lot less than before.

As I was about to go to the kitchen with the nanny to make him something to eat, he pulled me towards him and said: "Sister, there's no hurry for the dinner – I want to report something to you first."

I was amused by his solemnity: "Haha! After a few years working in a government department, you now speak with a touch of bureaucracy! Forget about the report – tell me what it is."

"My brother-in-law is the governor now, but I'm still a staff member in the County Department of Agriculture. Don't you think it's a little bit unreasonable?"

"Unreasonable?" I didn't understand his meaning at this point.

"Could there be any governor whose brother-in-law is still a common staff member? I've done some research and discovered that the brother-in-law of the county magistrate in our hometown is the commissioner of Inland Revenue. The brother-in-law of the Xinchang county magistrate is the director of the Bureau of Finance. The brother-in-law of the mayor of Jiuyuan is the director of the Civil Affairs Bureau. The brother-in-law of the mayor of Huangchuan is the director of the Bureau of Land Planning. Jiuyuan and Huangchuan are both prefecture-level cities, so the director of the Civil Affairs Bureau and the director of the Bureau of Land Planning are county-level cadres. Following this rule, shouldn't I at least be a vice mayor in a prefecture-level city? Or a deputy director-general of some department in the province!"

"Hey! You want to be an official?" I came to understand his real purpose of visiting. "Why don't you strive for it by your own efforts?" I was a little bit annoyed.

"Having a good brother-in-law is my good luck! Few people have this blessing in their whole life."

"Stop daydreaming!" I pulled a long face.

"I'm not daydreaming – it's my blessing. As the old saying goes – nothing is worse than having no blessing. When you're blessed, it'll come to you wherever you are."

"You're not your brother-in-law. If you want to be an official, work for it by yourself."

"Sister, you must be joking! Nowadays, how could anyone become an official through their personal struggle and abilities! Everyone looks for connections. Everyone relies on connections. Thank God I have a brother-in-law who is a governor. It's a rare luck that few people could have."

My nanny cut in when she heard our conversation. "Madam, he's your only younger brother. If you don't help him, who else will? You could talk to his brother-in-law and ask him to give your brother an opportunity.

Your brother is a man of feelings. He'll appreciate your help!" My nanny had been living with me for a long time, and she talked to me the way a family member would.

"Sister, how could an official post be given as casually as this? My brother should have the political integrity and professional competence that an official should possess. If he has, the county government will give him an opportunity. His brother-in-law can do nothing," I explained to her.

"Sister, you're now the wife of a senior official and talk like a bureaucrat. Nowadays, is there any official who doesn't use his own people? If he doesn't, he must be a fool! Once he's in trouble, who will help him then?"

"Stop talking nonsense!"

"In fact, it's not me who would feel embarrassed if I couldn't be appointed as an official, it would be my brother-in-law. People would laugh at him not me! They would gossip behind his back. Look at that Ouyang Wantong! He doesn't deserve his reputation in the province. How could he do great things when he can't even arrange for an official post for his brother-in-law? It must be that no one listens to him in the provincial government. He must be no match for those around him and have no ability at all. A loser indeed!"

"What is this false logic?" I was almost amused by him.

"What I just said is not unreasonable. It's the truth! Working in officialdom is just like hunting in the jungle. If you don't use your own people, you're sure to pay for it in the end. Haven't you seen how many officials use their own people? Not only their own brothers and brothers-in-law but also their paternal brother-in-law and maternal sister-in-law, and even their cousins and cousins-in-law. For what? For convenience and mutual benefits! Once inspections come, such as from the people of the Commission for Discipline and People's Procuratorate, all his relatives will protect him."

"You're talking about corrupt officials, aren't you? Only corrupt officials need protection."

"Sister, you've only been the wife of a governor for a few days and you've already forgotten how things really are. Do we have officials who don't take bribes? Go and check on their properties and you'll know how many of them dare to claim that what they have now corresponds to their income. Only fools don't play graft! Besides, it's human nature to be a little greedy."

"You show your true colours at last! Is it for these petty profits that you want to be an official? Who dares to give you the power then? Suppose you become an official and finally end up in prison, sentenced by the Procuratorate and the Court because of your corrupt practices. I wouldn't go to the prison to visit you."

"What? Go to prison?" He was frightened by my words, which were meant to scare him. "That wouldn't happen, would it? Just for taking some small bribes?"

I scared him again. "Just do your job well in the county and live a good life with your wife and your children. Stop thinking about being an official. People often say blessings and misfortunes are neighbours. It's not necessarily a good thing to be an official. You're the only son in our family, and if you become a corrupt official and go to jail, how could our mother accept it and live on? And you know she's always in poor health. Safety is the most important thing for anyone in this world. Don't you understand?"

I played on his fears of going to jail and successfully dissuaded him from asking Wantong for an official post. Failing to achieve his goal, he was unhappy, pulling a long face and insisting on going back without waiting to have dinner with Wantong. "You just said you missed us, but now you want to leave without seeing your niece, so you're clearly lying to me!" I smiled and teased him. He was embarrassed when he heard this and agreed to stay. After Wantong and my daughter came back, and when wines were served in front of him, and when my daughter innocently urged him to drink, he began to feel happy again.

That's all that I can remember and say to you.

Oh, there is another thing. He asked to resign a few years after we got married. It was on his own initiative, not because his superiors forced him to do it or because he had committed some serious errors. But his secretary, Mr Zheng, later told me that Wantong had a long conversation with the secretary of the Provincial Party Committee and then withdrew his resignation without handing it over to the central government. I was not clear why he wanted to do that, and he didn't discuss it with me before he made his decision. For some time, people in the provincial government talked about his possible promotion to become secretary of the Provincial

Party Committee and no one ever expected that he would suddenly request a resignation. He told me about it after the whole thing ended, and I asked him about the reason. He smiled and said: "I'm tired. Besides, something is wrong with my cervical spine, and I often feel dizzy. I'm afraid if I carry on, it'll do harm to my work. And, I want to have more time to be with you."

Since then, his mental state was not healthy, which made me accept that there might be some other reasons for his resignation, but he didn't want to tell me, and it was improper for me to ask him. You know, I couldn't interfere with his work too much because it might involve confidentiality, and this was a regulation.

He persisted in his work until he retired. I was overjoyed when he did retire. He could finally go to bed on time in the evening. He could go out for a walk in the morning. He could regularly go out to watch movies with me, and he could watch TV with me at home. We had much more time to talk to each other, and I often said to him: "There's no end to working as an official. It's wise to quit while you're ahead."

Never did I expect that he would have such a serious health problem after he retired. Just like that, he was gone, leaving me alone in this world.

Yes, of course I checked that key. Since he left it with me in the last hours of his life, it must have been very important to him. We have many rooms in our house. Some utility rooms are usually locked, but when I tried to open the doors, I found the key didn't work. So I tried it on the locks on the closets and it didn't work there either. I had no choice but to leave the key with my daughter Xiaoxiao.

Xiaoxiao is a smart girl. She guessed that it might be the key to a private safe rented in a bank. I was shocked. Did he secretly hide something valuable in the bank? Money? A bank account book? Gold bars?

Taking Xiaoxiao with me, I started the search at the Provincial Agricultural Bank. Then we tried the Industrial and Commercial Bank, the China Construction Bank, the Bank of China and finally the Provincial Bank of Communications. Xiaoxiao was right. The governor of the Provincial Bank of Communications recognised the key when we showed it to him. "Yes, it's a key for one of our private safes," he said. He called the manager of the bank vault, and very soon we found the safe.

Xiaoxiao and I and all of the people present in the bank thought there must be a fortune in the safe, but no one had expected that there would be nothing but a piece of old musical score for the suona, a brief letter without a signature and an inexplicable ink painting he had drawn.

It was after I read that anonymous letter that I decided to invite you to write a biography for him.

At present, only my daughter and I have seen the things in the safe.

I'll give them to you later, and you can see them for yourself.

2

OUYANG QIANZI

THE SON

WHAT DO you want from me? You want to write a biography for Ouyang Wantong? Do you want him to be immortal? Do you want his name to go down in history? Forget it! So many officials have wanted their names to be in the history books, but did they succeed in the end? It would be pointless to carve his name into a stone, let alone write a book about him. Don't waste your time! Let me tell you one thing. There's a rule for people who want their names to go down in history – the more they want it, the harder it becomes. Meanwhile, those who don't ever think about it would probably manage it. What's more, I cut ties with Ouyang Wantong a long time ago. We were like strangers. If you want to write about his glorious deeds, I'm the wrong person to turn to.

Who has asked you to do this? Was it her? Then you should go and ask her! She lives with the great people and must know him. Let her tell you more about his brilliant deeds!

Yes, he was my father – I can't deny that. But he was my father only in the biological sense. I know about his death. The funeral committee informed me. I would say he deserved it. He was in his sixties. Is there any reason for a man to live longer than that? Fortunately, God is fair and does not give him any privileges regarding death. God knows how many privileges a senior official like him would enjoy if he were given extra time! Of course, I didn't attend his funeral. Whoever wanted to attend is none of my business. I didn't want to go anyway. Such a noble man he was, 'a big mandarin' in this region, controlling the fate of nearly a hundred million people with his overwhelming power. It would be such a stain on his reputation if I, a common civilian, should attend his funeral!

My mother is dying. She had liver cancer shortly after she was released from prison. Why do people have liver diseases? Because they often get angry, and anger does great harm to the liver! Just think about her fifteen years' imprisonment. How could she feel at peace? It's unbearable when anger occupies your heart. At whom is she mad? Me first, of course. I'm a loser who has always caused trouble for her. Besides, she's angry with another person. Who is that? Do I need to tell you? A louse on a bald head is an obvious thing!

I want to remind you that nowadays people remember celebrities such as singers, comedians and movie stars, as well as news anchors and opinion leaders who frequently appear on TV shows and websites. They seldom pay attention to political figures, those busy officials who appear daily on TV and in newspapers, though few people can remember them at all. In the eyes of the public, these officials wear suits of the same colours, use almost the same words, have a similar look and walking manner, and completely lose their individuality. The respect that people have for them is extremely limited. The judgements that people make on them are extremely strict. They are forgotten extremely quickly. The worship for political figures in the middle of the 20th century will never happen again! Do you want people to remember Ouyang Wantong? It'll be quite difficult!

It's unlikely that you'll make that happen, isn't it?

I advise you to do something meaningful. Write valuable works that can be passed on. Don't write about things that no one wants to read. You're simply wasting your own time and energy, wasting online space and paper!

It's a total waste of labour and money!

I'm sorry. My words might be hurting your feelings.

Why did he ask to resign? I don't know. I don't even know why he became an official. How could I know why he wanted to resign?

Go and ask someone else.

See you, buddy.

Find another way to make money!

3

OUYANG ZHAOXIU

THE PATERNAL AUNT

YES, I heard about it. Never did I expect he would die before me! I'm more than eighty – fifteen years older than him – but I'm still going strong with good hearing and eyesight. I can manage two bowls of noodles plus half of a steamed bun for a meal. His childhood? Sure, I remember, but why do you want to know this? Write a biography? What's a biography? What's the use of writing a biography? To be remembered? What's the good of being remembered? A man goes off like a snuffed candle, his body becoming the soil. What's the use of being remembered? Besides, how many people in this world will be remembered? It's not always true that a man will be remembered because he's written into a book.

I was fifteen years old when he was born. I still remember it was near twilight when I came back from the field after picking green beans. The moment I entered the yard, a piercing scream burst into my ears. It scared me so much that I dropped my basket on the ground, the green beans scattering here and there.

Shocked, I seized the hand of my mother, who was standing in the yard, and asked: "What's wrong? Who's screaming?"

My mother threw a fierce look at me: "Stop making a fuss! Your sister-in-law is giving birth to a baby!"

With my hand clutching my chest, I sighed with relief and said to myself: "My goodness! How could a woman scream like this when she gives birth to a baby? It's horrible!"

It's probably because of this scream that I was particularly afraid of giving birth several years later. After I got married, I had been secretly praying that I wouldn't get pregnant. But eventually I did.

My sister-in-law screamed in agony for at least half an hour until she gave birth to him. When my mother and I heard the cry of the newborn baby, we hurried into the bedroom and saw that the midwife had just wrapped him up. As she handed it to my mother, she said: "It's a breadwinner!"

My mother exclaimed happily: "Great! Great! We have a new generation in the Ouyang family!" With these words, she shouted loudly to my father and my brother waiting in the next room: "Hey, it's a boy!"

I took the baby from my mother and looked at it. Its eyes were half closed, and its face was wrinkled. I couldn't help saying to my mother: "Why does it look like this? It's too ugly! It doesn't resemble my brother and sister-in-law at all!"

Grinning from ear to ear, my mother replied: "You silly girl! You know nothing! All newborn babies look like this. He'll change. In two days, you'll see. We in the Ouyang family are known for our beauty."

Staring at its little face, I said: "You little thing, your mother suffered too much to bring you into this world!"

On the day when drawing lots was held to celebrate his first birthday, I went to Zhao Mingxian's house at the east end of the village, borrowed his suona and placed it among the goodies for this little thing. You know, I enjoy listening to the suona quite a lot. His mother borrowed a drawing brush from Uncle Jiuchang, the painter in the village, hoping he could learn from him and become a painter when he grew up. Do you know what a painter does? In our village, a painter's job is to paint the eaves and roofs of newly built houses, door gods for villagers during the New Year celebration, Chinese paintings to hang on the wall of the living room of the households celebrating weddings, coffin paintings for those families conducting funerals, and paintings of dreams for those who want their dreams to come true. A painter, admired by every household in the village, lives a milk-and-honey life indeed. My father carved an official seal engraved with the words 'Liu Lin County Government' with a white radish, pressed it on a seal ink paste, and placed it in front of the boy, hoping that he would be an official when he grew up, which was also the wish of my mother and my brother.

Can you guess which one he eventually grabbed? It was a complete surprise! He got the suona in his left hand and the drawing brush in his right hand. I was overjoyed of course, thinking I could listen to suona music to my heart's content when he grew up and learned how to play, or even had his own band. Besides, it was a good way to support himself. You know, in our community, a suona band was indispensable to any wedding ceremony or funeral. My sister-in-law – his mother – was happy too. She believed being a painter was good enough to make a living, have a wife and start a family. But his grandfather – namely my father – was angry. He snatched the suona and the drawing brush out of his hands, threw them on the ground, stuffed the radish official seal into his hand and said to the confused little thing: "You're a man. What's the value of being a suona player or a painter? If you have guts, be an official when you grow up. Bring something new to the Ouyang family and win glory for us!"

Probably scared by his grandfather, Wantong immediately began crying loudly.

He could walk unsteadily when he was only eleven months old. Once he could walk, he began causing trouble. One time he pushed his grandfather's teapot away on the table so forcefully that it fell on the floor and broke into pieces. It was his grandfather's favourite teapot, and he had been using it for almost half of his life. If somebody else in the family had done that, my father would've scolded him without any mercy. But it was Wantong who did this, and my father simply sighed and said: "You naughty boy! You're trying to stop your grandfather from drinking tea, aren't you?"

When he was five years old, our dog began to be afraid of him too. I was married at that time, and whenever I came back from my husband's family, I would see him chasing that poor dog with a stick, not allowing the poor thing to sleep in his doghouse. My mother, unbelievably, backed him up and said to the dog as she also held a stick in her hand: "Since Wantong does not like you to sleep in your doghouse, would you please go out and take a walk."

His academic performance was good though. He started elementary school at six and kept winning all kinds of awards, one by one. He won prizes like exercise books, a writing brush and certificates of merit, and his teachers in the elementary school always praised him for his cleverness.

But he caused some trouble one day during the second semester when he was a second grader. I remember I was bringing my child back to visit my parents, and before I entered the yard I heard him crying inside. I pushed the door open and found my brother was spanking him on the bottom with one of his shoes. My father, my mother and my sister-in-law were all standing there, watching.

I hurried forward to stop him and asked why. My brother said madly: "This shameful thing dared to pull off the pants of one of the girls in his class!"

I was startled by his words and then took the whimpering urchin into the room, whispering to him: "Did you really do that?"

Wiping his tears, he admitted it with a nod.

"Why?"

He sobbed and said: "I just want to know why girls don't have pee-pees." His words made me giggle.

When he was eight years old, something unfortunate happened to my family. It was a small thing at the beginning. I remember it was during the drought period, and my elder brother was watering the cornfield with the water from the small ditch beside the ridge of the field. The Fang family, whose field was next to ours, came to stop my brother, saying he had used their water. Annoyed by this, my brother replied: "The water in the ditch was raindrops from heaven. How could it become yours?" They argued and shouted, and in the end the Fang family took advantage of having more people there and resorted to force. They broke my brother's left leg.

With tears of anguish in his eyes, my father took the Fang family to the county court on that very day. My family's argument was strong enough to win the case, but the Fang family had a nephew who was the county head, and they claimed that my brother was to blame and should be held solely responsible for his broken leg. My family eventually lost the case. My brother's leg did not heal completely, and he became a cripple with a limp. In his anger, my father got heart problems, and often pressed his hand to his chest, complaining of pain.

Although he was a child at that time, Wantong could understand what had happened to the family. I remember one day my father caught Wantong's hand and said: "Tong'er, you've already seen what has happened to us. If you're not an official, you're sure to be bullied like this.

Keep this in your mind when you grow up. You must be an official!" Wantong didn't say anything and stared at his grandfather blankly.

One spring, my father went to sell a calf belonging to my family, and he didn't come back until twilight. With him was a middle-aged man he met in the town. The moment he entered the room, he asked my mother to scramble some eggs and fry some pancakes. He ordered my brother to kill a hen and stew it on the stove, and he also told me to ladle two bowls of yellow wine from the wine jar. He warmed the wine, apparently entertaining a distinguished guest. After the wine and the dishes were served on the table in the living room, my father didn't ask my brother and my mother to eat with them. He and the man began eating and speaking to each other mysteriously in very low voices. I asked my mother and my brother whether they knew the man, but they both shook their heads.

After they finished supper, it was already dark outside. My father said to my mother: "You guys go and eat your supper, and I'll take this gentleman to the graves of our ancestors."

My mother was shocked: "It's pitch dark now. What can you see there?"

Father gave her a stare: "Woman, you're ignorant! Stop nagging and do your work." With these words, he left with the man.

After we finished dinner, we stayed awake, waiting for them to come back. My father's behaviour was truly confusing. Just before midnight, he came back alone. My mother asked him where the guest was, and he said that the man had gone.

I was so curious about the whole thing and couldn't help asking him: "Father, why did you go to our ancestors' graves at night?"

After a short hesitation, he said: "The guest we had today is a feng shui master. I've been thinking about inviting him to check on the feng shui of our ancestors' graves to see why we haven't had an official in the family for so many generations. As the saying goes, the worse luck now, the better luck next time. Why do we still not have an official after several generations? I have invited him many times but he always declined. He said the government believes feng shui is a superstition and he didn't dare to take the risk to practise it again. Recently, I heard he wanted to buy a calf, so I gave him the one we had. The gift was probably too much for him, and he finally agreed to come and observe the graves after dark. Just now, he walked around the graves three times, then took two hundred steps in four directions – to the north, the south, the east and the west – to study the location. He then opened a compass to check the position. He also looked up at the stars in the sky. Finally, he told me that the graves conformed to the surrounding environment and our ancestors' bones could be warmed by the *qi* of the underground, which in return would bless the descendants. However, there's a small canal flowing nearby, so our graves can't gather the *qi* of dragon and the *qi* of wealth, which pass over our graves and flow with the canal without stopping. That's why we haven't had officials for generations."

"What should we do?" My mother was anxious.

My father took a smoke from his pipe and replied calmly: "The master told me there are two methods to solve the problem. One is to stop the small canal from flowing beside our graves. The other is to bury earthen pots that can hold some water underground to the north, south, east and west of our graves. Either of the methods will work."

I thought it over and felt the first one was too difficult because we would have to get permission from the leaders of the village and the county government. As for the second one, it was only a matter of money! We could go to the town to buy the earthen pots the next day.

The next day, my father brought four big earthen pots back from the town, and my mother wiped them clean. After supper, my father and my brother secretly carried them to the graves and buried them according to the instruction.

It's probably because of this that our ancestors' graves have gathered the *qi* of the dragon and the *qi* of wealth. Wantong became an official when he grew up. I remember a couple of weeks before Wantong was admitted to university, Old Dong, who lived in the east end of the village, told me that when he passed by the graves of our ancestors he saw a thread of purple smoke rising straight from the middle of the graves, and it lingered there for quite a long time before it drifted away.

Wantong has had two strengths since he was a child. Firstly, he loved reading books. You know we didn't have many books in the countryside, and whenever he found one, he wouldn't put it down until he finished reading it. No one in the family needed to urge him to do his schoolwork, and he never let his parents worry about all the exams he took – the elementary entrance exam, the middle school entrance exam and the high school exam. It was often when he brought back the admission notice that the adults knew he had been successful, so all they needed to do was to provide the tuition for him.

The second gift he had was related to the suona and painting, which of course had something to do with me and his mother. I enjoy listening to suona performances – especially *A Hundred Birds Worshipping the Phoenix* – so I encouraged him to learn from Zhao Mingxian who lived in the east end of the village. Mingxian used to be the leader of a suona band. He played the suona, his younger brother and his wife played the vertical flute, and his younger sister played the wooden clappers.

At that time, a suona band was usually a family team, so it was easy to organise things like apprentice training, management and money distribution. Mingxian had two apprentices. One was Wantong and the other was his daughter Lingling, who was two years younger than Wantong. Wantong began to learn to play suona at the age of eight while Lingling was only six. The two kids were smart, and very soon they learned how to play. Though they could only practise the suona at dusk after school, they could both play quite well within two years. I had a selfish thought at that time – if Wantong married Lingling in the future, then the suona band of the Zhao family would become the band of the Ouyang family. If this happened, we would have a gold mine, and I could enjoy *A Hundred Birds Worshipping the Phoenix* any time I wanted.

Things just happened the way I wanted them to go. Wantong could already play the suona alone on the stage, and Lingling was a good flute player as well. In some evening shows when Mingxian and his wife were not available, Wantong and Lingling would step into the breach and give excellent performances.

It seemed Wantong was right on track to make money playing the suona, but unexpectedly, my father – Wantong's grandfather – stood up to say no. At first, my father didn't show any objection to Wantong learning to play the suona, thinking it was simply a way for him to relax after school. Later, when he found Wantong was becoming addicted to playing the suona, he worried that he might forget about his most important task – to be an official! He was therefore strongly opposed to it, especially objecting to his making money by performing in shows. Whenever he heard Wantong play the suona, he would smash plates and bowls, and sometimes he would even go to the show himself and aimlessly bang his walking stick. Wantong had no choice but to give it up. If he had continued, he would certainly have become a suona master when he grew up. His grandfather was obsessed with the hope that Wantong would become an official. But is being an official really that great? Is there anything wrong with enjoying one's life by playing the suona?

Wantong also learned how to draw from the village painter, Uncle Jiuchang. His mother had insisted on this. Wantong was clever, and very soon he could draw like a professional. His roof painting was great, and the door gods he drew were imposing too. One year before the Spring Festival, Uncle Jiuchang fell sick, but all the families in the village still came to seek door god paintings, so Uncle Jiuchang had to ask Wantong to paint for him. That year, all the pictures of door gods pasted on the front door of each household in the village were Wantong's work, and everyone said that he did a great job.

When he was in middle school, Wantong had already learned from Uncle Jiuchang how to paint dreams. Do you know what dream painting is? When people had good dreams, they liked to record them in the hope that they would come true. So how were they recorded? You would go and tell the dream to Uncle Jiuchang who could, based on what you recalled, paint it with his drawing brush. Then you would take the drawing home, put it up on the wall beside the bed, and stare at it every day. As you watched it, your dream would probably come true. This really worked and was verified several times. Many people in the neighbouring villages believed in this, and they came to invite Uncle Jiuchang to paint their dreams.

Also, if you had frequent similar nightmares and wanted to stop them from becoming true, you could describe them to Uncle Jiuchang and he would paint them according to your description. Once you got it home, you would spread it on the floor of the living room, sprinkle a handful of powdered cinnabars on the painting and then burn it. From then on, you would not be haunted by that nightmare anymore.

After Wantong learned how to paint dreams, he could do this work whenever Uncle Jiuchang was on a faraway trip or fell ill. One dream painting could earn Wantong two litres of corn kernels or even a meal of noodles with ground mutton from a generous family, making him the envy of many high school students in the village! But my father – his grandfather – not only forbade him to play the suona but also forbade him to become a painter. He threw away Wantong's paint brushes, preoccupied with the idea of encouraging him to go on with his study and become an official.

Capable of playing the suona and painting, Wantong soon became the target of many households with unmarried daughters in the nearby villages. Matchmakers began to visit our family. You know, at that time in the countryside, unlike what young people usually practise nowadays, marriages were often decided when people were in their teens, almost ten years earlier than is usual today, for fear that they might miss the right person. His mother – my sister-in-law – grinned from ear to ear when she saw the matchmakers, and she asked for my opinion. I said to her: "Can't you see Wantong and Lingling like each other. Nothing seems to separate them."

Alas, this is a mistake that I have made too. Wantong, though he had to give up playing the suona, couldn't give up his feelings for Lingling, and they secretly kept in touch with each other. I bumped into them several times when they had a date on the riverbank outside the village, and once I even saw them kiss each other in the woods outside the village. Of course, I just turned a blind eye and pretended not to see them. I wondered whether my father let Wantong see Lingling, even though he didn't allow him to learn the suona from Mingxian. What a graceful, pretty and ingenious girl Lingling was in our village!

When Wantong was a second grader in high school, his grandfather and grandmother were both sick in bed, and his two younger sisters and one younger brother were still too young to help with the housework. Short of money and labour, his father wanted him to quit school and help with the family. Hearing that, his grandfather was angry. Lying in bed, he hit the bedside with his pipe and scolded Wantong's father: "No one is allowed to ask my grandson to quit school! I would rather die in bed without taking any medicine to save money for my grandson's tuition. How can he become an official if he doesn't go to school? How can the Ouyang family change its fate if he doesn't become an official? Who will protect us from being bullied in the future?"

It was because of his grandfather's insistence that Wantong finished high school and was successfully admitted to Qinghe University.

In those days, being admitted to a university was equivalent to being listed on the emperor's releasing roll, becoming an official theoretically. His grandfather was overjoyed with the news and walked all around the village on his crutches, saying to anyone he met: "Good news! Good news! My grandson Wantong has been admitted to Qinghe University and has become an official. In future, anyone who goes to the provincial capital should visit him."

In the year when Wantong went to study in the provincial capital, every household in our village was starving because there was no meaningful work and not enough food was being distributed. Only the families of Mingxian and Uncle Jiuchang had money to buy food and didn't suffer from hunger. Wantong's grandfather wanted to sell his ancestral jade pot to get some money for Wantong, but in those years who could afford to buy this? No one came to buy the pot and the time for Wantong to go to university was arriving. As there was no money for him, the whole family became anxious.

If it weren't for Lingling's help, our family would have had no way out. It was she who got 30 yuan from her father and sent it to Wantong, taking the pressure off our family. Lingling was sixteen years old at that time, beautiful and sweet like a flower bud. She had a delicate and soft face, pointed and bouncy breasts, and curvy hips. She was a girl who was loved by everyone.

The night before Wantong departed, I returned from my husband's family with eight boiled eggs for him. After dinner, his grandfather began to tell him this and that while I could see his restlessness, looking outside from time to time. I knew he must have a date with Lingling, and I thought I should help them. So, I went out of the yard and shouted: "Wantong, come out! Some of your friends are calling you." After he ran out, I whispered to him: "Go and see her!" He bowed to me gratefully and then rushed quickly towards the woods outside the village.

It was not long after Wantong went to university that my father's illness became serious. At that time, no family could have any savings and it was very difficult to borrow money to buy medicine. Lingling's family helped us sometimes, but they themselves were always hard up. Eventually, my father was unable to fight his illness anymore. My brother knew how much my father loved his first grandson, Wantong, so he suggested sending him a telegraph, telling him to borrow some money from his teacher and come back home to pay a farewell visit to his grandfather. My father, however, didn't agree. He panted: "Don't distract him from his study! He's the hope of the Ouyang family. As long as he becomes a real official, I'll be happy in the underworld!"

Whenever Wantong wrote back, he would enquire about his

grandfather, but my brother and sister-in-law didn't tell him that he had died. Instead, they told lies. It wasn't until the summer holiday in his second year that Wantong managed to come back home for the first time. He even bought some snacks with what he had saved from his grant for his grandfather. The moment he arrived at the house, he knew his grandfather had gone because he saw the yellow paper couplets on the door frame. He went to his grandfather's grave and cried in front of it for quite a long time. It was me who finally dragged him back. I remember clearly that when he stood up in front of the grave, he said in a low voice: "Grandpa, I've always remembered your wish!"

Of course, Wantong bought gifts for Lingling too. She was eighteen years old at that time, and numerous matchmakers went to her family every day, but she declined them all. Her parents, my brother and sister-in-law and the other villagers knew she was waiting for Wantong. I asked him what he was going to do about Lingling, thinking he might have changed his thinking after having studied in the provincial capital and seen many girls in the city. To my surprise, he said Lingling would be prettier than those city girls if she were dressed in clothes city girls usually wore. He also said that once he was assigned a job after graduation, he would come back to marry Lingling and then take her away with him.

When my brother and sister-in-law and the Mingxian couple heard him saying this, they began to happily prepare an engagement ceremony for them.

Because of Wantong's status as a college student and the popularity of Mingxian's family for their suona performances, a lot of households in the village attended the ceremony with gifts. Uncle Jiuchang's gift was the most handsome one – a newly butchered pig! During the ceremony, I proposed that Mingxian play the suona for a while and he agreed. That day, the Mingxian family did something special. The suona music danced high up in the air, and everyone enjoyed the music to their hearts' content. Two families in the village were quarrelling at that time, but they were seduced by Mingxian's music and ended up standing there listening attentively. On that day, *A Hundred Birds Worshipping the Phoenix* seemed to come alive. It was as if the birds were chirping merrily in the tree. Everyone was refreshed by the wonderful music.

Later, two young men suggested Wantong and Lingling present an ensemble. At first, the two of them were shy but they finally agreed to perform after being pressured by the audience. Wantong took the suona from Mingxian and Lingling took the flute from her uncle. With Lingling's mother striking the clappers, they began to play *A Hundred Birds Worshipping the Phoenix* again. At the very beginning, the two were a little nervous, but very soon they were in time with each other. They probably felt the delight in their hearts, so the music flowing from the instruments was extraordinarily merry. This particular piece gives musicians enough space to be creative, so they can imitate the singing of any type of bird they choose or they can add to the original music. They have the final decision on how many types of birds they want to include in their performance. On that day, Wantong added almost all the birds that could be heard in our village. It was so vivid that it seemed like all the birds were coming alive and singing around us. Lingling complemented him perfectly. No matter how Wantong played, Lingling cooperated with him with her flute, and their performance was such a success that it seemed to have brought everything back to life. The villagers were so fascinated by their music that they simply stared at them and forgot themselves completely. The audience applauded vigorously!

After the congratulations, Uncle Jiuchang brought a paper and brush. After he spread the rice paper on the table and inked the brush, he said to Wantong: "You must have sweet dreams these days. Let me paint your dream and make it come true! Tell us, have you dreamed of a group of children playing around?"

Wantong was a bit shy at first, but then he said: "Grandpa Jiuchang, let me paint it myself!"

Hearing that, Uncle Jiuchang handed the brush to him hastily saying: "That's a great idea. You're a good painter yourself!" Wantong walked towards the table and began to draw. He painted a wood first, then added a few clouds in the sky over the wood and a goose flying in the sky. Everyone was waiting for him to continue, but he put down the brush.

It seemed that Uncle Jiuchang also felt that he hadn't finished his painting and asked: "Is that all?"

Wantong replied: "I've finished. I've had many dreams recently, and that is what I've always dreamed about."

Uncle Jiuchang smiled and said: "Great! It probably means that our Wantong will become a goose sailing in the sky in the future."

But when I looked at that picture, I had an ominous feeling. Of course,

I couldn't say it out loud. It was a time when the whole family was delighted, so how could I be the one to spoil it?

During the Cultural Revolution, it was the school revolutionary committee that decided where Wantong should be assigned to work. He wrote back home before the school issued the result, saying that he had two options – one was to work as a cadre in a factory in the Tianquan suburb, while the other was to go back to his home county and work as an official in the commune. They were both administrative government posts. He asked his parents for advice, so his father asked me to come home, hoping to get my thoughts.

I said: "When Wantong's grandfather was still alive, he had been looking forward to the day when his grandson could be an official. Wantong should choose the one that has power and the potential to be quickly promoted in the future."

His father wrote what I had said in the letter to Wantong, and that's why he finally chose to work in Guanqiao Commune in his home county. He indeed made the right choice! The day he reported to Guanqiao Commune, he became the secretary assisting the head of the commune with all kinds of work. He was finally a real official!

By this time, the family had begun to prepare the wedding ceremony for him and Lingling. He wrote a letter back and said it might be better to arrange the wedding ceremony on a day around the Spring Festival so that he didn't need to take leave. He also said he would take Lingling to Guanqiao Commune with him after the wedding.

My brother and sister-in-law and the Mingxian family were preparing for the wedding happily. At that time, traditional sedan chairs for the bride were not allowed to be used. The government advocated a new style of wedding ceremony – using a bicycle to take your bride home! I remember it was me who went to borrow the bicycle from Uncle Jiuchang's son. You know, few families in the village could afford to buy a bicycle, but Uncle Jiuchang's son bought a new Flying Pigeon bicycle. It cost me twenty eggs to borrow the bicycle, which meant that on the day when Wantong and Lingling had the wedding ceremony, Uncle Jiuchang's family couldn't use it no matter what urgent business they might encounter – they had to give the bicycle to Wantong to bring Lingling back. I met Lingling after I had reserved the bicycle, and joked with her, saying: "Ling, I, your future aunt, have reserved the most beautiful bicycle for you! Once you're married and you become a member of our Wantong family, don't forget your old aunt! Remember to honour me in the future!"

Hearing this, Lingling was so shy that she covered her face with her hands and ran away immediately.

No one expected what happened next.

The wedding was scheduled on the twenty-eighth of the last month in the lunar calendar, which, according to the person who picked the wedding day for them, meant celebrating the New Year right after their wedding ceremony. Double happiness indeed.

Wantong came back on the twenty-fifth, and I happened to be at my parents' home on that day. The moment he entered the house, I felt something was wrong. There was no happiness on his face. You know, there would definitely be some sign of happiness on any young man's face when his wedding day was only three days away, no matter how much he tried to conceal it. Wantong didn't have that look. Instead, there was a touch of worry and anxiety on his face. What happened? I was surprised and worried, feeling that something must have happened.

Sure enough, when we had supper together, Wantong told us the trouble he had met. He never told his colleagues about his wedding and planned to let them know when he asked for marriage leave. Things happened unexpectedly. It was just three days before he went back home that he was required to accompany the leader of the commune to attend a meeting in the county. After the meeting, his leader took him directly to the home of the county magistrate. He had thought the county magistrate wanted to give them some instructions, but to his surprise the magistrate was not at home. Instead, his wife and daughter were waiting for them. The commune leader chatted with them for a while and then took Wantong away. He was wondering what it was all about when the commune leader said to him: "The magistrate and his wife have a good impression of you and want you to be their son-in-law. Their daughter is very satisfied with you too now that she has seen you. What do you think about it?"

"Good heavens!" Wantong's grandmother shouted happily when she heard this and then asked: "What does the girl look like? She's not ugly, is she?"

Wantong reluctantly took out a photo from his pocket and handed it to his grandmother. "My leader gave me this," he said.

Taking a glance at the photo, his grandmother slapped her thigh and said: "Good! Good! Very agreeable!" Then she passed the photo on to Wantong's parents, and then to me. I looked at it closely. The girl in the photo looked good, but compared with Lingling, she was far behind. She simply looked fashionable and well dressed.

At that moment, Wantong's grandmother opened her mouth: "A county official likes Wantong and wants to marry her daughter to him, which indeed never happened in our Ouyang family before. It's a big happy event, an honour! It's the modern version of the traditional practice of choosing the emperor's son-in-law!"

"Have you thought about Lingling? What should she do? Their marriage has long been arranged!" I stared at his grandmother – my mother – unhappily.

"Can we reject the county leader?" asked Wantong's mother.

"Definitely not! It would mean we don't have the sense to appreciate favours?" said Wantong's father worriedly. "If we did that, the county leader would make life very difficult for Wantong, and there would be no hope for him to be promoted."

"Wantong, what do you think?" Wantong's grandmother looked at him and asked.

Burying his head in his hands, Wantong sat there brooding silently.

Then his grandmother announced: "Well, since all of you are keeping silent, I'll make the decision to break off the engagement with Lingling."

I was shocked by what she said and shouted as I looked at Wantong: "We can't do this! Lingling's family have already prepared the dowry, and they have bought wine and food for the wedding banquet!"

His grandmother gave me a stare: "You know nothing! Man struggles upwards, water flows downwards. We can't stand in the way of his future promotion! The Ouyang family hasn't had the opportunity to work as officials for generations. Since we have the chance now, we shouldn't let it slip by."

Wantong raised his head and said: "Don't say anything. I'll marry Lingling! In any event, the worst thing for me is to work as the secretary in the commune forever."

His grandmother sighed: "It's your own business after all. We respect your decision as long as you won't regret it later."

Since the wedding was going to be held as scheduled, my brother and sister-in-law and I planned to go on with the preparations the next day. But at suppertime the next day, Lingling came, eyes red and swollen. I had thought she might be unhappy with some details of the wedding arrangements, so I hurriedly offered her a seat. To my surprise, she sobbed and said: "Brother Wantong, I heard the county leader wants you to be his son-in-law. It's very important for your future promotion, and I don't want to ruin your career. Otherwise, you'll hate me for the rest of your life. Our marriage is off!" With these words, she wiped her tears and ran away.

The whole family was shocked.

Wantong pulled a long face and asked: "Who told her this?"

My brother looked at my sister-in-law. My sister-in-law looked at me. I looked at my brother. Then we all looked at my mother – Wantong's grandmother.

"I told Lingling's father," she said, "but I simply said Wantong would rather marry Lingling than be the county magistrate's son-in-law. Nothing else!"

"Ah!" Wantong slapped on his thigh.

I understood my mother's small tricks. I gave her a dirty look and then turned to Wantong, holding his hand and said: "Come with me to see Lingling in case she does something foolish."

I clearly remember the scene when we arrived at Lingling's home. Lingling and her mother were crying in the inner room, while Mingxian squatted outside in the living room smoking his pipe in silence. When he saw us, he rose unsteadily to his feet and said: "Go back home please. There's no need to say anything. Lingling understands what she should do, and she told us she couldn't ruin Wantong's career. She wouldn't force Wantong to marry her. It wouldn't be good for either family. I know it's not easy for a man to have the opportunity to be an official. We all understand it. Wantong, forget about this and go for your future. When you become an official in a high position, don't forget us and don't let others bully us ordinary people. That'll be good enough! Please go back!" He kept waving at us as he said this.

"Uncle… I… I never asked my grandmother…" stuttered Wantong as he tried to express himself.

"Go back home. The more we talk about this, the worse everyone feels! Go back!" Mingxian pushed us out of the front door.

Wantong left home very early the next day. It was already the twenty-seventh of the last month in the lunar calendar. Before he left, he said to me: "Aunt, I'll be on duty in the commune during the Spring Festival, and I won't be back to celebrate the New Year this year."

I went back to my husband's home on that morning as well. Since there was no wedding banquet, what was the point of staying with my parents? Upon my departure, my mother stopped me and asked me to have breakfast before I left. I didn't pay attention to her. I was angry with her. It was she who deliberately ruined Wantong and Lingling's marriage. She was obsessed with the idea of being the grandmother of a senior official!

"You stupid girl! You've become a mother, yet still you have no brains."

I could hear her cursing behind me, but I didn't turn back because I knew that if I turned my head, I would get into an argument with her.

At that moment I thought of the picture Wantong drew – the one about his dream. A goose flying over the sky. Yes, that was indeed ominous. One single goose. Why not draw two geese? If so, it might bless their marriage.

Lingling got married hastily three months later. Her husband's family was in Weijiaji, a small town a few miles away, not far from my husband's home. Her husband was a carpenter who often carried axes, chisels and saws to find work around the region.

Wantong and the daughter of the county magistrate had their wedding in the county. The county magistrate's surname was Lin, and his daughter was named Lin Qiangwei. She was tall and slender, like a tree crowded with other trees, trying to grow upwards in the woods.

His parents-in-law wrote a letter to invite my brother and sister-in-law to attend the wedding, but neither of them wanted to go. They had never travelled far and knew little about the customs of city people, so they thought their visit might bring disgrace on Wantong.

It wasn't until after the wedding ceremony that Wantong brought Qiangwei back to meet her parents-in-law. On the day they returned, all the villagers came to see them. It was indeed a glorious return to the village for Wantong. He himself looked fair and well fed. There was no sign of the worry and timidity that he used to have in his knitted brows, probably because he ate well and did not have to work in the field now that he was an official. He was dressed in a well-pressed standard cadre uniform and liked to walk with his hands folded behind his back – a very official-like appearance. As for Qiangwei, she was not bad looking, and she dressed fashionably with her long hair hanging down to the shoulder.

She wore a short coat, had a round and prominent bosom and two slender legs. Her clothes were adorable. The villagers had never seen such an agreeable daughter-in-law. My brother and sister-in-law kept smiling, and later they laughed so hard that they even forgot to cover their mouths, exposing all their teeth in front of people. The villagers made compliments all the time, saying it was the first time anyone had brought a princess back as a daughter-in-law there. They also said it was the first time our village had an emperor's son-in-law!

That night, my mother was so happy that she proposed to invite a suona band to celebrate. I said to my brother: "If you do invite one, please find one from a faraway village. Don't think about Mingxian's family – it would be like thrusting a knife into their hearts."

As I said this, I stared sharply at Wantong, who hurriedly waved his hands towards his grandmother and said: "No, no, Qiangwei and I prefer peace and quiet!" Qiangwei didn't understand what we were talking about and simply ignored our conversation.

Later, I heard that the Mingxian family went out to do some odd jobs the day after Wantong and Qiangwei came back. During that time, they mostly played songs about Chairman Mao's quotations, or the song called *Sailing the Seas Depends on the Helmsman*. They never met Qiangwei.

Qiangwei brought joy to the family, but there was a fly in the ointment. She appeared arrogant and hot-tempered and behaved contemptuously towards people. This might have been a result of her spoiled childhood. The very night when they came back, some young lads in the village who called Wantong brother came to tease the newlyweds for some fun. This was an old tradition in the countryside. No one ever expected that when one of the young men reached his hand out to push her, she would immediately raise her eyebrows and shout coldly: "What are you doing?" This made the young guys freeze on the spot. Another young man jokingly asked her to light a cigarette for him, but she just threw a matchbox to him and said: "Light it yourself!" These villagers soon left in low spirits. My brother and sister-in-law made apologies to them anxiously, and Wantong himself felt he was losing face, but he dared not get angry with Qiangwei.

Qiangwei had two more failings. First, she was quite picky about food. Whenever the food didn't agree with her, she would throw her chopsticks down and refuse to eat, claiming that she was not hungry. This worried my sister-in-law quite a lot. How could she, a rural woman who only cooked simple food at home, know how to cook the dishes the county officials usually ate? And when it happened, Wantong could do nothing but take out biscuits and cakes he had prepared and coax her to eat some. The other problem was that she was too particular about hygiene. She would rinse the bowls and chopsticks she and Wantong used with boiling water several times before each meal for fear that they were not clean. She thought that the toilet was dirty, so each time she went there she frowned as if she were on the way to the execution ground. She complained about the chicken droppings in the yard and would order Wantong to sweep it several times a day. I told myself secretly that this kind of daughter-in-law was not easy to please, and since Wantong had her in his life, it seemed that he would not have an easy time.

Their marriage was indeed beneficial to Wantong's promotion. Soon after Wantong and Qiangwei got married, Wantong was transferred to a new post in the county working as a secretary. His grandmother grinned from ear to ear after she heard the news. She said to me: "You see – who has done the right thing?"

I was disgusted by what she said.

When Wantong and Qiangwei's son, Qianzi, was born, my sister-in-law wanted me to go with her to see her grandson and take care of Qiangwei during her postpartum confinement. It was the first time I had been to the county. My goodness, the trip was indeed an eye-opener – the streets were so long, there were so many people and the shops were huge. I didn't know people in the city had such luxurious lives until I entered Wantong's house. The walls were painted pure white, the floor was spotlessly clean and the shoes were placed neatly in order.

Qiangwei's postpartum was, in a sense, an enjoyable experience. Her mother, the county magistrate's wife, arranged for a driver to do the grocery shopping, and he bought vegetables, chicken and fish. A nanny was hired to take care of the newborn baby. Wantong's mother and I were in charge of cooking and stewing soup. I still remember the soups we learned from the magistrate's wife. There were so many of them – chicken soup, pig trotters soup with soy beans, creamy cabbage soup, duck soup with mushrooms, mutton blood soup with vermicelli, and white fungus soup with lotus seeds to name a few. I learned so much. Qiangwei's only job was to feed the baby. She didn't sleep with the baby during the night – the nanny did that. Qiangwei was a princess and liked to throw tantrums without any reason. Back then, I thought that anyone who was born into a county official's family had a blessed life.

Wantong's path to pursuing an official career was not smooth. It was only two years after he had been transferred to the county that his father-in-law was removed from his post under the accusation of being a so-and-so '-ist'. Wantong was categorised among 'obedient sons and grandsons' and was forced to work in the County Cultural Centre. Luckily, the Ouyang family had a good background, and people there were not too hard on him. The Cultural Revolution changed Qiangwei's temperament too – she learned how to control her behaviour and be a considerate wife, to some extent.

After that, Wantong became the person he wanted to be in his own right. He passed the examination and went to study in the provincial capital. After graduation, he was assigned to work in Tianquan city. Eventually, he became the deputy mayor of Tianquan before his grandmother passed away. We checked our Ouyang family genealogy records and found that no one had become such a senior official for quite a few generations. It was totally beyond our expectations. His grandmother grabbed his hand and said to him before she breathed her last: "Tong'er, you have brought honour to our family and carried out your grandfather's wish. When I see him in the other world, I'll be proud to tell him all about it. You know, since you became an official, no one ever tries to bully us and there's nothing I can complain about. I'm very content with what we have..."

Looking at the contentment on her face, I felt for the first time that perhaps she was right to insist on making an official of Wantong. If they had followed my will and allowed Wantong to play suona and marry Lingling, today's Wantong wouldn't exist.

As you know, Qiangwei became an official too, which made the whole village happy. They all said the Ouyang family was a home of officials. But no one expected that Qiangwei would get into trouble and go to prison a few years later. This news shocked the whole village like a lightning bolt. We were all dumbfounded – how could this happen to an official?

Then we heard Wantong had been removed from his position. For me and my brother and sister-in-law, the days wore on like years. What I feared most was that Wantong would take this too much to heart. You know, my brother had problems with his legs, and my sister-in-law couldn't read or write so she dared not to go to Tianquan. Therefore, I had no choice but to go there myself.

I found him in his home and said to him: "Boy, don't take it so hard! At worst, we can go back to our hometown and be farmers! The Ouyang family have been farming in the countryside for generations, so can't we survive like this? A great man knows when to yield and when not to yield. Never lose your hope!"

Thankfully, Wantong was restored to his post, but his marriage with Qiangwei came to an end. When I was informed of their divorce, I once again thought of that dream picture Wantong had painted – a goose was flying over the sky, wasn't it? Wantong was the lonely goose, and that painting was indeed ominous!

When Wantong was the mayor of the provincial city, I went to live in his place for a few days. He hadn't yet married Xiaowen at this time. I didn't want to go at first, but my youngest son, Wantong's cousin Lianhe, pestered me to go. Lianhe didn't want to teach after he graduated from a normal university. Instead, he established some kind of cultural enterprise company selling some disc. I can't remember it clearly – oh, I got it, it's called a CD. What he could earn from this business was barely enough to cover the food and rent that he and his wife had to handle.

Why did he want me to go to see his cousin Wantong? His real purpose was to ask a favour of Wantong for the approval of a piece of land. He told me he wanted to start a new business. He wanted to be a property developer because property was the most profitable business, and anyone who did it would make a big fortune overnight. He said the most important precondition was to get the land. Once you had the land, your next step was to find an architectural designer to do the building plan, and then you could make money immediately by selling houses. Getting quick rich was a piece of cake! He said a piece of land could generate huge profits. Wantong had the power to approve the land, and as long as he gave the green light, hundreds of acres of land could come to him. He said all I needed to do was to count the money at home! He also reminded me of one more thing – tell his cousin that he would have a share in our profits. He promised to give Wantong fifty per cent of what he earned.

I was somewhat convinced by what he said, though I knew there might be some bluffing in his words. After all, who didn't want to make money and become rich nowadays. At his instigation, I took a bus and went to Wantong's home in the provincial city.

Wantong's house was much more spacious than before, but it was a big mess without a woman living there. I advised him to find a woman and remarry as I cleaned up the house slowly. He smiled and said: "Aunt, it's not easy for me to find a desirable one since I'm not young anymore." I knew he was telling me the truth, and I dared not push him either.

For the first few days after I arrived, I was too embarrassed to talk about Lianhe and his plan. It wasn't until a few days later that I opened my mouth and told him all about it. After he heard that Lianhe wanted to be a real estate developer, he said to me: "Aunt, there's no one except you in this world who treats me like my mother. You've been giving me so much care since I was a little boy. By rights, I shouldn't reject anything that you ask of me. I should give you the permission. Lianhe's right to say that I have the power to approve the land, and as long as I give him the land, he's sure to make quick money. But I can't do this! Why? Qiangwei is the perfect example! Why did she end up in prison? Money and land. Suppose I approve the land to my cousin Lianhe, I'm using my power to help my relatives gain benefits. Suppose Lianhe gives me half of what he earns from real estate. He and I are simply dividing up illegal benefits, which violates discipline and law. The final consequence of doing this, therefore, is Lianhe and I going to prison. Aunt, you don't want to visit us there at your age, do you?"

Hearing that, I was so scared that I stood up involuntarily, waving off my request. Qiangwei's imprisonment had been such a heavy blow on the Ouyang family. How could I allow this to happen again? I didn't say anything else – this reason alone was good enough to scare me.

I went back to Tianquan by bus that very day, and the moment I saw Lianhe, I scolded him: "You're so obsessed with being rich that you almost lured me into doing a bad thing. But for your brother Wantong, a great disaster could have struck the Ouyang family again! Go and sell your CDs honestly. No matter how much you earn, you should accept it as long as it's enough for both of you to feed yourselves. Don't you know that peace is a blessing?"

Of course, Lianhe didn't expect this. He curled his lip and said: "Brother Wantong knows you're timid, so he told you this to frighten you. Look at all the officials in the province. Could you find any who don't help their relatives seeking benefits? Have they all been arrested? Are they all in prison? Huh, who will be scared by this? The majority of them are enjoying their lives, aren't they? Forget about it! Since I have such a just and impartial cousin who is unwilling to help his relatives, I'll give up the idea to be a real estate developer. It's just my bad luck."

My youngest son had been much spoiled by his father, and he wouldn't listen to anybody. Look at the careless and arrogant way in which he looked at people. I was wondering whether he would suffer from it sooner or later. And things did happen as I expected – he got into trouble a few years later.

Do you want to know what happened to him? He was such a good-for-nothing that he dared to sleep with one of his salesgirls right under his wife's nose and made that girl pregnant. Well, the woman asked for 100,000 yuan as compensation. If he didn't pay, she would keep the baby and show it to his wife after she gave birth. Lianhe's wife was not the type to be trifled with – if she knew about this, she would definitely stab him with a knife. Lianhe was terrified and ran back home begging me to go and get help from Wantong. He said brother Wantong had been the governor and it would be quite easy for him to settle this down. He said as long as Wantong mentioned this to the chief of the Bureau of Public Security, the chief would call that woman to the police station and teach her a lesson. She would obediently have an abortion..." I hated doing this. How could I tell this disgraceful thing to Wantong? But though Lianhe was indeed a loser, he was my son, and I didn't have the heart to do nothing when he was in trouble.

Reluctantly and quite embarrassed, I went to see Wantong in the provincial city. Wantong had already married Xiaowen and began his normal life at that time. He enquired after my family, and I stammered out what Lianhe had done, including his idea to teach the woman a lesson. After listening to my words, Wantong pulled a long face and said to me: "Aunt, if we do it as he wants, we're obviously abusing my power, which is a kind of bullying, isn't it? It's Lianhe who did the wrong thing, and if we force the woman to have the abortion, isn't that bullying? If we were the family of that woman, could we accept a result like this? Why did my grandfather, grandmother and father insist that I should be an official? Wasn't it because they didn't want to be bullied by officials? Suppose I use my power to help Lianhe and bully that woman – won't I be cursed as a corrupt official too?"

Wantong's remarks turned my face red, but Lianhe, after all, was my son and I had to figure out a way to save him. Wantong told me later that the only way to solve this problem was to satisfy the woman's requirement and give her the 100,000 yuan she had asked for. It would be compensation for the harm her body would suffer when she had the abortion. Wantong was right – it seemed there was no other better choice. But where could Lianhe get such a large amount of money? This poor pathetic man never had any extra money saved since he began to work! Wantong went into the room, brought out a card and asked Xiaowen to withdraw 50,000 yuan from the bank. From the look on her face, I could tell Xiaowen was a bit annoyed.

Wantong handed me the money and said: "Aunt, that's all I can do for you. As for the other 50,000, when you go back home, ask Lianhe to borrow from his friends. You must let him worry about this. He must learn to face the consequences himself. Otherwise, the same thing will happen again. He is married now, so you should stop worrying about him. Let him be independent! Also, remember to let him know that he's lucky to get away with this because he's a businessman. If he were a civil servant, the Discipline Inspection Department would punish him!"

Lianhe, that pathetic good-for-nothing, has probably learned a lesson from this incident because in recent years he has done his business honestly and not made any more trouble.

I have talked quite a lot – probably too much. I don't know whether it will be useful to you.

4

REN YIMING

THE PROFESSOR

YES, I'm quite familiar with Mr Ouyang Wantong, or I should say we were good friends. When he was free, he liked to come to my place to sit, talk and drink tea with me. Because of my poor health, I didn't attend his farewell ceremony. We became acquainted at a 'Future Development Seminar' and he at that time was the mayor of the provincial city and the deputy secretary of the Municipal Party Committee.

At that seminar, most of the speakers were fond of saying nice words only, such as how beautiful our future would be and how smooth our development would be. On the contrary, I made some unpleasant 'warnings'.

I remember the first point in my talk was that precautions should be taken against major social unrest. Economic reforms have indeed greatly improved people's lives, and we enjoy more political and cultural freedoms, while there are fewer hardships. But it's right at this moment that the feelings of pain become more acute and harder to deal with. That's why social unrest usually doesn't occur when people are in the worst situation, but rather when things are improving.

My second point was that future development should focus on four new situations. First, quite a few high-ranking officials' families and a considerable number of rich people have applied to emigrate to other countries, while those who haven't are preparing to do so. Wealthy people are starting to transfer their property abroad, which indicates that the political and business elites have no confidence in the future of our country. Second, something has gone wrong with our faith. The total number of those who firmly believe in Communism, Buddhism, Taoism, Islam or Christianity is less than one-third of the total population. The vast majority don't have any faith at all – the only things they worship are power and money. There is a generally accepted idea that obtaining power and money is everything in life and the ultimate measure of a person's success. The third issue is that the natural environment has been destroyed. Our basic necessities, like water, air and land, have been seriously polluted. Mineral resources are the subject of predatory exploration. It's as if we have no intention of giving our children any chance to go on living in this world. The last one was China becoming a low-IQ society. In China, the number of books we're reading is rapidly declining – less than one book per person per year on average, compared to seven in Korea, forty in Japan, fifty-five in Russia and sixty-four in Israel. Everywhere, we can see mah-jong houses and internet bars. We can see people play games, chat, browse jokes and text on their mobile phones. Not many people hold a book and read attentively. Occasionally we'll see some people read books, but most of them will be preparing for exams. Think about this! How could our national IQ be improved? And how can we compete with other nations?

The last point I mentioned on that day was that we should keep in mind several sets of figures. The first set is the ratio of the number of officials to the number of civilians. You know, in the Western Han dynasty, the ratio of ordinary people to officials was 7,945 to 1. In the Eastern Han dynasty, it was 7,464 to 1. In the Tang dynasty, it was 2,927 to 1. In the Yuan dynasty, it was 2,613 to 1. In the Ming dynasty, it was 2,299 to 1. And in the Qing dynasty, it was 911 to 1. What about the number today? Someone said it's 67 to 1, which I think might be exaggerated – they might have categorised personnel in all public institutions as officials. But the indisputable fact is that nowadays the ratio of officials to ordinary people is quite large. A Bureau of Personnel and Labour at a prefecture-level can have several hundred staff. New York in the United States, with a population of 18 million and a GDP of 2.6 trillion dollars, has four mayors and deputy mayors, two council speakers and deputy council speakers. In Tokyo, Japan, with a population of 13 million and a GDP of 1.1 trillion dollars, there are two mayors and deputy mayors, five council speakers and deputy speakers. In our province, one prefecture-level city with a population of 5.65 million and a GDP of 10 billion dollars, has 39 municipal leaders, including a secretary and a deputy secretary, the minister of the Organisation Department, the minister of the Publicity Department, the minister of the United Front Work Department, the secretary of the Committee of Discipline Inspection and the secretary of the Committee of Political and Legal Affairs, nine mayors and deputy mayors, four assistants to the mayor, nine chairs and vice-chairs of the NPC Committee and ten chairs and vice-chairs of the CPPCC.

After each staff downsizing, the number of civil servants increases. The head of each government unit is looking for ways to increase its manpower quota. In the future, the management of manpower quotas of officials must be governed by the law. Whoever changes it violates the law – otherwise, the ratio of officials to civilians in our country will soon reach the limit.

The second set of figures is the ratio of administrative cost to GDP. In India, it's 6.3%. In the United States, it's 3.4%. In Japan, it's 2.8%. However, in China, it's 25.6%. Take government vehicles as an example. In New York, the number of government vehicles is 6,800, of which 95% are fire engines and police cars. In Beijing, the number is 700,000!

The third is the ratio of house prices to household income. The number in London is 6.9 to 1. In New York, it's 7.9 to 1. In Sydney, it's 8.5 to 1. In Seoul, it's 7.7 to 1. In Tokyo, it's 7.9 to 1. In Singapore, it's 5 to 1. But the number in Beijing and Shanghai is 30 to 1.

The fourth set of figures is the percentage of forest cover in our country. According to statistics, the present percentage of forest cover in China is only 16.5% while it's 67% in Finland, 66% in Japan, 64% in Korea, 60% in Norway, 44% in Canada, 30% in Germany, 33% in the United States, 23% in India and 20% in France. The world average is 22%.

The fifth set of figures is about rural areas. In China, rural areas produce about 120 million tons of solid waste every year, almost all of which will pile up outdoors, around the house, beside the roads and in pits or even water resource areas, spillways and village ponds. No one is in charge of collecting and processing that waste. Twenty-five million tons of domestic sewage is produced, and almost all of it is discharged without any treatment. This seriously affects the quality of the environment around villages. Also, we lose 10 billion tons of fertile soil every year. We know it takes 1 to 400 years to form one centimetre of arable soil naturally, and 3,000 to 12,000 years to have an arable layer. In China, the annual output of waste residues exceeds 500 million tons, which are all dumped in rural areas. By 1988, the accumulated amount reached 6.6 billion tons, and at present the figure is certainly higher. The accumulation of solid waste in China is nearly 8 billion tons. More than a thousand square kilometres of land has been occupied and destroyed by this waste. The amount of fertilisers used in rural areas is close to 40 tons per square kilometre – the standard application is 22.5 tons per square kilometre.

The sixth set of figures is the crime rate. Based on the relevant data of the Supreme People's Procuratorate and the Supreme People's Court, the estimated crime rate of ordinary Chinese citizens is 1 in 400. The figure for workers of state organs is 1 in 200. The figure for workers of judicial organs is 1.5 in 100...

When I finished my speech, Ouyang Wantong walked towards me. I instinctively thought he must have been annoyed by what I had just said. As one of the most senior officials in this city, he wouldn't want to listen to this kind of unpleasant talk, like the cry of a crow. He might want to give me a warning and embarrass me in public, but I was ready to refute him, and I didn't want to save his face. A senior official would never make any real contribution if he didn't have the grace to listen to different views. Didn't he know that freedom of speech was the bedrock of development and stability in a normal society? Officials should listen to different voices. A government should not be obsessed with the idea that everything it did was what a wise man would do. I was not afraid of him. I'm a teacher – if you won't allow me to teach, I can go back to do farming in my hometown. Just like the old saying goes – when one door shuts, another one opens.

Unexpectedly, he came over and held my hand, saying to me enthusiastically: "Professor Ren, thank you for being honest and speaking the truth with your warnings. It'll help us officials keep a clearer head."

It was from then on that he began to associate with me. At first, I was somewhat reluctant for him to visit my house. He was, after all, a senior official and I had the fear that others might talk behind my back, saying I was flattering him and trying to gain political benefits. Nowadays, quite a few intellectuals try to curry favour with officials, obsessed with the idea of tearing off the label of intellectual and becoming a member of the official team to bring honour to their families. In China, only officials have the privilege to leave their names in history, so entering the officialdom has become the goal most Chinese intellectuals strive for. I, however, only want to teach, and I don't want to leave others an impression that I'm trying to build some connection with officialdom and seek an official position from Ouyang Wantong. I look down upon people like this, and I don't want to become one of them. Gradually, however, I discovered that he was sincere, and I slowly began to accept him as my friend and welcome his visits at any time.

I once asked him directly why he wanted to be an official.

He didn't reply with some high-sounding words. He smiled and said: "My initial purpose of becoming an official was to prevent my family from being bullied by others, for the safety of my family and to change my life. When I grew up and began to understand things, I saw with my own eyes someone abuse his authority to bully my family, and they were unable to live in peace. I decided to become an official in order to change the vulnerable position of my family so that no one dared to bully us. After I became an official, I found that not only would no one dare to bully you and your family, but it also meant you could gain benefits. All officials have the power to distribute material benefits – both minor officials with small power and senior officials with huge power. In China, it's safe to say as long as you become an official, you're sure to gain more benefits than ordinary people. That's one of the reasons why I'm determined to work in officialdom. Later, as my rank in officialdom improved, especially after I became a county governor and city-level official, I began to realise I couldn't just think about myself and my family – I had to be responsible for the place I was entrusted to take care of. I had to seek benefits for the people for whom I was responsible. Otherwise, I would be a fatuous official. I would earn myself eternal infamy. I would leave a record in local chronicles. The awe I have for history and the fear I have of historical records makes me more cautious. It wasn't until I became a provincial-level official that I began to think of our nation and our country because by that time I have had so much power that I couldn't just think about myself and my family. I felt that I owed heaven and earth. We have about thirty provinces in China. If the top-level senior officials in those provinces and cities seek personal benefits, what will happen to our country and our Chinese nation? So many of our predecessors shed blood and sweat for this country. Shouldn't I learn from them?"

I didn't think he was being dishonest. It was hard for an official to avoid telling lies, and I liked to make friends with honest people. The second time he came to my home, he brought me an authentic writing brush made of weasel's hair. I was quite happy because I like calligraphy, and I'm particularly fond of great writing brushes. I tried the writing brush, and it was indeed a great one, so I thanked him again and again. He kept a straight face and said to me in a solemn way: "You don't have to thank me because I'm not giving it to you for nothing – I want one thing in exchange." I was a bit shocked and then asked him what he wanted. He said: "One piece of calligraphy."

I laughed. That was no problem. I spread a piece of four-foot long Xuan paper on the writing desk and wrote down two lines: "Play your role well when the stage is provided for you; When there is no stage, don't just be a spectator."

He smiled as he read it and said: "Good, I'll regard it as a warning to me. As soon as I arrive home, I'll frame it and hang it on the wall…"

When we were together, we had a lot of things to talk about, an extremely wide range of topics! He said to me: "In officialdom, most of what I hear on weekdays are praises. Subordinates usually dare not speak unpleasant words. My peers are usually unwilling to say anything against me. My seniors usually don't say anything unpleasant. So all I hear are pleasant words. You're not an official, so you don't have any worries, and it's only in your place that I could have the chance to know the truth."

I said: "Truth is harsh and unpleasant, and you might feel annoyed."

He smiled and said: "Many good emperors in history were overthrown amid enthusiastic praise from their ministers."

We seldom gossiped. It was something we weren't interested in. We always talked about issues on the governance of a country. To be honest, I, as a scholar and educator, knew very little about the governance of a country, so I was simply an armchair strategist, but he enjoyed talking with me. He said: "I'm more of an implementor and practitioner who must work out objectives, plans, measures and policies, while you're more of a spectator and judge whose remarks help me keep my head clear."

In our discussions, sometimes he put forward a question and I gave an answer, and sometimes I raised a question and he made comments. When we disagreed with each other, we would argue. In those instances, I was not a professor in his eyes, and he was not the secretary in mine. I was several years older than him, so he called me older brother and I called him younger brother. Sometimes, our discussions became so heated that my wife would intervene and say we had made too much noise and were distracting her from her painting. She also warned me more than once that Mr Ouyang was the secretary and if I annoyed him, I would suffer from it for sure.

I remember he once asked me a question: "In your opinion, for a large country like us, if a big problem should happen in the future, what are the possible reasons for that?"

I turned it over in my mind and said to him that domestically, there are three main reasons.

To begin with, financial management is the basic. If something should happen to it, big problems set in. Today, no matter which department of the national economy has gone wrong, we have the time to deal with it leisurely. But financial problems are different. People won't give us the opportunity to solve it calmly. Financial disaster spreads extremely fast and can cause panic. People are extremely sensitive to any negative information in this field. Once they hear their savings of many years could be in danger, their reaction will be lightning-fast. Perhaps within a few hours, tens of thousands of people would gather in front of banks across the country asking to withdraw their money. Suppose they fail to get their cash back – anger will sweep over the crowd, disturbances will start and a tremendous commotion will occur in the end. When a financial crisis breaks out in the United States, it's the government that panics because the ordinary people usually spend borrowed money, and the collapse of banks has nothing to do with them. However, in China, things are quite different. In China, even poor households can deposit in banks several thousand or tens of thousands of yuan for child-rearing, ageing and medication. If something happened to the banks, it would be such a heavy blow on them. It would be like a knife is stabbing their hearts.

Next, corruption of the ruling party. If the situation gets worse, big trouble will definitely befall. Needless to say, you're sure to know how appalling the corruption of our officialdom is! Nowadays, as for performance assessment, promotion, job transfer, price-setting, distribution of products and the implementation of construction projects – has any of those been done without sending money to people who are in charge? People all complain about this. If immediate measures are taken to stop this, perhaps the complaints will fade away. If not, people's anger will accumulate and it'll eventually explode, damaging the whole of society.

Third, if we continue making mistakes in managing the migrant population, big trouble is sure to come. Nowadays, there are roughly 200 million rural youth and middle-aged farmers working away from home. Migrants are the easiest group to be stirred and agitated – this has been proved again and again throughout history. The hukou household registration system should be reformed as soon as possible. Throughout the whole world, it's only us and the North Koreans who still have this hukou policy, isn't it? Migrants should be settled down as quickly as possible. On this issue, what we need is not some small steps but giant leaps forward.

As for the relationship with other countries, we must first deal with the United States, who right now is the head of the global village, a title not given by the villagers but obtained through his own power. In the village, he wants to intervene in every household's affairs. He often presses his ears against the windows of other households, trying to hear what's going on inside the house. He has incurred widespread resentment, but no one dares to speak it out. As for China, of course he wants to poke his nose into our life as well. But China, who has been financially well off recently, has a lot of brothers and has a bit of power, doesn't want to listen to him and follow his instructions anymore. The village chief is so annoyed by your attitude that he provokes your neighbours to stir up trouble and drive you crazy. In my opinion, we shouldn't fall out with this village chief. As the saying goes, he who fights and runs away lives to fight another day. The village chief has deep pockets and advanced weapons, so it's us who will suffer if we fall out with him. Someone has made an estimation that the comprehensive national power of China is only 48% of the United States, and science and technology strength is only 20%. We don't know whether these numbers are accurate, but it's certain that we aren't a well-matched rival to the United States in terms of national power, so we'd better not offend him. We have examples in history. Those countries – such as Germany, Japan and the Soviet Union – who dared to challenge the United States at the wrong time all suffered heavy losses. We should learn their lesson. We should honour the United States as the head of the global village, offer him a cigarette when we see him, and buy him a drink from time to time. We want to live peacefully, don't we? Of course, if he still insists on bullying us, that will be the last straw. To teach him a lesson, we could grab a stick from behind the door and hit him repeatedly on his forehead until he passes out. This would stun him and make him think about his behaviour.

Then there's one more thing we need to be cautious about. Japan, our neighbour, isn't happy with his lot and is always preying on us. He's supposed to be well off, but the traditions his ancestors have left for him aren't good. Whenever he sees the land and property of others, he wants to seize them and keep them all for himself. A member of his family once wrote an article in which he said: "Because of Japan's special geographical location and scarcity of natural resources, the ultimate form of our development is to wage wars. The only way for us is military expansion! Let's use our Yamato valour, wisdom and spirit to conquer Asia and conquer the world, to wash out the dishonour of the failed holy war breaking out decades ago, and to use our Yamato excellence to control the nations who are inferior to us, thus pushing forward the progress of the world."

There were two lessons for Japan from the holy war he lost several decades ago. First, he should not have offended the United States before he conquered Asia and consolidated his position. Second, to conquer a large country like China, he should not have tried to eat everything in one mouthful. Instead, he should have been patient and eaten it like sashimi, one slice after another. China should have been divided into seven or more separate countries, and then the power of the Han would have been weakened so that China had no room for manoeuvre.

Some Japanese even secretly made a plan to conquer the world within thirty years: "The first step is to conquer China and the rest of Asia. Let's use our powerful fleet to destroy China's large but not terrifying fleet and then inflict heavy damage on their air force. The United States will support this, the Taiwanese will be happy and the countries around the South China Sea will be happy. Next, we firmly control Taiwan and make it our military base. Losing air-sea power, the Chinese will be unable to react to our attacks on North Korea and South East Asia. As a result, their government will lose its prestige. The spirit and will of its people will be broken. Then we could take this opportunity to stir up ethnic discord in various regions. At that time, China will become weak without a war. As for our strategy of modestly weakening the power of China, neither will Russia send troops to support China nor would he make any objection to our action. Second, we should consolidate our position in Asia and rule the world with our ally Germany. After we wipe out China, South East Asia, North Korea, South Korea, India and Pakistan, we should eliminate their languages, customs and lifestyles – that is, all the deep-rooted depravity of those inferior nations – then force them to learn everything from us, making the whole of Asia a united country and a united nation, a Yamato nation at last. Next, we should use the United States to control Europe, and assist the German Nazi Party to regain its power so that it can conquer the whole of Europe. Then, we, together with Germany, can launch an attack from the east and the west and eliminate the Commonwealth of Independent States. When Japan, Germany and the United States are the only countries in this world, allied with Germany, we can destroy the United States to avenge our defeat in the second world war. The third step is to destroy Germany and dominate the world."

Of course, we must not take all these dream-like words seriously, but we must not totally ignore them either. The history of Japan goes round in circles, starting from state construction to launching wars, defeat, construction and then launching wars again. We should always remain vigilant towards him, and whenever we see him lift up his sword, we must strike first and mercilessly beat him, so that he chooses death over life. Only in this way can he remain honest for another decade. We must bear in mind the lessons the United States learned at Pearl Harbor, and we should foresee the possibility that thousands of Japanese jet fighters will suddenly appear in the sky over Qingdao, Ningbo, Zhanjiang, Shanghai and Beijing one morning and begin dropping bombs. If it should happen, what should we do? This is not impossible! The right wing in Japan became part of the mainstream long ago and has now become the majority. Right-wing politicians are very popular, and at some point could find an excuse to launch a pre-emptive attack against China.

When I finished my talk on that day, Mr Wantong stood up and walked towards the writing desk. He took up a writing brush and wrote a line on a piece of Xuan paper: "One term in power but a hundred years' peace is called for." I read it and invited him to sign his name on it. "I want to frame it and hang on the wall as a memento," I said. Did you see it? Yes, that was the one he wrote on that day. Although he hadn't practised calligraphy, the words he wrote presented very clear and forceful lines and strokes, well worth appreciating.

Am I digressing? No? Then I'll continue.

Another topic we talked about quite often in those years was the management of human society. We human beings are social animals who can't live alone, so we must form a society through association and interaction, which necessarily raises issues like systems, organisations, rules and administrators.

Wantong believed human society had reached the third stage of management. The first stage was the infancy of human beings. The management of society was handed over to the elders and tribal chiefs, whose authority was usually based on blood relations. People were willing to obey them because of their old age and their standing in the upper reaches of the river of life. The second stage was the childhood of human beings. The task of managing society was mainly given to slave owners and emperors. Slave owners' authority was built on sticks and slaughter, while emperors' was built on the deception of the divine right of kings and repression of state apparatus. Both reeked of blood. The third stage is the youth of human beings, with the management of society given to an elite group. People gradually realised that societies managed by slave owners and emperors were full of injustice and barbarism, so they eventually overthrew them by force and chose elite people to administer the society under the constitution, no longer giving their destiny to one person only.

Wantong believed human society was currently at this third stage. He said it was hard to say how long this stage would last or what kind of management would come in the next stage – it would be based on new creations of mankind.

Basically, I agree with his ideas. I told him three things must be dealt with properly if human society is left to the governance of an elite group. First, there must be a system to guarantee that those who are chosen to manage society are indeed elites. Second, strict rules must be followed to manage those elites to make sure they don't abuse their power. Third, the elites who govern the human society will certainly degenerate into ordinary people for various reasons such as age, knowledge and corruption, so there should be measures to guarantee regular personnel renewal and elimination.

I once joked with him saying: "You're now one of the elites governing society. When do you think you might become a mere mortal again?"

He smiled and said: "I am, right now. I have less time for reading books, my learning ability is declining, the efficiency of my new knowledge mastery is low, my body is prone to fatigue, my brain sensitivity is declining, my thinking mode is lethargic, I'm suspicious of new things, I enjoy visiting old places and old friends, and I'm fond of talking about the old times. I'm getting weaker each day."

He added: "It usually takes ten years or so to change all the knowledge stored in one's brain into skills and power to manage human society. After that, one might repeat oneself, lose energy and spirit, and become an ordinary person. Therefore, no matter how capable officials look, it's unwise to let them stay in their positions for too long. Nowadays, many countries have ruled that their leaders must serve the people for a term of four or five years, and then be reappointed only once, which I think really makes sense."

We talked about everything. In my place, he was not an official anymore, but a friend with whom I liked to discuss issues.

Having a friend like Mr Wantong who had supreme power, I also asked him to do me some favours. What favours? Change the age-old malpractice of higher education!

Once, when he came to my place for some tea, I said to him: "I have to ask you to do me some favours."

He asked: "Public affair or private one?"

"I have my son and daughter take care of my personal things. The help that I need from you is related to higher education."

I told him higher education in China had gone through many detours. In 1952, there were big changes in colleges and universities. We rigidly copied the industrial technical school models of the Soviet Union and cancelled secondary colleges in comprehensive universities. At Tsinghua University and Zhejiang University, the school of engineering was all that was left. Engineering was given too much emphasis. Science was ignored. Some humanities and social science courses – such as political science, law, finance and economics – were cancelled. This led to a serious shortage of legal and financial professionals. In 1958, a great leap forward in higher education began, with the proposal to establish a university in every county. One, two or several college students would be enough to set up a university. In 1957, there were 229 colleges and universities in China, while in the autumn of 1958, a total of 23,500 amateur red and expert colleges and part-work/part-study colleges were established. In Hegang, Heilongjiang province, a university was set up within seven days. This incredibly fast speed greatly deteriorated the quality of Chinese higher education. Next, higher education enrolment adopted a policy called Not Suitable for Admission, whereby admission to universities was not based on individual performance and academic records, but rather family background and social relations. Some high school graduates were labelled as Not Suitable for Admission, and a great number of excellent high school graduates were deprived of the basic right to be educated without any explanation. The unfairness and injustice of education policy have made our country lose many great talents, which made the quality of higher education even worse.

In 1966, the Cultural Revolution started, and China's system of higher education was literally closed, with no admissions at all. In August 1970, higher education resumed its enrolment and began admitting students from worker and peasant backgrounds. Political activism and Party recommendation remained the criteria for admission to universities regardless of education level and age. It was claimed that university was a place where everyone could come and learn. The academic level of those college students can only be imagined. After 1980, nationwide supplementary classes of high school courses and techniques were launched, and worker-peasant-soldier college students had to obtain a certificate for junior high school as a precondition of obtaining a college degree. This was indeed a strange tale in the history of higher education in the world.

Since the resumption of the college entrance examination in 1977, higher education in China should have developed healthily according to laws of education. However, a new round of turmoil started again in 1990 with university mergers. In total, there were more than a thousand universities and secondary schools involved in the merger, and they were reduced down to 412. This kind of merger aimed to deliver first-class education by expanding the scale, but without changing the system or improving the teaching. As a result, some universities lost their historical features, specialities and educational brands, and there was an excessive number of non-teaching staff. Responsibilities were unclear, and management efficiency was low.

In 1999, a policy was implemented to make higher education support domestic demand, resulting in colleges and universities blindly expanding the scale of enrolment. This led all national public universities to take out loans of up to 250 billion yuan. Under the stress of repaying the loans, presidents of universities prioritised the generation of extra profits, which consequently led to the decline of teaching standards and students' overall quality.

In short, during these years we've been ignoring the science of education in our practice, haven't we?

He sighed after I finished my words and said: "I've been paying too little attention to education, and I have a heavy heart now that you've told me this. Yes, we should learn a lesson. Higher education is the fundamental way to cultivate elites for our country and nation, and we must do this according to the law of education science."

I told him there were three urgent things for him to deal with. The first one is to work out a way to prevent university professors and associate professors from rushing to become officials. Nowadays, young and middle-aged professors and associate professors all want to quit their teaching positions and work as chiefs, directors, deans, and vice presidents in their universities. Why? School officials have the power to allocate houses, evaluate professional titles and distribute research funds. They have the final say on everything in a university, enjoy better lives and receive more respect than professors and associate professors. How can a university do well without a stable teaching faculty? In universities, it should be professors who have the final say. In a society, if everyone is lured into becoming an official, something will go wrong with the system, a sign of the decay and collapse of society. You know, society needs a lot of people to engage in every walk of life to produce material and spiritual wealth for everyone to enjoy. Officials are simply managers. It's impossible to make a society run smoothly with too many managers but not enough workers.

The second thing is to disqualify some universities from granting doctoral degrees. There are several universities in our province whose right to award doctoral degrees have been obtained through back-door practices between provincial and municipal leaders and the Ministry of Education. Many of those who have been awarded a doctoral degree have little competence. Many dissertations are a cut-and-paste job with no valuable content. That's why we have so many good-for-nothing doctors who have ruined the reputation of doctors. Besides, officials and businessmen are pouring into campus, pursuing master degrees and doctoral degrees. In western countries, the elimination rate of doctoral candidates is about 30%, but our universities have been giving the green light to officials and businessmen, many of whom neither attend classes nor work in the lab or review documents. Their elimination rate is zero. Businessmen pay universities money, while officials use their power to provide universities with convenience. What do these doctors do for our country?

The third thing is to abolish the self-taught examination system as soon as possible. This system played an important role when the gross college enrolment rate was quite low. But today, when the average enrolment rate has reached more than 20%, it has fulfilled its mission. In today's self-taught examination system, cheating in exams is a serious problem. In many places, teachers will write down the answers for students to copy during exams. What's the use of diplomas issued to these people?

On that day, he listened to me until I finished, keeping silent for quite a long time, but at last he nodded and said: "It makes sense! As for the first two things, I'll immediately ask people to investigate and come up with a rectification plan. As for the third one, it's the state policy, and I don't have the power to abolish it, but I can report to the higher level." It was about a month and a half after he left my house that day that a series of policies was put forward in universities in our province, all aiming at the two things I mentioned previously. From this, I recognise him as a friend, who didn't brush me – a poor scholar – off.

In the winter two years ago, I went out for a walk one morning. It was very cold outside, and I forgot to wear my hat. Blown by the cold wind, I felt blood vessels in my brain getting tight. Then, with a snap, one blood vessel suddenly broke. I felt my vision go black, and I fell back unconscious. I was told that someone who was out walking there called an ambulance and sent me to the emergency room immediately. After the brain surgery was done, I was transferred to the intensive care unit. After that, I was supposed to be sent to the neurosurgery ward, where beds were still available, but the man who was in charge of the ward told me there was no bed. His real purpose was to get some money from my family if I wanted to have a bed in the ward. My wife and my daughter are only good at teaching, so how could they know this? No money for him – no ward for me then. I was then placed in the corridor of the hospital.

Extremely anxious about my situation, my wife suddenly remembered Secretary Ouyang Wantong and the phone number he left for us. She called him for help, and he came to the hospital in his car the moment he hung up the phone. He first came to my bed in the corridor to see me and then he went to the ward to make sure there were beds available. Next, he summoned the dean of the hospital to meet him. He said to the dean: "First, expel the guy who is in charge of neurosurgery wards. In our hospital, there's no position for such a bastard! Second, a thorough investigation must be made immediately in every department! If any similar case should be found, expel! Third, arrange for Professor Ren to stay in a ward at once. You are a university graduate, so you should know how precious professors are. Without them, how could we have top talents? Didn't the students nurtured by our professors send rockets into space and submarines under the ocean? And the president of our country, and our premier! Who is not cultivated by our professors? Think about it! Dare you trifle with them like this?"

I received the best care after he came to see me in the hospital. Of course, I was very grateful to him, but he still often made apologies to me, saying he didn't do a good job with medical ethics and has made me and other patients suffer..."

That was the favour he did for me, and there were occasions he asked for my help too. Here is an example. For some time, he was obviously in low spirits. Every time he came to visit me, he simply sat there, drinking tea, speaking very little.

I said: "If you regard me as your older brother, tell me what is bothering you. Perhaps I could help a little."

He forced a bitter smile and then asked earnestly: "Brother, how do you get along with your wife? What's your secret weapon to maintain an intimate relationship? Teach me how to do that."

I was amused by his words and answered: "My wife is also a teacher. When we're at school, she teaches mathematics and I teach my history, neither of us meddling in the other's affairs. At home, she's a micromanager. She complains about my negligence of hygiene and orders me to take a shower every day – otherwise, I'm not allowed to sleep in the bed. She complains about my tobacco smell and orders me to smoke less – no more than three cigarette butts in the ashtray every day. She complains about my fondness of drinking and warns me not to drink too much – four cups a day at most, which is no more than an ounce. She worries about the distance between me and my female students and orders me not to go out with female students alone. I dare not control her because, to be honest, there's nothing for me to control. She doesn't smoke or drink, she cares about personal hygiene and she goes back home directly after class. Is there anything I could care about?"

He smiled bitterly after I finished my words and said: "It's much better to be a teacher! Well, no more talk about this."

Seeing that he was unwilling to continue, I changed the topic quickly in case he was feeling miserable.

We sometimes joked around with each other as well. Once I asked him with a smile: "I hear it has become a fashion among officials to have a mistress. Many officials have one, don't they? Those who haven't could even be looked down upon. What about you? Is it much easier for an official at your level? Have you ever tried this? Anyway, I'm not a member of the Commission for Discipline Inspection, and I'll admit to you first that I once had a lover but later we broke off. So, what about you? Tell me the truth."

He burst out laughing at my words, saying: "All men who are psychologically and physiologically healthy in this world have a common desire to possess as many beautiful women as they can. This is an instinct inherited from male animals. Because of my position, I have more opportunities to meet with beautiful women. If I tell you I'm not attracted to any of them, you definitely won't believe it – of course it would be a lie. But if you at last decide to step forward and make the one you fancy your lover, you have to get ready for three things. To begin with, prepare a lot of money. There is no free lunch, let alone free sex, which is actually very expensive. The reason why some officials become corrupt is that they bite off more than they can chew and are tempted to enjoy high consumption without enough money in their pockets. Next, prepare to accept a broken family or even death. It's hard to keep your wife in the dark, and when she knows you have a mistress, cries and screams and quarrels will come for sure. What's more, there's the possibility that one of the two women might end up killing herself. Finally, prepare for dishonour and dismissal. These days, with the improvement of surveillance methods, affairs have a high risk of being exposed. Businessmen can afford to pay to avoid misfortunes, but officials can lose their fame and official positions forever. As for me, neither do I have a lot of money, nor do I want to ruin my family. Besides, I still want to be an official, so I have to control my lust and perform my role as a husband honestly, as is required by society. Of course, I have to admit one thing to you as well. I once lost control after I had drunk too much. Fortunately, I came to my senses before I was completely out of control, but this still gave a girl a false impression, which consequently affected her life afterwards. I've been tortured by this for a long time, and I feel very sorry for the girl. My heart is full of guilt. I haven't seen her since then, and I dare not contact her. I guess she hates me, and I don't know what has become of her."

I once asked him what his greatest difficulty was. He told me it was choosing the right people. "The basic principle of recruiting is supposed to be very clear – that is, people with all-round talent, ability and integrity, who come from all over the country. But in fact it's very difficult to carry this out. Whenever a vacancy is available, you're bombarded with all kinds of back-door notifications, many of which are from your superiors. What should you do then? Say no? It might be all right for you to say no once but if you do it several times, you might be transferred to another position. Eventually, you have no choice but to compromise, employing a combination of talented and mediocre people. In the past few years, quite a lot of people like this have entered our team. Many of them are sons, sons-in-law, daughters, daughters-in-law, secretaries and friends of officials and leading cadres. I know people don't like it, but if you don't cooperate, you can't push forward with your work. What else could I do?"

I once asked him about his opinion of Chinese intellectuals. He said: "Intellectuals are the elite of our nation and most of them have intelligence, insight, moral integrity and talent, though some of them might bend in servility. Intellectuals are the ones who care about and love this country most, who are most willing to think about our country's fate and who worry about the universal benefits of human beings. It is, however, a pity that for many years we haven't had enough trust in them. We always regard their ideas as an attack on our government. We always keep an eye on them. We're never tolerant of them, and this has hurt their feelings. There is one more thing – intellectuals are always dissatisfied with the overall reality of society, which I think is right. It's their dissatisfaction that has contributed to the sombreness of officials. But some intellectuals who are dissatisfied with reality are prone to construct a utopian society and advocate radical politics, which will often lead to a result that is contrary to their expectations."

Later, I heard the news that he offered his resignation. It was out of the blue and indeed out of my expectation. When we spoke with each other, I could feel that his aspirations had not been fulfilled, that he still had a passion for his work and he still had a lot of things planned. There was not the slightest sign of his willingness to resign. I thought there must be some external forces that forced him to make such a sudden decision. What external forces? I didn't know exactly, but my guess is that it might have had something to do with that letter I wrote.

I wrote a letter to him before the Spring Festival of that year, in which I said: "Economic growth of a province can't always increase at a rate of about 10%. It is also difficult to rely on investment to create growth all the time. And it is even more difficult to do so by developing real estate. Otherwise, you will burn your fingers sooner or later, and it will cause great pain to the long-term development and people's lives in the future. As the governor, you must have the courage and boldness to change the current situation. Of course, amid a nationwide emphasis on fast growth of GDP, what you are going to do might be regarded as inappropriate and rebellious, and you might lose opportunities to be praised or even be promoted, but you have to take ordinary people into consideration..."

I heard Governor Wantong agreed with what I said after he read my letter, and then he forwarded the letter to the General Office of the Provincial Government, asking them to have a discussion on it quickly. After this letter was made public, Ouyang Wantong was accused of trying to manipulate public opinion and deflect from his incompetence and the provincial economic slowdown. The letter was deemed to be an argument against 'Development is the Absolute Principle', and it was suggested that Governor Wantong planned to threaten the secretary of the Provincial Party Committee with the economic slowdown in order to seize power. This probably placed great pressure on Wantong.

Could this be the reason for his resignation? I'm not quite sure about it.

There's another possibility – that is, he was making a protest by doing this. Protest against whom? Please allow me to keep it a secret for the time being.

5

JIN XIAOWEI

THE LANDSCAPE ENGINEER

Do I know Yin Qingqing? Of course, I know her. She's the child of my elder sister – my niece – so how couldn't I know her! How did you get to know her? Having watched her performance on the stage? Well, since my sister died of an illness, Qingqing lived with me for some years, and later she moved out after she was admitted to an opera school. God knows why the child would fall in love with singing Yu opera. She was obsessed with the idea of going to an opera school and learning how to sing. She's a beautiful girl with a great voice. She passed the entrance examination and was admitted. She later starred in several plays, earned quite a reputation, and her name and photos appeared in newspapers. The whole family was very happy for her. Just a second, I have a photo of her in costume. Look – this one. She's pretty, isn't she? At that time, a lot of boys chased after her, and they wrote her piles of love letters, but she was very choosy and didn't look at those letters at all. She was indeed a star for a while. No matter where she went, she was surrounded by a group of followers, all wanting to take a photo with her. But no one knew what happened to her – she suddenly quit singing, which made me quite confused.

You want to know whether she had any contact with officials? Of course she had. Whenever she had a new show, the officials all went to watch it. After the performance, they would come backstage to meet the performers, so how could she not have contact with them? Well, it seems to me that there are some implications in your words, aren't there? Please come straight to the point. What exactly do you want to know? Her relationship with Ouyang Wantong? Good heavens! How did you know about that?

Qingqing once told me there were only four people who knew this – herself, me, Ouyang Wantong and another man, but she didn't tell me who that man was. So, you're that man, are you?

Oh, you're not that man? Where did you get the information then? Confidential? All right, do as you please.

Anyway, Ouyang Wantong is already dead. Things change with the passage of time. It's not a big deal if I tell you the story of Qingqing and him.

Qingqing told me the story herself.

I remember it was a Sunday and Qingqing came to see me. I noticed something strange about her look. She knocked over one of my flower vases and broke it into pieces when she entered the room. She was somewhat incoherent when she sat down to talk with me. She was absent-minded when we had dinner together, stopping occasionally, eyes drifting and hands fidgeting. I guessed she might have experienced something disturbing or emotional.

So, I asked her with a smile: "Qing'er, you're not a young girl anymore. Don't be so picky. Find a suitable man to marry. Have you fallen in love with someone?"

She was shocked and shook her head to deny it. But I persisted in my questioning, and she finally nodded her head. I asked her who that man was. She said: "He's an official."

This made me even more worried. You know, nowadays, quite a few officials are fond of playing with girls. Hearing that the man was an official, I began worrying about whether she would be cheated. I asked her what rank that official was. She told me he was a senior official. I became more cautious. It was unusual for such an ordinary actress like her to fall in love with a senior official. Besides, he must be much older than her. My instinct told me there must be something strange in it. I therefore continued: "Does this official love you?"

She said: "I don't know."

Her answer made me anxious. I continued on: "How far has the relationship between you and him gone?"

She lowered her head and murmured: "Very intimate."

I didn't like this vague answer, so I asked her again: "What does very intimate mean? Can you explain it a little more clearly?"

Her face flamed. "Just very intimate," she said.

I felt I should put it directly if I wanted to know the truth, so I asked straightforwardly: "You've had sex with him, haven't you?"

She uttered a small cry unhappily: "Aunt!" Then she shook her head with shyness.

I was relieved when I heard this. As long as she was still a virgin, no one could find any fault with her and things would be simple.

I concluded the relationship between the official and Qingqing was still at the early stage of seducing and being seduced. He wanted to take advantage of Qingqing's innocence and ignorance of emotional issues to capture her and play with her. I required her to tell me the whole story. She had no choice but to talk about how they became familiar with each other and how fervent her love for him was. After she finished, I realised that she was the one who initiated the whole thing. She mixed gratitude, good feelings and admiration together, mingled them with rewards and love, and let herself get so tangled up that she couldn't get out.

I asked her what she planned to do next. She said: "I love him so deeply that I want to build a family with him, and I must. I don't care how people look at us, gossiping about some May-December marriage."

"What if he never has the idea to marry you, and the intimacy between you and him was simply a momentary impulse in which he forgot himself?"

She muttered through clenched teeth: "Then I'll make him do that! Threaten him with his reputation, which I guess any official will care about."

Looking at this young lady who was so desperate, I wanted to estimate the chances she had of winning the battle, so I kept asking her the name of that official. I even thought that if the official was not too old, perhaps I could work out a way to help her realise her dream. But never did I expect that the name Qingqing would speak out would be Ouyang Wantong. Such a senior official!

He was somebody everyone knew!

I was very shocked.

Seeing that I was staring blankly, Qingqing said in a low voice: "Aunt, do you know someone who could help discover how Ouyang Wantong feels about it, and persuade him to marry me. I swear I'll be good to him all my life, and I'll take care of him to his hearts' content."

I smiled bitterly and said gently to her: "Qingqing, you might as well forget about it. I should tell you directly that the story between you and him has nothing to do with feelings. The so-called intimacy between you and him is just a natural physical reaction of his body, which, in your eyes, might be something earth-shaking, while in his eyes, it might be a minor mistake. You've misunderstood him."

Qingqing said bitterly: "Aunt, wait and see. If he refuses to marry me, I'll ruin his reputation and make him unable to be an official anymore."

I looked at her, not knowing what to say.

In the days after she left my home, I followed the news on the internet, thinking that if Qingqing should attack the reputation of Ouyang Wantong, she would definitely choose the internet, which was the perfect place to spread such things quickly and make Ouyang Wantong pay for it.

But I didn't find any news. After a long time, I couldn't help but make a phone call to Qingqing, asking how things went. She sighed and said: "After thinking about it over and over again, I've decided to let it go."

I gave a long sigh of relief.

I didn't ask her anything more, and I felt she had made a wise decision. Later, she left the stage and got married. She gave me no explanation and no details about the reason why, and I didn't ask her about it either. We all have secrets, don't we? Though I'm her aunt, I should respect her privacy. If you want to know some details about her story, you should go and talk to her.

In this case, it was lucky that she retained her purity. Nowadays, could there be any officials who are willing to contain themselves when beautiful young bodies are presented in front of them?

Could they let go of such beautiful young women?

Do you believe it's possible?

6

WANG JIQING

THE CHAUFFEUR

I WAS the chauffeur of Governor Ouyang Wantong. I began to work for him when he was the mayor of the provincial capital. You know, I've never had an accident in these years. My acquaintance with him was somewhat legendary. One year, he came to visit military drills in my field troop division, together with some other provincial and municipal leaders. On the trip to the military drill base, they had to transfer to our military off-road vehicles, and it happened that he was in my jeep. On that day, the road was in a bad state caused by tanks and the other armoured vehicles during the military drill. The other jeeps encountered some problems, while my jeep was the first and the only one to arrive at the drill base smoothly. I remember he was very happy about that and said: "Young man, you drive quite well. If you want to transfer to civilian work after military service, come to me."

I kept his words in my mind, and I did go to see him when I was about to transfer. When he saw me, he said very directly: "Good, come and drive for me then."

After I became his chauffeur, I never let him and his secretary worry about transport. Any time, any season, no matter whether it was windy, snowy, rainy or foggy, or wherever we went, cities or rural areas, I would be there waiting for them on time – not even a minute late. After he became the governor, the regulations required that a police car should accompany him in case something should happen, but he liked to keep a low profile and preferred going out with just a few attendants, refusing to let a police car follow behind. So, I had to prepare to deal with accidents myself. Fortunately, I have had full-scale combat training in the field army, and I can handle the bad guys if I meet them. But to ensure his safety, I prepared pepper sprays, an electric baton and a dagger with the permission of his secretary. To tell the truth, when I was preparing these things, I never thought I would actually use them. Anyway, who would dare to pick on the governor's car and ask for trouble?

It seemed I had been wrong. These things unexpectedly came in handy one night. It was a drizzling night. After the governor listened to the report of the county secretary and the county magistrate of Gong county and had supper with them, we needed to go back to the provincial capital. The county leaders insisted on driving us to the national highway, but the governor refused, so I started the car and drove the governor and his secretary away. Before we got very far from the county, probably about ten kilometres, in the middle of the road ahead of us stood a woman and a man waving to us. It looked like the woman was holding a child in her arms.

I said to the secretary: "It's very late now – we don't need to stop the car, do we?"

The governor spoke up: "Stop the car! It looks like the child is ill and needs to be taken to the provincial capital. Let's give them a ride."

I slowed down and pulled over beside them. Rolling down the window, I asked: "What happened?"

The man came over and said: "My child is sick and my wife has just broken her leg. I was wondering whether you could give us a ride?"

"No problem," I said.

Then the man added: "Could you do me another favour and help me get my wife and child into the car?"

I unbuckled the seat belt, opened the door, got out of the car and walked up to the woman. Just as I reached her side, she suddenly pulled out something from inside her arms and slammed into me. I realised it was actually a man dressed up as a woman, and there was no child in her arms at all. Luckily, I had some skills and dodged aside immediately. The man standing beside me charged at me with a knife in his hand. I failed to jump aside in time and got stabbed on the arm. At that moment, I pulled out the dagger on my belt and, with several slashes of it in the air, the two guys fell to the ground. Then another man with a long stick dashed out from the dark roadside and jumped on me. With one tumble, I rolled over to his side and stabbed him on the leg. With a painful scream, he fell to the ground as well. The whole fight lasted two minutes. When Secretary Zheng and the governor came out of the car, the three scoundrels were all rolling on the ground, screaming in agony.

Later, the Public Security Department found out the three guys were regular car thieves who had offended several times before.

Am I blowing my own trumpet a little bit? Okay, thank you, let's continue.

I should say the governor treated me quite well. You know, he seldom showed his feelings and spoke very little. He was more likely to let you feel his love by his actions. He asked his wife to introduce my wife to me. We got along well from the first time we met. When my son was born, he and his wife came to the hospital to see my wife and the baby.

After that incident, Secretary Zheng and I both proposed a police car should accompany us whenever we go out, but Governor Wantong said it was only an accident and there was no need to be afraid of one's own shadow, still refusing to let a police car follow behind. He said: "Think about it – if whenever I go out I'm surrounded by people and followed by a police car, would any ordinary person dare to approach me? Would I still have the chance to listen to true voices?"

The security office, however, arranged for a police car to go along with him, following at a distance with no police licence plate or siren, so that the governor wouldn't notice it.

It was probably on the fifth day after his retirement was announced that a big accident happened. It was very dangerous. On that morning before daybreak, following Secretary Zheng's instruction the previous night, I came to pick up Secretary Zheng first and then went to pick up the governor in his house to attend a seminar on economic development held in Shanyang city. It was the first time for the governor to participate in an event since he retired. Secretary Zheng warned me to be particularly careful that day because the security level for a retired governor was reduced. The police car that used to follow us had been cancelled. I nodded understandingly, but inwardly I thought a retired governor was still a governor, and there would be no problem now that it was broad daylight. Unexpectedly, something did happen. When I drove past the governor's house and turned to the street, a big truck suddenly appeared and rushed right at us. Usually, trucks were not allowed on this street, so I pressed the horn forcefully as I tried to escape from it, but there were many street vendors on the roadside, and there was no chance for me to dodge aside and no time for me to reverse the car either. I desperately pressed the brake and knew an accident was inevitable. Just as we were about to crash head-on, the truck driver suddenly wrenched the wheel to the right and moved aside.

I broke out in a sudden cold sweat.

Secretary Zheng turned pale with terror as well. He was so angry and swore at the truck driver: "That bastard!"

Governor Wantong sat in the back seat, silently.

The truck had already driven away. Secretary Zheng called the chief of the Municipal Public Security Bureau, asking him to immediately find the truck owner and the driver in order to confiscate the driver's licence and punish him with a fine.

More than an hour later, the police chief called back saying they had checked the street surveillance video and the truck belonged to the Imperial Court Real Estate Company. The driver was called Hui San, and he had quite a lot of violations in his driving record. Jian Qianyan, the president of the Imperial Court Real Estate Company, made an immediate apology and condolence to Governor Wantong and then promised to severely punish Hui San. The Public Security Bureau prepared to confiscate Hui San's driving licence under the charge of violating traffic restrictions and speeding.

Governor Wantong spoke up calmly after he heard this: "It's a warning for me that they could take my life any time they want."

Both Secretary Zheng and I were shocked.

That is all I think worthwhile to tell you. What else do you want to know?

7

SUI CANLAN

THE FORMER CLERK OF THE BUREAU OF PERSONNEL, TIANQUAN CITY

GOVERNOR OUYANG WANTONG? Of course, I'm very familiar with him. If you want to know more about him, I'm the person you need. His ex-wife Lin Qiangwei and I were classmates at high school. We are very close friends who kept no secrets from each other. We're 'besties', as young people would say nowadays. You know, Qiangwei even told me about Ouyang Wantong's performance on their wedding night. Qiangwei said: "Sister Canlan, when he came up, at first he just sat there and dared not to move. With a flustered look in his eyes, he glanced at me shyly! I was wondering if there was something wrong with him. What if he were impotent? What should I do then? Unexpectedly, the moment I switched off the lamp, he became bold all of a sudden. He jumped on me. I was so anxious that he couldn't even undo my buttons. You know what? He started tearing my clothes, and the buttons on my coat were ripped off and fell noisily onto the floor. Gentle as he looked, he behaved like an animal at that time. He pushed himself into me, squeezing and thrusting, harder and harder until I felt as if I were torn apart."

All right, all right, let's talk about something else, something more serious.

After they got married, I was a frequent visitor to their family. As long as Qiangwei was free, she would send people for me or call me to her place. We did nothing special – just gossiped with a cup of tea and a plate of sunflower seeds. We chatted and laughed and had a lot of fun. What did we gossip about? Everything! Married lives of our classmates, events and rumours in the county, funny things about officials at all levels in the county, our female classmates having babies, the health of our parents, life plans – everything, you know, including topics like how to make men infatuated in bed.

At that time, there was one thing Qiangwei talked about most – she wanted Wantong to be an official. She said: "I must help Wantong climb the ladder by means of my father's connections. As long as he's on the top, I'll have nothing to worry about. And I want to have a go at making it in officialdom too."

I was happy to hear her say that, and I said: "As long as you and Wantong stand your ground, there's nothing for me to be afraid of. With you two to rely on, I don't need to worry about being bullied in my life. I won't starve while you two have something to eat."

Very soon, Wantong was transferred from the commune to the county, but when everyone said that he was going to be the deputy director of the County Production Office, Qiangwei's father was labelled as a rightist and removed from his post, which stunned Qiangwei and Wantong. I didn't know how to comfort them. Because of this, their family's status went down drastically in the county, and Wantong and Qiangwei, who used to be the most welcomed people, became very unpopular. You know, at that time I was the only one who dared to invite them to my home. My parents were both workers in the County Fertiliser Factory, so I was a descendant of the proletariat with a good class background, and no one dared to bother me. In those days, I often invited them to my house. If I didn't have something decent to treat them, I would cook a pot of noodles with garlic sauce, and they would break out into a great sweat as they ate.

They had a hard time in those years. Qiangwei's father was sent to be re-educated in May Seventh Cadre School, a labour camp, and soon he died of a heart attack. Shortly after her father's death, Qiangwei's mother fell ill and died too. Wantong was demoted to work as an ordinary cadre in the County Cultural Centre, subject to being denounced as the filial son and grandson of capitalist roaders. Qiangwei worked in the Bureau of Education sorting files and doing some cleaning. She was labelled as the daughter of a capitalist roader, and people talked about her behind her back quite often. What was even sadder was that their second child, who was very healthy and strong, died of meningitis. I often went to see them and comfort them. To be honest, I was quite afraid that they might do something stupid. During that period of time, you know, a lot of people killed themselves. Luckily, they came through. It was during that time that I discovered Wantong was a strong-willed person. Whenever I went to see them, Qiangwei would always sit there wiping her tears and lamenting there was no future for them, but Wantong didn't complain. He just sat under the window sill, reading books, his brows furrowed. When he saw me, he greeted me with a nod and then went back to his books. He just sat there reading all kinds of books. Many of them didn't have covers, and I didn't know where he got them from. Think about it – deprived of his power and his dearest son, he could still be at peace with himself and sit there reading books. Don't you think that's impressive? I remember I once told my husband: "Wantong is cut out to be a great person. If he is given a chance, he's sure to achieve something."

As I expected, when the graduate school entrance examination was resumed after the Cultural Revolution, Wantong, regardless of his age, passed with a high score and went to study in the provincial capital.

He was assigned to work in the Organisation Department of the Municipal Party Committee after his graduate study. After that, their life was good again.

Once he was settled in the Organisation Department, he transferred Qiangwei and his son Qianzi from the county to Tianquan. I went to visit them before they moved. Qiangwei took my hand and said: "Canlan, I never thought we could pick up the pieces and begin a new life. You were my true friend when we were in trouble, and I promise we'll transfer your family to Tianquan sooner or later." I smiled and didn't take it seriously, thinking she was just expressing her thankfulness.

You know what? About a year and a half later, Wantong did transfer me to work in the Municipal Personnel Bureau, and my husband to the Municipal Water Conservancy Bureau. Good heavens! We were both so overjoyed that we didn't know what to say when we received the posting. I called Qiangwei to express my gratitude, and she said on the phone: "Sweetie, it's a small thing. Nowadays, is there anyone who doesn't use his own people? Power has its expiration date!"

When Wantong was the county magistrate, Qiangwei was still a staff member. She told me: "In China, in every dynasty, official positions are the only measurement when people look at you. As long as you become an official, you're respected, recognised as smart and talented, and accepted as a good judge. I must be an official!" Within two years, she became a section chief with Wantong's help. Later, when Wantong was appointed deputy mayor of Tianquan, she pressed to be a deputy director. Wantong refused at first for fear that it might have negative consequences, so she wept and wailed and pestered on and on. I remember I encountered the cold war between them several times when I went to visit them. Qiangwei refused to cook for Wantong. Even an honourable official can find it hard to settle a family issue. All I could do was keep silent and help with cooking so that they might make up when they ate together. I discussed it with Qiangwei when Wantong was not at home and persuaded her not to be so anxious. I told her that if Wantong was able to promote her, he would be sure to do it. But she said that Wantong was not bold enough to do it willingly – if she didn't push him, he would never think about promoting her. Later, Wantong indeed made Qiangwei the deputy director. It could have been thanks to his social connections, or probably he was just fed up with her pestering. Who knows anyway!

After Qiangwei became the deputy director, I really basked in her light. Whenever I needed it, her government car would be arranged for me to use immediately. You didn't know? The deputy director of a prefecture-level city has long had a government car! Also, whenever she was invited to a banquet by someone who wanted to ask her a favour, she would ask me to go with her to eat some delicacies. Qiangwei told me it was called sticking together through thick and thin. When someone invited her to a beauty salon, she insisted that I come along to enjoy it with her. From time to time, she would send her chauffeur to my home with gifts she received from others. To be honest, I never thought her promotion would have brought me so many benefits.

After Wantong became the mayor of Tianquan, I could see a very obvious change in him. Firstly, he declined invitations to banquets – even from very close friends like us who would visit each other often. He would find all kinds of excuses to refuse. He once said to me very frankly: "After dinner comes reckoning. If I attend a man's banquet, how do I have the nerve to blame him when he does something wrong?" Secondly, he often visited ordinary people in their homes. Sometimes he would go to companies, factories or rural areas in plain clothes and without any attendants to find out what was going on. He solved many problems for ordinary people. He told me that he came from an ordinary family and what the ordinary people expected officials to do was to solve practical problems for them. What's more, he insisted on a strict control over the entry to municipal governments. He said: "We have many more officials than we need in municipal governments. One more official means one more mouth to feed for ordinary people."

These actions earned him a good reputation, and a lot of people praised him. I told Qiangwei what I had heard. She smiled and said: "He wants to be a good official! But there's one thing he doesn't understand – what's the use of compliments from ordinary people? What matters most is compliments from his leaders! In my opinion, he has taken the wrong path. Compliments from ordinary people might even bring him troubles. Why? If he takes ordinary people's benefits into consideration, it might do harm to the interests of the rich and the powerful. That is indeed not a good thing."

Shortly after that, Jian Qianyan, the owner of a paper mill who was familiar with my husband, came to see me, asking me to introduce him to Qiangwei, for which he brought us a lot of gifts. I didn't think too much about it, thinking it was as easy as raising my hand, so I gave him my promise. A few days later, Jian Qianyan arranged for a banquet, and I invited Qiangwei in the name of friends gathering. At the dinner table, I found that Jian Qianyan, young as he was, was good at observing people and knew how to converse. That evening, he kept Qiangwei amused with various anecdotes, and she giggled all the time, which made me feel it was a very successful gathering. I didn't know I was making a great mistake at that time, leading my bestie and my benefactor into a trap!

After this banquet, Jian Qianyan approached Qiangwei directly without us as the middlemen, and at that time my husband and I both felt we had helped Jian Qianyan and didn't owe him anything anymore.

Qiangwei later became a bureau director, and it was said to be the proposal of the secretary of the Municipal Party Committee. I had no idea how she made it, but what I did know was that after she became the director, she spared no efforts to send her son Qianzi to study in the United States. Studying abroad required a lot of money. In that period of time, the gifts Qiangwei and Wantong received were usually things like food, clothes and other daily necessities – people never sent them money. They therefore didn't have enough money in the bank to afford Qianzi's tuition fees. Qiangwei worried about it quite a lot. But one day, she told me her friends helped her with the problem, and I was very glad to hear the news because I sincerely hoped she could fulfil her wish to send her son abroad.

No one expected that it was the beginning of a disaster. Just after Qianzi had completed all the paperwork for going abroad and then flown to New York, someone suddenly reported to the Central Commission for Discipline Inspection that Lin Qiangwei had asked for bribes to send her son to study abroad. Attached to the allegation letter were a video and a voice recording of her receiving bribes. The higher authority launched an investigation, and it all proved true. After Qiangwei's arrest, I learned that Jian Qianyan had sent someone to a pre-arranged place to do the recording in advance before he gave the money to Qiangwei. Then he made a demand on Qiangwei that a piece of land in the suburb be sold to him to set up another paper mill. At that time, Qiangwei was probably eager to send her son to the United States, and she also felt it wouldn't be difficult for her to do him a favour since she was the director of the Land Bureau who was in charge of this. She eventually agreed. To her surprise, the secretary of the Municipal Party Committee intervened when the land was under approval as the site of a paper mill. He pointed out that the land was just beside the Tianshui river passing through the city and a paper mill would definitely pollute the river. Not knowing his son's studying abroad was related to this, Wantong firmly supported the secretary's opinion and objected to the construction of a paper mill on this land as well. When Jian Qianyan got the news, he thought Qiangwei was simply playing with him, and his anger turned into hatred. So he exposed Qiangwei's practice of extorting bribes.

On the day Qiangwei was taken away, I was stunned first, then I cried my eyes out. Wasn't it my fault that she got dragged into this? I blamed myself again and again for introducing that black-hearted boss to her. How could he set people up like this when failing to achieve his goal? Didn't he have any conscience? What's the point of sending her hundreds of thousands of yuan? To ruin her career and future just like that?

When Qiangwei was arrested, Qianzi was called back from America and then Wantong was removed from his position. That was really a big disaster! During that time, I kept going to the detention centre, wanting to see Qiangwei, but I was told that visits were not allowed because the case hadn't been concluded yet. I could only send her some clothes and daily necessities. When her case was tried, I managed to get permission to be present in the hearing. In the court, Qiangwei took all the blame on herself, getting no one else into trouble – neither Wantong nor Qianzi or anybody else. And very decisively, she also divorced Wantong. I never thought the court would give her a prison sentence as heavy as fifteen years – fifteen years! I guess Qiangwei hadn't expected that. I saw she reeled back and her face turned pale immediately when the court announced the sentence. Even today, it seems her sentence was too heavy. It was only hundreds of thousands of yuan! You know, nowadays bribery of more than five million yuan doesn't receive such a heavy sentence! Of course, in that year, most people didn't have much money, and hundreds of thousands of yuan was not a small amount.

I went to see her after she had been put into prison. I bought her the best underwear and the snacks she liked. I don't know whether she got them or not. In the meeting room, I noticed she had become terribly thin. I held up the phone and said to her: "Qiangwei, I'm really sorry for what happened to you. It's me who set the wolf to guard the sheep and dragged you into this. You need to eat something. Don't take this to heart."

She forced a bitter smile, saying nothing. On that day in the reception room, I kept talking and crying while she just listened to me quietly.

When the time for my visit was almost up, she opened her mouth and said: "Canlan, don't blame yourself for everything. The reason I'm in this situation is that someone wants to replace Wantong as the mayor. Jian Qianyan is just the front man."

I was very frightened by her words.

When I went to see her for a third time, she looked calm. When we were talking to each other through the phone, she suddenly added one line: "Canlan, remember to take care of Qianzi for me." I nodded hurriedly, thinking it was just an ordinary instruction. Never did I think she had planned to commit suicide.

Shortly after she told me that, she had a chance to go to the hospital, and when the prison guard was not watching, she rushed to the window of the sixth floor and jumped out. Fortunately, the prison guard rushed to her side and caught her in time.

It's me who has ruined Qiangwei!

8

XIA ZHAOFENG

THE FARMER FROM JINPO VILLAGE, FUNIU COUNTY

I CAN SEE with half an eye that you must be a city man. Look at you, well dressed and hair shiny with grease. You've used some hair oil, haven't you? Why do you city men worry so much about your hair? Just a few hairs, isn't it? Essence, creams or oil, is it worth it? Why have you come to our village? Guess? No idea. Come to cheat us again? You city people often do that to us farmers, don't you? Today, you sell us fake milk powder, and our babies' heads grow abnormally large after having it. The next day, you sell us shirts with something called formaldehyde, and our bodies itch badly after we put them on. The day after tomorrow, you sell us defective walking tractors, and they damned break down without even ploughing three acres of land. Or you come to seize our land at a very low price, and then sell it on at a very high price to make huge profits! Tell me directly – what have you come here for? Enquire about a person? Who? Ouyang Wantong? There is no such person in our village. Are you mistaken? The governor? Heavens! Why do you come to this small village if you're looking for the governor? Go and find him in the provincial capital. Don't you think you're entering a monk temple to look for a nun? What's the damn use of coming to our village? What? This governor came to our village before? Wait for a second and let me think. Oh, yes, I remember now. A few years ago, a provincial official did come to our village. Right, right, at that time someone called him the governor. Governor Wantong. We had a small contact too. Look at my poor brain! I could forget everything. Truly a pig's head! I even didn't remember whether I slept with my wife or not last night. Now I don't remember things. I'm old and useless!

Why did he come to our village? For the air. I won't forget this. You know what air is, don't you? It's just in front of our eyes. We can't see it, we can't feel it, but we can't live without it.

A few years ago, a boss surnamed Jian, with a given name of something like Qianyan, came to our village and set up a factory called Chao Tian Chemical Plant on the hillside to the west of our village. We didn't know what they would produce, but that Boss Jian was really generous. On the opening day, he gave our village committee 10,000 yuan so that every household in the village could have a drink to celebrate the opening of the factory. This never happened before, and all the villagers were very happy.

Gradually, however, we found the factory chimneys always blew out black smoke and gave off a very bad smell. At the very beginning, we didn't pay attention to it, but as time went by we found breathing the air from the chimney every day was making everyone in the village quite listless.

A man like me who was in his forties should have been in the best time of life to make a woman moan with pleasure during sex all night, but since the chemical plant went into operation, I found I couldn't do it. I felt sluggish and impotent. At night, when the woman snuggled up to you, you wanted to do it too, but you just didn't have the strength. You felt your legs soft, and your penis failed to erect. Even if it did erect, it lasted only a short time, and you finally found you were not in the mood for it.

The scarier thing was that women in the village often gave birth to disabled babies, either lacking arms and legs or mentally retarded. These children's eyes had enlarged white parts, and their lips were thick – fools indeed at first glance.

The villagers began to realise something must have gone wrong with the air. It had been damned polluted, and something must be done about it. So, some of us men in the village had a discussion, and we went to look for Boss Jian, hoping he could close the factory. Unexpectedly, Boss Jian was mad at us after he listened to what we had to say. He said this factory had been approved by the higher authority and he had invested a lot of money. How could it be closed simply because we came to complain about it? There was no way!

Since he was blind to our complaints, we had no choice but to go to report this to the township. We hoped that the township leaders could back us and do something about the smelly black smoke from Chao Tian Chemical Plant, which had already done harm to us. To everyone's surprise, the moment we arrived at the township, that Boss Jian arrived too with his people – and money! I heard they gave the township head and all the secretaries a stack of bills each. The head and the secretaries changed their attitude immediately and began to scold us, saying we should look at things from a broader perspective and stop making damned complaints without any proof!

Realising it was impossible for us to reason with them in the township, we therefore went to the county to report the pollution. You know what, before we arrived at the county by hitching a big truck full of cement, that Boss Jian had already been there in his private car – that is to say, when we represented our grievance to the cadres in the county, that boss had already met them. What was the result? I heard that Boss Jian treated them to a big banquet and then slipped a card into each one's pocket. You know what a card is, do you? A piece of hard plastic into which you can deposit money. After the county cadres accepted the card, they began to persuade us to overcome the difficulties and try to better understand the hard situation Chao Tian Chemical Plant was in.

When we heard this, we knew they had also been bought by that boss. Now we had no way out in the county either, so we made a decision to go to the city. The Municipal Petitioning Bureau received us. They promised to uphold justice and asked us to go back home and wait for the result. We went back to the village and waited patiently. We waited and waited, but we didn't get any result, nor did we see any improvement. Instead, more black smoke was vomited out through the chimneys of Chao Tian Chemical Plant. We reckoned Boss Jian must have bought off the city cadres who were in charge of this.

It seemed there was no more to be done. We made up our minds and went to the provincial capital as a last resort. We seventeen men each brought along a white plastic bucket full of smelly air inside. We bought the train ticket and went to the provincial city. In order to attract the attention of the officials, we went to the front of the provincial government building, all of us dressed in white shirts with the word 'qi' written in black ink on it. Seventeen men stood in line, each holding a plastic bucket of polluted air. The seventeen "qi" lined up in a row attracted a lot of attention. We succeeded at last. It shocked the people inside the provincial government and reporters who wrote articles. Some officials came out to receive us. They led us into a big room, brought each of us a clean shirt to wear and then listened to our story. After we finished, one of the officials said: "We'll report to our leaders immediately and try our best to give you a reply as soon as possible."

We were worried that we were being fooled again and they might be bought off by Boss Jian . Damn it! In those days, people's consciences were low and cheap, and anyone could be bought off with a little money. We forced the official to write a note promising to solve our problem within seven days.

The next day we went back home, and to our surprise a group of people came to our village, including the governor you just asked about. He didn't put on any airs in front of us, to be honest. He went to visit each family in the village one by one. At Lao Cai's family, he shed tears the moment he saw Lao Cai's newly born twin grandsons who had no noses, which made us feel he still had his conscience. At Lao Liang's family, he shed tears again when he knew the whole family had cancer. Lao Liang, his wife and his son were the closest to the chemical factory. After visiting each family in the village, he went to examine the Chao Tian Chemical Factory for a while. Then he summoned the whole village and said: "Dear fellows, I'm very sorry for being so late to come to see all of you. You've suffered a lot. You have my word today that the poisonous gas will never be discharged again from Chao Tian Chemical Plant to do harm to you." He didn't lie to us. On that day, he stood in front of the factory gate and didn't leave until he saw the machines were shut down and there was no black smoke coming out from the chimneys.

Later, we heard that Boss Jian was furious about this and didn't eat for a whole day.

Chao Tian Chemical Plant had to dismantle their machines and send them off quickly, plus all the workers. The land the factory occupied was to be sold back to our county government.

Not long after the factory moved away, the strange smell that surrounded the village was gone, and the sky turned blue as it used to be. People had strength again. At night, men found they were in the mood for having sex with women again.

In our eyes, this governor was good. He was able and willing to do things for ordinary people. I remember at that time some old grannies in our village went to the small temple in front of our village to burn incense and pray for him. The air in our village became better, and all the villagers said we should do something to thank that governor surnamed Ouyang. We had a discussion and then decided to send him some gifts as an expression of our gratitude. But what should we send to him? Some wheat, corns, sweet potatoes? He definitely didn't care about that. At last I had an idea – the jade pendant I wore. Look, this one hanging from my neck now. Don't look down upon my jade pendant. This jade pendant is a mini statue of Guan Yin carved out of white jade. Can you see it clearly? People say good luck will come when men wear Guan Yin and women wear Buddha. My jade pendant has a long history. It's passed down from my grandfather's grandfather, and whoever wears it will be blessed. It works very well! My great-grandfather wore this and lived to the age of ninety-one. My grandfather wore this and lived to the age of eighty-nine. My father wore this and lived to the age of ninety-two! I wanted to send this to him so that Guan Yin the goddess would bless him with a long life. Everyone said it was a good idea. So I went to the post office in the town, bought a wooden box, wrapped the jade pendant with newspaper, layer by layer, and then put it into the box. What's more, I asked my son to write a letter explaining how effective the jade pendant was. Together with the letter, I mailed the box, which was addressed to Governor Ouyang in the provincial government. I thought he probably wouldn't receive the box, but he did receive it. However, he sent a young man surnamed Zheng to my home to return the jade pendant. That young man said to me: "Governor Ouyang said he appreciates your kindness, but the jade pendant is a family heirloom and he can't accept it. It's better for you to wear it, and pass it down from generation to generation."

Why did you come here asking about him today? Has something happened to him?

Passing on? What does passing on mean? Wait, do you mean he passed away? You city men always speak like a book! To be direct, you mean he died, don't you? He did? Myocardial infarction? My goodness! Why do people like him die so early? I don't think he was old. Why did he die? Lack of a good diet? He should have lived a better life than me. Look at me – I'm still going strong! Great Lord, why did you take a good man away? Damn it! The King of Hell has probably checked a wrong number on the book listing every soul and allotted a death date for every life. That is very possible! The King of Hell has ruled the underworld for generations. Won't he get old? Why doesn't he retire? With his poor old eyes, he's likely to make a mistake. He should step down and let me take over the name book! Damn it! If I were in charge of that book, I'd be sure to let Governor Ouyang live to the age of a hundred. He was such a good official who never put on airs in front of us and who was willing to speak for us and do things for us. Do you believe what I said just now? You do? It's true. I'm a man who always keeps his word, even if I were dragged into the underworld. I would definitely let Governor Ouyang live to the age of a hundred! Damn it! Check a person's name without any serious consideration. What the blazes did the King of Hell do?

Well, he shouldn't have sent back the jade pendant I mailed to him! If he had worn the jade pendant, the goddess Guan Yin would have been sure to bless him and wouldn't let him leave us so early!

What a pity!

9

YAN FEI

THE NEPHEW

YES, Ouyang Wantong was my uncle. My maternal uncle. I'm the son of his sister Ouyang Wanlan. My mother died of some acute disease when I was only three years old. My father remarried shortly after my mother's death, so I was taken in by my Great-aunt Ouyang Zhaoxiu, with whom I grew up. You're right to come to me enquiring about him. I failed the college entrance examination when I was seventeen years old, so my great-aunt asked me to look for my uncle, hoping he could find a job for me. After we met, he said to me after thinking for a while: "Go and join the army! That's the best way to train your ability to live independently. Your mother died early, and your father doesn't care about you since he remarried. Your great-aunt is getting old, so in the future you'll have nobody but yourself to rely on. To do that, you must learn to be independent. The army is the best place to teach you this."

Therefore, I went to sign up for the army and was approved without any difficulty. Probably my uncle had notified them in advance, or perhaps I looked very strong. When I changed my clothes, I realised I was going to be a sailor, belonging to the navy stationed in Shandong province.

I felt fresh and new and went to say goodbye to my uncle in my new military uniform. He patted me on the shoulder happily and said: "Good! Quite a man in military uniform. Try your best when you're in the army. I'm not making any big demands on you. Do your best with the tasks given to you by your leaders, and finish these years of your service safely."

I nodded and said: "Uncle, believe me – I won't do anything to disgrace you."

That night he took me to a small restaurant on the street, and for the first time invited me to drink with him – three drinks. I knew my aunt-in-law was born into a county official's family. She disliked us poor relatives and didn't welcome us to her family, so my uncle could only take me to eat in a restaurant. The aunt-in-law I mentioned is my uncle's ex-wife, surnamed Lin, who looked very unfriendly and often quarrelled with my uncle. Not a nice person indeed. My great-aunt told me she sometimes didn't allow my uncle to sleep on the bed after they quarreled, and she even dared to kick him down to the floor beside the bed. Great-aunt told me my uncle had to sleep on the sofa for a few nights. He also paid for my tuition fee secretly behind my aunt-in-law's back, because if she knew that she would quarrel with him again. I don't like her, and I didn't say goodbye to her before I went to the army.

Sitting on the special train full of new recruits, we arrived directly at Qingdao – such a beautiful city. I only knew of Qingdao from books, and I didn't expect I would ever come here to be a sailor. It was probably when I saw the Qingdao Trestle that I made up my mind secretly that I would stay here. I would try my best. I would be an officer and settle down here. I wrote about my idea to my uncle, the second closest person besides my great-aunt in my life, and he wrote me back saying: "It's good, and I support you, but whether you can stay in Qingdao or not depends on your own efforts. Don't count on me to find any connection."

I was assigned to be a soldier in a destroyer after the training. You've seen a destroyer, haven't you? This was a big warship that could destroy the enemy! To be a soldier in a destroyer is so cool and high status! When the ship sails in the sea, parting the waves and pushing forward, you would feel so gallant and so heroic standing on the deck. Of course, it would make you feel dizzy too. The first time I was on the ship, I was seasick and threw up uncontrollably.

All right, that's enough about me. You want to know more about my uncle, and I should focus on his story. To cut a long story short, I was admitted to Dalian Naval Academy after I painstakingly went over all the reviewing materials. Then I heard something had happened to my uncle's family and my aunt-in-law had been arrested for bribery.

To be honest, I was deeply shocked by the news. In my hometown, my uncle's official position gave him great seniority, so it was indeed a big surprise that his wife could be arrested. I could never have imagined it. Of course, there was another funny and unfilial feeling in my heart – that is, I was secretly happy for my uncle. No one would quarrel with him anymore, and he wouldn't have to put up with her. At that time, I was a bit worried about my uncle too. Would he become embroiled in my aunt-in-law's case? I waited for the school holiday anxiously, and when the holiday finally started, I took the train heading for my hometown. I wanted to see my uncle.

When I arrived at my hometown of Tianquan, I discovered that my uncle had indeed been dragged into it. He had been removed from his position. Alone, he was reading a book at home. My cousin refused to go back home to stay with him because he thought if his father had stood up and done something to save his mother, she would not have been put into prison. I was angry with my cousin about this. You know, he shouldn't stand in his mother's shoes only.

My uncle nodded when he saw me and asked: "Holiday from school?"

My tears came down before I opened my mouth.

Uncle said calmly: "No need to be so sad! Learn from your uncle's lesson."

I whimpered and said: "It's all my aunt-in-law's fault. What did she want the other people's money for? You've been wronged too."

He shook his head and sighed: "It's not your aunt who implicated me. It's I who implicated her. If I had not been an official, been such a mayor, she would not have become a director. People would not have bribed her. I'm to blame for this. I should have reminded her to curb her desire. I should have told her the importance of self-discipline for an official in China. You know, there was never any person or regulation that could restrain her or show her the pitfalls of being an official."

Uncle blamed himself alone on that day, without the slightest complaint about my aunt-in-law. This surprised me a lot.

My uncle was later restored to his position and transferred to work in the provincial city, which made me feel relieved. After I graduated from Dalian Naval Academy, I went back to work as a deputy captain in the flotilla branch of Northern Seas Fleet. Then I was transferred to Fleet Command as a staff officer. All right, less about me, more about my uncle.

After my uncle was restored to his position, I went back to visit him during my holiday, and I noticed that he had become quiet and restrained. He declined all social engagements except some official ones, and he often read books at home alone, welcoming no visitors except family members.

He said to me: "Yan Fei, your aunt-in-law's lesson must be learned by all of us. In China, people tend to regard the promotion of an official as the improvement of his morality as well, so they seldom supervise the officials, which makes it the easiest thing for them to become corrupt and accept bribes. Besides, we Chinese are used to associating being an official with making a fortune. In the face of money, officials are likely to lose sight of what's important. But once the authorities find that you have done something wrong and prepare to deal with you, people might abandon you because there are big differences between officials and ordinary people, and you could find it hard to regain your trust and reputation within society. You might feel that you would rather be dead than alive. The contrast is extremely sharp and painful! Young as you are, you're an officer now with a little power in your hand, so you must be very careful!"

His words shocked me greatly, and I knew he was sincere. I memorised his words in silence.

My uncle once attended a meeting in Weihai, Shandong province after he had been transferred to work in the provincial city. I went to see him with my girlfriend Xiao Yang, who was also a soldier working in the Communication Department in the Northern Seas Fleet. Uncle said: "Shall the three of us go to Liugong Island?" I agreed, telling him we had troops stationed on the island and I would call them to get ready for the reception. He shook his head and said: "You want to use your power as a staff officer to seek some special privilege for me? That's not right. It's better not to bother them. Why don't we go there freely and have a look?"

On Liugong Island that day, we showed him around the Admiralty Department of Beiyang Fleet, the iron pier and the fort. We visited the monument of Beiyang Loyal Souls in memory of the heroes of the War of Jiawu, the residence of Admiral Ding Ruchang, the Beiyang Fleet commander and the Commemorative Museum of the War of Jiawu.

Wearing a solemn and heavy look, he finally looked at the eastern waters of the island and said: "Beiyang Navy was defeated in that area. Yan Fei, you and Xiao Yang are both soldiers, and I, as a representative of the Party Committee of the Provincial Garrison, am a soldier in a sense, in plain clothes. Should we three feel shameful for the failure of the War of Jiawu?"

I replied to him in a low voice: "Yes, all Chinese should feel shameful for this."

Uncle said: "We should all do our job well and strive not to repeat the failure of the War of Jiawu. I read some reference materials, one of which is a speech delivered by a senior official of the Japan Maritime Self-defence Force. He said in his speech, 'If China and Japan start a war again, I promise to eliminate the Chinese navy within four to six hours!' Of course, he was somewhat bragging or trying to cheer up his troops, but why would he dare to talk so wildly? Yan Fei, have you ever thought about it?"

My uncle's words sent my blood running faster at that moment, and a kind of indignation rose immediately from the bottom of my heart. Since then, I began studying command skills in naval battles with intensity. I had learned about it in the past – you know, assignments from my senior leaders – but I never paid great attention, just did what I was told. I felt an urgency to study hard for the first time in my life after he told me this, and I thought about what I would do if a war should happen tomorrow.

In those years, I gulped down knowledge with unmatched enthusiasm. I researched almost all the naval battles in history. I learned by heart all the tactical strategies of almost all combat arms of the navy. I read books and knew about the seabed topography in the main areas of the Bohai Sea, the East China Sea and the South China Sea. I knew the performance and combat characteristics of our major rivals' warships like the palm of my hand. I became the famous Mr Know-it-all in our Naval Fleet Command. No matter which question a commander asked me about naval battles, I could quickly answer. No one would beat me! I even won first place in the staff officers' military competition.

One year in the Spring Festival, I went to Qinghe and paid a visit to him. After he treated us to a meal, he said: "Since you're now the deputy director in charge of combat in the Fleet Command, what about giving you a small test today?"

I smiled and replied: "No problem, go ahead, Uncle," thinking secretly that he wouldn't have any challenging questions for me to answer. You know, my uncle knew very little about the navy – he was a complete layman.

He took out a large-scale map, pointed to a place in the Yellow Sea with a pencil and asked: "Your superior commands your unit to ambush a submarine here, and prepare for a surprise attack on an enemy aircraft carrier. What are you planning to do?"

I quickly estimated the map by sight, did a simple calculation in my head and then answered: "I would immediately make a suggestion to my superiors that we should move the place of ambush about three kilometres to the north, because in the area you just pointed out lies a set of reefs which is not suitable for submarines because of its depth."

My uncle smiled after he listened to my answer. He said: "Your answer is right. You know, half a month ago I went to National Defence University of the People's Liberation Army in Beijing to study military knowledge with a batch of local cadres. We were observing naval table-top exercises, and during the break I heard a minister use this one to test his staff officer. So I memorised that place on the map, hoping to test you with it too. I never thought you would give the right answer. Great! You have proved that you're worth your salt."

My uncle was very happy on that day. He said: "You're a soldier and I'm an official. Both of us should do our work meticulously. We must be clear about what we should know. We must know this in our hearts before we give orders to others. If we rely on assistants and secretaries, we'll be sure to pay for it. My carelessness could deprive ordinary people of their money and peaceful lives, while your carelessness could result in your soldiers losing their lives."

Our fleet holds a few large-scale naval exercises every year. I remember in exercise, the director suddenly presented us with a new situation. Our flagship was hit by a ship-to-ship missile, and the chief of staff and the chief of combat were both seriously injured. The chief commander issued an order at once that a deputy chief staff officer and I, the deputy director, take their places. I was very nervous because it was the first time for me to carry out a combat mission alone at sea. Happily, however, thanks to the studying I did in my spare time, I assisted the chief staff officer and successfully completed the task given by the headquarters, winning praise from the chief commander and the director section.

It was also after that naval exercise that a senior officer surnamed Wei from the Beijing Headquarters came to our place for an inspection. My leader asked me to accompany him. Well, that senior officer certainly put on quite a show, with many attendants, a long line of cars and strict security measures.

When I reported combat readiness to him, he recognised my Qinghe accent and asked me kindly: "Boy, what's the name of your hometown in Qinghe?

"Tianquan city."

He was very glad to hear this and said: "You're my authentic country fellow! Who else is in your family?"

I told him that my mother died early, my father remarried, and I was raised by my great-aunt and my uncle, and that my uncle is now working in Qinghe provincial government.

He then casually asked: "What does your uncle do in Qinghe provincial government?"

I replied: "His name is Ouyang Wantong, and he's..."

He immediately stood up in surprise: "Hey! You're the nephew of Ouyang Wantong! Good boy! Your uncle and I are good friends. I didn't know you're a soldier here."

On that day, when we had lunch together, he insisted on having me sit with him at the main table. When the banquet started, something unexpected happened. After he sipped a mouthful of Maotai, he suddenly said: "This wine is fake! I have authentic Maotai with me, thirty years of cellaring! My treat for all of you. Secretary Qiu, please go to fetch it from my car."

All our leaders at the table were very embarrassed when they heard that. Secretary Qiu brought the wine back and asked the waiter to serve our cups again. The banquet went on, but I noticed a subtle change in the atmosphere at the table. One of our officers didn't change his cup and insisted on drinking the original wine, and he also made no attempt to toast Uncle Wei during the banquet.

To be frank, I also felt Uncle Wei had overdone it. How could he make such a scene for the sake of some wine?

When I toasted Uncle Wei, he patted me on the shoulder and said: "Whenever you need my help, come and look for me."

On that very night, I made a phone call to my uncle and talked about his friend General Wei and also the wine incident. My uncle laughed a bit and said: "This friend of mine has become so particular about things since he moved to Beijing. There is something about him that I disapprove of!

You could only learn how to win battles from him. As for the other matters, never follow his lead."

A while after that, I went to Beijing on a business trip. After I finished my business, I felt I needed to visit my uncle's friend Uncle Wei. He was at the top level, and it would be good for my future if I could establish contact with such an uncle. You know, social connections are very important in one's promotion. I called Secretary Qiu first, expressing my hope to visit Uncle Wei. He said Uncle Wei had an appointment that night and asked me to go there after dinner.

I had my supper very early in a small restaurant on the street, then I carried my pre-prepared gift, which I thought was pretty good – two bottles of Lanling liquor, a very famous wine in Shandong province – and took a taxi to his home. He had a large yard, one side of which was a room with sofas inside. Secretary Qiu asked me to wait in that room, saying Uncle Wei was meeting some important guests in the living room of the main house. I nodded with a yes and sat on the sofa waiting. Shortly after I sat down, the desperate cries of a sheep suddenly erupted outside the door. I was pretty shocked – how could there be a sheep inside the senior officer's yard? And what's more, such a horrible bleat!

I rushed out to take a look and found two men were slaughtering a sheep. I went forward and asked: "Why are you killing it here?"

One of them, a middle-aged man, who was skilfully skinning the sheep, glanced at me unhappily and said: "If not here, tell me where I should go?"

The other one, who was a young fellow, perhaps recognised that I was Uncle Wei's guest and explained to me very politely: "Our senior officer prefers eating fresh mutton taken from newly killed sheep, so we kill one almost every day. These sheep are all specially bought from the Inner Mongolia prairie – juicy and delicious."

I returned to the room without saying a word and couldn't help sighing in my heart that Uncle Wei was indeed particular about food.

Very soon, some other guests came into the room, each of them waiting to see Uncle Wei, and each of them carrying a bag or a box, seemingly gifts. They all waited on the sofa like me, but Secretary Qiu didn't appear any more.

About an hour later a sound like a reversing truck suddenly came from the yard. A soldier ran into the reception room and said to those of us who were waiting: "Please do us a favour and help unload the truck." Upon hearing that, I stood up at once and went out to the yard with the soldier, followed by the other guests. I looked into the truck, and my good heavens! The carriage was filled with hundreds of boxes of Maotai! My eyes popped out in great shock! You know, it's a luxury for us to have only one bottle of Maotai – now here was a whole carriage of it! I took a box of wines, followed the soldier and moved towards a basement behind me. I almost shouted out with surprise when I entered the basement – it was full of boxes of Maotai, hundreds of boxes, some of which were labelled as having been cellared for fifty years! My grandmother! When could he finish drinking all this wine? How much money did all this wine cost?

After I helped with the unloading of the Maotai, I waited in the reception room for almost another hour. Finally, Secretary Qiu came to call me to the living room to see Uncle Wei. After having seen his wine cellar, I was so embarrassed to bring my two bottles of Lanling liquor to him, so I secretly kicked the two boxes of wine under the coffee table and followed the secretary to the living room.

When I was inside, Uncle Wei stood up and shook hands with me, saying: "Welcome, my young country fellow!" Compared with my uncle's living room, his was much more spacious and lavish, with a set of mahogany furniture. Though I had no idea of what kind of mahogany this set of furniture was made of, I could immediately recognise the luxury and quality when I saw the lifelike dragons, phoenix and flowers carved into it. It was incomparable. On the wall hung the paintings of Zhang Daqian and Qi Baishi. On display cabinets high and low were ornaments of jade carvings, exquisite porcelain, unearthed crystals and ivory – a big feast for the eyes.

Seeing my curious face, Uncle Wei said: "Few of these are valuable things." I came close to bursting out and saying how could these be worthless! Uncle Wei asked about my work in the army and encouraged me to try my best. I noticed he was very tired and yawned from time to time while he was talking with me. There were a few more visitors waiting to see him, so I dared not to sit for a long time. With some greetings and blessings, I got up and left.

That night I couldn't help calling my uncle after I returned to the hostel. I told him what I had experienced in Uncle Wei's house, especially those Maotai in his wine cellar. My uncle sighed: "One spring a few decades ago, your Uncle Wei's family wanted to apply for another homestead to build two more rooms. For this, his father invited the branch secretary to have dinner at home. His father killed a chicken, scrambled some eggs and also used the only five dimes the family had to buy five *liang* of liquor made of dried slices of sweet potatoes. His father sat with the branch secretary and served him the wine from time to time, while he himself dared not take even a small sip. His father had thought half a catty of wine would be enough for the branch secretary to drink, but that man drank like a fish, and he asked for more after he had finished all of it. However, there was none left for his father to pour into the secretary's wine cup. The branch secretary didn't drink to his heart's content, so he was very unhappy and left Uncle Wei's family, swearing all the way. As a result of this, the branch secretary didn't approve the homestead for his family. Your Uncle Wei witnessed the whole thing, and he told me later, 'When I become rich in the future, I swear I'll build a huge wine cellar and fill it with wines.' It seems he has made it."

After my uncle finished this story, he continued in a rare and harsh tone: "You'd better not get too mixed up with him! You should strive for progress by your own performance, not his help. Never get yourself involved into trouble blindly. If you can't get promotion in the army, return to civilian work. It's not a big deal."

I felt very strange at that time, wondering what my uncle meant by saying this. Did he mean visiting Uncle Wei would get me into trouble? Anyway, I would keep some distance from him – there was no need for my uncle to exaggerate like this! I came to understand it after some time. A note of discord had already crept into the relationship between my uncle and Uncle Wei at that time. I should be very grateful for my uncle. If he hadn't stopped me from keeping a close connection with Uncle Wei, I might have got involved in some trouble when later Uncle Wei fell down because of corruption.

When I became the captain of a destroyer, my uncle phoned me to express his congratulations. He said: "I'm the first in our family to have a career in politics, and I disgraced our family. You are the first in our family to be a soldier, and you would never bring discredit on us." I gasped, wondering why my uncle told me this on such a happy occasion as my promotion.

It turned out my uncle's warning came true. In an important naval exercise, a warship was almost involved in a serious accident because of my careless mistakes in command. Still frightened, I called my uncle to report what had happened, and he said: "Learn from the lesson, and never let it happen again. I must warn you beforehand – if a sea battle should happen in the future and you lose the battle, you're not allowed to come to see me if I'm still alive. You aren't allowed to visit my grave if I'm dead!"

His words stunned me.

My uncle's reaction after Uncle Wei's case? I know a little.

I remember it was on the day when I attended a commendation meeting at the Beijing Navy Headquarters. My destroyer was honoured for its outstanding performance in a joint sea exercise with the navies of other countries. During the meeting, my mobile phone vibrated. I quietly glanced at it and saw it was from my uncle. He knew I was in Beijing. I texted him back in a hurry, telling him I was in a meeting. Very soon, he sent me another one to say he heard something had happened to Uncle Wei, and he wanted me to check it out as soon as possible. I was greatly shocked when I read the message, thinking what could happen to such a senior officer like him. I guessed at that time he might have fallen ill or had a car accident. The moment the commendation meeting was over, I made a phone call to Secretary Qiu, but his phone was out of reach. Could it be that Secretary Qiu had been injured in the accident as well? In a moment of desperation, I took a taxi to Uncle Wei's house.

When I arrived at his house, I found two sentries standing outside the yard, forbidding anyone to go into the house. Not far from the house, someone was pointing towards the yard. I went over to them and asked what had happened. One of them spoke up: "This officer Wei and his secretary have been taken away by the Disciplinary Committee. I'm afraid he'll not be a senior officer in the future."

Great shock nailed me to the spot, and I said nothing for a long time.

Later, I found a private place and made a phone call to my uncle, telling him what I saw and what I heard. For quite a while there was no sound from the phone, and I thought he probably hadn't heard what I said clearly. As I was about to repeat, my uncle gave a long sigh and said: "I knew this day would come, but I never expected it would be so soon." That was my uncle's immediate reaction after Uncle Wei had been taken away.

Later, when I went back to my hometown to visit him, my new aunt-in-law said: "Since your uncle heard the news that Uncle Wei has been under detention and interrogation, he's been saying to himself, 'You watched him constructing a tall building, playing and singing loudly. You watched his building standing there, and the beautiful dancing. You watched his building collapse, cries bursting out. You could only watch all of this, unable to do anything.'"

When I was with my uncle, there was one more thing that left a deep impression on me. He told me many times that he had done something wrong when he was a county magistrate. I wonder whether you would like to hear about it? You do? All right!

My uncle said that when he was a country magistrate, a director in the county government office surnamed Pang was very capable – not only good at coordinating work but also writing official documents. No matter what kind of materials he was given, the final paperwork he presented would be very impressive. My uncle appreciated his talents very much. During his second year as the magistrate, he strongly rejected others' opinions and made Pang the deputy magistrate. On the ninth morning after Pang was promoted, a young cadre in the county government named Ruan Ruo suddenly broke into my uncle's office and said that Deputy Magistrate Pang had harassed and insulted his wife the previous night, and he wanted my uncle to punish Pang. My uncle said: "I was very surprised at that time, so I asked him how Pang had insulted his wife. He said he had taken his child for a walk after supper, and his wife stayed at home alone. Just as she had finished having a shower, Pang knocked on the door and asked for some sort of document. His wife had thought it was him and their child returning, so she came to open the door without any clothes on. She was taken aback when the door opened, and that Deputy Magistrate Pang put his arms around her, groping and kissing wildly, though he didn't rape her."

After hearing that, my uncle asked him immediately whether he agreed to let the Public Security Bureau handle this, but that young cadre shook his head and said he didn't want the matter to be made public – they had to live in this small city and what they wanted was a punishment for that Pang within the Party so that he would never bully them again.

After Ruan Ruo left, my uncle immediately called Pang for a meeting. To his surprise, Pang jumped up to defend himself after he heard this. He said that was a complete slander because he had been working overtime in the office that night, and he had two witnesses. He also added that he had criticised that Ruan Ruo a few times in his work, but he had never thought he would fabricate stories to slander him. After Pang left, my uncle asked the two witnesses in his office, and they both testified that they had been with Pang during the time in question.

My uncle said he had made a judgement at that time that the young cadre Ruan Ruo had made it up to deliberately ruin Pang's reputation as some sort of revenge. He therefore called another deputy magistrate who was in charge of institutional affairs and arranged him for a talk with Ruan Ruo, giving him some criticism and putting an end to the matter.

To everyone's shock, one night three days later, that young cadre Ruan Ruo and his wife both committed suicide, leaving their young daughter alone in this world. In their farewell letter, they said that Deputy Magistrate Pang had in fact raped Ruan Ruo's wife that night. The young couple worried that if this news had spread, it would be too shameful for them to live in such a small city, so Ruan Ruo didn't tell the truth to my uncle. Even though they hadn't revealed the whole truth, they didn't expect the evildoer to receive no punishment at all. They didn't want to live in this ugly world anymore where officials stuck together against ordinary people.

My uncle was stunned by the news and issued an order that the Public Security Bureau thoroughly investigate the case. Two days later the truth was revealed. Pang had indeed raped the young cadre's wife, and the two witnesses who provided him with an alibi were actually collaborating with him. Pang had long been obsessed with that young woman, and after many fruitless attempts at seduction, he finally sought an opportunity and raped her. He had thought the young couple would swallow the bitterness down.

After my uncle learned the truth, he stayed in his office for a whole day, refusing to go out and refusing to let anybody in. He just sat at his desk and smoked quietly thinking about the whole thing carefully. He said it was the first time he understood the weight of the power he had. It indeed could kill people indirectly and had the final decision on life and death. My uncle reflected that if he had been a little bit more discreet and taken a different approach, the young couple probably would not have chosen to end their lives – two breathing lives! But because of his hasty decision, and his failure to recognise the force of the negative strength of power, he ruined these two lives and ruined a family. My uncle said that when he reflected on the way he dealt with this matter he found the reason why he had been so hasty. There was already a conclusion in his heart before he handled it – that is, officials at higher levels generally had a more noble character than officials at lower levels. He said he mistakenly thought of officialdom as a place to train one's personality. He had failed to make a distinction between official ranks and personalities. Besides, there was a hidden psychological motivation in his mind – he was unwilling to admit that the official he himself had promoted would do this. He believed he wouldn't have chosen the wrong person. If that Pang did do something wrong, he himself would of course feel disgraced, and that's why, when Ruan Ruo came to report this to him, he was biased at first.

Uncle said he felt deeply in debt to the young couple and tried many times to find their young daughter in order to give that child more care, but unfortunately he couldn't find her. It was said that her adopted family intentionally cut off contact with all her acquaintances, unwilling to let the child know where she came from to avoid her being hurt again.

10

ZHENG FANGFAN

THE SECRETARY

MY TIME with Secretary Wantong was not short. It started from the time when he was the provincial mayor. After graduating from the Department of Economics and Management of Qinghe University, I stayed there and took a teaching post, working as a lecturer. One day, our president asked me to go to the mayor's office, telling me that the mayor was looking for me. I was very surprised. What did a mayor of a provincial city want from me, an unimportant lecturer?

When I went to see him, he held my hands and said: "I know you from your article 'The Economic Breakthrough of Central Cities in China' in *Economic Reference*. I've asked you here today to discuss one thing. What about coming to work as my secretary?"

Of course, I was very surprised, but I knew it was a chance for me to turn my knowledge from books into social practice, so I didn't hesitate for a minute and replied with a nod: "Yes, I agree!"

He smiled and said: "Good! Very decisive! Come to report here in three days' time."

I sat at the desk of the mayor's secretary three days later. Since then, many years have passed, and I've followed him from the position of secretary of the Municipal Party Committee to deputy secretary of the Provincial Party Committee and the governor. We got along very well.

When I worked with him, he once said to me jokingly: "I hear there's a saying going around that a 'three-types-of-men criteria' is very popular in promoting cadres – that is, if a man wants to be promoted, he should be either a young master, a son-in-law or an adviser. You, in a sense, are an adviser. So what kind of promotion do you want in the future?"

I replied with a smile: "I want to go back to teach at Qinghe University."

Hearing that, he said: "I'm very glad to hear you say this. You know, there are too many secretaries who go on to become officials. Some very important positions have been occupied by secretaries of important people. I don't mean they shouldn't be officials – I'm just saying the fact that all the secretaries of senior officials later work as officials proves there are some problems with our system. It's another kind of nepotism. Just think about it – if a country's important powers end up in the hands of a group of secretaries who haven't received any practical training on governing, what will happen then? Don't you think it's very dangerous? You're different – you've thought about going back to teach in the university, which is really refreshing."

Before he retired, he once asked me whether I would like to go back to Qinghe University to work as a vice president and teach part-time. To be honest, I definitely wanted that. You know, I was not young then, and it was improper to be a full-time secretary, but at that time he was in poor physical condition, and his mood was also not good. I felt embarrassed to say anything and decided to stay with him for the time being. But I never thought I would be with him until he went to another world.

Last autumn, I accompanied him to a maple forest in the suburbs to enjoy the leaves, which had turned red. We got out of the car and walked to a maple tree that was covered in red. However, as I was about to take a photo of him, he suddenly pointed at the sky and asked me to take a look. I looked up and saw a team of geese flying south. He said: "Xiao Zheng, this scene is very similar to a dream I have often had recently. But in my dream, it was one goose flying in the sky, not a team of them."

I laughed and said: "That is very interesting. Does it mean you want to go to the south for a rest like these geese? If you really want to go, I can arrange for that. We could go to live in Hainan for a while."

He shook his head and said: "No need – dreams aren't true. And no matter where you go, the best place is home."

He asked me to take a photo of the geese flying south, but they were far away by the time I was ready to do it.

He had Alzheimer's disease? That's nonsense! I don't know where that news came from. I worked with him for so many years, and he had always been sharp in thought, showing not the slightest sign of dementia. I don't know whether that news had some connection with that absurd medical report.

It was in one spring when he was still in his post that the General Office informed all the provincial leaders to take part in the annual medical examination in the Provincial People's Hospital. I went there with him. It was a routine examination and went very smoothly. He was in good physical condition except for his high cholesterol. We went back to the office, talking and laughing.

But in the evening on the third day after we got off work, a friend from the Finance Department, who was about my age, stopped me in the corridor and whispered to me: "I heard Governor Ouyang has got Alzheimer's disease?"

I laughed and said: "Nothing of the sort! Where did you hear that?" He discretely took out a piece of paper from his trouser pocket and showed it to me. It was a medical report with the name Ouyang Wantong written on it. The list read: "Based on a psychological test, a haematology test and a neuroimaging test, the patient is suspected of having mild Alzheimer's disease. Prescribe a small dose of cholinesterase inhibitors, and keep the patient under observation. Encourage the patient to take part in social activities and daily family activities."

I remember I was very angry after reading it. I threw it onto the ground and said: "Sheer nonsense! Governor Ouyang hasn't got Alzheimer's disease!"

With these words, I left angrily.

Never did I expect that the rumour would spread in the Provincial Party Committee and provincial government, so that all of the government officials would believe Governor Ouyang had Alzheimer's disease. Then I realised I should find out where the rumour came from. I went to look for that friend from the Finance Department and asked him for the so-called medical report. He said: "On that day we met, after you told me it was not true, I tore it up and threw it away."

I asked him where he got the medical report, and he said he found it on the floor when he opened the office. I found this very strange and thought that someone might have been making a joke, so I didn't pay much attention to it.

Governor Ouyang had been kept in the dark about this – I didn't tell him about it, and neither did anyone else dare. If he had known that, he would have died of rage.

I felt very relaxed when I was with him. He was not the kind of person who wore a solemn face all day long. Whenever he had time, he would talk with me about almost anything.

Once, we talked about people's toughness, and he said: "As for this, my mother was the most strong-willed in my family. When I was a child, I often saw my mother borrowing things blushingly from neighbours, like mixed flour powder or ground corn. Once, she asked me to borrow some cooking salt from an uncle living to the east to us. Holding a small bowl, I came to the door of that uncle and shouted, 'Uncle, my mother has asked me to borrow some salt.' That uncle sullenly took out his pipe from his mouth and said, 'Again?' With this, he walked towards the salt jar, fumbled out three large salt particles and threw them into my bowl, saying, 'Enough for one meal. Lending anything to your family amounts to hitting a dog with a meatball – nothing will come back!' I was eight at that time and could understand what he meant. I went back home, pouting, and handed the bowl with three salt particles to her, shouting angrily, 'Don't ask me to borrow anything again!' My mother just lowered her head and wiped her tears without saying anything. My father at that moment came back holding the bullwhip in his hand. When he saw the salt and the bowl, he yelled at my mother too, 'Who asked you to borrow salt? Will we die without having salt for one meal? You damned woman!' My mother didn't say anything in response. She just went to cook for the family as she wiped her tears. If my mother had not been so strong, my family wouldn't have survived that difficult time."

He also talked about his early ambition with me. He said: "I could have been an ordinary person, rather than an official. My mother said I grabbed a suona and a painting brush during the drawing lots celebration. How interesting my life would have been if I had pursued the suona or drawing. If I could play skilfully, I could have been a suona performer in a folk orchestra, playing accompaniment or solo – either of them would have been wonderful. Whenever I feel bored, I can just pick up my suona and play *A Flower, Carrying the Bridal Sedan Chair, Celebrate the Harvest, Ode to the Loess, Zhuyunfei, Ode to Rivers and Lakes, The Dance of the Golden Snake, Lingering Snow on a Broken Bridge* and *Wind from the Lotus Pond in the Drizzle*. Any of these would be refreshing to play and listen to. If I had chosen to be a suona performer, I might have made a lot of money."

I reminded him with a smile: "Then you wouldn't be a governor. It's difficult to promote a suona performer to be an official."

He said: "You really talk like my grandfather. When I was a child, my aunt invited an uncle from our village to teach me how to play the suona. My grandfather grabbed the suona from my hand and threw it away, saying, 'Is there any promising future for a boy to play this when he grows up? Playing music won't help him enter the officialdom.' My aunt of course was annoyed when she saw that. She argued, 'Is there any need for such a little child to know things about being an official?' My grandfather said, 'As a man, he should go into officialdom to make something of his life.'"

When he talked about the past, he always narrowed his eyes and looked at the sky outside the window. It was as if he wanted to have a better view of those past years one more time.

We all think it's glamorous when a man becomes a governor. With cars and houses, with people flattering and applauding, and with everything done for you by others, it seems that life can't be any better. In fact, that's only one side of the story, and there's another side that few people see. I, as his secretary who stayed with him all day long, was lucky to see the other side of being a governor. What's the other side? The loss of freedom. Take eating as an example. We generally eat our meals until we're full, but for a governor, a meal sometimes takes four or five times longer to finish. When important leaders from Beijing or the neighbouring province come to visit, the governor should be present to have dinner with them. Sometimes, he would have to attend five banquets at the same time, so he could only sit for ten minutes at each table. When you take away the time spent chatting with the guests, he was only able to eat a few hasty mouthfuls of food at each table. What's the fun of this kind of life? Another example is going to the toilet. When we ordinary people need to go to the toilet, we can do this easily for as long as we want. But for him, the moment he went to the toilet, a lot of people wait outside for him to give advice, receive reports, have meetings, issue instructions or get in a car. He had constipation, which meant he needed more time, so what could he do? I often saw him walk into the toilet painfully and then walk out painfully. Changing clothes is another example. We ordinary people usually don't need to change clothes during the day, but a governor does. One occasion might call for casual clothes like a jacket, while others might require a suit. Sometimes, the interval between the two occasions was so short that he didn't even have the time to change his clothes, so he had to do it in the car on the way to his next destination. It was extremely troublesome to change trousers in the car, and the slightest carelessness would result in embarrassment when he got out of the car.

Yes, I know about his resignation.

He made a sudden decision, and I knew nothing about it beforehand. Half a month before his resignation, he still talked with me about the similarities and differences between Chinese officialdom and foreign officialdom, and he was very cheerful at that time. I remember he said the similarity between China and foreign countries was that officialdom was the place for people to realise their self-worth, to show their political talents and administrative abilities, to satisfy their inner desires to rule others, to fulfil their aspirations for entering middle or even higher social class, and to realise their hopes to serve their nation and country. The difference was that officialdom in foreign countries was strictly controlled by the law and closely monitored by news media. Anyone who entered officialdom was first of all treated as a potential offender, whose actions were under strict supervision, and there was clear regulation on what you could and couldn't do. If you did something that was not allowed, you immediately faced the danger of being fired and punished – even if you were the president, you would suffer impeachment. But in China, officialdom was regarded as a melting pot and higher ground of morality where great people could be trained. Officials were regarded as the most intelligent and most virtuous people. The official was the one who had the wisest thoughts, whose words and deeds were the most virtuous and who had the authority to rule over the people in the same way that parents ruled over their children. Officials had the power to judge everything, and no one dared to question their decisions and words, especially the top local leaders in certain locations. Even when officials were jerks, no one could control them except for their superiors. Secretary Wantong said this must be solved in the future. Without supervision of officials and without restrictions on the power they had, they would sooner or later become corrupt. Their powers would sooner or later be used to do evil things, and the ultimate victims would certainly be ordinary people. He said he was prepared to conduct a test in Qinghe province to see if he could find a solution for this problem.

How would the test be conducted? He did tell me his vision. He said: "We can start with the reform of the function of the Provincial

Committee of the CPPCC. Nowadays, the members of the committee are selected by the Organisation Department, and they only have the right to participate in discussions and give suggestions after being elected. They have no supervisory powers. In future, the number of committee members from various sectors could be determined by the Organisation Department. As for who finally becomes a committee member, it should be completely determined via elections within the various sectors. Officials should be forbidden from being candidates. Once committee members are elected, their job is to supervise the officials in their sector – so members of the financial sector, the cultural sector, the commercial sector and the agricultural sector supervise the officials in their respective sectors. It's necessary to ensure that officials in each sector are supervised. The main task of these committee members is to find fault with the officials – not only in their work but also in their lives, especially their violation of law and discipline. It's also better for the Provincial Committee of the CPPCC to have a newspaper whose main function is to publicise the supervision work, especially the violations of law and discipline. Of course, it will publish stories about some good officials who perform official duties honestly. In this way, with people and means to supervise, those officials will have a sense of urgency every day so that they have to serve the people honestly instead of sitting back quietly as a master. Officials who are under supervision would have no right to decide whether the members of the CPPCC leave or stay, and any official who retaliates against CPPCC members by any means, once verified, would be immediately removed from office and investigated."

I remember I was very happy after listening to this and said: "I hope this idea can be realised very soon." But unfortunately, just a few days after we talked about this, he suddenly proposed his resignation.

Why did he resign? It's hard for me to explain it clearly. The day before he resigned, he was taking part in the provincial rural work conference in high spirits and said with a big grin that he would go to visit the ten main wheat producing counties before summer harvest. But in the afternoon the next day, he asked me to go to Provincial Secretary Liang's office with him to deliver his handwritten resignation personally. After he entered the secretary's office, he began talking before the door was closed by Liang's secretary. He said: "Secretary Liang, after careful consideration I've decided to step down and retire. This is my resignation."

I was shocked, and I could see that Secretary Liang was too. He stared at Governor Wantong and asked surprisingly: "Why?"

"I want to change a lot of things. But I've found there's little I can do, and I feel powerless in the face of social atmosphere and power itself. A very strong sense of powerlessness..."

Governor Wantong then waved towards Liang's secretary and me, signalling us to go out for the time being.

On that day, he talked with the secretary of the Party Committee until it got dark – two solid hours – while Liang's secretary and I waited outside. We secretaries usually chatted happily when we met, but that day we were not in the mood. We both knew his resignation would be an earth-shaking event in the political arena in Qinghe province. We were thinking about possible causes and effects of this incident, especially me because Governor Wantong's resignation would have the greatest impact on my future. Everyone in political circles knows the fate of a secretary is closely connected with the fate of a leader. When a leader loses his post and his power, his secretary's fate will change accordingly, and there will also be some unpredictable changes as well.

When you become a governor after having struggled as an ordinary cadre, life will be glamorous at first, according to secular evaluation. Usually, at this stage, you would consider how to go further, either to be the Party Committee secretary or go to Beijing for a post in a ministry or commission directly under the State Council. He, however, suddenly announced his resignation, and this not only surprised the outside world but also surprised those of us who had been working with him. He never told me the real reason for his resignation. The so-called powerlessness was just what I heard about, and I didn't understand what exactly it meant. I carefully reflected on it and felt there were a few reasons for his sudden resignation. The first one, I guess, would have something to do with his wife. Perhaps she had done something. Well, you can't write this into the biography.

His wife Chang Xiaowen had a good reputation during the first few years after she married my old leader Ouyang Wantong. Among the wives of the leaders of our province, she was the one who earned the best comments. I also had a good first impression of her. At that time, she didn't interfere with political affairs, she didn't intervene in her husband's work, she kept a low profile and she declined money and gifts from others. She was also kind and polite to us staff.

Nobody knew when it started, but she gradually changed. I was the first to notice this. I saw that she became more and more particular about her dress. You know, she was born into an ordinary family, and she used to pay no attention to what she wore. She usually went to work in a police uniform and wore casual clothes when not at work, occasionally a skirt, which was no different from the other wives of government cadres considering the style and fabric. Everyone who met her felt she was very amiable and addressed her as Madame Chang casually. Slowly, however, she wore the police uniform less and the fashionable clothes more often. At first, she bought women's clothes made by a local company in the province, then from two famous domestic companies and then famous international brands. She spent more time shopping for designer brands, and no matter where she went – in the province, in Beijing or abroad – most of her time was idled away in those fashion stores. We staff members spent more and more time with her buying clothes. At the very beginning, the chauffeur did it, then it was the guards and then it was me. She bought more and more designer clothes. Secretary Wantong somewhat doted on her because of the age difference, so he didn't intervene. Honestly, she was younger than the wives of the other provincial leaders and she was pleasing to the eye, so she was indeed beautiful when dressed in the brand-name clothes. You know what, the wives of the other leaders all learned how to dress from her, wearing the same brand that she wore. We might say she was leading the fashion trend in the circle of the wives of provincial leaders. Some people in the government offices would always figure out a way to send her some clothes at festivals or New Year. Secretary Wantong gradually noticed this and reminded her of the negative effects, but she didn't care about it at all, saying: "What's the big deal of wearing beautiful clothes! I'm not doing a bad thing, so what should I be afraid of?"

Perhaps it was because she wanted to show off her beautiful clothes and didn't want to wear a police uniform anymore that she asked to be transferred to a different job. She wanted me to ask the Provincial Committee whether they would accept her, and she told me not to let the governor know about it before it was done. The leaders of the Provincial Committee immediately expressed their sincere welcome when they heard she wanted to work there. It was I who helped her with all the transfer procedures. At that stage, she told Governor Wantong, who was of course unhappy about it, but since what was done couldn't be undone, he could do nothing but frown to show his disapproval.

When she started work in the Provincial Committee, she was in charge of the contact with members of the business community, so she had more chances to deal with entrepreneurs. When some people discovered she was the governor's wife, they tried every means to curry favour with her. At first, she was very cautious, trying to avoid those situations. Later, a brand clothing manufacturer in the province invited her to visit a new production line in their factory. It was what she liked, and she had good reasons, public or private, to go and have a look, so she went there in high spirits. The factory manager showed her around the production workshop, then took her to the new apparel fitting room, inviting her to try on a newly-designed autumn dress, which aroused her interest quite a lot. She had a lot of fun in the fitting room. When she was about to leave, the manager put two sets of clothes she liked into the car that was taking her back. She politely declined a little bit and then took the clothes with her.

After that, the manager regularly invited her to try new clothes and sent her newly-designed clothes quite often. She became more and more fond of that manager, more and more valued him, and more and more wanted to offer him help. Later, that manager said he wanted to have another piece of land near his factory for expansion. He asked her whether she could do him a favour and say some good words about him in front of the provincial leaders so that they would give him a green light. She agreed without any hesitation and said: "No problem, I'll arrange for Zheng, the secretary, to do this." Hearing that, I felt terrified because Governor Wantong had told us that no one was allowed to meddle in the field of real estate, saying it was a world of money that could easily destroy a person. But since his wife asked me to do this, I had no choice but to comply. I called a deputy mayor who was in charge of real estate in the provincial capital, asking him whether he could give that manager the convenience of expanding the factory. That deputy mayor agreed for my sake.

After that, she went to try new clothes more and more often, and I dared not interfere. Later, I heard that manager had asked his designers to record her height, arms, bust, waist, hips and shoulders so that the clothes could be tailored to her needs. Sometimes, designers from foreign countries would be invited to make clothes for her, so each time she went there and tried the clothes on, they fitted her nicely, which made her particularly happy. Eventually, that manager indeed got the piece of land he wanted. To thank me, he sent a set of clothes to my wife and a bank card with 500,000 yuan for me. I immediately returned the clothes and the card. I, as a small secretary, dared not to ask for trouble.

The day after I returned the clothes and card, the governor's wife came to me with a set of clothes. She said: "Please return the clothes and the card to the manager." I saw that the card read one million! Good heavens! Something was sure to happen if she should accept. She came to tell me specifically: "That's the end of the matter. Governor Wantong is very busy. Don't report this to him." I understood what she meant – don't tell the governor in case he becomes angry and criticises her.

But out of my expectation, the manager of that clothing factory didn't expand his factory after he got the land. Instead, he had several commercial residential complexes built there, which of course aroused the attention of the Department of Construction because in that place the construction of commercial residential property was not allowed. The factory manager again came to the governor's wife with several sets of brand-name clothes asking her to grease the wheel for him to get the approval of the Department of Construction. She might have realised the seriousness of the matter. She hesitated for a while, criticised him for the lack of discipline and then ordered him to take the clothes away. She later came to me and said that the factory had already invested a huge amount of money on the construction, and if they stopped halfway, they were sure to go bankrupt. She wanted me to go to the Department of Construction and say a good word for them. I knew it was a violation of discipline, but I was afraid to annoy her in case she spoke against me in front of Governor Wantong, so I did it against my will again. The Department of Construction thought it was Governor Wantong's idea when they met with me, so they didn't follow up any more. In fact, Governor Wantong didn't know anything about it. That's the truth – I'm not covering for him. He has passed away, so what's the point of telling lies for him anyway?

As for staffing matters, she was very cautious at first. She barely intervened, and she didn't even get involved with her own brother's promotion. But she made an exception once. The boss of a jade factory in our province is a member of the committee. One day, he sent her an invitation to the opening ceremony of their exhibition building. She thought it was her duty to go, and she asked me to go with her. I was free on that day, and I'm interested in jade carvings, so I decided to go along to feast my eyes.

The exhibition building was presented in a very grand way, and almost all the fine jade carvings from the factory were on display. She, however, had no interest in the large jade carvings and just glanced at them quickly. But when she entered the jade bracelets exhibition hall, her eyes lit up. A variety of jade bracelets made of various materials were placed inside the showcase, and their beauty was reflected under the spotlights. She stopped in front of the showcase, intently studying those jade bracelets. Noticing that, the boss hurriedly rushed to her side and began to introduce them to her: "This is a special jade bracelet of safety and auspiciousness for ladies. Jade bracelets can be divided into colours – usually white, sapphire, jadeite and agate – with each type having some special functions. White jade bracelets help to calm one's mind and nerves. Sapphire bracelets help one to avoid evils and make one feel more vigorous. Jadeite bracelets can relieve disease of the respiratory system and help overcome depression. Agate bracelets clear away heat and improve eyesight. Jade bracelets have various origins including Xiuyan, Hetian, Dushan and turquoise. Xiuyan jade is produced in Xiuyan county in Liaoning province. Hetian jade comes from the Xinjiang autonomous region. Dushan jade comes from Nanyang in Henan province. Turquoise jade is from Yun county in Hubei province. They are all famous Chinese jades. Styles of jade bracelets include round bangle, oval-shaped, bamboo weave pattern, braided, carved and so on. You have rounded wrists and delicate skin, and you have an elegant bearing, so this round bangle Hetian jade bracelet suits you best."

As he said this, he took out from the showcase a crystal-clear jade bracelet containing quite a few jadeites inside and presented it to her. She put it around her wrist and lost herself in appreciating it, forgetting to look at the price tag. I had a look and couldn't help but gasp – 880,000 yuan! This lady didn't know anything about jade, and she had no idea that this jade bracelet could be so expensive. She probably thought it was only a small gift, so she didn't decline, but instead put it around her wrist and walked out. The boss then asked someone to fetch an exquisite jade bracelet box, put the tag price inside the box and gave it to me.

I whispered to the boss: "How could she afford such an expensive thing?"

The boss smiled: "It's only an expression of our goodwill, a small gift. How could we ask her to pay for it? What's more, gold is valuable while jade is priceless. I just wrote a price randomly on the tag. Please set your mind at rest!"

When we returned to the governor's home that day, I hesitated for a while but eventually placed the box with the price tag inside on the sofa. I wanted her to know the price of the bracelet, so she might be clear about what to do. As I expected, she called me the next day and asked whether the number on the price tag was accurate or not. I told her it should be accurate based on the current price of Hetian jade on the market. I also told her that reserves of Hetian jade were running out, so the output was diminishing and the price on the market was getting higher and higher.

She asked: "What should I do? Return it to him?"

I heard a kind of reluctance in her voice, so I said: "Well, you accepted it, so if you return it, they might feel embarrassed."

"Oh..." she responded and then remained silent for quite a long time before she spoke again. "Take me to his place and return the bracelet. I can't accept such a valuable thing."

I guessed that boss wouldn't give such a valuable bracelet away for no reason – he must have some motive. Sure enough, when we went to give the bracelet back to him, he sighed and said: "To be honest, I do want you to do me a favour. Now that you insist on returning it to me, I feel embarrassed to mention it."

She asked: "What on earth is your problem? Anything I can do, I will. It rarely has anything to do with whether I receive a gift or not."

That boss told us his son had been the deputy director of the Provincial Industry and Commerce Bureau for three years, and recently the director had been promoted, leaving his post available, but there were too many candidates. He wondered whether she could put in a good word for his son.

She listened and, after some deliberation, she said: "I usually never bother myself with things like that, but in your case, I could have a try."

When we got back home, she said to me: "Make a phone call to Deputy Minister Jiao of the Organisation Department. Tell him that I want him to do me a favour. I'll talk about this with Wantong later."

Of course, I had to listen to her. It turned out everything went smoothly, as she had expected, but I assumed she didn't tell Governor Wantong. It was perhaps after this case that she felt it easier to handle things like that. She began to make exceptions from then on and took care of things in this way more and more. Later, some of her country fellows, classmates and friends, who dared not go to the governor, all came to her secretly whenever they wanted to be promoted. Usually, she didn't meet those people at home – she was invited to go out and made promises to them at tables. Then she either asked me to do the work or she herself went to see some leaders. I didn't know whether she accepted gifts or not, but there was sure to be a hangover from it – that is, evidence against her. Could it be the case that someone had some evidence and gave the governor no choice but to resign?

But in the end, Secretary Liang persuaded him to take back his resignation, which itself indicated it was probably not because of his wife.

Another reason for his resignation was perhaps the big trouble caused by the treatment of water and soil pollution along the Qianlong river. For a period of time, the number of cancer cases in some counties along the Qianlong river increased hugely, and newborn infants' deformity rate was very high as well. A reporter from the provincial newspaper conducted an in-depth investigation and found it was because the Haifu Mining Group, located in the upper reaches of the Qianlong river, had been discharging too much polluted water into the river. This polluted not only the Qianlong river but also many fields on both sides of the river, which directly led to the excessive content of cadmium, lead and arsenic in the farmland nearby. It was because people ate the food produced from those farmlands and drank the groundwater connected with the Qianlong river that the incidence of cancer cases and deformed babies in those counties became so high.

That reporter wrote internal reference documents based on what he had found. After reading this, Governor Wantong immediately gave out his instruction that an expert group should be formed by the Provincial Environmental Protection Department at once to verify this and, if it was discovered to be true, a solution must be found quickly and reported to him. Very soon, the Provincial Environmental Protection Department submitted a document stating that everything the reporter had written was true and suggesting the Haifu Mining Group be forced to stop discharging polluted water into the river. The next day, after Governor Wantong read the document, he took me, together with the director of the Provincial Government Office, the director of the Information and Industrialisation Office and the director of the Provincial Environmental

Protection Agency, and drove to the Haifu Mining Group in Qian county without informing their leaders in advance.

When we arrived at Qian county, we didn't go to their headquarters first. Instead, we went to some mines where we saw how the polluted water was being discharged directly into the Qianlong river. Haifu Mining Group was a famous large-scale private enterprise in the province, whose annual output amounted to nearly 10 billion yuan. Hai Chengui, the president of the group, is a famous rich person in the province who usually behaves quite arrogantly and imperiously. After his subordinates reported to him that a group of people were inspecting their sewage again, he hurried over aggressively with a bunch of security guards in order to drive us away. When he saw it was Governor Wantong, he forced smiles on his face quickly and said he was just coming to invite the governor to deliver a speech to all the employees in the group headquarters. The governor came straight to the point when he saw him, telling him with a cold face: "First, immediately stop the production line and close all the mining fields. Second, install sewage equipment as soon as possible – the resumption of mining will only be approved when all the sewage equipment has come into operation and there's no discharge of polluted water. Third, provide financial aid to the local government for the treatment of polluted water and soil to make the river clear again and to reduce the content of heavy metal in the soil. Work with the Provincial Environmental Protection Agency and make a careful assessment to determine how much money it needs."

At first, Hai Chenggui listened with smiles, but gradually his face hardened as he listened. After Governor Wantong finished, he said briefly: "All right, I appreciate the governor's concern about environmental protection."

Governor Wantong then went to inspect the most polluted villages and towns along the Qianlong river. On the very evening of that day, his wife phoned me from the provincial capital. She said it was urgent and asked to speak with the governor immediately. I handed the phone to the governor, and her voice came from the phone: "Just now, Deputy Director Lin of the Provincial General Office came with a vice president of Haifu Mining Group to deliver a large statue of Gautama Buddha packed in cardboard. At first, I thought it was made of ceramic, and I felt it might be unwise to refuse a Buddha admittance to the house, so I allowed them to put it down. When they left, I opened the package and found the Buddha was made of pure gold – over fifty kilograms! What should I do? I called them, but they didn't answer the phone."

With a sullen face, the governor told me to inform Director Pang of the Provincial Public Security Department and tell him to immediately send a person to his home to move the statue to the Public Security Department for storage. Just as he finished dealing with the first phone call, we got another one from the director of the Environmental Protection Agency of Qian county, who said all the mines of Haifu Mining Group resumed production after closing for only one afternoon. After listening to my report with a livid expression, the governor asked me to make a phone call to Hai Chenggui at once, and when the call was connected, he yelled at him angrily: "Why did you agree overtly but oppose covertly? That is two-faced behaviour! Is it because you sent me a gold Buddha? Let me tell you, I've sent it to the Provincial Public Security Department. You must stop all the mines immediately!"

Hai Chenggui responded with a bit of pleading at first: "Governor, close all the mines? So many mines! Closing for one day means a loss of over 10 million yuan, which is not only a loss for my Haifu Mining Group but also a loss for industrial production in our province. My shareholders and I will lose money, while the provincial government will lose the increased GDP – for you, that means a loss of your political achievement. Please allow me to go on with the production while installing sewage equipment at the same time."

The governor said coldly: "What about those cancer patients and deformed babies? When a family member has caught cancer or given birth to a deformed baby, you tell me, how do they continue their life? I don't need this political achievement, and you don't need to have so much money, do you? How much money in your estimation would be enough? Close all the mines at once! Resume your production when all the sewage equipment has been installed."

I, along with all those leaders of provincial offices who went to inspect with us, thought that Haifu Mining Group would definitely shut down its production since the governor had been so angry about it. To everyone's surprise, three days later, a report came from the director of the Environmental Protection Agency of Qian county that Haifu Mining Group had not shut down all of its mines! The governor became furious. To be honest, I was very angry too. I called Hai Chenggui immediately, but his phone was switched off. When I called his office, the receptionist told me that he was not in. The governor then asked me to inform the Qian county government to cut off the supply of electricity and water to all of Haifu Group's mines.

This order at last shut down all the mines of Haifu Group. Governor Wantong told me that the Qian county government should report Haifu Group's pollution control progress every ten days to the Provincial Government Office, without giving any leeway.

I thought that since the governor was so firm, the Haifu Group would definitely obey the order. I didn't expect that Haifu Group would not want to spend a large sum of money on the treatment of pollution. They didn't purchase or install any sewage equipment at all. Instead, they exploited all their connections trying to soften Governor Wantong's determination. From the third day, I began to receive phone calls from various officials speaking good words for the Haifu Group. They ranged from vice-provincial officials to provincial officials of neighbouring provinces and even officials from some ministries of the central government. I had to let him take those phone calls. How dare I not? But I could see every time he answered, his anger accumulated. He couldn't take his anger out on those people, so he slapped the table in a rage and walked back and forth in his office after he put down the phone. He told me: "This Hai Chenggui is showing me how powerful his connections are and trying to force me to give up the pollution treatment! Great, show me what he's capable of!"

On the evening of the thirteenth day after the shutdown of the Haifu Group, the confidential telephone connected directly to Beijing on Governor Wantong's desk suddenly rang before we left. I saw him lift the receiver, so I rushed out of his office and went to mine. You know, I wasn't allowed to listen to this type of phone call, but there was only a thin wall between my office and his, and though I couldn't hear the voice of the incoming call clearly, the governor's voice could be heard. What's more, his voice was pretty loud – probably because of his strong emotions – so his words came into my ears voluntarily. It sounded like the governor was defending himself: "...I'm not prejudiced against the Haifu Group. Still less am I prejudiced against private enterprises or unconcerned about the decline of GDP. But I'm worried about the greater consequences of water and soil pollution, I'm worried about more cancer cases, and I'm worried about more deformed babies. Yes, I should examine myself. I know my working methods are problematic. I know that since I became the governor, the economic development in our province has slowed down…"

I knew the call was about the shutdown of the Haifu Group.

That evening, Governor Wantong didn't move for a long time after he replaced the receiver. The working day had finished. I peered into his office through the crack in the door and saw him slumped over the desk, his face buried in his arms, motionless. I knew he was feeling miserable, so I left him alone. That evening, he just stayed in that position for about an hour, while I stayed in the outer room still. It wasn't until he stood up to wash his face that I entered the room to tidy up the documents. Before he left, he told me in a low voice: "Tell the provincial EPA that the Haifu Group can resume production while installing sewage equipment at the same time. But they must install the equipment – otherwise, I'll shut down their mines again in a month's time."

Was this the reason for his resignation?

I don't know.

I thought about his resignation for some time. The third possible reason is something that happened in Beijing. Very few people know about this. I can tell you, but you must promise not to write it into the biography.

Once, I accompanied Governor Wantong to go to study in the Central Party School in Beijing. He stayed on campus while I stayed in a hotel outside the school. Almost all the secretaries that accompanied their leaders like me lived in that hotel. We were there to provide services like drafting speeches that the leaders would use at campus seminars, organising banquets in the leaders' spare time, contacting the ministries, commissions and offices, and some odd jobs like laundry. In addition to a secretary, some of the provincial and municipal leaders brought with them the most effective writers from their provinces to draft papers that were published as part of their studies.

I would say, among those secretaries, I was the one who had the lightest workload because Governor Wantong was a graduate student who wrote quite well. He didn't like what I wrote for him, so he wrote his speeches and articles himself. Also, he didn't like to send his underwear to the laundry, so he washed his clothes himself, and therefore saved me a lot of work. My work there was mainly about getting various construction projects for our province. I needed to arrange for the governor to meet leaders of some ministries and commissions and to coordinate and negotiate with cadres at the level of department or bureau. You know, if you don't build connections with them, you'll lose a lot of projects.

One morning, some secretaries, who happened to have some free time, asked me to play cards with them. To be honest, I like reading books, and I don't have much interest in playing cards, but I couldn't decline the invitation. Playing cards and chatting among secretaries was the best opportunity to exchange information and ideas about some big issues. It's said that many political decisions in Beijing start with secretaries sitting together and trying to take in the situation, then reaching an agreement and persuading their leaders to make the final call. And it was on that very morning, playing cards and chatting with those secretaries, that I got some important information – a highway trunk line in the national plan would be under construction ahead of schedule this year, and nearly four hundred kilometres of this road would be in our Qinghe province. There were already many sons of senior officials chasing the tender contracts, and fierce competition was expected to begin very soon.

I told this to Governor Wantong and reminded him that someone might ask him for help on this. He listened, reflected for a moment and said: "Tell the director of the Provincial Department of Transportation that if I have to ask someone to go to them for help, they must do their work according to the regulations. Don't give any special treatment, but try not to use any insulting remarks."

My judgement and estimation were correct. Ten or so days later, the director of the Beijing office of Qinghe province called to report that a toff in Beijing wanted to invite Governor Wantong to a party. Governor Wantong frowned when he heard this. I knew it was a dilemma for him – if he should decline, he would offend that man's father, but if he should go, there might be some unreasonable requests about highway construction. It would indeed be an uncomfortable banquet. He hesitated for a long time and eventually said: "Let's go to the banquet. My refusal would make people lose face, which equals an immediate offence. A late offence is always better than an earlier one, isn't it? Let's go and see what he has to say."

The banquet was held in a private club in the city. It was not eye-catching from the outside, but the interior was decorated luxuriously. Governor Wantong and I were both shocked by the level of splendour, though we had visited quite a few high-end venues. There were pavilions and pagodas, a flowing stream with fish, red sandalwood furniture and famous paintings hanging on the wall. Indoors, objects from the Qing dynasty were on display. On the floor were silk carpets. Beautiful girls served the tables. The host was that toff who had made the invitation, and another famous toff was also present. They warmly invited us to take our seats, made a few conventional greetings and polite remarks first like: "We've heard so much about Governor Wantong, and now we're so glad that we finally have the chance to meet you in person!" Then they said their fathers had very good impressions of Governor Wantong and often praised his political achievements. They both believed Governor Wantong was sure to be promoted. Next, they urged us to drink the wine, and after the first three glasses, the four of us took turns to make toasts.

After the toasts, that toff at last got to the point: "Governor Wantong, I'm wondering whether you could do me a small favour. For you, it's like taking candy from a baby. For me, it's a matter of feeding my family."

Governor Wantong had been silent but smiling all the time, and at this moment he knew he should speak. So he said: "You're welcome. Anything I can do to help. I'll try my best."

The toff then continued, and sure enough it was about his plan to have contracts for the highway in Qinghe province. After the governor listened to him, he said: "I knew this when the highway was still in its planning and designing stage, but until now we haven't received any official notification about its construction date. If the news you have got is true, we'll give you what you want. Anyway, whoever helps us with the construction is a good thing, let alone you! Secretary Zheng, mark this down."

I nodded my head at once.

When the banquet was over, the host toff clapped his hands, and immediately two girls wearing traditional Chinese dresses came in. They were really very beautiful – plump breasts and round hips, willow eyebrows and large eyes, slender and tall figures, eyes looking around in a charming manner, smiles attractively blooming on their faces. Their long white legs were partly hidden and partly visible inside the dresses that slit up to the thigh. The fragrance of perfume drifting from their bodies was tempting, making me dare not to look at them, especially their legs.

"Ladies, accompany the two bosses to take a bath and relax. Serve them well!" The host gave a solemn order to them.

"Gentlemen, please." The girls walked towards us separately.

Governor Wantong smiled as he shook his head, saying to the two toffs: "We appreciate your kindness, but I'm delivering a speech at the school conference tomorrow. I have to go back to prepare the draft. Please excuse us – we're leaving now. We can come again some other time."

With these words, he stood up and walked out, and I followed him in a hurry. In the car, Governor Wantong whispered to me: "The reason why he wants the tender is not to do the construction himself – he wants to resell the contracts. Tell the Provincial Department of Transportation, to inform that toff before the bidding starts, but treat him the same as the other bidders. No special treatment! By then, he might find it's too late to seek some other connections."

I had butterflies in my stomach at that time. This of course would stop them from reselling the contracts which was indeed good for the construction of the highway, but no good for the governor himself. There would be some consequences!

Later, the Provincial Department of Transportation followed our instruction and informed the toff in advance to take part in the bidding. He came in high spirits, thinking that it was a mere formality for him to go through before taking the contract away. He was dumbfounded when he found he had to bid for the contract like the other bidders. How could he win the bid when he was simply trying to fool people with an empty proposal! He left Qinghe with resentment towards Governor Wantong. Upon his departure, he called, saying he wanted to see the governor. I told him the governor had gone to Hong Kong to attract investment. He yelled at me hatefully: "Tell Ouyang Wantong, how dare he play tricks on me! He has bitten off more than he can chew! Shit! Who does he think he is? A fucking governor! Who does he think he is? He's just a pathetic commoner! Shit! Let's wait and see."

Governor Wantong, sitting beside me, heard all his curses on the phone. I saw his face turned livid with rage, and then he picked up a tin tea box and crushed it until it was flattened.

After this, a few phone calls came from Beijing. Every time the governor answered the phone, he would sit in the chair saying nothing for a long time.

I knew there must be a hundred things running through his head.

There is another thing that might have led to Governor Wantong's resignation, but I can't tell you in detail because it involves a living provincial leader. I could give you a general description, but it's only for your reference. You must promise that you'll never make it public or write it into the biography – otherwise, you and I would both be in trouble.

It was a small incident at the very beginning. The Ministry of Education sent a working group to inspect the higher education in Qinghe province. The working group was staying in Qinghe University Hotel. At 10 o'clock one night, a young lady surnamed Liao, who was part of the working group, heard someone knocking at her door. She looked outside through the door viewer and saw a stranger standing there. She didn't know him and needn't have opened the door, but she thought it might be someone from Qinghe University who had come to report something. Besides, it was a standard hotel in the university, so she wasn't suspicious.

When she opened the door, the man said: "Come with me."

Ms Liao felt a bit strange and asked: "Where should we go?"

Hearing this, that man got mad and said aggressively: "You'll know when you're there."

Ms Liao was surprised and wondered why this man would behave so rudely, so she replied angrily: "I won't go anywhere unless you tell me clearly."

The man didn't explain more when he heard this. Instead, he walked towards her, held her in his arms and covered her mouth with a wet towel. Ms Liao struggled but suddenly fainted and leaned softly on the man. The towel was soaked with ethyl ether. The man held Ms Liao and prepared to walk downstairs. Fortunately, a male colleague from the working group was returning from visiting friends and saw what was happening. He asked: "What's going on here? Is Xiao Liao sick?" The man who was holding Ms Liao got scared, pushed her towards her colleague and ran away.

The next day, the news spread around Qinghe University. It was a coincidence Governor Wantong would meet with all the members of the working group of the education ministries as planned that day. Before he went there, I told him what I had learned about the previous night's incident, advising him to make an apology to the working group during the meeting. He was mad as he listened and immediately called the police chief of the provincial capital to Qinghe University, asking him to crack the case on the same day. The good news was that there were cameras in the hotel corridor and the man's face and figure were both clearly recorded. The man parked his car on the campus, and the number plate was photographed too. The campus gatekeeper said he had met this man many times. With all these clues, the Public Security Bureau caught the man, whose name was Big Bear, without much effort.

After questioning him, the police found out what had happened that night. Big Bear was ordered to pick up a young woman in room 411. He had been drinking wine and mistakenly knocked on the door of room 311, where coincidently a young lady was staying. So this is what happened with the case that shocked the governor.

The case might have ended there. After all, there were no serious consequences. But the inspector in charge of Big Bear's case thought there was something suspicious because of the ether on the towel. He went on questioning Big Bear about the girl he was going to pick up in room 411.

Big Bear stammered: "A junior female student at Qinghe University."

The inspector continued: "Where did you take this girl?"

"Nan Song Garden in the eastern suburbs."

"Why did you take her there?"

"I don't know. I just pick up the person and drive her there. Nothing else. It used to be quite smooth. Knock on the door, take the girl and leave. Never thought I would make a mistake this time."

"How often do you take girls there?"

"Sometimes every two days, sometimes every three days, or once a week. It's not fixed."

"A different girl each time?"

"Yes, always new faces."

"Who asked you to do this?"

"My boss."

"Who is your boss?"

"Jian Qianyan, president of International Feiteng."

"Which villa did this President Jian ask you to send the girl to in Nan Song Garden?"

"Jinxiaoju"

"Who is living there?"

"I don't know."

"You don't know? Do you want me to treat you as a criminal who abducts and trafficks women?"

"No, no, a provincial leader goes to stay there regularly."

"Which provincial leader?"

"A deputy one… I dare not say who he is…"

Outraged, Governor Wantong reported this to the higher authority, but there was no response.

11

WEI CHANGSHAN

THE COUNTRY FELLOW

THAT THE ADMINISTRATIVE division agreed to let you interview me proves you're pretty capable. I don't mean because I'm of any importance. You know, I'm actually a living corpse that stinks. I'm only waiting for the day when I have thoroughly decayed. What I mean is that no writer or reporter has ever been here before. You're the first one.

What do you want to know? Stories and facts about my corruption? I've already spoken about these many times, and most of that has been reported in the newspapers and on the internet. You're still interested in that? Stories about money and gold bars? Houses? Wines? Works of art? The people those things were sent to? What kinds of gifts? Stories about women? Or the story about that female singer and me – about how we met and so on? You writers are all fond of that stuff. Why would such a beautiful female singer want to be with a plain-looking guy like me? Thanks to power! It was power that gave me an aura of physical appeal, a handsome man. What? You don't want to write about this? You want to know something about Ouyang Wantong? He died? You're going to write a biography for him? How could he go so early?

Of course, I'm very familiar with Ouyang Wantong. I'm clear about what you want to know about him. We were born in the same village, and he was a few years older than me. In our childhood, we often took a bath in the pond together, and we even knew where each other's birthmarks were. According to the hierarchy in our village, I called him elder brother, and the two of us had the highest ranks. He was sort of my first teacher and mentor in life. We were blood brothers, but later we gradually grew apart and then lost touch. The main responsibility for that is mine. Of course, look at me now. How fortunate that I broke off with him. Otherwise, he might have got involved in my case.

It was good for him. Yes, breaking off with me was definitely good for him.

Our relationship goes back a long time, and I have so many stories about him. Where should I begin?

Well, let's start from that September in 1976, from the day when Ouyang Wantong came to tell me about the death of Chairman Mao. He was a secretary in a commune in our county at that time. One late afternoon, he suddenly returned to the village. When I went to see him in his house, he was discussing something excitedly with his father. When I entered the room, he stopped and began to chat with me about ordinary things, but I could see there was an unnatural expression on his face, and I left.

At dinner time on that day, when I was sitting under the locust tree in front of our house, drinking my gruel as I watched the stars falling into my bowl, Wantong came. He said: "Changshan, there's some important news. I hesitated for a while, and now I've decided to tell you."

I was hungry at that time, so I just looked at him enquiringly as I drank my gruel.

"Chairman Mao passed away!"

I stopped, looked at him in great shock and said: "Don't talk nonsense!"

"It's true. The commune is about to broadcast."

I uttered a low cry and stood up in panic.

"What do you think about it?" he asked.

"Think about what?" I didn't get what he meant for the time being.

"Lessons from past dynasties tell us that when emperors die, changes are sure to happen."

I stared at him in shock. "What changes?"

"Any change! The more the better. Whoever is in power knows that people like change. Take land for example. That's the area that needs to change most. Think about it – what do we rural people care about most? Having enough food to eat is the most important thing! But in recent years, has there been any farmer, including you, who has eaten his fill?

Why haven't they had enough to eat? It's because nobody has the right to use the land!"

"Shh! Don't speak so loudly! Don't you want to live?" I looked around hastily.

"Take it easy. They don't understand what we're talking about."

"But who dares to make a change?" I lowered my voice and asked him.

"Not you and me, of course, but there must be someone."

"Did your father-in-law tell you this?"

"He has passed away. This is my prediction."

I stared at him in the darker and darker night. I knew he had gone to study at the university in the provincial capital. He liked reading books and newspapers. He was a cadre in the commune. He was very knowledgeable.

"It's very likely there'll be bloodshed."

Bloodshed? For a fleeting moment, I felt something cold crawling up my back.

"Those who want to change are sure to encounter resistance from those with vested interests who don't want to change."

"Who will bleed?"

"I don't know."

"You don't know? Then why did you come to scare me?"

"Though we have no influence on the world, we should learn to predict. In all things, success lies in preparation – without preparation there's sure to be failure."

"What should we do now then?"

"Do nothing. Just like what you're doing now, drinking your thin gruel quietly. We only need to wait and see."

Later, the Gang of Four in the central government were arrested, and I couldn't help but admire his foresight. It indeed turned out to be a court upheaval. It was probably from that point I was more convinced by what he said. I didn't dare not to listen carefully.

When Wantong returned for the Spring Festival the next year, he came to me and asked me to go over what I had learned in high school. I followed his suggestion. I remember when he advised me to review my books, he said: "For you, the most important thing in your life is likely to happen very soon. You know, since the Sui dynasty recognised the problems with the recommendation system and established the examination system in the seventh year of Kai Huang, a comparatively fair system of appointing officials became the consensus of leaders to consolidate their rule, and it was adopted by all subsequent dynasties. Chairman Mao Zedong's scrapping of the college entrance examination in China, no matter how many reasons he had, was definitely an unwise decision. This policy won't last long now that he has passed away – it's sure to change. Get ready for the college entrance examination."

He was once again right.

On 21 October 1977, the news media announced the resumption of the national college entrance examination. One month later, the examination was conducted nationwide. Because I had prepared in advance, I wasn't nervous and entered the examination room calmly.

I was admitted to Qinghe University's history department. In that year, I was 23 years old. You know, at that time, college students were quasi-officials, and after graduation they could work as cadres in Party and government organisations at all levels. On the day when I received the admission notice, I went to his office, held his hand joyously and said: "Brother Wantong, without you, I couldn't have made it. You're the one to whom I owe the deepest thanks. If it hadn't been for your prediction, I would never have thought about preparing for the examination, and I wouldn't have been admitted by college so smoothly. Tell me, how can I return the favour?"

He smiled. "How can you reward me now? Treat me with steamed sweet potatoes? Don't mention it again. Reward me when you're ready in the future!"

There is not much to say about my time in college, attending classes, completing assignments, reading books and taking exams – it was quite similar to your college life. Of course, as the first college students after the resumption of the examination, our lives were quite different from the ones of today's college students. The first difference was our age. On average, we were older, and I still remember the oldest one in our class was about thirty years old. That's why few of us would play idly, and we spent most of our free time reading books. You know, we had wasted ten years during the Cultural Revolution, and every one of us felt there was too much to learn. The second difference was that many of us were married. In my class, one-third of the students were married. During winter or summer holidays and festivals, we always had spouses of our classmates come to visit. The third difference was about dating. Unlike today's college students, we dared not be open about being in love. In those years, relationships between men and women were a serious matter. Anyone who got too close with the opposite sex would become the victim of gossiping and criticising, so dating between classmates had to be kept extremely confidential.

In 1978, Wantong quit his job in the county government and was admitted to Qinghe University's history department as a graduate student, becoming the oldest student in our university.

We were good friends, and at that time we became college mates, so we naturally got together quite often. One night after dinner, he called me out of school and whispered to me in a very solemn tone: "Have you done it?"

"Done what?" I didn't understand what he meant.

"Found a girlfriend."

I shook my head. "Do you think I could do that? Plain looking, born in the countryside and not a penny to my name! Is there any girl who will have a crush on me?"

"Do you know what a man is most afraid of?" He looked at me seriously. "Lack of confidence! You should dare to pursue girls boldly!"

"Who could I chase after?" I asked him with self-ridicule in my laughter.

"I have found one for you! You've got to be quick."

"Who?" My smile faded since it seemed he was not joking.

"Wu Zi in your class. She's twenty-one years old. No boyfriend yet."

I froze for a second. I was quite familiar with her, a quiet and ordinary-looking girl in class who often sat in front of me.

"How do you feel about her?" Wantong asked me with a smile.

"Not bad. Though not pretty at first sight, she looks good after careful appreciation."

Wantong said: "I noticed almost every other week and always on Thursday night after supper, a jeep with a military plate will stop in front of the school gate, bringing her food and other things."

"So what?"

"It means she has some background. Her family is not ordinary. I guess her father is probably an army officer."

"If so, it's even less likely she would have a crush on me."

"Oh, you're such a good-for-nothing!"

I was a little offended by his words and didn't say anything for a while.

"Take my advice and hurry up!" With those words, he turned and left.

I raised my head slowly, looking up at the distant and limitless night sky, not a single star to be seen because of the light. I was already in my twenties. How was it possible that I wasn't interested in women, and how was it possible that I didn't dream about having a girlfriend? But look at me – except for some miserable food tickets the university issued to us, I didn't even have the money to buy a bowl of stewed noodles for a girl! Did I dare to chase after an officer's daughter? Forget about it. When I graduated from university, found a decent job, had a regular wage and an urban registration, it would be possible for me to find a girl from an ordinary family and get married. You know, it's important to recognise who you really are.

The next day, I totally forgot about this. But to my surprise, Wantong pulled me aside after class and whispered: "I have already put a note for you in Wu Zi's backpack, inviting her to watch the movie *The Great River Flows On* at the cinema in Huanghe Road."

Greatly startled, I asked: "What? How could you..."

"I'm really worried that you might lose this opportunity. If you don't do it quickly, someone else will. I've heard there's another man who is interested. Come on – go to the movie."

"Why are you pushing me like this?" I was a bit annoyed at that time. Though we were best friends, how could I let him decide on my marriage?

He said in a low voice: "Changshan, you should be clear that we both have a new social status. I'm an official, and you're a quasi-official – that is to say, we will both go into the battlefield of officialdom in the future, which is not the same thing as tilling the land. The entire history of China has told us that officialdom is the place where social connections are essential, and you'll need people who can back you up. But my father-in-law was killed in the Cultural Revolution. What should we do in the future? Fight alone? Since you have an opportunity right now, why don't you seize it?"

Good heavens! I stared at him in amazement. He could even think that far!

"Come on, do me a favour! Besides, Wu Zi is a good girl. She's worth pursuing. Look, I've already bought the two cinema tickets for you."

I felt quite warm when I received the tickets. Yes, he was somewhat arbitrary in doing it like this, but was there any one of my classmates and friends who cared more about me than him? Meanwhile, I admitted in my heart that what Wantong said was right. If we should enter officialdom, social connections are truly needed!

"All right, I'll try! Anyway, it's not such a big deal to lose face."

After supper that night, I walked towards the cinema with a beating heart. I had been prepared to wait in front of the cinema for a long time and then go back to school alone. But to my surprise, the moment I got there, Wu Zi came over to me with a smile on her face and said: "Hey, Wei Changshan, thanks for inviting me to the movie."

I remember my face flushed at once, murmuring a few words even I didn't understand, while Wu Zi appeared very generous and graceful, saying: "Let's go into the cinema."

After we took our seats in the cinema, there was still a period of time before the movie began, but I didn't know what I should say to her, worrying that I might annoy her. Fortunately, Wu Zi was very chatty and went from one topic to the next. She asked what I thought about some of our teachers, the assignments and the history of the Song dynasty, which we were discussing in class. When she raised the Song dynasty, I relaxed at once because I had read so many books about it, and what our teacher taught in class was far less than one-third of what I knew. I spoke fluently, one sentence after another, and most of it consisted of my own ideas. Wu Zi perhaps felt it novel and was fascinated by what I told her.

When the movie started, she whispered into my ear: "It seems you're not a nerd." This flattered me, so I turned to her and smiled. She unexpectedly continued: "Wei Changshan, don't you know you look great when you smile."

Encouraged by her compliment, I became emboldened and said: "Compared with you, I'm miles behind. You're the most beautiful girl in our class."

"What a sweet-talking charmer you are! I've never before heard such flattering words!" She lowered her voice and laughed softly in my ear.

"I'm not flattering you – they are my true feelings! In my eyes, you're the most beautiful girl in our class, like a fairy!" I whispered into her ear, as she had done.

She slapped my hand and said: "Enough! Don't be so sickening! I'm getting goosebumps on my body. Of course, I'm very happy to hear these words. Is there any woman who doesn't like to hear that?"

The way she talked filled me with anxiety. I grabbed her hand and said seriously: "I'm not soft-soaping you. I mean it."

"All right, take it easy. I believe what you said is true..."

To my surprise, she didn't withdraw her hand, which made me joyous. My courage grew. I started whispering things to amuse her, and I continued until the movie ended, the lights came on and the audience stood up to leave.

I reluctantly let go of her hand. Under the light, I saw her face brimming with happiness and shyness. We dared not to go back to school together. When we parted at the entrance of the theatre, watching her small and delicate back, I was filled with joy, excitement and gratitude to Wantong.

When I got back to school that night, I went to the shared bathroom with my wash basin and toothbrush set, ready to wash. Wantong came in and stood there looking at me without saying anything. I smiled and nodded at him, and just as I was about to speak, he turned around and left with a knowing look.

After going to see that movie with Wu Zi, I had the confidence to pursue her. I no longer felt inferior or scared. I realised that some women didn't care about how poor your family was – they were mainly interested in your abilities and character. From then on, we spent time together whenever possible. We would go to the library to read books, take a walk outside the campus discussing papers I wanted to write about the Song dynasty, or go to a public park where I taught her how to swing.

I just had one principle to follow when I dated with her – we never went to places where I needed to spend money. I never dared to take her to shopping malls or restaurants. I usually limited our dating time to three hours to make sure we could get back to school in time for the cafeteria opening times.

We maintained the relationship like this for about one semester, and I felt I could win her heart. She began to ask me to give comments on her assignments, revise her papers, help choose reference books, and borrow and return books for her. She wanted me to accompany her to the hospital when she was sick. She often brought me snacks to eat. She even bought me a short-sleeve shirt in summer. She confided in me when her roommates annoyed her in the dorm...

By the end of the first semester of the third academic year, we had become very intimate, and there were no secrets between us.

One day after supper, Wantong called me to the playground. I thought he might want to know how the relationship between Wu Zi and me was going, but as I was about to tell him, he suddenly stuffed ten ten-yuan bills into my hand. A hundred yuan! You know, in those years, that was indeed a fortune! To be honest, I hadn't had so much money since I was born. I was very surprised and asked: "Why are you giving me this money?"

"You haven't taken Wu Zi to visit Songcheng yet, have you?" he asked me with a smile.

I shook my head. "No."

"You both like the history of the Song dynasty, so it's inexcusable not to go and visit the capital of the Northern Song dynasty, isn't it? We don't have class this Saturday afternoon, so take Wu Zi to Songcheng and come back on Sunday afternoon."

I was moved by his words. Was there any other friend who could be more considerate? Although his family was richer than my family, he was always hard up because his father-in-law had died, and he had his mother-in-law and his child to feed. How could I have the heart to accept such a large sum of money! I hurriedly put the money back into his hand and said: "We're okay, we can wait to visit after I graduate and work. Besides, Wu Zi never said she wanted to visit Songcheng. Why should we do that now?"

"Listen to me. It's better to set out on Saturday afternoon, so you can stay there for one night."

"A hotel costs more. If we go, we could leave on Sunday morning and come back on Sunday afternoon. One meal and two round-trip tickets," I suggested.

He laughed and pointed at me. "You're indeed obsessed with money. Have you ever thought of cementing your relationship with Wu Zi before graduation? You guys are graduating very soon! Go and stay there one night. I've checked the price – an average guest house in Kaifeng costs a little more than 10 yuan for one night. After this night, make her yours! It's indeed worthwhile to spend such a small amount of money."

I went blank at first. Then I asked: "What's the connection between staying one night in the hotel and making her my girl?" Then, all of a sudden, I knew what he meant. I flushed and mumbled: "Do you think Wu Zi is that kind of girl? She wouldn't do that."

Wantong smiled and turned around, laughing as he walked away. "Just go and you'll find out."

In my heart, I had been thinking about taking Wu Zi to spend a few days in a place outside of the provincial city. Now, with Wantong's encouragement and financial support, I was quite happy. I went to have a discussion with Wu Zi about a trip to Songcheng that coming Saturday. She agreed without any hesitation, saying: "Great! You have finally decided to take me out to have some fun."

That trip to Songcheng turned out to be exactly as Wantong had said. When we checked into the hotel, I had to order two single rooms because if a man and a woman wanted to stay in one room with two beds, they had to show their marriage licence. But after a long kiss with Wu Zi before we went to sleep in our separate rooms, we were both sexually aroused. Wu Zi didn't urge me to go to the other room, so I stayed with her and didn't worry about the consequences. Luckily, no one came to check on us that night. The next day, we didn't get up to go and visit Dragon Pavilion, Iron Tower, Pan Lake and Yang Lake – we just went out and bought some bread and boiled eggs to fill our bellies and slept till four in the afternoon. Then we got up, light-headed, went to the bus station, bought the tickets and returned to school. Never had I expected that night would make such a big difference! One week after we returned from Songcheng, Wu Zi came to me and officially told me she would marry no other man but me.

My heart sang with joy. I hurried to Wantong's place and told him the big news. He first gave a long sigh of relief and then uttered one word: "Congratulations!"

When the Spring Festival holiday came that year, Wu Zi wanted me to meet her parents and stay in her house. I was hesitating about whether to go or not. To be honest, I was afraid I couldn't afford some decent gifts for her family, which might make her parents look down upon me. I went to seek advice from Wantong, who said immediately: "Of course you should go. A son-in-law should go to see his parents-in-law. I'll prepare the gifts for you. Though we couldn't afford expensive ones, a small gift from afar will convey deep feelings."

That evening, Wantong brought a bag to my dorm. He took out a man's sweater first, saying it was for my father-in-law, then a woman's sweater for my mother-in-law, then two headscarves for Wu Zi's two sisters. I was moved to tears at that time. Even my own brother couldn't be so thoughtful and so considerate! I remember I held his hand impulsively and said: "I can't thank you enough for your kindness! I can only return your favour in the future."

I had thought Wu Zi's home was in a unit stationed near the provincial capital. I only discovered her family was in Beijing when she handed me a train ticket on the departure day. I was very surprised and asked her why she didn't tell me she came from Beijing. She smiled: "I'm sorry. My father instructed us kids not say anything about our family in case it should have some influence on our relationships."

Nervously, I took the train with Wu Zi. In my heart, Beijing was a holy place. I had never been there before. You know, I had already been worried about going to meet Wu Zi's family, but I was even more worried when I found out that she lived in Beijing. But Wu Zi eased the tension by talking with me about people and things in Beijing.

Based on my life experience in rural areas and my understanding of city life in recent years, I had imagined what Wu Zi's family would look like – only thinking the best, of course. But when I arrived, the reality was beyond my expectations.

Our train arrived at the Beijing station at six o'clock in the morning, and the moment we got off the train, a PLA officer came to us and called out: "Hello, Wu Zi."

She immediately replied: "Hey, good morning, Uncle Yu."

"This is Changshan, right? Welcome to you on behalf of Wu Zi's parents."

I later discovered from Wu Zi's introduction that Uncle Yu was her father's staff officer. As I speculated on the military title of this staff officer, I observed the Beijing railway station curiously. Following Uncle Yu, we left the station and got into a black car. From the car window, I enjoyed the scenery of the early morning in Beijing greedily. It was the first time I had sat in a car, and the first time I had been on the road in Beijing. The scenery outside the car window made me dazed, while my inner anxiety betrayed my fear. The sedan finally stopped in front of a small courtyard in a military compound. Guards with guns stood motionlessly outside. Wu Zi rushed into the yard after she got out of the car, and I, led by Uncle Yu, passed through the guards and went into a living room – the largest I had ever seen. The furnishings shocked me. Besides a sofa, there were two huge cannons and an ancient military motorcycle!

Uncle Yu signalled me to sit on the sofa, and then a laughing voice of a man came from the neighbouring room: "Good, my sweetheart has grown up and found a boyfriend all by herself! Let's go and meet our future son-in-law!"

Hardly had the voice faded away when Wu Zi and a thin old man wearing casual clothes appeared hand in hand at the doorway connecting the living room to the inner room. They were followed by a kindly looking elderly woman.

I knew they must be Wu Zi's parents, so I hurriedly stood up and bowed to them.

"Your name is Wei Changshan?" said Wu Zi's father. He looked very thin and spoke in an extraordinarily loud voice.

"Yes, uncle," I greeted him as Wu Zi had instructed me in advance.

"Good! This young lad looks smart and will be an excellent soldier if given enough training! My daughter is indeed an excellent judge of people."

"Father!" Wu Zi said petulantly. "He's a college student, not your soldier."

"Go and wash your hands, son," Wu Zi's mother nodded to me. "Let's have breakfast first! You two have been on the train for a whole night so you must be starving!"

I didn't expect that Wu Zi's family would have a dining room. It was so big, with a dining table and ten or so chairs, but that morning only Wu Zi's parents, Wu Zi and I sat at the table having breakfast. On the table were various dishes including porridge, soybean milk, steamed buns and deep-fried dough sticks. In the cabinet against the wall were wines and cutlery, all of a style that made me overcautious. Wu Zi handed me a steamed bun, and just as I was about to put it in my mouth, Wu Zi's father suddenly announced solemnly: "Wei Changshan, I have no objection to my daughter's choice. But I need to warn you that if you don't treat my daughter well or lose your temper with her, you should beware of my gun!" When he finished speaking, he slapped the table hard.

Greatly shocked, I trembled and dropped the bun on the table. My face must have turned pale at that time.

"Do you have to speak like this? Scare the child on purpose?" Wu Zi's mother hurriedly stood up, picked up the bun and handed it to me, saying: "Don't take offence at your uncle! He's as stubborn as a mule with a fiery temper!"

Wu Zi, at my side, was embarrassed and squinted at me as an apology.

"Eat! Help yourself to more!" Wu Zi's father was now smiling. "I just wanted to speak frankly first. You know, Wu Zi is my youngest daughter, my treasure!"

I nodded my head to indicate I fully understood him and finished the bun quickly in order to end this extremely suffocating breakfast. This annoyed Wu Zi's father again – he was very displeased with my eating only one steamed bun! He said: "Only one bun? Are you really a man? What can you accomplish in the future? Let me tell you – when I was your age, I could have twelve buns like this for one meal! Eat!" As he said this, he placed two buns onto my plate, without giving me a chance to reply.

I glanced at the old man, whose hospitality was indeed quite different from others. I had no choice but to lower my head and stuff the two buns into my mouth. I have to admit I was really full after eating those two buns.

I was given a room on the second floor, and Wu Zi was next door. There were so many rooms in her family home – the second floor alone had five rooms! Wu Zi told me that she and her two elder sisters had a room each, the nanny had one, and the remaining one was the guest room that I was staying in. Her parents' bedroom, the large living room, the small living room, her father's study and the dining room were all on the first floor. On the third floor were some storerooms, and in the basement was a table tennis table where they went for some exercise. In the bungalow on the left side of the building lived the guard platoon leader and twenty soldiers. In the bungalow on the right side lived two drivers, one cook and Uncle Yu the staff officer. Her father's secretary, Uncle Cao, had two offices in this bungalow too.

I was amazed at the status of her family. I had thought they would be living in a terraced tile-roofed house – never did I expect it to be like this. It seemed her father's rank was higher than Wantong and I had imagined. If I had known the real situation of her family, I wouldn't have dared to date Wu Zi, no matter how much Wantong encouraged me to do so. There were huge differences between my family and hers – a world of difference!

After breakfast, Wu Zi's father went to work, and the yard quietened down. Wu Zi came to my room, asking me whether I wanted to go out and have a look around. I didn't answer her question but instead asked her unhappily why she hadn't told me about her father's official position.

"What's wrong? Are you mad at my father's words?" Wu Zi smiled.

"My parents don't allow us to reveal the situation of our family. Haven't I told you that my father always speaks frankly like that, and you'll gradually get to know him after you've lived with him long enough? In fact, he's very nice to people, especially to his son-in-law. You know, he's very good to my two brothers-in-law!"

"If I had known the real situation of your family, I would rather be killed than date you."

"Well, I'm glad I didn't tell you earlier. If I had done, how could I find a man like you!" said Wu Zi as she patted me on the shoulder. "What my family has right now could all be taken away at any time. In the Cultural Revolution, we didn't even have a place to sleep. My father told me that an official position is just a piece of paper. With it, you're an official. Without it, you're a civilian. All you can see in my family is merely worldly possessions. Only the feelings between us are real because they can't be taken away by anyone."

A strange incident happened during my first night with Wu Zi's family. I was preparing to go to bed when I suddenly heard the noise of a motorcycle being started up downstairs. It was very late, and I was surprised, wondering who was going out at that time. I walked to the window and looked outside – nothing in the yard, no people, no motorcycle. I listened carefully and was shocked to find the sound of the motorcycle came from the living room downstairs. It reminded me of the military one I had seen earlier that day. Who was starting up a motorcycle in the living room at night? For what? Driving out? The continuous sound of the motorcycle made me restless, so I sneaked out of my room and walked down a few steps along the stairs to check the living room.

Under the faint light of a small lamp, I could see a soldier sitting on the motorcycle. Without moving his body, he pressed the throttle gently to keep the motor running. What was going on? It was so late, so wouldn't it prevent the whole family from going to sleep? As I stood there confused, Wu Zi came behind me silently, patted me on the shoulder and whispered: "I realise you might be confused about why he's starting the motorcycle at this time. He's helping my father to go to sleep. It's a kind of hypnotism. During the war, my father got used to sleeping in noisy places, especially on a jeep, listening to the roar of the engine and smelling the burned gasoline. After the war, he couldn't fall asleep when it was quiet, and he suffered from very serious insomnia. He tried all medicines, but none of them worked. Later, his soldiers came up with this idea. Every night after my father washes and has gone to bed, they start the motorcycle in the living room, making him feel like he's sitting on a moving jeep and smelling the burned gasoline he used to smell when he was on the march during the war. This way, my father will fall asleep within half an hour, and as long as you don't wake him up, he will sleep on."

"Oh?" I looked back at Wu Zi in amazement. At that moment, the soldier who was on the motorcycle gradually throttled down and the motorcycle got quieter. A few minutes later, the noise faded away. The soldier walked out of the living room quietly and closed the door behind him gently. The main building regained its serenity completely.

"My father is asleep. Go and get some sleep!" Wu Zi whispered and gave my hand a gentle pull, signalling me to go back to my room.

As I lay down on the bed, I was still fascinated by what I had just seen...

In the following few days, Wu Zi took me to visit scenic spots and historical sites in Beijing, which to an extent relieved my depression, and I started to relax. I thought no matter how high the official position of Wu Zi's father was and how influential he was, I was his daughter's boyfriend and he would have to accept me as a member of his family one day.

On New Year's Eve, Wu Zi's eldest sister and second sister came back with their husbands and children for the Spring Festival, and I therefore became the target of their inspection. They asked a lot of questions about my family and me as if I were a bad guy who had planned to abduct their little sister. This made me feel uncomfortable, and I had no appetite for anything at the New Year banquet. Luckily, Wu Zi's second brother-in-law saw my displeasure. He whispered to my ear: "Don't get upset! I understand your feelings because the same thing happened to me when I first came to their family. As long as you two get married, they would not dare to treat you like that."

On the morning of the second day of the New Year, Wu Zi's father sent the nanny to call us to the small living room. The moment we entered the room, Wu Zi's mother came too. They sat down on the sofa, and a sense of tension pervaded the room. Obviously, this was going to be a very formal conversation.

Wu Zi's mother spoke first. "Changshan, there's only one semester before you and Wu Zi graduate. Have you thought about what you're going to do after graduation?"

"I heard we're probably going to be assigned to Party and government departments at all levels," I said. I realised that this conversation was going to have a big effect on my long-term future. I thought of Wantong at that moment. If he were by my side, I would definitely ask for his opinion before giving my answer.

"You're not thinking about doing something else?" asked Wu Zi's father.

"I could take a teaching post and join the faculty at Qinghe University. But I don't know whether I could make it or not."

"What about joining the army?"

"Join the army?" Surprised, I turned around to look at Wu Zi, hoping to see her attitude from her expression. You know, I never thought about being a soldier, and neither did Wantong, I guessed.

Seeing that I was looking at her, Wu Zi smiled and said: "Dad is asking for your opinion. Say yes if you want and no if you don't. He won't push you to do that, and neither will I."

Wu Zi's mother explained: "Changshan, your uncle has been serving in the army for a lifetime and he would like one of his children to take over and be a kind of successor. It's a pity we don't have a son, while our three daughters and two sons-in-law all refuse to join the army. So he wants to know how you feel about it."

I didn't know whether I could be a good soldier or not, and I knew nothing about life in the army. I couldn't make up my mind at that moment. If I agreed, what if I should regret it in the future? If I declined, would it affect my relationship with Wu Zi? You know, at that time, it was very hard for me to stop loving her.

Wu Zi's father explained: "As long as you're willing to do it, you're sure to do it well. After training, any man will eventually become a good soldier. Of course, you're a college graduate, and you wouldn't be an ordinary soldier – you would be appointed as an officer based on administrative rankings. The overall educational level of our army is not high, and that's why I'm eager to recruit college students directly from local universities."

Become an officer? Hearing that, I felt relieved somehow. What's the difference between being an official in a local Party or government department and being an officer in the army? Both are working as an official to support the family! Since Wu Zi's father wanted me to be an officer in the army, which, according to Wantong's idea, meant someone was backing me up, I would do it. So thinking, I nodded and said: "Okay, I'll do it."

"Are you sure? You won't regret it?" Wu Zi's father responded immediately.

"No regrets!"

"Great! That's settled!" The old man slapped his thigh happily. "Finally, I have someone to take over my career! Well, when you graduate, make a statement that you will comply with Party decisions on job allocation, and someone else will take care of the rest for you."

When we had lunch on that day, Wu Zi's father asked me to fill my wine glass and clinked glasses with me three times in a great mood. Her mother also said: "When Changshan and Zi'er graduate, let's hold a wedding party for them."

Never had I imagined that things would go so smoothly after I agreed to join the army...

When I returned to school after the Spring Festival, I hurriedly told Wantong that I had agreed to Wu Zi's father's request that I join the army. I had thought he might be very upset about this, thinking I wouldn't be able to help him in the future, but he grabbed my hand and said: "Good! The two of us – one in the military and one in politics – can help each other! This is the perfect result."

Do you want to listen to all this stuff that has little to do with Ouyang Wantong? You like it? That's great. To tell you the truth, I'm so happy that you're here listening to me. In this place, loneliness is the most miserable thing. No one talks to you, nor are they willing to listen! But you know, in the past, so many people invited me to speak, and countless people came to talk to me willingly. It's indeed a sharp contrast, and I really can't bear it. Thank you for listening to me! Then I'll continue my talk, and you can go on listening. Whenever you get bored, you can find some other topic for me to talk about. Have pity on me!

Graduation season finally came. At that time, university students were guaranteed a job by the country, unlike today when you have to hunt for a job by yourself. In our time, if you had some social connections, you would be allocated to a good workplace, but even if you had no connection, you would still be given a job. I followed the instruction of Wu Zi's father and stated that I would comply with Party decisions on job allocation, then I went to ask Wantong whether he needed any help from Wu Zi's family for his job. He said: "Not now. You and Wu Zi haven't got married, and if you go and ask her father for help right now, he might feel it a little too much. What's more, I'm a graduate student, and I'm sure to be given a job. Help me after you've secured your position."

The final allocation came out. Wu Zi would report to the Ministry of Personnel in Beijing. I was allocated to the Cadre Department of the General Staff in Beijing. Wantong, as a graduate student, would report to the Organisation Department of the Tianquan Municipal Committee. At that time, graduate students were rare and seldom assigned to work in a place at the county level or below. When we got the dispatch card, Wantong smiled and said: "I can finally work in departments at the municipal level!"

It was time to say goodbye upon graduation. The night before I would go to Beijing to report, with the money left after I had bought the ticket, I invited Wantong to have dinner with me.

He said he would pay for it, but I didn't agree. I said: "It must be on me at least once or I'll feel very uncomfortable."

He said: "All right, let our future officer treat me this time."

I didn't drink wine – my family never had the money for that – but that night I bought a bottle of Baofeng liquor and drank with Wantong. I remember I held the wine glass and said: "Brother Wantong, I'll never forget what you've done for me! Soon I'll have the ability to assist you. Tell me, what can I do for you now?"

Wantong smiled: "What you need to do is be a good soldier and establish yourself in Beijing, then you'll have the ability to help me. Right now, I don't need you to do anything for me – do your own things well!"

I threw up after drinking wine that night, and Wantong took me back to the dorm. It was the first time I had ever been drunk.

I went to report to Beijing with Wu Zi. After she reported to the Ministry of Personnel, she was assigned to the office of the Personnel Department as a secretary, while I was assigned to the Military Training Department as a staff member. On the day when I put on my new military uniform, I was indeed very excited. You know, I'm a farmer's son and never had I dreamed that this day would come.

Wu Zi and I had our wedding ceremony on the first National Holiday after we started work. It was a simple ceremony held in the hall of the Minzu Restaurant, but a lot of people came to celebrate our wedding, and the names of some of them surprised me quite a lot – they were names that often appeared in the newspapers! Wu Zi's parents repeatedly invited my parents to attend the wedding, but I declined on the excuse of their poor health. You know, never in my life had I seen such a scene, let alone my parents who had never even been to a county. If they should come, they would definitely feel helpless, and I couldn't let them make a fool of themselves on this occasion.

With Wu Zi's careful instruction in advance and the kind consideration and guidance of the master of the wedding ceremony, I behaved well at the wedding, and no one in Wu Zi's family could find fault with me. After I went through the wedding test, the Wu family changed their attitude towards me. They completely accepted me as a member of the family, and we became very close.

During our honeymoon, I proposed to take Wu Zi back to my hometown in Henan. Wu Zi of course agreed very happily, and her parents were also very supportive. Her father said: "Zi'er should go to visit her parents-in-law as an expression of filial love."

Wu Zi and her mother went to the shopping mall and bought a lot of things for my parents and the other family members, such as clothes, food and some daily necessities. I wrote back home in advance, asking my younger sister to tidy the house and buy some delicious food and some other good stuff with the money I had posted to them beforehand.

On the train homeward, I explained to Wu Zi: "You know, my family is very poor. My parents are ordinary farmers, and the basic needs of living in my family, such as food, clothing, daily necessities and housing are totally different from your family – we're poles apart! I hope you're ready for this. You're not going to enjoy a comfortable life in Qinghe, but you'll gain an understanding of the truth of the lives of people on the bottom of the social ladder."

She smiled at my words, saying: "Stop exaggerating! I went to visit my two sisters when they had settled and worked in the countryside, and I know what it looks like. If you can grow up there, couldn't I be happy to stay there for a couple of days?"

Though I had given her a warning and got her prepared for the poverty of our village, I still noticed the shock in her eyes when she saw the poverty-stricken house with nothing inside but bare walls. We had three main rooms and a small kitchen. My parents lived in the east room, while Wu Zi and I took the west one. My younger sister, who usually slept in the west room, had to sleep in the living room in the middle, so my two younger brothers, who usually slept in the living room, had to carry their quilts and spend the night at their friends' house after supper. We had nothing else in the house except three beds – two king size and one single – passed down from our ancestors, a dining table made when my parents got married, a few small wooden chairs and two old wooden chests.

Wu Zi, however, didn't reveal any disgust on her face but instead had the manner of a woman following the man she had married, be he fowl or cur. She helped my mother do the dishes and sweep the yard and helped my sister wash clothes and trim vegetables, sharing the chores as a daughter-in-law should do, a genuine daughter-in-law in the countryside. No one in the village could tell she was a daughter of a high-ranking official. To this day, I'm very grateful to her!

Well, I'm getting totally off the point talking about Wu Zi and me. All right, let's go back to Wantong.

After Wantong reported to the Organisation Department of the Tianquan Municipal Party Committee upon graduation, he was kept there instead of being allocated to another department. You know, at that time, graduates were quite precious, and what's more, Wantong had worked as the secretary of the commune and county government, and he was quite familiar with the grass-roots issues, so the Organisation Department appointed him as a staff chief. Three years of training in graduate school gave Wantong an edge in writing official documents. Most of the work of the Organisation Department of the Municipal Party Committee consisted of drafting documents, so he quickly stood out among his peers. After two years of working as the staff chief, he was promoted to be a deputy minister, entering the world of cadres of department level.

Wantong had helped me enormously, but the chances for me to return the favour were quite rare. I can only remember three times when he turned to me for help. The first time came when he worked as the deputy minister of the Organisation Department for two years. The county governor of Xigong, a small county subordinate to Tianquan, was promoted, leaving his position available. He called me on the phone and said: "It's an opportunity for me. I'm qualified for this post, but there are a lot of candidates, and I'm afraid it will be hard for me to win by relying on my talents and social connections. I need your help." I instantly gave him my word that I would try my best.

On that very day, I went to Wu Zi's family and talked about Wantong with my father-in-law, who just asked me one question: "Does he truly have the ability and quality to govern?" I nodded. He immediately made a phone call to the secretary of the Qinghe Provincial Party to recommend Wantong officially. Soon, Wantong took up the new post. He was indeed an expert in his work! The second year after he became the county governor, the output of the food production of Xigong county jumped to first place in the province.

When he worked as the county governor, I went to visit him once with Wu Zi on my holiday. He showed us around the experimental fields of hybrid wheat and maize that he had proposed to develop, the chestnut forest he had proposed to plant, the red jujube processing and packaging factory he had established, the Hong Kong-funded flour mill he had supported, the bakery and confectionery factory and so on. I got a sense of the ambition he had to do his job well and to benefit the people in his county. At the dinner table, I confessed to Wu Zi that the first note she had received was actually written by Wantong. On discovering the truth, Wu Zi first punched me petulantly, then she stood up and bowed to Wantong very solemnly: "Brother Wantong, thank you! Without your help, I wouldn't have found such a good husband."

The second time he came to me for help was when he worked as the mayor of Tianquan city. At that time, his family was experiencing major problems – his wife had been arrested, and he had been removed from his position. I remember it was at night, and I had already gone to bed when the phone rang. The moment I heard his voice, I knew something terribly wrong had happened. It was a voice full of pain, frustration and despair. You know, he was always cheerful, smiling and laughing with me, and never did he talk to me like that. The first sentence he said on the phone still lingers in my ears: "Changshan, my family is finished!" After I heard about the situation, I knew it was very tricky, but I didn't hesitate, and I firmly believed he was innocent.

At that time, I was a civilian military cadre with the rank of major general, and I leveraged all my connections, but none of my friends could do anything. I had no choice but to turn to Wu Zi, asking her to go to her father for help. You know, it was difficult for my father-in-law to help Wantong at that time because he was ill in hospital.

Wu Zi went to the hospital and asked her father: "Dad, how do you feel about my husband Changshan?"

Her father said: "Changshan? He's good, and I'm very satisfied with him."

Wu Zi continued: "So, should we thank the person who introduced us?"

"Definitely!"

Wu Zi then told her father about Wantong and the case that had resulted in him being removed from his post. She begged her father for help. He hesitated for a long time but eventually struggled to pick up the phone beside his bed and spoke to a senior leader about Wantong. This contributed to Wantong's subsequent reinstatement.

After he was rehabilitated, I went to see him again on a business trip. When we talked about life in officialdom, he didn't have the vigour and militancy that he once had. Instead, he wore an imposing face and kept sighing. He said the longer he was an official, the more evils he could see in officialdom. It might not be the best choice to be an official, but once you walked in, it was difficult for you to walk out.

I was in officialdom for many years, and I did have some sympathy for his words.

The third time Wantong came to me was when he was about to be promoted from the deputy secretary of the Provincial Party Committee to the governor. The appraisal team heard some unfavourable opinions about him, which were mainly about his second wife who had been very close with some businessmen and might have taken bribes. He wanted me to explain his innocence to some relevant departments. My father-in-law had passed away, but at that time I was already a general. I had friends all over Beijing – both inside and outside the army – and I had the ability to do him a favour. I arranged a few banquets, invited some friends who worked in key positions, gave an account of Wantong's case, gave assurances about his innocence and requested them to inspect it again. It worked. The appraisal team investigated the whole thing again and finally proved his innocence, which removed their doubts and led them to nominate him as the candidate for governor. Wantong was elected soon after.

We met many times after he became the governor. Each time, we talked about ourselves and our families, but what we talked about most was the safety of our country. Perhaps it was because we both held high positions and defending our country had become our common responsibility. He would always ask me to talk first about the development of army construction, and then he would move to the issues concerning national security he had encountered in his work.

There were four things he talked about most. The first one was buying US treasury bonds. He said buying US debt was actually a case of we Chinese producing goods with our own resources, then exporting to the US for them to consume, and then the US giving us a bunch of papers with numbers on them, namely paper money. Then they depreciated the dollar to shrink the numbers on the papers. They nominally told you that you could buy things in the US with these papers, but in fact you were not allowed to buy high-tech items – you could only buy things they didn't care about, which actually meant hollowing us out by every means. That was a hidden long-term ploy that we must have a clear idea about.

The second one was cybersecurity. The root servers of the internet were basically located in the US, making them the controllers of the internet. Think about it – the internet had entered hundreds of millions of households in China, and some well-known websites in China were not owned and controlled by Chinese. Hidden security risks should never be underestimated.

Another one was the exporting of rare earths. Europe and the US sued China at the WTO, forcing us to export rare earths in the same volume as in previous years. This will result in most of China's rare earths being mined and exported within a decade, destroying our ecological environment and preventing us from manufacturing sophisticated weapons. In addition to this, they implemented an arms embargo, a technology blockade and a ban on the sale of strategy resources. Doesn't this place China in a dangerous military situation?

The last one was about GDP. In his opinion, the concept invented by American economists had some advantages, but it also engendered a false sense of security. It seemed that with the increase of GDP, our country would surely be strong and influential, but in fact these were two different things. In 1840, China's GDP accounted for one-third of the world's GDP, while the UK's was one twentieth, and the sum of the entire Europe was still less than China. So why was China divided up by the Europeans? In 1894, the GDP of China was nine times than that of Japan. So why was China defeated by Japan? We all should have a clear idea about this concept.

I felt that all his worries deserved attention. As for army construction, he had served as the first secretary of the Party Committee of the Tianquan Army Division and the Provincial Police Garrison, so he was qualified to speak about these issues.

I asked him about his opinion on army construction, and he said there were at least three things to lay emphasis on.

The first one was about using people. We must place those who think about the issues deeply and who have the talent to command in battles in the key positions, instead of using those who only know how to flatter you all day long and who sent you money, gifts or even women. Only in this way can we have the confidence to win once the war starts.

The second thing is to update weapons and equipment as soon as possible. Most of the military spending must be used to purchase and develop advanced weapons and equipment – not on luxurious banquets and costly buildings – to try to keep our capability the same as that of the US. Build a few more aircraft carriers and more advanced submarines. Get stealth fighters flying in the sky. Develop sophisticated drones. Increase the reach of the intercontinental ballistic missile. Never be afraid of accusations that you're a threat because they'll dare not to lay hands on you if they feel threatened.

The last point was to enhance military training. Focus on basic training, rather than putting on a show for the leaders or the TV cameras. Train hard to develop real abilities required in real battles.

These were very good points! I thought he was saying all the right things. Even though he was not a soldier, he got right to the point.

As a senior official, he was very perceptive.

It was also during this period of time that we began to have disagreements, and we eventually became enemies. To be honest, looking back now, the first time that I was unhappy with him was when he came to attend a meeting in Beijing. I invited him to my home, and he proposed to visit my basement. I was surprised – why was he so interested in going there?

I led him into my basement where he found hundreds of boxes of Maotai liquor piled up inside, fifteen or thirty years of cellaring. He asked me why I saved these wines.

"This is my hobby! I like drinking wines, and I like sending people wines too," I said.

I remember he shook his head and told me solemnly: "Changshan, it's not good! It's definitely not you who have bought these wines. Either someone else bought them for you or they have been bought at the public expense. It won't do you any good. Even if you drink to your heart's content, how much can you drink in a day? Keeping these wines could only paralyse you. You're a general now, not a farmer, and you should not always think about keeping good stuff at your home."

I was very upset with him, especially his reprimanding tone. After all, I was a general. Couldn't he stop talking to me the way he lectured his subordinates? Why was it such a big deal? Had keeping some Maotai in my basement become a matter of principle? Besides, how much did he know about the social life of officials in Beijing? He was only a governor at provincial level! Take the Spring Festival as an example. I had to go to visit dozens of leaders and friends during the Spring Festival, and wasn't it necessary for me to take some boxes of wine to each of them? He was simply a governor at provincial level, a frog in a well. How could he understand the officialdom in Beijing! You know, though I didn't refute him that day, I did put on a long face. I just wanted him to know I was no longer his younger brother in the village who had never seen the world. He couldn't just criticise as he wanted. I was a general of the Republic, a person who was equal to him. He needed to learn to respect me.

The second time I bore a grudge against him was about my taking a private jet. I was on a trip to investigate the garrison unit in Qinghe province. I took a private jet on that day. You know, I liked to go on a private jet because it was fast, time-saving and safe. You couldn't avoid dealing with ordinary passengers if you took a train or a civilian aeroplane. What if something should happen? Of course, that was my consideration at that time.

Before my plane took off from Beijing, I asked my secretary to contact Wantong's secretary, as I was thinking about visiting him that night – after all, my destination was Qinghe, his place. I didn't expect that he would come to greet me at the airport personally. When my plane landed at a military airport in Qinghe, I saw him come over to welcome me, and I knew he would probably pour scorn on my extravagance. Indeed, as soon as we met, he smiled and commented: "What a grand manner our dear general has! Such a beautiful private jet! So many guards, and so many people to greet you! Congratulations!" It was not funny at all. I was a bit annoyed by his tone, which was tinged with irony and sarcasm! What the hell did he want?

In the hotel, with nobody around, he continued and criticised me to my face: "Changshan, is it necessary for you to put on airs when going back to your hometown? It's not a long journey, and there are so many civil flights and trains available. Why did you bother so much to take a private jet? The common people will swear at your lavishness when they see that."

I retorted him at once: "That is for my work! No one would want to fly around in a private jet unless his work required it." I was really mad at him. I was a general, and I came to meet him out of kindness, while he talked to me the way he talked to his directors! What kind of courtesy was this?

My biggest displeasure at him was his interference with my family affairs and my divorce. Yes, Wu Zi is a good woman, but even a good woman will sometimes turn you off. She always had a suspicion that I had another woman when we were both in our fifties. She kept warning me not to be so close with this actress or reminded me to be cautious about that female news anchor, nagging and suspicious and making me sick! Of course, she didn't make a fuss about nothing. Well, now it's impossible to hide it from you. I had a very intimate relationship with an actress surnamed Zan. What could I do? She was so pretty, and she was such a coquettish young woman who was always ready to snuggle up in my arms. I had no choice. I'm not a perfect gentleman who could never be disturbed in the face of a pretty woman. What's more, who can say monogamy is really human nature? Is it such a virtue to settle with someone for whom you obviously have no feelings? Yes, my father-in-law passed away, and I had moved out of the original family home, but I still felt depressed and restrained, as if my father-in-law were still laying his eyes on me all the time. I felt like a fish out of water. I felt oppressed. I was in my fifties. I was longing for a free life, body and soul! I didn't want to live under the shadow of my father-in-law.

I had no idea how Ouyang Wantong knew I wanted to divorce Wu Zi. Perhaps Wu Zi called him, or perhaps my daughter asked him to mediate. You know, even an upright magistrate cannot easily resolve family disputes. In this situation, it's better to pretend that you don't know anything, even if you've already heard about it. Who the hell wanted to get involved in things like this? But he did. He was in Beijing for a meeting, and he came to my home to persuade me to give up the idea. I became very angry upon hearing it. Who was he to tell me what I should do? Did I bother him when he divorced Lin Qiangwei? Why couldn't I do this when he could divorce his wife and marry a young and pretty one?

He didn't get mad though. He said: "Yes, I shouldn't interfere with your life. It's after all very personal, and you are a general. You understand that I'm also divorced. I'm not qualified to persuade others not to divorce. But I have to. There are three reasons. First of all, I was your matchmaker, and since you want a divorce, the matchmaker should be present based on the custom in Tianquan. My role as a matchmaker requires me to help you guys make up with each other instead of getting a divorce. Secondly, I'm your country fellow and your friend. I should be here when a big event happens to your family. I have the feeling that you're the assertive one in the family and you should be responsible for Wu Zi. You can marry a young woman after you divorce her, but she's old and has lost her charm with the passing years, so it will be difficult for her to remarry. Thirdly, as a man who divorced once, I want to let you know that you shouldn't do it unless you have no other choice. The kids will suffer most. You know, it was my wife who filed for the divorce, and I knew she wanted to protect me by doing that..."

My divorce had been put aside because of him. I had been angry with him whenever I thought of this before I was detained and interrogated. But now it seems he was right. My son and daughter have been put into prison because of me. My daughter-in-law and son-in-law have been disciplined as well. I know they all have a grudge against me. At present, the only person who is willing to visit me and send me daily necessities is my old wife Wu Zi, while those young women who used to be close to me all put the blame on me when I was under investigation. They completely denied the money I had given to them! And now, only heaven knows where they have gone. I'm totally forsaken!

You want to know my opinion on power? Well, power is good indeed. It's a commission, a piece of paper to be honest, but when a person gets this piece of paper, he'll become a new person in the blink of an eye. He might be very ugly, someone an ordinary woman would never want to look at, but once he has that piece of paper and power, people immediately change their opinion of him. Women all feel he's special. Many young women, including very beautiful ones, want to get close to him. Power makes him handsome! Don't you think it's weird? Next, power brings majesty. A person who used to bend over and cower silently will immediately stand erect and become very confident. Even the way he walks will change once he's given that piece of paper. He'll look majestic, and those who used to look down upon him or ignore him now give him respect. They'll even become timid and awed in front of him! Don't you think it's strange? What's more, power makes you rich. I don't need to elaborate on this. Given power, a poor man will make his family rich quickly. Great power brings immense wealth. Look, power can bring you so many benefits, so how can people not fall in love with it? How could I not like it? Now, so many people criticise me and say I'm desperate for power regardless of anything. Yes, I admit it, but I'm not the only one. Is there any man who isn't?

My opinion on money? As for money, although it's always connected with power, it's independent – or to use a modern term, it's subjective. What does that mean? It means it doesn't need to rely on power. That is to say, once you have money, you don't need to worry about anything. Money can buy you anything! Think about it, is there anything in this world that money can't buy? Land? A house? Delicious food? Beautiful clothes? Fancy cars? Only if you have money, can you have all of these. Even a woman's body and a man's conscience – buying those is never a problem. The price for a conscience? It's expensive nowadays! Based on my personal experience, for men with low social status, the price for their conscience is sometimes a bit higher than those with higher social status. It sometimes takes you about 10 million yuan to buy the conscience of a man with high social status, while those with low social status generally will cost more than 20 million yuan. In short, as long as you have money, you can handle almost anything. So my suggestion for you is try your best to make more money. You don't think I'm planting some unhealthy ideas in your mind, do you? Since you've raised this question, I have to share the truth I've found with you. You know, it doesn't make any sense for me to tell lies here.

My opinion about fame? I don't care too much about it, nor have I done any research on it. Personally, I'm more concerned about practical things. Fame, in a sense, is empty. When a man has power and money, fame follows behind. People will gossip about who has huge power and who is incredibly rich. Isn't that fame? You don't need to pursue fame in particular because it'll come to you when you have power and money. Let's put these theoretical issues aside. I usually don't like to talk about them. Shall we go back to Ouyang Wantong? Let's go on with the story between him and me.

There are quite a lot of stories that have made me very dissatisfied with Ouyang Wantong. For example, his stepdaughter Chang Xiaoxiao came to visit her classmate in Beijing during a Spring Festival, and she stayed in my home. According to the custom at Spring Festival, I, as her uncle, should give her some lucky money. As usual, I gave her three gold bars wrapped in a red envelope – that is, three 500-gram gold bars. The child was quite surprised but very happy indeed. Probably she had never received lucky money like this. I was happy too. To my annoyance, Wantong asked his secretary to send the gold back a few days later after the child returned to Qinghe. I was furious. It was hard to believe that he would return the lucky money back. I questioned his secretary, who stammered: "The governor thinks the gift is too expensive, and he can't accept it. He said he appreciates your kindness." That was too much. I was infuriated. I believed it was a heartless act of breaking off with me. From then on, I seldom contacted him. Whenever he called, I would answer, but never did I take the initiative to call him.

There was also an issue with my plan to build a house in my hometown. I argued with him face to face once, and we both were red-faced with anger. You know, after he became the governor, I asked him to approve a piece of land, telling him that I wanted to build a house. He said: "If you're going to build a house, build one in our village. I'll ask the director of the village committee to give you a homestead. They are sure to help you with that. Though you work in Beijing, your hometown is in the village after all. It's very reasonable to have a home here. When you're getting old and miss your hometown, you can go back to live in the village for a period of time, which the villagers will understand."

I told him I was not going to build the house in the village. I wanted it built in Tianquan, and what I needed was not a piece of homestead – I wanted at least 20 acres. I would have a few decent buildings for each of my brothers and sisters. There should be a water system in the yard to set up the landscaping and build the pavilions, like some of the private gardens in Suzhou. I had been serving the country and the army for most of my life, and I wanted to enjoy my life now. What's more, I intended to leave my children a legacy and a memory so that my future generations would always remember they had a general in their family and they were the descendants of noble people.

But Ouyang Wantong flatly refused. "Heavens! 20 acres? That is quite a lot. You know, land is highly prized. How could I approve such a large area of land to you? Besides, what's the point of building so many houses? Aren't you afraid of being cursed by people who are jealous of you?

"Tell me yes or no?" I was quite annoyed.

He said: "Changshan, don't force me to make mistakes! I know you've helped me many times in the past and there's no reason for me to turn you down, but this is beyond my competence, and I don't have the right to grant you this. It would be an obvious violation. I hope you can understand. You just think about it – suppose all the military leaders at provincial level working outside Qinghe ask for this much land to build houses? How terrible it would be!"

I knew he just wanted to give me a lecture and it was useless to beg him anymore. I retorted loudly: "Be a good governor as you please!" With that, I turned around and got into the car. His secretary came over to persuade me to stay for dinner. I stared at him and signalled my driver to start the car...

I later found someone in Beijing to complete all the procedures of land requisition in Tianquan. When it was done, I hired one of the best architects in China to come to Tianquan and draw the building plan based on the location of the land and surrounding environment. After the blueprint was finished, I invited some feng shui masters to check the chosen site, and construction of the houses didn't begin until all the design and layout followed the rules of feng shui and would be sure to do good to my future generations. The construction team I hired was from Beijing too. To tell you the truth, I even invited a master in ancient architectural coloured drawings from the Summer Palace to do part of the eaves. You know, I'm someone who does things properly or not at all.

On the day when the main building was completed, I went back to Tianquan to inspect the construction. Ouyang Wantong happened to be working in Tianquan on the same day. When he heard I was back, he came to the construction site too. Seeing all the carved beams and painted pillars throughout the courtyard, he said with overwhelming alarm: "Changshan, you're not building a house to live in after you retire, are you? It's indeed a general's mansion – a palace! Aren't you afraid of what people will say? Don't you worry about being criticised behind your back?"

I replied coldly: "Whoever wants to gossip is none of my business. What's the big deal if people talk behind my back? Should I stop what I'm doing simply because of criticism? You should go to Xidi in Anhui and

Yangcheng in Shanxi. Look at those big mansions. In the past, those who did business or worked as officials outside their hometown would always build a big mansion when they went back. Why shouldn't we do this today? Go and visit the House of Huangcheng Chancellor in Yangcheng county, Shanxi province. Doesn't it look magnificent? Suppose there was no such fortification-like official residence compound – how many of us today would know the name Chen Yanjing, the grand secretary of Wenyuan Library and the minister of personnel?"

He was choked by what I said and was speechless for a long time. Then he asked: "Where did you get the money? How much will it cost to build so many magnificent houses?"

Again, I retorted: "You don't need to worry about it. I'm not grabbing from others anyway."

His face flushed with embarrassment. He said unhappily: "Well, then you're good! Take your time. Goodbye!" He didn't invite me to dinner, and I didn't see him out. The relationship between us faded away.

You want to know where I got the money to build the house? Everyone knows that because there have been reports in the newspapers! I don't need to find any excuses any more.

Part of the money was kickbacks. My position gave me control of funds allocation. Suppose your work unit wanted to have more funds. Yes, I could do that for you, but you would need to do something to show your gratitude. It would be ungrateful of you not to give me kickbacks! What was my percentage? Well, it was not fixed. Suppose I allocated 50 million yuan to you. It would be quite proper for you to give me three to five million as the kickback. To be honest, I never mentioned the percentage of the kickback. They all paid me voluntarily, and I never complained about the amount. I truly appreciated their kindness, no matter how much they gave to me.

Cash gifts from my subordinates was another source. I was the principal leader, and my subordinates always prepared a red envelope for me in the New Year holidays or festivals. They would also do this whenever they got promoted or transferred. When I was ill, they would come to visit me with an envelope. I've always believed the money they sent to me for the New Year holidays or festivals and the money they brought along when they came to see me in the hospital shouldn't be included in my bribes. It was just social relations!

How large was this proportion of the money? About two or three million yuan a year. Not too much, right? I would like to point out one thing in particular – I never took the initiative to ask for any money from my subordinates. They all did it willingly. Sometimes, when you insisted on saying no, people would feel hurt. In the early years, people usually sent actual goods like meat, fish, cigarettes, wines, snacks, turnips and even green onions. For example, during the Mid-Autumn Festival, all of the work units sent mooncakes, flowers and fruits. Then you would find your room was piled up with these things. It was impossible to eat them all, and there was no place to store them. Most of it went rotten. I don't think it's a good way to send gifts.

Later, they figured out a better way. They put money into an envelope and sent it to you, so that you could buy the mooncakes and fruits, making both sides feel at ease. The sender avoided the embarrassment of being recognised by others when driving to your house, while the receiver didn't need to worry about how to keep it.

At the very beginning, envelopes were quite popular – usually with 500 yuan inside, then a thousand – but later, cards replaced envelopes. A card containing 2,000 yuan was quite a decent gift. It could get you a piece of clothing in the shopping mall. Then, they deposited more money in the card, 5,000, 10,000 and 20,000. Later, sending cards was banned by the Commission for Discipline Inspection, so they went back to cash gifts again – 50,000 bundles, 100,000 bundles, and the figures increased upwards. It was almost impossible for you to stop accepting the money since you had done that in the past. If I refused to do that, I would offend more people. Eventually, cash gifts became so common that they began to send gold bars.

The last part came from the retention of the land and properties that the army didn't need anymore, a kind of kickback. You know, we would sell land and houses that the army no longer needed to some local bosses, who were generally very loyal to their friends. After the transactions, they felt they owed you and would secretly send you some money as a reward. I consider this part had something to do with emotions, and it was a bit unfair to be totally regarded as bribes.

The money they found underground when they confiscated my home? Did I have a choice? You had to find a place to keep the money you had. In the bank? I didn't have the nerve to do it. I wonder who came up with the idea of the real-name personal savings account system! It's goddamned wicked! This rule should be scrapped. Nowadays so many officials have to keep their money at home, which, you know, does no good to banks! Leave the money with relatives? It won't work. They would be sure to let it out within a few days. They wouldn't be able to keep their mouths shut – especially the women. Women can't keep secrets. It's said that a woman can only keep a secret for three months at the most, and I totally agree with that. You never know when they may disclose it. So you have no choice. You can relax when your money is at home. What's more, keeping your money at home will make you feel particularly comfortable when you look at it every few days.

Remember what I told you just now? When I was a child, all the money I could see were very small bills, cents or a few yuan. My father's savings never exceeded five yuan, and they were always wrapped in his shabby handkerchief. My father always carefully put his savings of a few yuan into the handkerchief and hid it in a wall crack because we didn't have a safe place to keep the money – there were no cabinets or boxes, and he couldn't afford a lock for the two desk drawers. When I was in elementary school and middle school, the most terrible day for me was when the tuition fees were due. Whenever I told my father the amount of money I needed to hand in, wearing a sad face, he would always unwrap the handkerchief and count those cents and a few yuan again and again. If there was not enough, he would gloomily go out to borrow from neighbours. After this happened a number of times, all the other villagers were afraid to see my father. In my memory, there was almost nothing in my family except for a few old wooden beds, two cooking pots and some rough porcelain bowls. All this motivated me greatly, and I've had a strong desire for money ever since I was a child. When I saw it, I wanted to possess it. When I put it in my pocket or in my home, I would feel quite at ease. That's why I like to put it beside me.

At the very beginning, I didn't have much money saved, so I put it in a wooden box under the bed. Later, when I had more, I bought a safe. Then one safe was not enough, so I bought another one. But you simply couldn't keep buying more safes when your money grew. Think about it – a row of safes with money inside along the wall would be eye-catching enough to arouse suspicion. Finally, I came up with the idea of burying it underground. But still there was one thing that troubled me a lot – how to properly bury money underground without damaging it. You know, it was quite humid underground, and if it was not done carefully, your paper money would decay and fall apart. To solve this problem, I read a few books that explained how the landlords in the past buried their valuables underground. I bought a few vinegar and soy sauce porcelain jars, put the money in, sealed the opening with wax and buried it underground. It was safe, but one jar couldn't take too much. If you buried too many jars, it would be too easy to find! What a great loss it would be if someone else dug it up.

Later, I heard of a new type of safe that had a burglar alarm and a fire alarm, and it was water- and damp-proof. I hurried to the mall to investigate and found that they did have such a safe. I was very happy and ordered a few. My house in Tianquan had already been completed at that time, so I asked my architect to design a secret chamber under the lawn in the courtyard, and I told him it was for storage of odds and ends. In fact, it was a place for the safes. After it was completed, I rented a big truck in Beijing, wrapped all the safes stuffed with money with plastic sheets and straw ropes, layer after layer, and loaded them all into the truck. They didn't look like safes at all! Then with my son and my daughter accompanying me, the truck went all the way back to the new house in Tianquan. At midnight one night, my son, my daughter and I moved all the safes into the secret chamber. You know, I didn't trust the others – even my daughter-in-law and son-in-law. This could only be done by your bloodlines! I covered the opening of the chamber with soil and the next day had the workers plant the grass on it. After that was done, I finally felt relieved. With this money, I thought my children and future generations would never suffer, no matter what would happen in society. They would never have to live a life that was always lacking money, like I had when I was a child. Alas, I didn't expect that things would end up like this. I didn't expect that they would confiscate my house and find that money. What a big waste of all my hard work! I'm so unlucky!

Why didn't I give the money to others? Of course, I did – if not, how could I get promoted and be put in an important position? You have to give money to your superiors! I don't remember in which year people began to give money for promotion. At the very beginning, tens of thousands of yuan could buy you one promotion. Later, when the river had risen and the boat was floating higher, you could only get a promotion if you gave hundreds of thousands. Though there was no tag price for some posts, everybody knew how much they would cost. If you wanted the progress, you had to follow the rules and pay the price. If you didn't play the game, you were simply wasting your money – that is to say, if you paid too little for the post, it was impossible to get promoted.

What's the largest amount of money I've ever given? Well, I actually have already confessed, but if you want to know, I can say it again – 20 million yuan! I deposited 20 million yuan in a card and sent it as a wedding gift to one of my superiors when his daughter got married. You're shocked, aren't you? Yes, that was indeed a huge amount. How much can you earn by writing a book? Oh, well that almost amounts to what you could earn by writing books all your life.

Of course, I wouldn't give all of my money away. At most, it was one-third of what I had. The ultimate goal of promotion and being an official was to get money anyway, so you have to leave yourself with the lion's share. I've given away a lot of money to a lot of people. I've already revealed their names to the relevant organisation. I heard some of them have been arrested. Good for them! I can't be the only one who is corrupt. I can't be the only bad guy, while they are all honest and upright gentlemen. How could it be? Is it possible that I alone could bring about the deterioration in the standards of social conduct? Suppose I were the only one who was corrupt – I would've been exposed long before. I have access to newspapers here. When I discovered that some people – quite a lot actually – were attacking corruption so indignantly with an awe-inspiring righteousness, I almost laughed my head off! How couldn't I know them? They were corrupt too, but they hadn't been exposed yet! I have a strategy now – whenever I report a person who is corrupt and who has ever received my bribes, I always ask them during the next interrogation whether they've arrested the guy I exposed the previous time. If they haven't made an arrest – sorry, I refuse to give any new names. That's my attempt to push them to quickly arrest those corrupted officials like me. It's good for their work. What I'm doing is an act of anti-corruption, an act that is responsible for our country. You know, I shouldn't be the only one who feels sad, hurt and heartbroken here while they are outside happily drinking wines and eating delicious food! That is unfair!

All corrupted officials should be treated equally, and all their true colours should be revealed. Since I came here, I've disclosed quite a lot of embezzlers for the country. They are all moths that have eaten our country. I've made a contribution, haven't I?

There are many anti-corruption fronts, and I can be counted as one.

Of course, I'm a criminal first.

I admit I kept most of the bribes for myself. How could I give all the money that I had collected so painstakingly to others? To this day, I still believe it's reasonable for an official to make a small fortune. Otherwise, who would want to be an official? Being a faithful public servant with clean hands? Do you believe in this? I don't. Who could be that foolish to work hard simply to be a public servant? The servant is the one who has to listen to his master. Is there any official who wants to listen to ordinary people? Can you find one for me?

There's another point. Since ancient times, there's a saying that being an official means making a big fortune. Don't you remember the story that working as an honest magistrate for three years would still bring about a hundred thousand pieces of silver? We have a precedent in history. Could you cut off history at once? Impossible! Honestly, it's not easy to be an official. It doesn't work if your superior is dissatisfied with you, so you have to maintain a good relationship with them. It doesn't work either if your subordinates always make trouble, so you have to fool them. You have to be very careful when dealing with your peers because if anything should go wrong, they'll secretly scheme against you! What's more, you have to think about all kinds of questions day and night, and try to find solutions for them. You have to attend various conferences and deliver speeches, carry out investigations abroad and have a dialogue with the grassroots. It's very hard work! I'm getting off the point. Let's not talk any more about those who have nothing to do with Ouyang Wantong, shall we? Let's get to the point and continue the story of Ouyang Wantong and me.

What finally made us completely turn on each other was a meal – a banquet to be exact. A director of a large state-owned enterprise had invited me to dinner. He heard Governor Wantong was studying in the Central Party School, so he proposed to invite him to the banquet as well, since he knew we were country fellows. Of course, I couldn't show my objection to his face, so I accepted his suggestion, saying it was a good idea to have more fun. They invited him that night. When I reflect on that banquet now, the man who arranged it had gone too far, as it was a bit lavish. Three main courses and some side dishes for each person would be good enough, about four or five thousand yuan per person. But that boss probably worried about looking stingy, so he added one more dessert for everyone, with a platinum necklace on the dessert plate, which was perhaps worth a few thousand yuan. We had some young and beautiful ladies at the banquet, so it was understandable why he did that – a gift, you know. When the main courses were served, I had already noticed Wantong's displeasure. He said the price of the main courses would be equal to a farmer's harvest from two acres of field, which made that boss, who enjoyed similar benefits as a leader of the ministerial-level of the State Council, feel a bit embarrassed. Those young ladies were also amused by his words and kept laughing. To be honest, I also blushed with embarrassment, thinking how he could be so old-fashioned like this! Begrudge a meal! He was not a bit like a governor!

I had thought about stopping him, but I was afraid he might say something even harsher, so I had to play deaf! When the last dessert with the neckless was served, he stood up and went to the bathroom. I had thought he would be back very soon, but to everyone's big surprise, he left without saying goodbye, leaving all of us there – me, that boss, some guest officials and those ladies. I fumed with anger! You were a governor, so how could you have been so impolite? No manners at all! We were all in the official circle, so what was the point of being aloof in front of us? If you didn't want that neckless, couldn't you have just left it there? Couldn't you have just told me and put it on the plate? Or given it to one of the ladies sitting beside you. Why did you play this game and put everyone on the spot?

From then on, we stopped seeing each other, and probably that's why I didn't enquire about his illness and how doctors had treated him.

You want to know whether I talked with him again on the phone? Yes, but I didn't call him – he called me. You know, it would be improper if I didn't take his call. We were country fellows after all. I remember once he called me after the Sino-Japanese Diaoyu Islands dispute broke out. He asked me what the future development of this event would be. When I told him the superior leaders would take care of this and officers at my level didn't need to worry about it, he began to reproach me again. "Changshan, you're a general now. How many generals do we have in our country? If cadres at your level don't worry about these events, who else will? Yes, you're not the one to make a decision on how to handle this, but you need to think about it, consider what to do and report any good ideas you might have. If it's improper for you to publicly report it, you ask a reporter to write an internal document, which could be useful for decision-makers."

I tried to listen patiently as he continued his nagging: "This dispute is ostensibly caused by the Japanese right-wing island purchasers, but in fact the United States is the provocateur behind it all. It seems to be a territorial dispute between Japan and China while in essence it's the US-led economic war. The most serious problem in the United States is the huge debt. At present, it's impossible for the US to reduce debt, so the only way to develop the economy is to increase capital, and the way to increase capital and ensure the recovery of the American economy is to make sure that the US dollar becomes the global settlement currency and reserve currency. As long as the US dollar maintains this status, the US quantitative easing policy will have negative consequences for the other currencies around the world. But nowadays, the euro, the renminbi and the yen are challenging the status of the US dollar, so the United States must launch a war against them to eliminate the threat. In order to defeat the euro, the United States has identified fragile Greece as a weakness, the entire EU faltering as the result of the burning of chained barges, leaving the currency shaken. As a result, European capital quickly flowed to the United States and repaired the balance sheet of the US. In order to crack down on the renminbi and the yen, the United States has provoked the dispute over the Diaoyu Islands. The original currency exchange agreement between China and Japan has been shelved. The foreign exchange of the two countries who have the most reserves flowed to the United States under the influence of the potential war, which enables the United States to recover from the crisis rapidly. The economic and social structure of the United States is based on its debt expansion. When the United States can't pay the debts, they have to print banknotes to cover them. Once its status as the global settlement currency and reserve currency is shaken, the US economy and society will collapse."

He always treated me as a subordinate and gave me lectures as if teaching a young brother who had never seen the world. He was getting above himself, and this annoyed me. He forgot how many years I had lived in Beijing, and he forgot my present social status!

Another time he called me and talked about the danger of war. I was simply listening to him perfunctorily. He said: "Changshan, my work is restricted to the local area, and I can do nothing about war. Even if I worry about it, no one will listen to me. But you're different. As a general who leads your soldiers to fight, you should make one thing clear – war is actually very close to us. It might happen within a couple of years! You must take this into consideration."

He continued: "Recently someone sent me a speech given by Clinton. It was a secret speech delivered at Congress under the request of its members after the bombing of the Chinese embassy in Yugoslavia. I read it, and regardless of whether the content is true or not, something in the speech deserves our attention. Clinton said in that speech, 'The goal of the new strategy I'm about to describe is from now on, the United States will become the last and only empire of mankind. We have already made a detailed plan. The first step is NATO's eastward expansion. I believe you all have already seen that. In the Kosovo War, we were still awed by the Russians, but now they are almost naked beggars. But I want all of you to clearly understand that our eastward expansion is not just to make a spectacle of Yeltsin – our purpose is to control the entire Eurasian plate. In that region, and in Southeast Asia, we have a headache, which is China. In short, although it's still risky to do this, we basically don't have any enemies to stop us. A new 21st century under the leadership of the United States will soon arrive.' When Clinton replied to a question asked by a member of the Congress about how long the Kosovo War would last, he said, 'Looking at the history of America's development and prosperity, war conforms to the interests of the United States. This has been sufficiently proved by the rapid development of our economy after the second world war.' When Clinton answered the question put forward by another Congress member about whether the Kosovo War would drag America into the mire like the Vietnam War did, he said, 'The Gulf War has also proved our casualties during war are almost zero. It's like playing a video game, but the difference is they are gambling with their lives and the few possessions they have.' When a Congress member asked how the bombing of the Chinese embassy conforms to the interests of the United States, Clinton said, 'Besides Moscow, further away, there's another country – also a nuclear power – that we should be more concerned about. Yes, it's China. It should have split into seven countries ten years ago, but it still seems unbreakable. We've exerted many pressures on it, but its development is quite amazing, and it's unlikely to be broken up by internal means. There's one reason why we should let it follow the old route of the former Soviet Union, that is to say, obsessed with the arms race which will eventually drag it down. In the near future, China will be unable to say no to us because its economy will collapse and it will become an international beggar.' When Clinton answered the question about whether China would use a nuclear counter-attack, he said, 'Before we bombed the Chinese embassy, we carried out a very careful study and analysed various possibilities. Our conclusion was, firstly, an 'accidental' bombing will certainly offend the Chinese, but it won't provoke them to press the launch button of the nuclear bombs. Besides, they have made a stupid promise that they'll never be the first to use nuclear weapons. Secondly, what the Chinese want most from us is technology, so the United States is the last country it wants to offend. Thirdly, in view of this, protesting is the only thing they can do. Finally, we're prepared for the worst. Even if they should wage war against us, we have nothing to fear since the most advanced weapons all come from the United States.' When a Congress member asked whether the anti-American sentiment will influence the interests of the American business community, Clinton said, 'I think that the Chinese leaders will be more eager to restore the Sino-US relations than us. We have some strong cards in our hand, such as the issues surrounding Taiwan, Tibet and Xinjiang. Whenever we want to do something, it's easy to find a reason.'"

He repeated this topic on the phone, which irritated me quite a lot. Suppose there were such a speech – what's the big deal? Is there any need for you to worry about it?

He continued on the phone: "The United States now has less than 20 trillion in debt, and it could continue raising the debt limit and borrowing more money. But when this total debt reaches 20 trillion, the annual interest will be 600 billion dollars. Then, even if Congress allows the government to borrow 600 billion dollars a year, the money will only cover the interest! At this point, it will be impossible to borrow more money. What will the US do when its reliance on borrowed money ends? Deal with the debt peacefully? Refuse to pay off the debt? Of course, it could do that, but it would become isolated in the world, losing all face and prestige. The United States won't do this. There are two choices. The first one is to block trade. To China, the United States could offer Taiwan in return for debt forgiveness. To Japan, it could offer sole control of the Diaoyu Islands in return for debt forgiveness. If this happens, the whole world will see it, and the United States would still lose face and prestige. There is a particularly simple option for the Americans – provoke Japan to fight with China, and side with Japan. Once the war starts, the United States can erase all the debt it owes to China and at the same time tell

Japan that the debt should be erased in return for its help. We must pay special attention to this simple option!"

I was thinking to myself as I listened to him. You are a governor – can't you take it easy and concentrate on doing your own work in Qinghe province. What's the use of thinking about all these things, which in fact have nothing to do with your work? What good will it do you personally?

There was another time when he called me to recommend a professor at Qinghe University of Technology. He said when he was studying at that university, he found this professor's research project could be used for either civilian or military purposes, and that if it was used by the military, it was very likely that a brand-new weapon would be created. He said the United States wasn't afraid if you followed it and made weapons it had already had, like aircraft carriers, stealth aircraft and so on. You couldn't compete with the US as far as technology was concerned. The Americans knew all the weak points of those weapons and how to deal with them. What they worried most was if you took a new path and made new weapons they didn't have. Think about it. When they had drones, you made things that could destroy remote-control capability. When they built satellites and spaceships, you invented something that would cause them to lose connection with the ground. When they took a knife, you didn't have to have a knife of your own – you'd have to bring something that could accurately damage their eyes, making them nervous and frightened.

He said that because he was a governor and had no position in the military, he wanted me to report the information to the leaders of the headquarters as soon as possible. Honestly speaking, I wanted to tell him at that time there were institutions and generals in the military who were in charge of scientific research. Couldn't they be more professional than you? Did they need you to find talent in the local area? Of course, I didn't pay attention to his recommendation. Was I a well-fed person with nothing to do? It was probably a coincidence that the professor was later recruited by a research institute of the General Staff headquarters, and he indeed created a new weapon in a short period of time. Its power is beyond our imagination. It's confidential, so I don't have any detailed knowledge about it, but what I can tell you is this kind of weapon can be called the 'ultimate weapon' that will make any enemy who dares to play with us taste the bitterness of the terrible consequences and make them tremble with great fear.

To be honest, on this matter, I once again admired him from the bottom of my heart.

That's all I can tell you. In short, as I look back, I was a fool to break off with Ouyang Wantong. I threw away a true friend. If he had been around, a friend who would give forthright admonition, I wouldn't have been so far down the road of corruption and crime. I really regret it.

After having listened to what I've said, you can probably tell that Ouyang Wantong was not a mediocre governor, not a man who only knew how to recite a speech draft. He kept telling me there were too many wise men in China and the task for a leader was to find those people and establish a system for them to come to the forefront. I guess he might have some kind of anxiety in his heart. He always worried there was a force in the world that intended to put our nation in an unfavourable situation, and he always felt that time was pressing, so he was constantly looking for solutions and competent people. What's more, he was always in a hurry to do everything, which was totally the opposite of me. Before I was held here, I would say I lived an easy life and enjoyed myself every day!

Of course, his anxieties were not without foundation.

He was a person who always had worries, so I feel he lived his life with a heavy load.

Now he is gone. He is free.

12

HUA XIAOYU

THE NANNY

WHY DID you come to me? You've heard some rumours, haven't you? I know some people have been gossiping about Uncle Wantong and me. They ask why should I, such a beautiful young lady, be willing to work as a nanny for Ouyang Wantong for such a long time, especially during that period when his ex-wife was arrested, and he remained unmarried and lived alone? How could I be so steadfast in following him? There must be some shady affairs between us! I want to find the bastard who spread those rumours. I would go up to her and rip out her tongue!

I went to work in Uncle Wantong's family when I was 18 years old after dropping out of high school. In that year, a family in our village was building a house, and they invited my father to do some carpentry work. When they were constructing the beams, my father fell and broke a leg and an arm. As a result of this accident, he was crippled for life. You know, he used to be the breadwinner in my family, but after that he couldn't work to earn money. What's more, my mother had to find ways to borrow money for his treatment. I have two younger sisters and one younger brother. The whole family became so poor that we didn't even have enough food to eat. I had no choice but to drop out of school and help my mother at home. I couldn't make much money farming in the rural area. It was too difficult to feed such a big family.

As my mother and I ran around borrowing money and the whole family were in helplessness, a great-aunt named Ouyang Zhaoxiu came to see my mother. My mother told me this great-aunt was a very nice person who lived in the same village as my grandparents. When Great-aunt Zhaoxiu saw my family's poor situation, she said she wanted to introduce me to work as a nanny for a family in Tianquan. She didn't say which family, but my mother agreed. I therefore went to Tianquan with her, and at that time I didn't know I would be working for the deputy mayor of Tianquan, nor did I know his name was Ouyang Wantong. I just felt this family was quite generous because they were going to pay me three hundred yuan a month! You know, three hundred yuan was indeed a big fortune! The other nannies who had been working in this field for a long time in Tianquan only got 100 yuan a month. I later learned Ouyang Wantong and my mother, Zhao Lingling, had had a relationship when they were young. Great-aunt Zhaoxiu wanted to help us, so she introduced me to work for her nephew. I understood it was out of the care for my mother and my family that Uncle Wantong gave me the highest wage at that time. After Great-aunt Zhaoxiu helped me settle down in Tianquan, she told me not to let my mother know I was working in Uncle Wantong's family. I didn't quite understand why at that time, but later I realised she was afraid of hurting my mother's pride.

To be honest, I was criticised quite often when I first arrived at Uncle Wantong's family. Of course, it wasn't Uncle Wantong who blamed me. He didn't have much time at home, and when he saw me, he just nodded to greet me. It was Uncle Wantong's ex-wife Aunt Lin Qiangwei who liked to criticise me. Aunt Lin was an official too. I remember she was a section chief, an official like a town mayor. She really had the look of an official. Every day, Uncle Wantong's car would drive her to and from work. The driver would usually take Uncle Wantong to work first and then come back to take her to the office. She was in charge of everything in the family. She had a bad temper, and as well as criticising me quite often, she also criticised Uncle Wantong and Brother Qianzi. When they became her target, they had to listen to her patiently. I was criticised mainly because I did housework badly. Sometimes I didn't sweep the floor properly, sometimes I didn't clean the bathtub thoroughly, and sometimes the clothes I had washed were not clean enough. Besides, I was not good at cooking. The dishes were either too salty or lacking in flavour. Sometimes, even the rice would get burned! Well, I should say my mother had to be responsible for this! She never let me do these things at home, so I didn't have the chance to learn how to cook, which caused me embarrassment when I worked in Aunt Lin's family. As for the criticisms, I always admitted my mistakes honestly. Did I have any other choice? Yes, sometimes I got angry too, feeling she was too critical and she was making a mountain out of a molehill. I often thought about quitting the job and going back home, but I was unwilling to give up the 300 yuan payment because my family really needed the money. So I had to grit my teeth, swallow the anger and try hard to learn how to do household chores well.

Although Aunt Lin had a hot temper, she was not stingy and had a good heart as well. I remember when she gave me the payment for the first month, she handed me 350 yuan. I said that was too much. Great-aunt Zhaoxiu had told me my payment was 300 yuan. Aunt Lin said: "Take it. This 50 yuan is for you to buy clothes! You're willing to admit your mistakes, and I like that."

Within about half a year, I had sort of mastered the basic skills of a qualified nanny under the patient guidance of Aunt Lin and my humbleness to learn. I would say Aunt Lin taught me a lot of things. For example, when cooking pork rib soup, add a teaspoon of vinegar to the soup to help the phosphorus and calcium in the bones dissolve into the soup and preserve the vitamins at the same time. Or put in some fresh orange peelings to make it taste delicious and reduce the greasy feeling. When cooking beef, put a small packet of tea wrapped in cotton muslin into the stew to make the meat tender and delicious within a short period of time. When scrambling eggs, add some sugar into the liquid egg to keep the moisture inside and reduce the heating time. This will make the scrambled eggs fluffy and soft. With a few more drops of vinegar, the eggs will be even more delicious and soft. The more skilful I became, the less Aunt Lin would criticise me and the more she trusted me. Later, she gave me the money to buy food and daily necessities. She would also ask me to come along and advise her when she was shopping for clothes. After a year, she began to treat me as a member of her family and talked with Uncle Wantong about both public and personal issues in front of me, paying no attention to whether I could hear it or not.

At that time, the issue that she and Uncle Wantong discussed most was her position. She thought she had a junior position and that that was unreasonable, so she asked Uncle Wantong to work out a way to get her promoted. Uncle Wantong seemed reluctant and unconcerned about this matter, and this resulted in a few battles between him and Aunt Lin. One day when they were having supper together, Aunt Lin asked him whether he had talked with the secretary of the Municipal Party Committee about her promotion. Uncle Wantong said he found it difficult to say anything. Aunt Lin flew into a great rage. She slammed the chopsticks on the table and said: "My father went to a great deal of trouble on your promotion in the past. When he received public criticism, he was still going around to find connections for your position! Without him, you wouldn't be who you are today! Now you dare to treat me like this. Do you still have a conscience? Is there anybody in officialdom who doesn't know the rule about using your own people? Only in this way could you be free from impediments and trouble made by others in your work. It's also easier to divide benefits when they come. Besides, a lot of things nowadays are determined according to your position, such as houses, cars and salaries. I don't have a certain position, and I can't enjoy any benefits. As for you, you don't care about your wife at all. What on earth are you thinking about? You're thinking about divorcing me, aren't you? Thinking about finding a young woman?"

Brother Qianzi had gone to study in the provincial capital at that time, and no one else could step forward to calm them down. I wanted to do that, but I didn't dare. I was afraid of annoying them.

Aunt Lin's curse that night made Uncle Wantong's face contorted with rage. At first, he could still eat his noodles one string after another, but later he was so angry that he couldn't continue at all. He just held the chopsticks and sat there motionless. When Aunt Lin began to swear at Uncle Wantong, I quickly left the table and went into the kitchen for fear that Uncle Wantong would feel embarrassed in front of me. When at last Uncle Wantong stood up and left the table, Aunt Lin gave him an ultimatum: "If you don't get me promoted as an official at the deputy county level within three months, you're going to jeopardise your position as the vice mayor! Believe it or not, I mean it."

As it turned out, Aunt Lin was appointed the deputy director of the Municipal Bureau of Land and Resources within less than two months!

On the day when Aunt Lin's appointment document was issued, she was on top of the world! She at first proposed to book the best room in Bixi Building to have a celebration, but Uncle Wantong was firmly opposed to her idea, saying if she should show off like this, he would never participate! Aunt Lin listened to him this time. She asked me to prepare four cold dishes, six hot dishes and a soup at home. The whole family celebrated her promotion at home, and I remember Brother Qianzi was called back too. Sitting at the table, they talked and drank wine while I was busy in the kitchen. Aunt Lin drank quite a lot that night. Holding her wine glass, she said to Brother Qianzi with an expansive gesture and a wide smile: "Qianzi, you should work hard and graduate smoothly, then ask your father to get you an official position while he still has the power. Then we'll all be officials. A real official family!"

The second day after Aunt Lin got promoted, she raised my wage. She said: "Xiaoyu, from this month, I'll give you a hundred more every month. We should stick together through thick and thin."

For a period of time after Aunt Lin became the deputy director, life at home was quite peaceful. Sometimes I could even hear her singing. Uncle Wantong was in a good mood too when he came home. He didn't knit his brows anymore, and he began to talk a lot. From time to time, loud laughter would come out from their bedroom when they were inside.

Benefits also followed after Aunt Lin became the deputy director. She got a car to pick her up and take her back every day, and she didn't need to use Uncle Wantong's car anymore. I basked in her light too. Whenever her driver was available, a phone call could bring him to drive me to the local market to buy some meat and vegetables, which made me feel it was right for Aunt Lin to quarrel with Uncle Wantong at that time. She indeed had good reason to be a deputy director.

Another benefit she had after becoming the deputy director was more gifts and goods – much more than she got in the past. You know, when the officials' organisation offered the staff members some food and other daily necessities, only Uncle Wantong had a share in the past, but Aunt Lin was included after her promotion. When people from the counties came to give gifts, they brought two instead of one. Aunt Lin would place the costly gifts in a safe place while leaving the others in my care. In fact, they didn't need so many things, and they couldn't eat so much food. Every time when I went back home, Aunt Lin would ask me to take a lot of her gifts to my family. No matter what others think about her, I would say Aunt Lin is a very generous person.

Before long, Uncle Wantong became the mayor of Tianquan, the head of the municipal government. That was such a happy event. Just think about it – a city with a population of 10 million, and Uncle Wantong would take care of all his people's basic needs, including healthcare, everything! Wasn't it a great blessing? Aunt Lin again wanted to celebrate his promotion, suggesting inviting friends to a banquet in Bixi Hotel, with everyone getting good and drunk. Uncle Wantong resolutely refused, saying: "There are two sides to this – you just see the sweet side while ignoring increased pressure on me! Now I'm one of the heads of Tianquan, and I must guarantee a comfortable life for everyone in the city. Isn't it a heavy burden on me? When something goes wrong, I'm the one who will be blamed…"

Not very long after Uncle Wantong became the mayor, Aunt Lin was again nagging him about helping her with another promotion. She said she had enquired about this and there was someone who got promoted to become a division-head level official after only one year as a deputy director. Some people were pretty good at doing this. The key was to find a way in, such as letting her temporarily act as the head in that post, and then find a chance to get her promoted.

Uncle Wantong listened to her very impatiently and said: "It would be ridiculous for me to give my wife a promotion first after I became the mayor? Aren't you afraid that people will curse us behind our backs?"

Aunt Lin retorted: "Whoever wants to do that, go ahead! They won't say it to our faces anyway, so it makes no difference whether they swear at us or not! What's more, power has an expiration date. If you don't use it when you have it, you never will. If you don't help me now, you won't be able to do anything when you're no longer the mayor! Besides, if I were promoted to be a director of a certain bureau, you wouldn't need to worry about that bureau anymore. I'll definitely support your work wholeheartedly, and this will boost your performance in office. If you give the chance to someone else, you're just letting your own fertile water flow into someone else's field! What good will it do for you?"

Aunt Lin kept pestering Uncle Wantong with this. Later, he tried every means to avoid her whenever she mentioned it. He said he had work to do in the office or he needed to go to another room to make a phone call. At that time, I had the feeling that they would quarrel with each other over this again sooner or later.

A few days later, Aunt Lin came back home at noon in very high spirits. When she saw Uncle Wantong, she asked eagerly: "Do you know our Director Yin is being transferred to the provincial department? If his position becomes available, I want to be the acting director. You know, it's an important position, and you could feel at ease if you give this position to me!"

I remember Uncle Wantong thought for a while and replied: "Why should both of us work in the political field? It's not necessarily good for the family, is it?"

Aunt Lin lost her temper: "None of your high-sounding words! Who in China doesn't know that the success of one's life is evaluated by one's official rank! You're the mayor now, a successful man, but why don't you want me to be successful as well? Why do you want me to live under your shadow? Let me tell you – I don't want to be addressed by others as 'Mayor Wantong's wife'. I want them to say, 'That is Lin Qiangwei, the director of the Bureau of Land and Resources in Tianquan.' Is there anything wrong with me for wanting this? Don't you guys claim to liberate women? Why doesn't it work when it comes to my case? Why do you always try to find an excuse to avoid doing something that is in fact a piece of cake for you? Am I still your wife? The mother of your son Qianzi? And your closest person in this world? Why do you want to give the power to someone else instead of me? Are you afraid of being accused of favouritism? Look around yourself – is there any leader who doesn't use his own people?"

Aunt Lin nagged Uncle Wantong relentlessly that day. In the end, Uncle Wantong shook his head, sighed and said: "Alas, it's true that everyone wants to be an official, but seldom do I see such a person like you who is so crazy about it!"

Worrying that Uncle Wantong wouldn't make a sincere offer of help, Aunt Lin prepared a special gift and went to visit the secretary of the Municipal Party Committee herself.

Her efforts were not in vain. A few months later, Aunt Lin truly became the acting director of the Bureau of Land and Resources. She called me from the office on that day and asked me to cook more dishes for supper. At dinner time, Aunt Lin asked me to open a bottle of red wine. She happily raised her glass and said to Uncle Wantong: "Wantong, thanks. Here's a toast to you. This is not a celebration about my becoming the director of a bureau – it's a toast to express my thankfulness. Thank you for being brave enough to use your own people!"

Uncle Wantong shook his head before he drank the wine. After he had emptied his glass, he said solemnly: "Qiangwei, I must make it clear to you. This time, it's the secretary's proposal to appoint you as the acting director, so you must prove that you deserve the trust of the organisation. Behave yourself, especially when dealing with money issues! Look out for yourself!"

That night, Aunt Lin asked me to fill the bathtub and give her a good bath. After that, she applied a lot a perfume, carefully put on the newly bought semi-transparent nightwear I had taken out for her and walked into the bedroom with a big smile. That was her happiest night I had ever seen during those days.

Aunt Lin became the director of the Bureau of Land and Resources over half a year later. From that point onwards, more people came to report their work at home, and more and more people came to send gifts. They used to visit the house during New Year festivals and holidays, but now people came with gifts almost every day – all sorts of gifts, ranging from something to eat like sea cucumbers, gelatin or cordyceps, something to wear like suits, leather shoes and dresses, to something to drink like brand-name tea, chrysanthemum tea and coffee, to something to have fun with like golf clubs, ivory mah-jong and swords with carved gold, to some ornaments like necklaces, bracelets and jade pendants, and even bedding stuffs like sheets, quilt covers and pillowcases. Aunt Lin didn't like most of the gifts, or she didn't even want to look at them. She asked me to send some to her relatives, some to her neighbours and some to my family. Honestly, Aunt Lin was indeed very generous in this respect. I should say I totally supported her promotion at that time.

After Aunt Lin became the director, I could feel she and Uncle Wantong got on better with each other, but unfortunately it didn't last long. I don't know from which night it started, but they again argued with each other in an angry whisper. One night, I was abruptly awoken by a loud bang coming from their bedroom. I got up and went to the living room, straining my ears to listen to what was going on. Uncle Wantong and Aunt Lin were growling inside. About what? I don't know. I just vaguely heard some words like "land", "money" and "America". I wasn't sure whether I should go into their bedroom to calm them down. Luckily, they stopped a few minutes later, and I went back to my room.

Everything seemed to be all right until Aunt Lin was suddenly taken away on that day. I could tell she hadn't expected it at all. You know, the day before that horrible event, she asked me to go to the mall after lunch to buy a chain for her watch. Honestly, her old one was quite new, but she didn't like it because she thought it was too fancy. No one had expected that the Procuratorate and the Public Security Bureau would make a surprise visit at noon the next day after Aunt Lin came home after work. I remember clearly she gave me her handbag as I hurriedly gave her the towel to wipe her hands and face. Then I served her a cup of hot Maojian tea. As she drank it, she asked me whether I had any fried luffa for lunch. I said no but offered to cook some at once if she wanted. She nodded and was about to say something, but then the doorbell rang. We both guessed it would be more people bringing gifts. Completely unprepared, I went to answer the door as I heard Aunt Lin muttering: "So annoying! They won't even allow me to rest for a minute!"

After I opened the door, I was taken aback when a man and a woman rushed into the room! You know, most of the people who came to the mayor's house were either asking for an official position, a piece of land or some help with their problems, so they usually wore a look of trepidation or put on fake smiles with much bowing and scraping. Never did I see anyone be so daring! Instinctively, I thought they must be robbers, so even when they showed me their identification and said they were from the Procuratorate, I still didn't believe it. I wanted to cry out for help, but I was afraid that they would beat Aunt Lin and me. It wasn't until Uncle Wantong came back and agreed to let them take Aunt Lin away that I came to understand they were not robbers and Aunt Lin was in such great trouble that even Uncle Wantong couldn't save her. A calamity was coming to this family!

It was the first time I had witnessed someone being taken away by force, and this was a someone with whom I was so familiar and so close to, and who used to be so powerful! That indeed made me feel what fear was!

That lunchtime, Uncle Wantong didn't eat the food on the table at all, and neither did I. How could such a calamity befall this family?

In the afternoon, the driver came to pick up Uncle Wantong as usual. He got dressed and left the house on an empty stomach. I saw him walk with faltering steps, so I hastily grabbed a packet of biscuits, ran downstairs and put it into the driver's hand, signalling him to give it to Uncle Wantong. Apparently, the driver had already heard the news. He nodded to me and took the biscuits silently.

After Uncle Wantong had left for work, I immediately called Brother Qianzi who was in the United States. I wanted him to come back, but I couldn't get through. Later, I learned the Procuratorate informed Brother

Qianzi that his mother was ill, and when he arrived at the Beijing Capital Airport, they arrested him as well. I was so scared by the news that I held my hand to my chest and was unable to breathe! Good heavens! How could this family suffer from such great misfortunes?

The next evening, when Uncle Wantong came home after work, he seemed a lot older, and the driver helped him inside. It was as if he had contracted a serious disease. When I showed the driver out, he whispered to me: "Mayor Wantong has been removed from his office and is not allowed to leave Tianquan. He's in a great depression, and you need to look after him carefully. Call me whenever you need my help!"

I stood paralysed at the doorway for a long time. How could a prosperous family suddenly become like this? How changeable life was!

That night, I cooked four dishes and made his favourite sesame leaves noodles, but he just sat there motionless, not eating. I cried and said: "Uncle Wantong, it will do harm to your body if you don't eat anything..."

That night, he just drank some hot water and then lay down on the bed.

I didn't know what to do. I called his secretary for help, but he didn't answer the phone at all. In the past, he came to visit several times a day, but now he was nowhere to be seen. Not knowing what to do, I suddenly thought of Great-aunt Ouyang Zhaoxiu, and I felt I should go back to my hometown and invite her here. She was sure to know how to handle this. The next morning, I got up very early, cooked breakfast, kept it warm in the pot and left a note for Uncle Wantong on the table in the living room that read: "Uncle, breakfast is in the pot." Then I ran to the bus station. When I arrived at my great-aunt's home, it was already lunchtime. I felt like crying the moment I entered her house, but to my surprise, she was ill in bed, and someone was helping her to drink a bowl of herb decoction. Seeing her pallid look, how dare I cry in front of her? I just said I had come back to visit my family and everything was all right with Uncle Wantong.

After leaving my great-aunt's family, I went back to my family home – the two villages were not far away from each other. I couldn't help but cry when I saw my mother. At that time, my mother knew I worked as a nanny in Uncle Wantong's family. When she saw me crying bitterly, she anxiously asked me what had happened. After I had told her everything, she said to me in a low voice: "Xiaoyu, your uncle's family is now in trouble. The other people can stand back, but you can't. You're in debt to his family. Go back now and take care of your uncle and his family too. We shouldn't be snobbish. Snobbish people aren't respected by others."

As she said this, she gave me two hot buns fresh from the steamer, broke off part of a green onion and handed to me, saying: "Go back at once. Eat as you walk. Don't miss the bus for Tianquan. Work out ways to make him eat something first. Remember to tell him everything that has a beginning has an ending. There are no setbacks that we cannot overcome. Ask him to hold on!"

It was getting dark when I returned to Uncle Wantong's house that day. I saw him sitting at the table eating noodles the moment I entered the room. I was a little relieved. When Uncle Wantong saw me, he said: "Xiaoyu, I don't need to work for a period of time, and I can take care of myself. You can go back home during this period if you want. I've put your wages on the nightstand in your bedroom."

I wiped my tears and said: "I just came back from my hometown. My mother wants me to look after you here."

Uncle Wantong of course knew who my mother was. He remained silent for quite a while and then said: "Thank you and your mother."

From that day on, I took care of him. He seldom went out during the day, but rather sat in his bedroom reading, pondering or writing at the desk. He usually took a walk after supper. Worrying he might do something silly, I always tried to follow him secretly, but quite often I failed to keep up with him. Once, I caught up with him and saw him making a phone call in a public phone booth on an obscure street. I was very curious about it. We had a phone at home, so was there any need for him to do that?

After a long time, his position was finally restored.

As soon as he resumed his position, our home bustled with visitors again. Looking at them, I was quite surprised. Where were they when my Uncle Wantong had been removed from his office? Honestly, I look down upon them, though I'm a country girl. They are too snobbish, especially that secretary, who later came to visit with a big smile on his face. I said to Uncle Wantong privately: "This secretary is really ungrateful. He's useless! You've got to get rid of him!"

Uncle Wantong didn't say anything at that time, but before long he had him removed.

Later, I heard Uncle Wantong and Aunt Lin got divorced. Uncle

Wantong didn't tell me this in person – it was his driver who told me. He said Aunt Lin filed for the divorce and Uncle Wantong agreed.

Brother Qianzi went home once after he had been acquitted. For that occasion, Uncle Wantong took a day off and waited for him at home, but Brother Qianzi seemed full of hatred for his father, and he didn't even look at him when he entered the room. Uncle Wantong spoke to Brother Qianzi in a very cautious tone but Brother Qianzi ignored him, just packing his clothes and the other stuff. I made a table of dishes as Uncle Wantong had instructed, but Brother Qianzi didn't sit at the table, let alone eat anything. He finished packing his stuff and dragged his luggage towards the door. I hurried forward to pull him back to eat something, but he threw off my hand at once. Someone told me Brother Qianzi ate in a small restaurant on the street and then went back to his work unit on that day. I never saw him come back again after that.

I was responsible for sending things to Aunt Lin regularly after she had been sentenced and jailed. Every few days, I would also accompany Uncle Wantong to visit her. I always felt like crying when I saw Aunt Lin come out slowly in a prison jumpsuit with a pallid look to meet us and when I saw them staring at each other in silence.

Things changed greatly! How noble and arrogant Aunt Lin used to be, dressed in good clothes, with an elegant manner and surrounded by a crowd of people whenever she was out!

After this sudden change, I lost my admiration for Uncle Wantong's job because I began to understand his work was dangerous too. In fact, it was similar to my father's work as a carpenter. What's more, this kind of danger is much scarier. Uncle Wantong once asked me whether I would like to go with him and continue to work as his nanny when he was about to be transferred to the provincial capital. He said that he would raise my wage if I came. I shook my head. I had got married but this wasn't the reason why I didn't want to go, and neither was the wage a consideration. My unwillingness to go with him resulted from my fear. I was afraid of being involved in another accident. I was afraid of being scared again. I wanted to live a peaceful life. I was happy to live a poor life as long as I could have peace and security. That's all I can tell you. What else do you want to know? What happened after Uncle Wantong got divorced?

Yes, quite a lot of people from the Municipal Party Committee and the municipal government came to the house as matchmakers after the news of their divorce spread, but Uncle Wantong declined them all. He said: "I appreciate your kindness, but at present I have no consideration for this." He refused to meet the women introduced by those people. He lived quite a regular life during that period of time, going to work alone, eating his meal when he returned home, and then working on documents or reading books and newspapers in his bedroom, or talking about work with people in the living room. He told me no matter who rang the doorbell, those who were seen through the door mirror carrying any type of gift should never be allowed in!

Women did come to visit him at that time. Whenever there were phone calls from women for Uncle Wantong, he would ask me to say he was not at home. Some women knew I was telling lies and they came straight to knock on the door instead. Whenever this happened, he would ask me to stay in the corner of the living room serving tea during the visit until the woman left. I remember once, a woman from the General Office of the Municipal Government came with some documents one night. She was less than thirty and prettier than Aunt Lin when she was that age. She didn't leave after she put down the documents. Instead, she began to chat with Uncle Wantong, keeping the conversation going. Uncle Wantong mentioned several times that he had a speech draft to revise that night, suggesting that she should leave, but she just didn't get it and continued to sit there rattling on. She even took off her coat as she talked, revealing her exquisite underwear inside and two large breasts! You know, I was not a child anymore so how could I not understand what was going on? I stood up quietly and went into my room. I thought that since Uncle Wantong felt miserable at that time and he had divorced Aunt Lin, he might feel better if he did something with that woman. To my surprise, he called me again to serve the tea for her. After I filled her cup, she got up and left reluctantly.

I thought Uncle Wantong probably felt repulsed by women at that time.

As for the rumour that Chang Xiaowen was Uncle Wantong's mistress, I think it was nonsense. If they had been in that relationship, I wouldn't have been kept in the dark. What's more, it seemed a group of people in Tianquan had been watching Uncle Wantong, trying to find fault with him. Uncle Wantong must have known it, and he would never give them an excuse. It was after Uncle Wantong went to work in the provincial capital that he began a relationship with Chang Xiaowen.

I'm sure about this.

13

SHEN RUYU

THE FORMER MEMBER OF THE YELLOW RIVER COMMITTEE OF THE REPUBLIC OF CHINA

I HAD some dealings with Mr Ouyang Wantong. I heard the news of his departure from the TV. He left so early. He went to heaven too soon. He should've gone after me at least. But it's better to die early than go on like this, like me, an old man who is over a hundred years old, with ears that can't hear clearly, eyes that can't see clearly, teeth that can't bite and legs that can't walk! It's torture to live in this world and be a burden for everyone around me.

At the very beginning, Mr Ouyang Wantong came to me to discuss a water control programme. He wanted to know what I thought about it. I said to him: "As the governor, you're a man of great vision who is concerned about water control. What is water? The blood of the earth! The most important asset of a nation and a country! If something should happen to a nation's water, it will never become prosperous." I told him there were two problems with our water assets – a water shortage and the deterioration of water quality.

As for shortages, I told him to get two things done. First, save the existing water resources. Make everyone in the whole province know that water is not inexhaustible and we must use it as carefully as oil and food. Never should we be lavish with water resources – otherwise, more and more gutters, lakes, ponds, wells and even rivers will run dry. Then groundwater levels will decline, and it will become increasingly difficult for people to get water. Second, learn to save rainwater and snow water, the generous gifts from heaven for human beings. People should learn to preserve and cherish them. As they do in Israel, each family here should prepare equipment at their home to keep rain and snow. Villages, communities, cities and regions should have facilities to store rain and snow. Never should we allow them to flow into the sewers and filthy ditches in vain.

As for the deterioration of water quality, his feelings were similar to mine. I reminded him that the priority for water control programme was pollution prevention – that is, to control the water deterioration and to stop the pollution of water immediately. He admitted there was no longer a clean river in Qinghe, which itself was a bigger problem than the pollution control and water development of the Yellow river and the Huai river.

I said to him: "Water is the thing that enters our stomachs every day. How terrible it would be if it got polluted! Won't it affect people's life span? Won't it do harm to the reproduction of human beings? Won't it influence the future of China?" He agreed with me.

You know, once he set his mind on something, he would immediately command people to work on it. He worked truly hard on water pollution control, and he spared no expense on the problem. The main rivers in the province began to run clean again!

The two of us developed a friendship because of this. Later, he would come to visit me when he was free. I remember we once talked about longevity. He knew I was more than a hundred years old, so he asked what my secret was. My answer was three words – don't get angry. There are so many things in this world that will annoy you. If you easily get mad, you'll often feel unhappy, and this can make your internal organs lose their rhythm. And those who lose that balance will definitely get sick, which in turn damages your internal organs and makes longevity a mission impossible! You know, a hundred diseases result from anger so we should learn to relax. How? Keep calm when problems arise. Nothing must be done hastily. Make a concession first when dealing with people, and step aside first in the face of profits.

He said my words did make sense but he admitted that it was difficult for him to put them into practice because working in officialdom without getting angry was not easy. He therefore said that he probably wouldn't live a long life. I remember I laughed and stopped him from talking like that because it was quite ominous, but I didn't expect his words would come true! He didn't live to the age of eighty! That is indeed a great pity!

Another issue we discussed together was human development. He asked: "Based on what you've read, ideas you've developed and research you've done, how many years do you think we human beings have been living on the earth?"

Traditionally speaking, in China, about 1.7 million years ago, Yuanmo Man began living in Yuanmo county, Yunnan province. Lantian Man in Lantian county, Shanxi province was 800,000 years ago. Peking Man in Zhoukoudian, Beijing was between 20,000 and 70,000 years ago. The Upper Cave Man formed the clan society about 18,000 years ago. A maternal clan phase like Hemudu and Banpo culture began between 5,000 and 7,000 years ago. The middle and late paternal clan phase like Dawenkou culture was between 4,000 and 5,000 years ago. And the legendary period of the Yellow Emperor began about 4,000 years ago. In short, human beings have a history of about 200 million years. According to international anthropologists, human society began in eastern Africa where people derived from the big family of animals and broke away about 800 million years ago.

He said that both of these ideas seemed reasonable, but they failed to explain some newly unearthed fossils and relics, such as a fossil found in Antelope Spring, Utah, USA by the American amateur fossil expert William J Mist in the summer of 1968. On that fossil, a complete shoe print was left on a trilobite. The shoe print was about 26 centimetres long and 8.9 centimetres wide. The dent of 1.5 centimetres left by its heel, indicated that some shoes were quite similar to the casual shoes that modern people wear today. But the trilobite lived between 200 million and 600 million years ago! How can we explain this finding? Another example. In a 2.8 billion-year-old stratum on Clarke Slopes in South Africa, hundreds of metal balls with grooves were found. How can we explain this? Here's another one. The French discovered an ancient nuclear reactor in a place called Oklo in Gabon, Central Africa in 1972. It was estimated that the Oklo uranium deposit might have been formed about two billion years ago, but the nuclear reactor seemed to have been established shortly after the formation of the deposit! How do we account for this?

He wanted to know how I looked at these phenomena, and I told him my views were somewhat similar to the Mayans. Never do human beings appear on earth only once. Whenever a human civilisation has developed to a certain stage, it has been destroyed because of its own problems or the external environment. After that, a small number of people would be left, and they would begin a new life from the primitive society once more, and gradually a new civilisation would reappear. He smiled and said he kind of agreed with this idea. For example, science and technology could advance to such a high level that a new life species that is invented to benefit mankind unexpectedly mutates and destroys human beings instead. Or another asteroid leaves its orbit or drops from the universe and then hits Earth, ruining civilisation.

In short, it's quite possible that human life will be destroyed. This kind of speculation made us more aware of the miserable situation of mankind, and perhaps this is why we had so much respect for the way our species stood up again and again after falling down, rebuilding our world after being destroyed repeatedly and unyieldingly dreaming about establishing our existence and position on Earth and in the universe.

What we most frequently talked about was facing up to the weaknesses and problems of our people. He once said: "You've lived longer than any of us in this world, for several generations, and you're sure to know better than I. In your opinion, what are the main weaknesses of the Chinese people?"

My answer was that Chinese people have four very obvious weaknesses.

First, they are fond of infighting. Chinese people are used to regarding conspiracy as wisdom and the killing of their rivals as a heroic act. In officialdom, this creates internal strife, elimination of political opponents, the formation of cliques and the downfall of the weakest. The spirit of mutual respect, forgiveness, tolerance and cooperation haven't been deeply rooted in the hearts of Chinese people.

Second, they have a strong mentality of servility. You know, the suppression of those rebels in dynastic succession was particularly cruel. Beheading became common practice, so Chinese people are fearful of power. They've developed the mentality of obedience no matter who is in power, and they are willing to flatter the man in power with the most sickening words.

Third, they like doing things by connections. All sorts of connections. In China, no matter who you are or what you want to do – being an official, doing business, school enrolment, title evaluation or job transfer

– your social connections determine everything! Without those relationships, whether they are between blood relatives, teachers and students, country fellows, classmates, colleagues or even neighbours, it's ten times more difficult for you to achieve your goal!

The last thing that Chinese people are obsessed with is nostalgia – worshipping the people of the past as saints, regarding objects of the past as national treasures and calling the past times good old days. But they are very critical of the wise today, they disapprove of modern inventions and they always complain about today's life.

He listened and said with a smile: "It makes sense. The second point you just mentioned has an alarming significance for me. As a man in power, I should be very cautious when I use my power. Never should I take for granted that people must be obedient. I should listen to what they say, know what they think about, give them the right to speak and cultivate their community spirit. Laws must be established to ensure that people can speak to officials with a straightened back and have the right to alter and replace those officials, all of which will help to gradually reduce the servility of Chinese people. At the same time, I should always stay sober and try not to be carried away by flattery, compliments and words that are pleasant for the ears. These represent the speakers' intentions to keep out of trouble, and they aren't at all truthful or sincere."

That's what we talked about with each other. I guess it has no practical value, nor does it have any direct connection with the governance of his province or anything to do with my present life, but we both enjoyed chatting like that. We had a lot of fun. He was quite different from the ordinary political officials, and I liked him.

You know, most officials are very practical, and they only meet people who are useful for them. But he did not seem to be very utilitarian when he came to visit me. I think he wanted to relax and chat with me, an old and useless man! We don't have many officials like him. He was indeed an unusual character!

14

BAO JIANSHAN

THE CHIEF OF THE DEPARTMENT OF NEUROLOGY AT THE PEOPLE'S HOSPITAL

I DID SEE Governor Wantong many times when he came to our hospital, but I was not the doctor who treated him. To be honest, he was more of an acquaintance than a close friend. You know, he once felt a slight numbness on his right cheek and right thumb, so he came to see me, probably via the recommendation of our dean. I cured him, and he therefore trusted me. After that, whenever he felt uncomfortable, he would ask his secretary to call me or he himself would come to my office directly. Sometimes, when there was a case I couldn't handle myself, I would advise him to go to another doctor in another department or I would organise a consultation for him to finalise his treatment plan.

Generally speaking, he was in good physical condition. No major problems were found after many examinations. He didn't smoke and drank only very occasionally – usually just dry red wine. He insisted on taking a walk every morning, and nothing wrong had been found with his heart and blood vessels in the past. It was totally out of my expectation that he died of a heart attack! I was very surprised. My negligence! I should have reminded him to do a more detailed cardiovascular examination. I felt very guilty about it, but heart attacks are difficult to detect until just before they strike. In any case, he trusted me, but I failed to find that he had such a serious heart problem. I did owe him a lot.

When he came to see me, we sometimes chatted about health and disease, but never about his work. So I'm afraid I don't have anything that will interest you. Oh, there is one thing you might find interesting.

It was in winter several years before the death of Governor Wantong. One late afternoon, I received a patient who registered with me at the specialist clinic. It was nearly closing time, but that patient just sat in front of my desk without saying a word, quite different from the other patients who usually talked about their problems enthusiastically. A little bit surprised, I looked up and saw a strong man sitting there, wearing sunglasses and a mask. When I asked what was wrong with him, he suddenly said: "Director Bao, my appointment with you today is not for any disease."

Shocked by what he said, I asked: "What do you want to do then?"

He lowered his voice and continued: "I want to do some business with you."

I was even more shocked and asked again: "How could a doctor like me do business with you?"

He said: "You can, and you're sure to make a profit!"

I thought he might have some mental problems, so I stood up and said: "It's about closing time, and I have things to do. If you don't have any health problem, would you please leave the clinic."

He sat there and didn't move at all. Very calmly, he said: "The business I'm talking about with you, the director of neurology, has something to do with one of your important patients, namely Ouyang Wantong!"

I was taken aback by his words, and I realised this man was not a neurotic patient but a person I should take seriously because not only did he know my work, but he also knew Ouyang Wantong had once come to see me. "Ok, tell me what your business is," I said to him.

"Someone wants to hear a rumour that Ouyang Wantong suffers from mild Alzheimer's disease, and though it won't affect his work, he needs to start treatment at once."

"Are you serious? Who? Who wants to hear this?" I was very frightened.

"You don't need to know this."

"You mean you want me to announce that Ouyang Wantong has slight Alzheimer's disease?"

He nodded.

"But how could I alone identify this disease in him, a cadre at his level? You know, this couldn't even be done by a hospital."

"You don't need to write a diagnosis statement – you only need to tell his secretary and the people in the provincial government your concerns. What we need is simply a rumour to spread to the public."

"Oh? Couldn't you guys create this rumour yourselves?"

"It won't be authoritative unless it comes from you."

"Oh!"

"Then you'll get a sum of money."

"How much?" I asked him with a smile.

"One million!"

"Wow! That's quite a lot!"

"You've got nothing to lose and everything to gain."

"What if I don't want this money?" I stared at him.

"If you really don't want it after you've thought it over, forget I ever came to your specialist clinic."

"We doctors have lines that we can't cross. I can't take the money."

"All right. But I hope our conversation today will be a permanent secret between us. Otherwise, you'll pay the price. I know your son teaches in a normal university and your grandson is a second grader in the experimental high school and your wife takes a walk along the same path every day. If you reveal what I have said to you today, each of the three people I just mentioned will probably lose a right foot!"

I stared at him, shocked and feeling a biting chill all over.

I sat on the chair motionless for a long time after the man left. My first reaction was that Governor Wantong had offended someone. My second judgement was that these people were quite vicious and capable of doing anything. I had wanted to tell this to Governor Wantong, but I worried it might bring disaster to my family. I was too cowardly!

After thinking it over, I couldn't believe a decent governor would be afraid of such a rumour about his personal health?

But after this incident, I felt a little uneasy in my heart. I thought I owed Governor Wantong something.

Later, I searched newspapers, magazines and online news and found there were a few events presided over by Governor Wantong. The first one was the policy of heavy penalties on food counterfeiters. The governor said the penalty would make them bankrupt, and sure enough some enterprises closed down because of the tremendous fine. The second was about the investigation into the issue of real estate developers stretching steel bars and making them thinner in order to save money.

This had weakened the steel and consequently affected the firmness of the buildings. In the end, a few real estate developers were arrested. The third was the anti-corruption storm in the provincial government. Three corrupt directors and four deputy directors who asked for bribes were arrested one by one. That man who came to see me that day was probably sent by one of the three groups I just mentioned.

After a while, I heard the news that Governor Wantong had Alzheimer's disease. I have no idea to whom they finally turned, but they succeeded in their evil plot.

15

ZHAO LINGLING

THE RURAL WOMAN

WHY DO you come to see me? An old woman who tills the land in the countryside, and who has lost her teeth and hearing. What could I say to you? Do I know Ouyang Wantong? Of course I know him. My parents and his family lived in the same village, and we used to play with each other when we were children. How could I not know him?

You know, he was apprentice to my father learning how to play the suona. He was smart and learned very fast. Within two years, he could perform quite well. I learned to play the sheng at that time. Have you ever seen one? There's one hanging on the wall over there. The sheng is an accompaniment instrument for the solo suona. Sister instruments indeed. The suona has a high-pitched sound that's loud, crisp and sharp, while the sheng is low-pitched, sounding soft, silvery, rich and deep. Put together, they are pleasant to the ear.

Wantong was older than me, so I called him brother. During that time, we would forget everything when we played the suona and the sheng together, feeling so happy and sweet like eating a slice of watermelon iced in the cool well water in the hot summer. The music piece we played most was *A Hundred Birds Worshipping the Phoenix* – that is, a hundred types of bird come to pay their respects to the phoenix, flying around chirping merrily. What a lovely melody it is! Every time I played it, my heart jumped for joy, leaving all worries and grievances behind!

The feelings between us? Don't mention that again! It's ancient history. Look at me now, dim eyes and blurred vision, thin and grey hair, and rough skin like elm bark! Still want to know the story between us? All right, since you're so curious, let me tell you something. Anyway, both Wantong and my husband are no longer alive, so they can't feel annoyed since they can't hear me anymore. You know, we were young at that time. Just think about it – how could a young man and a young woman not develop tender feelings for each other when they had been together all the time, playing melodious music and exchanging looks from time to time? Certainly, he chased after me. I was thinking about him every day, but I was shy. The most I did was secretly bring food for him from my family, like stuffed buns, peaches, apricots, melons and so on. Watching him gobble up the food, I was filled with sweetness. He was more daring than me.

I remember the first time he touched me was on a summer night when we were on a return trip to our village. That night, we had been invited to perform at a wedding ceremony of a family in Chen village. When the performance finished, it was almost midnight, so the host treated us – him, me, my father, my mother and my uncle – to a bowl of noodles in addition to our payment. We walked back together, and as we moved on, Wantong and I fell behind, by accident or by design – who knows? The moon shone in the sky that night, but the thick cloud darkened everything under the moon and made it impossible for us to see each other clearly beyond dozens of steps. When my father, my mother and my uncle were out of our sight ahead of us, Wantong suddenly grabbed my arm and pulled me into his arms before I could figure out what was going on. Yes, I was surprised, but I was not scared. Honestly, I had been secretly looking forward to it. But what he did next was far beyond my expectation. He slipped his hands under my blouse all of a sudden and sucked my lips! It was summer, and you know, with only a single garment on, how could I put up with his groping around? I kicked him to stop his attempts, but never did I expect that my reaction would encourage him to go further instead! He lifted me up, laid me down on the ground and then pressed his body along the length of mine! He was too daring! He undid my clothes in a few moments, and I was unable to resist because if my efforts to stop him were any louder, my parents and my uncle in front of us would hear. Honestly, I didn't want to stop him from the bottom of my heart. You know, at that time I was sure I would marry no other man except him, and since he wanted to do this, let him be! Suddenly my mother ahead of us shouted: "Lingling, you and Wantong must hurry up!" We both panicked. Wantong helped me up immediately and asked me to answer my mother...

Shortly after that, Wantong's aunt came to my family to propose a marriage officially. My mother asked my opinion of this marriage, and of course I was overjoyed, but I could only say I would listen to her. My mother said: "I have talked with your father and we both think Wantong is a smart and honest young man on whom you can rely. Let's accept his proposal, shall we?" Hearing that, I buried my face in my hands and ran away cheerfully.

After the marriage was fixed, my parents began to prepare my dowry, and I secretly got myself ready. I mainly prepared my undergarments. I knew Wantong liked lotus flowers in particular, so I wanted to embroider some lotus on my bra and panties. I believed on the wedding night when he undid my coat and saw these vivid lotuses on my underwear, he would be very happy. You know, I was famous for my embroidery work, which was some of the most outstanding in the village! I secretly bought the silk thread for the embroidery work and some fine white cotton cloth for the underwear. I washed the cloth, dried it in the sunlight and made it into underwear. Then I began my embroidery work – one on the front of the bra and one on the front of the panty. The one on the bra was a lotus in full bloom, petals all open, red petals and pink pistils, all bright and vivid. The one on the panty was a lotus bud, swelling as if ready to bloom. I did my work so meticulously, needle and thread into and out of the cloth, stitches after stitches with all my affection for the lotus and my love for Wantong going into the embroidery. On the night when my work was done, I tried it on after my parents and brothers and sisters fell asleep. Holding an oil lamp in my hand, I stood in front of the old cracked mirror, looking at myself. Good heavens! I got dazzled when I saw myself. The two lotus flowers came alive, as if their fragrance was drifting from them. I felt I looked prettier with this underwear on...

Never did I expect something would go wrong with the marriage. You know, on that day when Wantong's grandmother sent a message that she would like to have a talk with me, I had thought she wanted to teach me how to behave at the wedding. I came to see her happily, but she told me instead that the county leader planned to marry his daughter to Wantong, who right now had no idea what to do. By saying yes to the county leader, he would feel in debt to me. By saying no, the county leader might make life difficult for him, and his future promotion would be even tougher, depriving Wantong of the opportunity to climb upwards as a cadre. She also said Wantong was the first cadre in their family after so many generations, the only one who could bring prestige and honour to the family, so the whole family didn't know how to handle this. Think about it. I was not a fool, so how couldn't I know what she really meant? Wasn't she forcing me to declare my position?

I cried and ran away covering my face with my hands. I lay on the bed at home for a whole day, crying and thinking, thinking and crying. After turning it over in my mind, I eventually realised I had to let it go! If not, Wantong would marry me with a grievance about the end of his prospects, which might make him either swallow the bitterness and get sick or find fault with me and make our life together unhappy. I would rather let him go and marry the daughter of the county leader! If he truly became a big official, it would be a good thing for his family and a good thing for our village too! An honour for his family and an honour for our village!

Later, I went to his family and told them the engagement was off.

I didn't know how Wantong felt about this, but I heard afterwards that his parents and grandmother were relieved and happy. Ah, I felt so miserable for quite a long time, but in the end, I let it go and moved on. Man struggles upwards, water flows downwards, and you should let it go when you have to!

You want to know whether I still hate him or not? What difference does it make? It's all gone! Like water, the life of a person flows away without being noticed. Now that Wantong has been burned to ashes, why should I still complain about him?

After the marriage was off, I pleaded with my mother to marry me to some family as soon as possible. One more day in the village meant one more day of heartache. Whenever I saw Wantong's house, I felt pain in my heart! My sole idea was to leave the village quickly even if it meant marrying a fool as long as I didn't have to face anything to do with Wantong's family and their house. You know, it was a pity that we didn't know there was part-time work outside the village at that time. If rural women had been allowed to work outside the village, perhaps I wouldn't have got married so quickly. I would have gone out to get a part-time job and see the world like the girls do today. For girls in the village at that time, the only way for you to leave your family and your village was to get married.

Later, I got married and moved to this village. How did my husband treat me? Well, we were an ordinary rural couple, nothing special. We were both busy during the day. He did carpentry work, and I had my hands full with the work in the field. At night, we did that thing – you know, human reproduction. You're a married man, aren't you? Surely you know what a husband and wife would do in bed at night! My husband was illiterate, he didn't talk the way Wantong did, and he wasn't particular about his clothes the way Wantong was. How could I be happy with him as I used to be with Wantong?

You know, when I was with Wantong, I always felt I was flying and weightless.

When Xiaoyu, my oldest daughter, was 17 years old, my husband fell to the ground from a beam at a house where he was working. He broke a leg and an arm and was crippled afterwards. It was a disaster, and life became so hard that we almost couldn't go on. Wantong's aunt, who lived in the neighbouring village, heard about what had happened to my family and came to my house. She told me to let Xiaoyu work as a nanny for a family. I agreed, and Xiaoyu went to Tianquan with Wantong's aunt. At first, I didn't know which family Xiaoyu was working for – I only knew her employer was very generous and paid her well, which was a great help for my family during our most difficult period of time. Later, I discovered Xiaoyu was working for Wantong. You know, after I knew this, an indescribable mixture of feelings tumbled through my mind. I wanted Xiaoyu to quit, but that meant no money for the family to move on! So there was no choice but to do it. Well, poverty stifles ambition!

Then something went wrong with Wantong's family. I could do nothing but tell Xiaoyu to take good care of her Uncle Wantong after I heard the news. Luckily, Wantong narrowly escaped and survived. When he was transferred to the provincial capital, Xiaoyu came back. You know, at that time, Xiaoyu had got married and become a mother. She had someone of her own to care for.

After Xiaoyu came back, I completely lost track of Wantong. We rural people didn't read books and newspapers. We got our hands full with food from the field, and we had no inclination to enquire about his whereabouts.

The first time I met him again after I broke off the marriage was the spring sowing time in that year. One day, the head of the villagers' committee came to my house with a group of people from the township government and county government. Without any explanation, they installed a TV and a washing machine in my house, moved in a set of wooden sofas and a decent-looking table, and even gave the place a thorough clean, both inside and outside! I was shocked and asked them why they had done this. Did we truly realise communism? Then, the head of the villagers' committee and the county head explained everything to me. It turned out that a big official from the provincial capital would be coming to visit our village the next day and he would probably come to my house, so they just temporarily made some arrangements for that.

I said in a hurry: "Could this big official go to visit someone else? I'm an old woman, and I don't know how to talk to him."

The county leader said: "Based on what we know, it's probably because of you that the leader wants to come back and visit his hometown. Please cooperate with us." He also told me that when the leader asked questions, I only needed to say good words for the village and the county, like good harvest, good social atmosphere, good life and good cadres who are eager to help the villagers. No bad things anyway. How could I dare say no to them at that time? I nodded to agree.

Early in the morning of the next day, the township head and the county head arrived at our village, together with some people who were asked to replace the villagers and work in the field. All the villagers took a day off to go to the town, and no one was allowed to come back until lunchtime. I was told to stay at home after breakfast and wait for that big official. Never had I seen such a ceremonial display. My heart was jumping with fear.

I waited until mid-morning when I saw a few sedans drive to the edge of the village and a big official get out of a car. Surrounded by a crowd of people, he firstly went over to the field and spoke with the people working there. I couldn't hear clearly what they were talking about, but there was some noisy chat and laughter. Honestly, I was wondering at that time what shame it was that none of the people working in the field were real farmers!

When the big official, led by the head of the village and the head of the county, arrived in front of my yard, I didn't recognise who he was until he shouted loudly: "Hello, sister!" His voice sounded familiar, so I looked at him carefully and then realised it was Wantong! Good heavens, he was chubby! Apart from some wrinkles and grey hair, he hadn't changed much, so I could still recognise him.

"Sister, I've come to see you and the other villagers on behalf of the Provincial Party Committee and the provincial government. You have a very clean yard," he said as he entered the yard before me. He didn't recognise me at all. I knew he wouldn't, and there were two reasons for that. First, I had changed a lot. At that time, I was an old rural grandmother, white-haired and full of wrinkles. How could he make the connection between that old woman and the young and pretty Zhao Lingling? Second, he couldn't remember the name of my village after so many years, though my daughter Xiaoyu had told him I had married and moved here. Also, this village was dozens of miles away from our parents' village.

He then entered the house and said happily: "Your family is well-equipped with electrical appliances! I heard your village had a good harvest this year and it seems true! How many people are there in your family?"

I thought I shouldn't pretend anymore – otherwise, I would have lost the opportunity to tell him the truth. I uttered a cry: "Wantong, don't you recognise me? I'm Lingling!"

Hearing that, he froze for a moment. He then hastily adjusted his glasses, stared at me and eventually asked in surprise "Is it really you? How…"

The other people who accompanied him all left the house when they saw this, leaving us two alone.

"I'm sorry I didn't recognise you," he said as he rubbed his hands uneasily. I didn't know they would arrange this. I had no idea about it." He seemed to be apologising to me. He was so embarrassed that he didn't even know where to put his hands and feet.

However, I, an old woman, was quite calm and I said to him: "They've done a good thing because now we can see each other. Otherwise, I would probably never have seen you again. Look at me! Old and weak, not too much time left for me."

"How could it be?" He calmed down and comforted me instead. "Your family are living a good life, aren't they? Take care of yourself, enjoy your life and live much longer – a hundred years' longevity!"

I smiled and asked him: "Good life? Are you talking about the electrical appliances, the table and the chairs? Unfortunately, they don't belong to me. When you leave, they'll take them away."

"Who will take them away? Aren't they yours?" He was very surprised.

"The township government put them here temporarily, especially for your visit, to show you that we common people have a very good life under their leadership. Do you understand? You should have known the villagers here know nothing except farming in the field. In the summer, you can harvest a few hundred kilograms of wheat from an acre of land. In the autumn, it'll be thousands. Wheat and corn are generally sold for a few coins – one or two yuan at most for half a kilogram, but you have to minus the money you've spent on seeds, machine seeding, fertiliser, pesticide, gas for the watering machines during drought, and hiring a combine harvester! How much money could be left? Kids' education, healthcare, clothes and daily necessities as well! At the end of a year, you could simply feed your stomach. In the past few years, my children have worked part-time outside the village, and their earnings can be saved. But who would dare to spend money on electrical appliances? You have to save the money for the future in case of fatal diseases, building houses or the cost of your children's marriages."

"Oh!" he shouted. He seemed both surprised and annoyed. His brows knitted and he looked like he was about to lose his temper.

I hurriedly calmed him down. "You should never criticise the head of the township and those other people. Yes, you could do that and then walk off, but I'll be the one who suffers. I'm an ordinary villager – wouldn't it be easy for them to deal with me, an old rural woman?"

He sighed a long sigh and said: "I'm very sorry to let you and my country fellows live such a life. I didn't do my job well, and I should take the blame for it. Take care of yourself. I'm leaving now," he said, eyes reddening at the edges. He took out a roll of money and placed it on the table. "I didn't bring much money with me today. This is a humble expression of my goodwill. Please accept it." With these words, he turned and left. Looking at the money, I thought about going after him and returning it, but I was afraid of embarrassing him. I stayed where I was and didn't say anything. Later, I went out, and I saw him walking towards the car with a scowling face, followed by a group of nervous people, all silent.

The next day, a truck came to take away those items the town government had placed in my house. The driver whispered to me that

Governor Wantong had scolded those accompanying cadres before he left. Do you know why they arranged for Wantong to visit my house? They made a wrong guess! They thought it was to see me in particular that Wantong had planned to visit our village! They had done some research before Wantong came and discovered that there was something between us when we were young. They wanted to play up to him, but they tickled the wrong place.

That was the last time I saw him. Later, the news came that he was removed from his office. Xiaoyu told me that he had died when she came back to see me from her husband's home. Well, maybe I'll see him again when my time comes at last!

16

MASTER ZHIXIAN

THE ABBOT OF YUANSHAN TEMPLE

I'M VERY familiar with Mr Ouyang Wantong. When he was a governor, he would come to visit our temple with a few people from the Bureau of Religious Affairs on the eve of Spring Festival every year. He didn't notify us in advance, and nor did he put on airs when he came. Like the other guests who came to burn incense and pray to Buddha, he usually arrived quietly. When he saw us chanting scriptures, he would stand there silently until we had finished, and then come to speak with us.

Once, when we renovated the hall, the donated money we had was not enough, so he asked the Bureau of Religious Affairs to make a special appropriation for us.

Sometimes, I would invite him to eat with us – he never declined with any excuse and would eat with all the monks. You know, we aren't particular about food like people are in the secular world. One bowl and one plate for each of the four monks sitting at a wooden table. All vegetarian food. Mr Wantong, like we monks, was not picky at all and he just sat down and ate heartily, which immediately narrowed the distance between us. Some young monks even dared to ask him questions.

Everyone in the temple respected him a lot. He once came to the monastery and chatted with me. He said: "Master, you're far away from the temporal world and you can observe life calmly and clearly. In your eyes, what is the main obstacle people have in this world?"

I smiled and replied: "At present, people come to the monastery to burn incense and pray to Buddha, usually for official posts and wealth. Not many of them do this for a peaceful heart, which indeed is not a good sign, a manifestation of being in a state of confusion. It tells us that a lot of people regard Buddha as the protector of personal desire, not the very incarnation of compassion that could save people from suffering. Whenever I hear people pray to Buddha for titles and money as they burn the incense, I always feel bitter in my heart. In the historical records of our Buddhist temples, a chaotic period has always ensued after a year when many people came to us for wealth and official titles. That isn't a good sign."

He remained silent for quite a while and then continued: "Since Buddha is concerned with saving people, why do you think there's so much suffering in this world?"

I told him, in the eyes of a monk, suffering came from three things. First, the heaven and the earth, like storms, flood and earthquakes. Second, the society, like wars and turmoil. Third, personal reasons, like betrayal and diseases.

He then asked: "In your opinion, which occupation will bring the least suffering?"

I somewhat understood why he asked this question. I smiled and said: "Well, any kind of occupation will be painstaking and laborious. All of them require you to deal with people and handle interpersonal relationships, which places a ladder in front of you to climb up, and which provides you with a payment to worry about. Therefore, could there be any less suffering in any occupation? Take you for an example. You're an official in the political field, glorious and brilliant when people look at you from afar, but in fact, you have many hardships too. You go to great lengths to make government policy, but any minor errors will attract criticism from the people. You work meticulously with your peers and senior leaders, worrying about betrayal and remaining calm in the face of all kinds of temptations. The slightest carelessness will lead to your ruin."

He laughed and said: "The abbot is indeed a saint who knows the way things work. I really admire you!"

Well, there was a little incident involving Governor Wantong that I want to tell you about. We have an eminent monk who travelled here from Yinshan Temple in the early years, who in a sense is my senior brother. He's good at reading faces, and he can quickly tell a person's past experiences and future life with one look. It is said that he learned the skill from a folk master who used to take refuge in Yinshan Temple. When he first came here, he didn't show his skill to us, but he sometimes read faces in his spare time for the monks in our temple. He would always be very accurate in doing this, so word spread and the number of people who came to him for face reading increased gradually. He asked me what he should do and whether he should accept those people or not. I thought since the followers had made this request, it would do harm to the reputation and the incense of the temple if they were to be completely refused. I gave him a separate room to receive a few people who wished to have a face reading on a daily basis.

Once, Governor Ouyang Wantong came to visit us. When I walked with him in the temple, we happened to pass the door of that senior brother's room, so I introduced them to each other. However, my senior brother thought the governor had come to him for face reading, so he said: "Mr Ouyang has broken two women's hearts and has been hurt by two women. Am I right?"

Governor Ouyang Wantong was stunned at first. Then his face suddenly turned red. I felt somewhat embarrassed as well and said immediately: "The governor hasn't come to visit us for a face reading."

With that, I was ready to invite the governor to some other places, but unexpectedly the governor's curiosity was aroused. He stood there smiling at my senior brother and asked: "What else did the master see from my face?"

"You have a disaster in the future."

"Oh, what disaster?" The governor still smiled, but my heart beat like a drum, worrying that my brother was speaking out of turn.

"There are many interpretations of a disaster. Please work it out by yourself."

"What else can the master see?"

"Have you been worrying a lot recently?"

"Oh?" The governor's expression changed, and his smiles disappeared. "Can the master see what kind of worry I have right now?"

"I need you to tell me one dream you had recently."

"A goose flies past in the sky, and there are clouds in the air."

"You're worrying about..."

I was afraid my brother would say something that might annoy the governor, so I took him away in a hurry.

There was a time when he came to take a walk with me in the temple. He asked: "Master, in your opinion, how can we measure the length of a life?"

"Well, in your world, people like to measure life with time – years to be specific – so we would say someone is 80 years old, for example. We monks, however, like to use Buddhist service times for the measurement. Let's take an example. When an eminent monk has done 29,200 Buddhist services, he's said to have lived in the temporal world for 80 years. We have 365 days a year, and if there's one service a day, that will be 25,550 over 70 years. Usually, a monk begins his service in the temple at the age of 10, so it would be roughly 29,200 services plus 3,650 services done symbolically. That's a monk's lifespan. I heard that in the western regions, people use the distance a person has walked in his whole life as the measurement. Whoever has covered 90,000 miles will have no regrets."

He listened and nodded. "Good, good. Measure the lifespan with the distance of walking. That's interesting."

He didn't say anything more on that day. Though he wore smiles all the time, I knew there was some reason why he was talking about lifespan. He must have been suffering. I don't know how to read faces, but I could see he was unhappy. He certainly wasn't in the realm of joy. He needed someone to save him.

I wanted to save him from his suffering, but he was unwilling to tell me more, so I had no idea where to start.

Later, I heard he considered resigning, and I felt secretly happy for him. If he did that, he might have set himself free from his pain. But it was said that he failed to do that and had to continue his work.

When the news came to our temple that he had passed away, all of us at the temple chanted for his soul for three whole days. I believe he must have arrived at the world of celestial bliss by now.

No more suffering.

17

DUAN DEYUAN

THE FORMER DEPUTY GOVERNOR OF QINGHE PROVINCE

I WAS THE DEPUTY GOVERNOR. Governor Ouyang Wantong's deputy. Yes, of course I know something about him. What do you want to know? It's up to me? Well, let me tell you my impressions of him and some memories about him then.

I still remember the first meeting he presided over after he took office. On that day, he came straight to the point and said: "I believe that fate has brought me to work with all you deputy governors, in addition to the arrangements made by the organisation. The world is crowded with a lot of people, but each of us will only meet a few that we can get close to, and even less that we can work with productively. And it's very rare to find someone who can work with a group of leaders in a provincial government. I'll cherish my fate of doing things together with you."

He continued: "Although we have not been chosen in a general election by all the people in the province, but rather appointed by our superiors, we should regard it as a privilege given by ordinary people who have entrusted us to manage this province. We should be responsible for them."

He also said: "When we start our careers as officials at the town or county level, it's understandable that we might regard our posts as a means to make a living and give more considerations to ourselves and families. At the level of department, office, bureau and city, it's tolerable to regard an official post as a symbol of personal success and family glory.

But when we're officials at the provincial and ministerial levels, we're criminals if we're still unable to break away from the constraints of ourselves and our families, and still aim to seek personal fame and benefits instead of thinking about our country and people. Do you know how many provincial leaders, ministerial leaders and military officers we have? At most one to two thousand, isn't it? Wouldn't it be the saddest thing if those two thousand people never think of our country and nation?"

He also pointed out that in China, working in the political field should be a lifelong career for cadres at provincial level, so in a sense they are statesmen. And that means they should have the code of conduct of statesmen. He continued: "We provincial cadres live in larger houses than ordinary people do, we ride better cars, and the same goes for food and clothing. Our personal interests have been guaranteed. In these circumstances, if you still don't direct the main efforts of your work towards the welfare of the common people, you not only lose the trust of our organisation and the common people, but you also fail your own conscience. You are nothing but a low politician, a passer-by in the political field."

He also added: "Today I want to let you know I'm not someone who is always right. I've made a lot of mistakes. The most serious one is that I didn't manage my family properly and my wife committed the crime of bribery. She's been sentenced by law while I've been sentenced by my heart. I hope you can all learn a lesson from me. Always keep a clear mind and draw a line that you'll never cross. You all know that we have defects in our existing system."

Honestly, I was shocked by what he said on that day.

After he took office, he demanded that all the members of the provincial government pay attention to the collection and analysis of data. He said: "All the policies and measures we use to govern our province in fact come from data. Without truthful data, how could we make the right decisions? Take population for an example. How many people do we have in the province? How many men and how many women are among them? What are the proportions of old people, adults, young people, teenagers and children respectively within each gender group? How many men and women respectively are migrant workers? How many children have they brought with them? Without the data, how could we determine the size of the labour force? How could we predict the birth rate? How could we determine how many hospitals we need? How many nursing homes, middle schools and primary schools? How to organise the rural residential areas? How to determine the scale of urban construction? How to adjust the family planning policy? Another example – how much arable land do we have in the province? How many paddy fields and upland fields? How much farmland will have stable yields regardless of drought or waterlogging? How much farmland has been destroyed every year? Without these numbers, how could we distribute the planting areas for grains, oil crops and vegetables? How could we predict agricultural output? How do we determine the grain warehouses we need to build? How do we organise the import and export of grains and vegetables?"

I think his words were very reasonable!

After he became the governor, he would go through three procedures before he made a decision. The first procedure was investigation and research, through which problems were found and preliminary solutions were worked out. The second procedure was expert analysis on the proposed solutions, and he would always select experts who dared to voice different opinions. The third procedure was a public opinion poll on the solution approved by the experts. This would be taken among different groups of people, and demonstrated a reverence for popular public opinion.

After assuming office, he mainly focused on four things.

The first was agriculture. He said: "Agriculture is a matter of stability. We're a big agricultural province with a population of nearly 100 million, and we can't expect the other provinces to feed us, so agriculture is the basis we must hold fast to. If we fail to do that, we'll be short of food and the whole province will be in chaos." For agriculture, he placed much emphasis on the following things. Arable land should never be used for other purposes, and the planting area must be guaranteed every year. The income of farmers should be increased year on year in order to attract them to the fields. Farmland irrigation, water conservation and scientific cultivation should be done to increase the yield per *mou* every year. Pollution of land and rivers must be controlled to ensure the production of green food.

The second was the development of industry and information technology. He said: "This is a matter of getting rich, which we can't achieve by depending on agriculture alone. If our province wants to get rich, we must develop industry and information technology. We should not only support the existing key enterprises to become bigger and stronger but also encourage people to build microenterprises. We should support local people to establish enterprises but also encourage investment from other provinces and foreigners."

The third was the business environment, which he said was a matter of vitality. He said: "Without a good business environment, no one will come to invest and do business. If so, how could our economy thrive? How could the economic development in our province obtain vitality?" He stressed the importance of construction of commercial facilities and premises where businessmen could establish a firm footing, of public security so that businessmen could feel safe, of the crackdown on triads in the commercial field to ensure fair competition, and of providing sufficient preferential policies to attract businessmen to swarm in.

The fourth one was the prosperity of education, which he believed to be essential for sustainable development. He questioned how a province could develop sustainably without enough talent when its education is underdeveloped? He stressed the development of primary schools, secondary schools and universities. He also supported private schools, hoping to establish a private university, like Harvard, in the province.

The deepest impression he left on me was his desire to do something extraordinary and take the economic and social development of Qinghe province to a new level during his term. He was not the kind of person who muddled along in officialdom and in his work. He had courage. He dared to make the decisions and took responsibility for them.

Let me tell you a story. Someone wanted to build a nuclear power plant in our province, claiming that in addition to the convenience of power transmission, it would greatly increase our financial revenue. However, Governor Ouyang Wantong refused to approve this project. He thought Qinghe, a big grain producing province with a dense population, was located in the heartland of the country, and if something bad should happen to the nuclear power plant, it would be impossible to isolate it – the result would be a huge disaster for both Qinghe and the whole country. His decision annoyed some people at the top. They turned on us, fiercely questioning who had blocked it. The office workers who dealt with this were scared witless. He stood up and told them it was his decision and that they shouldn't criticise others. He handed over a stack of research materials to them and announced: "That's why I disapprove of this project. Please take a look. If you don't agree, we can go to Beijing and have a discussion there."

As his subordinate, I respected him very much. If I have to point out his mistakes, I think the biggest one he made was the discord between him and Qin Chengkang, the deputy secretary of the Provincial Party Committee. This cost Governor Wantong dearly. I hadn't worked in Qinghe before and had no idea what had happened between them, but I knew they worked together in Tianquan city and I guess it was very likely that there were some unresolved conflicts from that period of time. The disharmony between him and Deputy Secretary Qin had brought him a lot of trouble, and I think his attempt to resign probably had something to do with that. Now times have changed, and I can say openly that Deputy Secretary Qin had a connection at the top. That's all I can say, and I hope you won't write this into the biography. You know, it'll just create trouble.

The relationship between Deputy Secretary Qin and Jian Qianyan? I'm not very clear, but I know one year when the Provincial Public Security Department investigated the triad leaders and their organisations throughout the province, Jian Qianyan and his company ranked first on the list. But later, his name was wiped off the list for no reason. I was not in charge of crime crackdown, so I don't know the details.

Of course, I had some disagreements with Ouyang Wantong in the course of my work. We had disputes over some issues, and we did get mad at each other, but he never harboured any resentment against me, let alone made life difficult for me. He said something that I'll never forget: "Today we're engaged in modern politics, which means we need to respect our opponents and bear no grudges because not all of our opponents are bad people."

18

LIN QIANGWEI

THE EX-WIFE

YOU COULD STILL FIND ME? You're truly great! This place where I live is very remote, and few people here know who I am. You know, except for my son, my daughter-in-law and my grandson, I haven't met anyone for many years. My daily routine is to feed those chickens, water these vegetables and flowers, and read books about the Lord. I have no interest in anything in this world, and I hope the tumour on my liver will grow faster so that the Lord can take me away quickly. Strangely enough, the Lord somehow always forgets to circle my name and send his people to take me away. I want to kill myself, but I don't have the courage to do that, and I worry about scaring my son and making him even more miserable. So for now I'm still dragging on in this world, neither dead nor alive.

Yes, I heard about Ouyang Wantong's death. The death of a celebrity usually makes a loud noise. I thought I would die before him, but unexpectedly he took the lead. He did this with everything. Even in death, he would compete with me and come first. Fine, he won! I have nothing to say.

Does it make any sense to talk about things in the past? Leave a memory? For whom? Forget about it! You may go now and leave me alone. What I like most now is peace. You should leave him in peace too. I'm guessing the biography is not something he decided before he died. It couldn't have been his idea! It was most probably Chang Xiaowen who arranged it. Oh, I'm right? I knew he wouldn't be so stupid to allow people to dig up his stories after his death.

Why are you still here? You must get something from me? You're quite stubborn, aren't you? How much is Chang Xiaowen paying you to do your work so seriously? All right, all right, what do you want to hear from me about him? Anything? I don't need to talk about the things he did after he became an official, like his efforts on grain production, industrialisation, water conservation, construction, the tertiary industry, caring for the people and anti-corruption. You can go and check all the documents, materials and records you need in the archives at all levels. Also, there are a lot of his speeches, instructions, articles and press interviews. You can begin your writing after checking all these. What? You think those are meaningless? They couldn't show the real side of a person? You want me to say something about him? Well, all right, let me tell you about the things that happened between him and me a long time ago.

It was because of my parents that I agreed to marry him at first. You know, they wanted to find me a husband who had a promising future in politics. To put it bluntly, a man who was suitable for the work of an official, so that I could rely on him. My father used to be a county magistrate, and my mother was the director of the County Women's Federation. During the period of the 'three-in-one combination' in the Cultural Revolution, my father worked as the director of the County Revolutionary Committee, but later he was stricken down. That's why they wanted to find a son-in-law who had the potential to be an official. When Ouyang Wantong worked at the commune, they saw him handle things neatly and maturely, and he was especially tenacious and unobtrusive in his work. Also, he was willing to work hard, and he was good at writing documents, so they both felt he was a talented young man and would have a promising future. They highly recommended him and urged me to meet him. When I met him for the first time, I thought his appearance and temperament seemed all right, and his underlying arrogance somewhat attracted me. You know, most boys of my age in the residential courtyard of the old county government and county committee were a bit flashy, which I despised, so I eventually nodded my agreement. I didn't really have a crush on him at first. I was a little bit attracted to him physically, and he met my parents' criteria for an ideal son-in-law.

After we got married, especially after the honeymoon period was over, I found the conditions of our families were so different, and living together had its problems. Up until then, I felt our ancestors' well-matched marriage was indeed reasonable. You know, in my family, I was used to taking a shower every night before going to bed, while Wantong would go to bed without even washing his feet. As for each meal, I would like to cook a few dishes plus a hot soup, while he would just take the noodles out into a bowl and eat them with only some pepper or a clove of garlic. As for drinking tea, I would usually leave the tea to draw for a while in the cup or the pot, sit down and sip it slowly, while he would pour the boiled water into a bowl, let it cool for a little while and gulp it down. It was very offensive to the eye! There were so many things like this! Gradually, I began to bear a grudge against him. Like most couples, we had frequent quarrels, and of course each quarrel ended as his apology and my victory. You know, at that time I had a psychological superiority to him because he claimed ties of kinship with my family and it was with my father's help that he could be transferred to the county, so he had to listen to me.

Later, things changed. After my parents were struck down one after the other, my position at home had a disastrous decline, and my superiority to Wantong was gone. Fortunately, Wantong still listened to me as usual, showing not the slightest contempt for me. He shouldered all the responsibilities for my family and tried his best to take care of my parents and our relatives, which filled me with gratitude towards him. My true feelings were developed from that time, and my true love for him officially began.

After the Cultural Revolution, he was admitted to graduate school, and I did my best to support him. I stayed at home looking after the children, went to work and did the housework all by myself. He lived up to my expectations and established himself in officialdom in the end. Then he climbed up step by step, and countless praises and words of admiration came to my ears, making me very happy. I secretly thanked my parents for their insightful choice – they indeed found me a precious piece of jade, a real treasure.

Then I wanted to try my luck in officialdom by using his power. You know, in China, nothing is more glorious for a woman than being an official. You should go and count how many high-ranking women are in officialdom!

Wantong, however, disapproved of my plan. He said: "It'll be better for you to be an ordinary staff member in the organisation. If we both work as officials, there will be no place for us to hide if something dangerous should happen."

I was obsessed with the idea of being an official, so how could I understand him at that time. Since he didn't help, I began to make life difficult for him, leaving him no moment of peace, which eventually gave him no choice but to allow me to go around fishing for help via his influence. I made it in the end. Of course, reflecting on what I have done in the past, I realise I was pushing myself into the quagmire. I was driving myself onto the road of death.

My pestering him during that period of time damaged our relationship. Think about it. Every day, I gave him the cold shoulder and quarrelled with him. How could I allow him to sleep with me? When this became something habitual, he would of course turn his eyes to other women, especially those sweet and obedient ones who were younger than me. My pressure on him simply meant giving the other women the chance to get close to him. Yes, I finally understand this.

When I began to feel that he had no interest in my body at all, things had already got worse. Though I had become an official, I had lost my husband's heart. As his wife, how could I turn a blind eye to this? I began to check on his life after work like a spy and observe those pretty women who associated with him. I finally discovered the truth and found that woman.

Who was she? I might as well tell you because it's no secret at all. She's Yin Qingqing, an actress of the Henan Opera Troupe in Tianquan.

Yin Qingqing was not a famous actress at that time, but she was born with an air of seduction and coquettishness, with slanting eyebrows as long and drooping as willow leaves, almond-shaped eyes, long slender legs, big breasts and a big butt. She knew how to dress herself, she always looked trendy and she was good at flirting, which had seized the eyes of countless men who all became lovesick puppies around her. I didn't know how she hooked up with Ouyang Wantong. After I discovered it was she who was trying to steal my husband, I was consumed with the idea of catching them red-handed, catching them in the bed so that I could teach that bitch a good lesson. But I never succeeded, and I didn't know why. Whether they stopped seeing each other, or they played hide and seek with me, I just couldn't get any evidence. When I questioned Ouyang

Wantong, he just denied it, and I was really busy after I became a chief official, so eventually I had to let it go.

It wasn't until Ouyang Wantong and I divorced that I learned Yin Qingqing wasn't going to marry him, and I realised I had treated them with groundless suspicion. Like many women who have never been an official, I had been blinded by jealousy. Of course, when a woman has been blindfolded, there's nothing to be ashamed of.

You know, I silently cursed them many times when I was filled with suspicion, but later I felt I had overreacted a bit and I was a little sorry for them.

It feels so good to be an official, especially when you become the chief official of a unit. All your subordinates, men in particular, are under your control, which makes you feel omnipotent! That was really cool! I was so happy!

I met that boss Jian Qianyan when I was feeling like this.

Jian Qianyan was a friend of my female classmate Sui Canlan. He was about 37 or 38 and looked quite clean and refreshing. He arranged a banquet for our first meeting, and he made a good impression on me. Canlan was my closest friend, so I had no reason to be wary about the person she wanted me to meet. Later I realised anyone who desired to make friends with you actually wanted to ask for something. The only difference was how much they wanted, how difficult it would be and how risky it would be. As an official, you should always be vigilant and read those people like a book.

But how could I understand it at that time? I muddled on, enjoying smiling faces and flattering talk, and thinking the meeting with Jian Qianyan was just an ordinary banquet like I used to have.

After that, Jian Qianyan called regularly. His greetings were simple and friendly, and I didn't get bored with him. And then he began to send gifts which didn't bother me. The deep impression he left on me was an invitation to a newly opened beauty store. I had only been to regular hair or beauty salons before that, so I went there out of curiosity and discovered what it was about – it was a store that would offer a set of body beauty services. It started with feet, massaging and applying toenail polish. Then the belly, removing fat by massaging and applying Chinese herbal ointment. Then breast beauty, rubbing and sucking your breasts with an instrument to make them bigger and rounder. Then face care, and finally hairdressing. When you were finished, you just felt so relaxed that you were almost a different person. That was indeed a wonderful feeling, and I fell in love with this body beauty service immediately.

When I was about to leave there on that day, Jian Qianyan stuffed a card into my handbag and said: "Sister Lin, come to do body beauty anytime you want. Remember to bring this card." I had thought it was a discount card with a little deposit in it, so I didn't think too much and got in my car with a thank you.

I went to that body beauty store many times after my first try. Each time I finished the treatments, I would take out the card, ask the waitress to swipe it and then leave. It was so easy, and I felt very happy. I had thought it would be at most a few hundred yuan for one visit, until one time when the waitress reminded me after she swiped the card: "Madame, remember to top up your card! There are only a few thousand yuan left, not enough for the next service." I was startled and asked her how much each service cost. She said the one I did cost 9,999 yuan each time, which shocked me quite a lot. I made a rough estimation and found I had spent nearly 200,000 yuan!

The next day, I called Jian Qianyan and asked him to come to my office. I handed the card to him as I said: "Thank you for the card but I don't want to go there anymore. Anytime you need my help, just let me know."

He shook his hand and said: "I have nothing to ask for from you. I only want you to be prettier and younger, to live more happily and comfortably."

Hearing that, I was relieved. He impressed me more after that.

Sometime later, he called and said a group of kids in Tianquan would be going to study abroad in New York. He asked me whether I wanted to send my son Qianzi to America too. Of course, I did want that, but Qianzi's academic record didn't meet the requirement of full state-funded scholarship, and he had already graduated and worked in Tianquan. We didn't have enough money to send him to study in the United States.

When he heard this, he said: "Don't worry. As long as you want him to study in America, I can pay for his tuition now, and he can pay me back when he returns. I'm sure he'll make a big fortune."

I was tempted by his words.

I told this to Wantong after I went back home. Wantong shook his head and said: "The cost of studying abroad is not to be sneezed at. We don't have the ability to pay the money back, so things could become difficult later on. What's more, Qianzi majors in human resource management, which in fact can be done here in China. Why should he have to go to study in the United States for improvement when he can do his job well here?"

However, I believed Wantong's fear was unwarranted. It was Jian Qianyan who offered to help me, and it would not only be unreasonable to turn him down, it would also make Qianzi lose an opportunity to broaden his horizons in the United States. I decided to do this by myself.

After I made up my mind, I went to see Jian Qianyan in his office. He put 700,000 yuan into a bag and handed it to me. I offered to write him an IOU but he smiled, waved his hand and showed me out of his office.

With this money, I immediately started organising Qianzi's study abroad

After a period of time, Jian Qianyan called me to say that one of his paper mills had been fined more than one million yuan for pollution discharge by the Environmental Protection Agency, and he wondered whether I could speak for him in front of the agency's leader so that his penalty could be reduced a little bit. You know, I took his money, and I definitely had to help him, so I agreed immediately.

Luckily, I was quite familiar with the director, and what's more he was under the jurisdiction of Wantong. When he received my call, he readily agreed and said: "Well, since Jian Qianyan is your friend, no fine for him this time, but you must tell him that he can't do it again the next year."

I told Jian Qianyan the good news, and he was very happy. He came to my office and said: "Sister Lin, you've done me a great favour. The money I gave to you a few days ago is my personal support for Qianzi to study abroad. Never mention it again."

After that, the pressure of having borrowed money from him was gone. We were even now. However, I underestimated his desire. Within only half a month, he came to me again and said: "Sister Lin, please do me one more favour. I want to buy the Silver Triangle land and set up a new paper mill." With these words, he handed me a land requisition application.

My heart jolted when I heard this. Silver Triangle, a place adjoining the urban area. How could it be possible to build a paper mill there? Even if I approved it, the municipal government wouldn't agree. I told him directly that this was not going to happen.

He didn't say anything and just smiled and left. I thought he might understand my words and give up his idea willingly.

A few days later, he came to my office again. He immediately took out a folder from his bag and handed it to me. Surprised, I asked him what it was.

He smiled and motioned me to open the folder. Confused, I opened it and found the deeds for a two-bedroom apartment in New York and a key. The title of the property was clearly written with the name Ouyang Qianzi. I was greatly shocked. "What do you mean by this?" I asked

"I know you're completing the formalities of Qianzi's studying abroad, so this is a small gift for him. You know, when he arrives in New York, he needs a place to live. I have asked a friend there to get a small apartment for him near his school, on the 26th floor, 80 square metres, two bedrooms plus one small living room – not big but basically good enough for him. And it's for you to stay when you go to see him."

"What? That is too much. How could we accept this?" Holding the folder tightly in my hand, I was surprised but pleased. How wonderful it would be if Qianzi should have an apartment in New York! He didn't need to worry about renting anymore!

"Sister Lin, it's nothing! We're friends, aren't we? I can only do this small thing for you. But your help for me is a big deal. Sister Lin, I've got to go." With those words, he stood up and left my office.

Sitting on my chair for quite a while, I felt I owed Jian Qianyan a lot. I hadn't helped him to get the Silver Triangle but he didn't hate me and prepared such a big gift instead. I felt guilty and upset.

I decided to figure out a way to help him.

One morning a few days later, I called him to rewrite his application with no mention of building a paper mill, but instead a training school for technical workers. He understood immediately and did it happily.

During that period of time, all the formalities of Qianzi's studying abroad had been completed, and his ticket had been booked as well. I thought it was the perfect time to tell Wantong about it. You know, I had to keep it a secret from him for fear that he would object, refuse to accept Jian Qianyan's money and spoil the whole thing. Now that the die was cast, it was time to let him know. Of course, I wouldn't tell him that Jian Qianyan had bought an apartment for Qianzi. I remember it was one evening when we were going to have supper together that I told him the news. He was going to fly to Guangzhou after supper for the launch of a big commercial project. We three sat at the table. I asked Qianzi to open a bottle of red wine, filled three glasses and served one to his father first. Then I said: "Wantong, let's raise our glasses to our son. He's going to study in the United States!"

Apparently, he was shocked. Holding his glass, he turned to Qianzi and flared up at him. "Why didn't you tell me earlier?"

Qianzi flushed and turned to me for help.

I smiled and said: "We wanted to surprise you."

"Be careful! This might not be a good thing!" he replied coldly. Then he drained his glass and got ready to stand up and leave.

I was a little annoyed. This was after all a big thing for our son. It had been nice of me to arrange it all without bothering him. What a cold manner he had! I said to him loudly: "Don't worry! This won't stop you from being an official! I did it by myself, and I didn't use your power and fame and I don't need you to lecture me."

He picked up his bag and left without saying a word. Qianzi looked at me with fear. "Mother, what should we do?"

"Do nothing! Ignore him! Let's drink the wine. Without him, the earth will go on turning all the same! Come on, Qianzi – cheer up!" I raised my glass and touched his.

A few days later, I took a day off and accompanied Qianzi to Beijing for his international flight. When Wantong came back home from Guangzhou, Qianzi had already arrived in America safely. He moved into the apartment bought by Jian Qianyan and finished his registration in the school. I felt relieved at last.

After that, I began to work on Jian Qianyan's paper mill project.

I talked with some of my deputy directors first. You know, at that time, we didn't have any regulations on land sales, and the attitude of bureau leaders was the crucial factor. I had to let them know this in advance. After this was done, I got it successfully approved at the bureau meeting that was held particularly on the issue of land transfer. Next, I checked with the deputy mayor in charge of the Land Bureau, and asked him to take care of this project. Eventually, he approved it, probably for the sake of Wantong. Finally, I had to face Wantong. I told him that an entrepreneur wanted to build a training school for technical workers in the Silver Triangle and that the Land Bureau had agreed to transfer the land at the current market price. The report would be sent to him soon, and I needed his help.

He frowned as he listened: "Secretary Fang of the Municipal Party Committee and I have discussed building a children's hospital in that place, so I think your proposal will probably be declined."

I therefore told him directly that it was Jian Qianyan who wanted to set up a training school there, suggesting that he must help him this time. He didn't say yes or no when I told him this, which made me think he had agreed to help. But to my surprise, when the report was sent to his office, he wrote: "I still insist on using this land for the construction of a children's hospital. Please follow the instructions from Secretary Fang!"

When Secretary Fang received the report, he read it and wrote: "Agree with Mayor Wantong. This land will still be used to build a children's hospital."

What's done couldn't be undone!

I sat with helpless anger for quite a long time.

There was nothing I could do. I called Jian Qianyan to come to my office, wanting to explain to him in person that it was Secretary Fang who had declined his project and ask him to choose another piece of land. Also, I wanted to make an apology to him face to face. To my surprise, Jian Qianyan was very cold when he answered my phone call. He said: "I didn't expect it would be Mayor Wantong who refused to sell the land to me! To whom else I should complain?"

I was shocked to hear that. How could he know this since all the instructions of the leaders were confidential! I laughed and said: "Don't listen to them. It's all rumours! How could Mayor Wantong object to you?"

He raised his voice and said: "Stop lying to me! Secretary-General Qin of the Municipal Party Committee has told me in person! Could it be a mistake?"

As soon as I heard the name Secretary-General Qin, my heart tightened. This man had competed for the mayor position with Wantong and had taken his failure to heart for a long time. They were friends only on the surface. I hoped that he would not stab him in the back on this matter.

As I was thinking about finding another piece of land that Jian Qianyan would like to have, he reported me. I learned afterwards that when he lent me the money, he recorded everything in advance on video. As for that apartment in New York, he also kept a copy of the deeds. He said it was I who asked for all those things. When I heard about his heartless behaviour in the detention centre, I couldn't help kicking myself. It was at that time that I understood everything Wantong had warned me about was so reasonable and how terrible it would be when a man suddenly turned on you.

It was too late for regrets!

Later, I discovered that the moment I was arrested, Qianzi was also arrested at the airport after he flew back to China because of a phone call saying I had been seriously ill. Wantong was soon removed from office as well. I hadn't listened to his warning, and the whole family was ruined.

During my questioning, I found the investigators intentionally led the whole thing to Wantong, which aroused my vigilance and also made me realise their real target was him. It was likely that Secretary-General Qin was controlling things behind the scenes, while Jian Qianyan was only the performer on the stage.

So in the following investigation, I didn't say a word about Wantong and insisted I had done it all by myself, which was indeed the truth. The only thing I could do inside those walls was protect him. I knew how much he had sacrificed to be an official, and I knew how important his career was to him. I couldn't destroy him. In order to put an end to the investigators' wishful thinking, I firmly requested a divorce with him and demanded it be done immediately. Wantong refused at first, and he even asked someone to visit me in the detention centre to persuade me to reconsider, but I had made up my mind. In front of the investigators, I purposefully depicted him as a worthless good-for-nothing, throwing muck at him in every way, from his character to his personality and from his lifestyle to his mental state. I said he was worse than an animal. Also, I made up a vivid story about him and Yin Qingqing. Although I didn't catch them once, I was good at telling stories. At last, I succeeded in making them believe that Wantong and I were through and that our marriage was merely a piece of paper that helped to keep up appearances in officialdom.

It was good that I didn't ruin him in the end.

I took responsibility for everything which saved my son as well. Qianzi was only subject to a punishment. Though he could never go abroad, he kept his job.

I'm sure the one who stabbed Wantong in the back must have been very disappointed. I heard he got a promotion too. Well, I hope he gets rich! Just think about it! How frightening and chilling it was that a person would entrap his colleague and beat him to death for an official position!

I live alone now. My son and daughter-in-law come to visit occasionally. They bring me some food and daily necessities, which are good enough for my life. When I was released from prison, Wantong was still in his post, and he sent word to me that he wanted to come to see me. I firmly declined. What would come of seeing each other again except bitter feelings and sadness? What's more, it wouldn't be good for his new wife. Alas, life has turned over to a new page, and there's no need to make more trouble.

Now I would say I'm disillusioned with the world and I've lost interest in everything. I've already become a disciple of the Lord, the only one who lives in my heart. That's all I can say. It might not be of any use for your biography. I'm sorry about that.

May the soul of Wantong have entered heaven!

May he be with the Lord too!

Amen!

19

WANG MANGHU

THE FORMER DEPUTY SECRETARY OF THE COMMISSION FOR DISCIPLINE INSPECTION, QINGHE PROVINCE

I WORKED with Governor Ouyang Wantong for some time. When he was a member of the Standing Committee of the Provincial Party Committee and the secretary of the Provincial Party Committee, I was the secretary of the Commission for Discipline Inspection. We had a lot of contact in the course of our work.

He told me many times that we should do some research on power structures. He said: "We both have experienced what power is on our journeys through officialdom. When you're the second or the third in command, the power you have is somewhat limited, but once you become the first in command, no one can set limits on you, which of course is totally unacceptable. Power itself means control and being controlled, an unequal 'evil' force invented by mankind to maintain the normal operation of society. Power is permeable and expansive, and it can seduce and corrupt humanity greatly. If there's no limit on it, it will avail of its resources and violence anytime it wants. Then it will quickly swell and hurt people, even changing good people into bad ones and making bad people worse."

I thought his idea was great, but at that time the whole country paid no attention to this issue. It was very difficult to implement the system we had designed, and many regulations were simply hanging on the wall or printed in documents, never being put into practice. His ideas didn't materialise in the end.

Shortly after that, there came the case of Guan Yuejie.

Guan Yuejie was the youngest deputy director of the Municipal Finance Bureau. His case was the most difficult we ever handled.

The initial clues about Guan Yuejie's case were not discovered by our Disciplinary Committee – it was transferred to us by the Public Security Bureau. Two police officers from the Public Security Bureau found a strange thing when they tracked three prostitutes at the Crown Nightclub. They discovered that every two days, one of the three prostitutes would secretly leave the nightclub at 9pm, take a taxi and go to apartment 1018, building 9 in Changhe Community. She would stay there for two hours and then go back to work in the nightclub around 11pm. The three girls were among the most beautiful in the nightclub, and they were said to be the club's brand. They would spend a lot of time drinking wine or dancing with you, and to sleep with them for one night would cost you as much as 5,000 yuan! The price of asking them to visit your place would therefore be higher.

The two police officers concluded that someone must be procuring women in apartment 1018. A rich man with a good background. They went to check with the property management company and found the owner of this apartment was an elderly person. They quietly brought in one of the prostitutes and asked her who the whoremonger was. The girl said he was a very rich young man who was quite generous and would pay an extra 500 yuan as long as you complied with his eccentric sexual requirements. Realising that the man she spoke of was not the owner of this apartment considering his age, the police officers applied for a secret search.

Once the application was approved, they searched 1018 quietly during the day and found that it was a two-bedroom apartment with a living room. One bedroom was in use while the other one had a locked iron door installed. They opened the door and saw a huge safe built into the wall. After they opened the safe, they were very surprised to find cash inside – about 10 million yuan. So they began to monitor the guy who lived in this house. To their surprise, it was not a foreigner who came to stay in this apartment for two hours every two nights, but Guan Yuejie, the 35-year-old deputy director of the Municipal Finance Bureau. They therefore transferred this case to us.

After they reported this case to me, I first decided to check whether it was Guan Yuejie alone who visited the house. If another young man had the key to this apartment, we couldn't conclude that it was Guan Yuejie who procured women. It took them a month or so to establish that Guan Yuejie was indeed the only one who went to that apartment, which had been purchased by him with the ID card of his uncle, who actually never went there. I went to report this to Secretary Ouyang Wantong, asking whether we should take action. Even if there was no need to do anything about his using prostitutes, he was probably involved in corruption since there was so much cash inside the safe.

After I finished my report, Ouyang Wantong asked me: "Is there a possibility that the cash belongs to another person, like an entrepreneur? It might not belong to Guan Yuejie. It might be merely stored in his place."

I was shocked by his question.

The secretary continued: "Taking strong measures against a civil servant will have a great negative impact on his reputation and family. We can't be too cautious about this. We had better not to do this unless we're quite sure about it."

I knew what he meant – we shouldn't take any action unless conclusive evidence had been obtained. I therefore assigned some smart and capable regulatory personnel to the audit team that was in charge of the accounts of the Finance Bureau. We eventually found that Guan Yuejie had illegally loaned 350 million yuan to a businessman named Jian Qianyan, who used the money for a period of time and then returned it to the Finance Bureau. The money in the safe was probably the interest or a kind of gift given by Jian Qianyan. We also found that Guan Yuejie was the son-in-law of our Secretary-General Qin. Guan Yuejie, who usually kept a low profile, never told anyone about his family background, so not many people knew he was Secretary-General Qin's son-in-law.

After I presented this evidence and the identity of Guan Yuejie to Secretary Wantong, he hesitated for a while and then sighed: "I haven't been on speaking terms with Secretary-General Qin, and if I should take actions against Guan Yuejie, he might think I'm taking my revenge! What a coincidence!"

Hearing that, I thought he would probably close this case. I tentatively asked him whether we should put the case aside for a while and wait for new developments.

He stared at me. "Why should we put it aside? If it involves embezzling public funds and corruption, anyone, no matter who he or she is, will be punished. Take immediate action against Guan Yuejie!"

We did it at once.

This young deputy director had thought himself mighty clever, never expecting that his secret would be brought to light and someone would dare to take measures against him. What's more, he was not worldly wise, and he was quite vulnerable in the face of interrogation. Only three days later, he broke under questioning and confessed everything. The safe in apartment 1018 was his. It was he who loaned 350 million to Jian Qianyan. The money in the safe was the so-called interest that he asked for.

A few days after we took control of Guan Yuejie, phone calls enquiring about him bombarded me from all quarters – local calls, calls from the neighbouring province and calls from Beijing, all from officials with certain positions. They all claimed to enquire about the case, but in fact they were trying to put in a good word for Guan Yuejie. I put them off by saying that it was still under investigation and there was no result yet.

When I went to Secretary Wantong's office to report this, he said: "Since he's corrupt, he must be punished according to the law. We shouldn't let him go simply because he's someone's son-in-law." As he said this to me, he asked his secretary to bring a wooden box to him. After the secretary opened the box, I saw a model of a ship made of pure gold, shining brightly with golden light.

"Where did you get this golden ship?" I asked

He smiled and said: "Last night I had a guest come to visit. She left this wooden box before she went, and she insisted that it was for me. Now I hand it to you, the secretary of the Disciplinary Committee."

I found a note inside the box that read: "Saving a life is better than building a giant ship." I went over to feel the weight of that ship, and it turned out to be 30 kilograms or so.

The case of Guan Yueji was quickly handed over to the Procuratorate. To my surprise, I received an express delivery the very next day after the case transfer. As my secretary opened the envelope, a photo of my daughter taken in front of her school gate fell out. Two deep knife cuts were left on the photo on the position of my daughter's neck. I was appalled by this and went to report it to Secretary Ouyang Wantong, who immediately asked his secretary to contact the Public Security Bureau, urging them to arrange for two plainclothes police officers to provide my daughter with 24-hour protection. He then took a courier envelope out of his desk drawer and handed it to me. I opened it, and a bullet, bright and new, dropped out.

I stared at him, stunned.

He just calmly asked me: "Are we scared of them?"

I don't want you to record what I'm going to tell you next. It's just between us. I'll dictate, and you listen. Don't put it into any book or written material. If you do, I'll deny that I ever said it. Understand?

20

YIN QINGQING

THE FORMER YU OPERA ACTRESS

I KNEW someone would come to me sooner or later for the so-called story about Governor Wantong and me. And sure enough, you're here now. You're not from the Disciplinary Committee? I thought you were sent by them to do this investigation. Tell you what I know? Of course, I will. Who am I afraid of?

When I met Governor Wantong, he wasn't the governor yet. He was the mayor of Tianquan city. And I was not working at the Provincial Theatre Research Institute – I was studying at Tianquan Traditional Opera School. You know, students of Tianquan Traditional Opera School would always figure out some ways to earn a little money at the weekends. Some would perform on the stage in a merchant house, some would do some opera singing in bars, and some would go to teahouses where guests would pick performers to sing for them. As for me, whenever the weekends came, I would go to sing for guests in Wuquan Teahouse in Huaiyin Street with some of my female classmates. You know, at that time, I was not as good a singer as I am now, but I had a good voice and had been praised by my teachers many times. So in Wuquan Teahouse, a lot of guests would pick me to sing for them. In that small teahouse, I was sort of famous.

I remember it was on a Saturday night. Together with several female classmates, I went to sing in Wuquan Teahouse again. At first, we took turns to sing scenes from an opera, and then we waited for the teahouse guests to make their orders. At that time, my attention was directed towards a table on the side of the stage, where a middle-aged man in a jacket was sipping tea quietly with two young men, a sharp contrast with the other guests who were talking very loudly. The middle-aged man looked familiar to me – I had thought I had seen him before, but his name just slipped my memory. As I was thinking it over, the order of the guests came, and I was asked to sing an episode of the Yu opera *Hua Mulan*. The moment I opened my mouth and began to sing on the stage, there was a burst of applause. And then one order after another came to me. Of course, I was more enthusiastic when I performed on the stage because the guests would pay 30 yuan for each order and I would get 10 yuan of that. The more I sang, the more I would earn.

While we were singing happily in the teahouse, six or seven young men rushed in, swearing and reeking of alcohol. They stumbled along and sat down at a tea table. One of them shouted: "Where's Yin Qingqing? We want her to sing a scene from the Huangmei opera *Fairy Couple* – 'The Husband and Wife Return Home Together'"

I was startled. What bad luck! I had never learned how to sing a Huangmei opera. You know, I majored in Yu opera at school and studied some Shaoxing opera and Quju opera. If guests wanted to listen to any of them, I could handle it, but as for this foreign opera, I was no good at all. I hurriedly asked Miss Liu, who was responsible for guest orders, to explain to them that I couldn't sing Huangmei opera well, to apologise to them for me and ask them to order something else. But when Miss Liu took the microphone and explained this on the stage, those young guys yelled and insisted on my singing 'The Husband and Wife Return Home Together'. I had no choice but to force myself to sing for them. It wasn't something I was good at, and it was inevitable that there would be some flaws in my performance. Before I even finished, one of them staggered on the stage, grabbed the microphone from me, put his arm around my wrist and said: "Come on my pretty sister, let me teach you how to sing Huangmei opera!" Never had I experienced this before! I was so scared that I didn't know what to do. I just stood there like a fool while that man was groping me and howling the lyric: "A pair of birds singing in the tree..."

"Hey, that's no way to behave, is it?" At that moment, the middle-aged man with whom I felt familiar stood up from his seat beside the stage to come to my rescue.

"Why the fuck are you butting in?" The young man who offered to teach me how to sing Huangmei opera was annoyed. He waved his hand to his friends and yelled: "Bring that meddlesome fool here! Let me teach him how to behave since he asks for it!" With a roar, his gang sprang up and rushed towards the middle-aged man. My heart flew into my mouth. It seemed he was going to suffer! They were just a gang of hooligans who were looking for trouble.

"Who dares to move?" A young man sitting beside the middle-aged man suddenly jumped onto the tea table and shouted: "I'm Jiang Zhaodong, the deputy director of the Municipal Public Security Bureau!" He showed his police ID card and continued: "This is our mayor, Ouyang Wantong!"

The troublemakers were stunned to hear this, while the other guests who were about to run out of the teahouse all stopped to see what would happen next.

"Hurry up and run!" The man on the stage who had his arm around my waist threw the microphone down and retreated in panic. But as he ran to the door of the teahouse, policemen with guns arrived. They stormed into the tea house, efficiently overpowered those hooligans and took them away.

"I'm sorry. I have failed to maintain law and order in our society and disturbed everyone here." With that line, Mayor Wantong stood up and bowed to all the guests packed full in the tea house.

That was the first time I met him. Before that, I had just seen him on TV, quite often, which was the reason why I felt him familiar.

The next time I saw him, I had already joined the municipal Yu opera troupe. I remember our troupe was rehearsing a new historical drama in which I played a supporting role, a bullied young daughter-in-law. On the night when the city leaders were coming to review the show, I arrived early and did my make-up backstage. Lao Tong, the suona player, came over to chat happily with us. At that moment, the sound of the suona rang out suddenly from the direction of the orchestra pit, playing *A Hundred Birds Worshipping the Phoenix*. It was very pleasant to the ears and sounded professional.

Lao Tong was very surprised and shouted: "Who is he? How dare he touch my suona?" As he said this, he turned around and ran to the orchestra pit. We young actors were curious too and followed him to have a look.

When we arrived there, Lao Tong was scolding a middle-aged man: "How could you play my suona without my permission? Don't you know how to behave?"

The man hurriedly apologised: "Yes, yes, I'm very sorry. I just wanted to know whether I could still remember how to play suona..."

After I took a close look, I was surprised to find it was the mayor, Ouyang Wantong! I stopped Lao Tong immediately and introduced them to each other. That night, after the performance was over, Mayor Wantong came over especially to shake hands with Lao Tong and me before saying goodbye. Lao Tong smiled and said: "Please forgive me, Mayor. Whenever you want to play the suona, come to our troupe, and we can play together!"

After the first two encounters with him, I felt there was a connection between Mayor Wantong and me, so whenever I heard some good news about him, my heart would be filled with joy for no reason.

In spring the next year, a modern rural drama, for which I had the leading role, was going to be performed on the stage after the rehearsals had been completed. The entrepreneur who sponsored the show was lecherous. He invited me to dinner and then asked me to come to his hotel room. The moment I entered his room, he started pawing me. Of course, I refused and told him that I was an actress, not a prostitute! But he replied solemnly: "The reason I'm sponsoring this show is to get you. If you don't listen to me, I'll immediately withdraw my investment!"

I ran out of the room angrily with the words: "As you please!"

I went home and cried the whole night. You know, it was very difficult to make a living singing opera, and the good old days when a troupe could survive by selling tickets at the box office were gone. You had to humbly look for a sponsor in order to stage a new drama. You were blessed when you met a kind sponsor, but you had to accept your bad luck when encountering those who harboured evil intentions.

The show was abruptly cancelled, and the people in the troupe wanted to know why. Lao Tong was worried about me after he discovered the reason, and he thought of an idea. He said: "I remember you're familiar with Mayor Wantong. What about asking him to do you a favour by having a word with the leaders of the Cultural Affairs Bureau. I heard they have some funding for developing local dramas. What if they could give you some help?"

I had no other choice but to try my luck. It would not be a big deal if he paid no attention to me. After all, how could it have turned out any worse? Determined, I went to the reception office of the municipal government asking to see Mayor Wantong. I also told them I knew him. The receptionist knew I was a well-known actress from the municipal Yu opera troupe, so he didn't drive me away. Instead, he told me he could make a phone call for me to Mayor Wantong's secretary to see if the mayor had time to see me. Shortly after the phone call, Mayor Wantong's secretary came and led me to his office.

I knew his time was precious, so I got straight to the point the moment I entered his office. As I spoke to Mayor Wantong, I couldn't help shedding tears when I thought of all the wrongs I had suffered at the hands of that entrepreneur. He smiled as he handed me some tissue and said: "Why are you crying over such a small difficulty? Let's work it out together!"

Two days later, the director of the Municipal Cultural Bureau came to see the rehearsal of our play. And the day after that, they agreed to fully fund it! When the play was presented on the stage, it was greatly welcomed by the audience, and the critics praised it highly too. I became famous overnight! All the media rushed to interview me. Photos of me on the stage appeared in the newspapers. Parts of my performance were broadcast on municipal and provincial TV stations. I was a success.

The first person I wanted to thank was Mayor Wantong. The last time I went to ask for his help, I ventured to ask for his office number, so this time I called him directly, telling him that I wanted to visit him after supper. It took him quite a while to remember who I was when he received the phone call. He hesitated when he realised who I was, and he told me he had a meeting to attend at night. I could tell he was simply looking for an excuse to refuse me, so I told him straightforwardly: "Mayor Wantong, I just want to express my gratitude in person, nothing else. I need at most five minutes, which won't inconvenience you!"

Hearing this, he had no choice but to agree. "All right, would you please wait for me at the entrance of Bixi Restaurant at 7.30pm? I got an official reception banquet in that restaurant, and I guess it will be over at that time."

I replied joyously: "Great, see you there then."

I brought him a jacket and a tie as a gift. Of course, I myself got dressed up before I left. You know, Mayor Wantong was my benefactor and my guardian angel. I had to make a good impression on him."

That evening, I stood in front of Bixi Restaurant, holding a bag. I knew I was a bit noticeable standing there, so I wore sunglasses and a hat. It was already late spring and a bit hot.

At 7.30pm, Mayor Wantong's secretary walked towards me and said: "The mayor has finished the banquet. Please come with me."

After thanking him, I followed him to the restaurant happily. I was only pleased because I could immediately express my gratitude to the mayor in person – I didn't have anything else on my mind.

It was the first time I had been to the Bixi Restaurant. Following his secretary inside the labyrinth-like building, we finally arrived at a room full of sofas, where the luxurious furniture and the blazing lights made me feel a little stressed. I was a little relieved to see that Mayor Wantong was the only one in the room.

He greeted me as soon as he saw me: "How are you, Yin Qingqing?" As I hurriedly reached out to shake his hand, I could smell alcohol on his body. He probably noticed me sniffing because he then said with a smile: "I'm sorry. I drank some wine tonight because of this official reception banquet."

I shook my head immediately. "It's okay. Yes, indeed. My father and my elder brother both like drinking wine. As for me, I've long been used to its smell." I knew his time was very precious, so I took out the gifts I had prepared from the bag and said: "Mayor Wantong, you've helped me a couple of times, and I'm very touched by that. In order to show my sincere gratitude, I brought you a humble gift. Please try this on to see whether it fits you."

He seemed to be a little surprised by my gift. He waved his hand at once and said: "No, no, thank you, but I have clothes. Please take it back for your father or your elder brother."

I was a bit anxious when I saw him react like this. At that time, his secretary had already gone and closed the door, so we were the only people in the room. I therefore summoned my courage and said to him directly and with a touch of playfulness: "Try it on. I've run around to several shopping malls and eventually chose this according to your height and weight. How could you not accept it?"

As I said this to him, I tried to hold his arms and pull him up from the sofa. He probably didn't expect me to be so stubborn, and it would have been impolite for him to pull a long face in front of me, so he finally said:

"All right, all right, I'll try it on. If it doesn't fit, you must take it back, okay?"

Seeing that he was going to get up from the sofa, I tried to help him up. The wine must have been taking effect, and he suddenly fell to the side of the sofa. I didn't expect this at all, so I lost my balance and fell on top of him. He collapsed on the sofa, and I was in his arms. Both of us were only wearing a shirt and a thin jacket, and we were somewhat shocked when our bodies came into contact. For a brief moment, neither of us dared move, and that sensation of physical contact quickly passed right into my heart. I was a little panicked, wanting to stand up at once, but as I tried with all my strength to rise, his arms went around my body.

I was 21 years old that year. I sang dramas about love between young men and women. I'd been in love, so I of course knew what he meant by doing this. I couldn't move anymore, and I knew his bold behaviour meant that he was fond of me. This brought me no feelings of discomfort or humiliation, but rather a kind of joy and pride in my heart. A famous mayor could be fond of me, an unknown actress! Could it mean that I would have a real backing from now on? I wouldn't need to be so careful around the head of our troupe. Thinking of this, I softened my body, snuggled deeply into his arms, found his lips with mine and offered him a long kiss. This was like throwing a match into a petrol can, and it set him on fire immediately. I didn't need to do anything else. He kissed my face and my neck like crazy, murmuring hot words and touching my body wildly with his hands. I only needed to encourage him to keep going.

Things were about to move to the next stage, and he was thinking about unbuttoning my shirt. I regretted having opened my mouth at that time: "Mayor Wantong, let me do this."

This woke him up and he stopped at once, staring at me in great surprise as if he had woken up from a dream. He was flustered and whispered to himself: "Oh dear! How could this happen? It's terrible, really terrible!" He then looked up at me and apologised to me eagerly in a low voice: "I'm awfully sorry! I shouldn't have offended you. I was out of my mind. Please forgive me!"

I smiled at him coquettishly and began to unbutton my blouse. You know, I was willing to please him, and I really hoped I could satisfy his desire. I saw the eagerness in his eyes just now, and I was sure I was right. I knew he liked me and wanted me. At that moment, to my surprise, he said to me urgently: "Leave, Qingqing, Go and leave here quickly!" He then stood up and shouted towards the door: "Secretary Hong!"

Scared, I hastily buttoned my blouse. I looked at him in panic, not knowing why he had suddenly changed his mind. Was it because it wasn't a proper place to do that?

Secretary Hong came in upon his order. Mayor Wantong said to him: "Please show Xiao Yin out."

I gave him a look full of regret and then followed Secretary Hong to the door.

That was my first intimate contact with him.

That very night and the next day, I was consumed by a wealth of joy and sweetness. A mayor who was in charge of a big city of tens of millions of people could have feelings for me and utter so many wonderful words to me. That was incredible! Since that day when I saw him again on TV, I would particularly feel close, excited and proud. At that time, I desperately wanted to share my experiences and my happiness with my girlfriends, but I instinctively knew that I couldn't. It had to be kept a secret – otherwise, it would have brought him trouble.

After that day I waited for his phone call. I firmly believed he would call me and want to see me because I had seen the intoxication he had when he hugged and kissed me and the lust for my body in his eyes. I firmly believed it was the beginning of an intimate relationship and we had a long future together.

But the days dragged on, and there was no call from him.

I was a little anxious and decided to take the initiative to call him. Since he was embarrassed to make the first move, I needed to be active. Was there any need for me to maintain a so-called reserved manner? Since it was something I wanted to do, since he was the person I truly liked, I should be decisive, and I shouldn't hesitate. I called him from a public phone booth. When it was connected, I said: "Hello, Mayor Wantong, it's me."

I had thought he might not recognise my voice immediately, but he actually did. He whispered into the phone: "Qingqing, I'm sorry. I've been too busy to contact you. Is there anything I can do for you?"

"No – I just want to see you. I miss you!"

He continued with a lower voice: "Qingqing, I was totally out of my mind last time we met. I'm really sorry about that. From now on, try your best to perform on the stage and be an excellent actress. Make your contributions to local drama. If you need my help, you can call me any time you want, and I'll do my best for you. But there's no need for us to see each other. You know, I'm worried I won't be able to control myself when I see you. It would definitely do harm to your life. You're so pretty, so young and there must be quite a lot of young men who are chasing after you. Don't hesitate to make up your mind when you meet someone suitable. I want you to live happily and wish you happiness."

I understood what he meant but I thought it was just his embarrassment to ask me and he was waiting for me to take the initiative. Was there anything I should be afraid of? I really liked this man, and I couldn't afford to lose this chance. I should be more direct and clear. "Mayor Wantong, I truly appreciate you and miss you very much. I'm living in a rented apartment. The address is Room 206, Unit 1, Building 27, Fanli Road. I hope to see you there. You can come any time tonight, and I'm sure you won't be disappointed. It will not cause you any trouble, and there won't be any danger."

I heard very clearly on the phone that he took a deep breath and then a long sigh. Then silence. He eventually said in a trembling voice: "Xiao Yin, it's getting cold. Take care! Goodbye!"

I feared he would put down the phone and that he hadn't understood what I meant, so I whimpered back: "Didn't you understand me?"

"I understand!"

"You don't want me, do you?"

"Yes, I want you."

"Then why don't you..."

"I'm afraid I'll ruin you."

"I'm not afraid of ruin. I'm just an unknown actress, so what is there to ruin?"

"It will ruin your life. Probably your entire life. That is too much for me. I'll feel guilty forever. It's best for us to stop right now. I'm older than you, and I know how serious it will turn out to be. I have to control myself."

"I'm not afraid. Even if it should ruin my life, I'll embrace it!"

"It will ruin me too. I still have a lot of things to do."

His last words filled me with fear. You know, I didn't want to ruin him. I would never do that. I called him because I wanted to make him happy, but since it would ruin him, there was no reason for me to persist. I should stop! In the end, I put down the phone.

After that, we didn't have any contact with each other. Even if there would be a chance for us to see each other – for example, if he should come to see our play – I would avoid meeting him. I was afraid of losing control of my feelings in front of him.

That is the real story between him and me.

You know, I even thought about forcing him to begin an intimate relationship with me, but after repeated consideration, I eventually gave it up.

I thought about him for a long time after this. You know, he has always occupied a special place in my heart, even when I began to accept Jian Qianyan's pursuit of me.

Yes, Jian Qianyan. Do you know him? He was a well-known entrepreneur in Tianquan city. A celebrity too. He later went to the provincial capital to develop his business. When he was in Tianquan, he loved to listen to Yu opera and came to see our show in the theatre quite often. I don't know whether it was the role I played in the show or my good looks that attracted him, but he began to look for chances to get close to me. At first, he would send flowers before the show. Then he would find all kinds of reasons to invite me to dinner. At that time, I was still caught up in my deep feelings for Ouyang Wantong, so I often gave him the cold shoulder. The head of our troupe said he wanted me to be polite to Jian Qianyan. He told me this man was rich, loved local operas and was willing to sponsor local artists, which might benefit our troupe in the future. After the talk, I started to accept his invitations.

I still remember the first time when we had dinner together. He was so cautious because he didn't want to offend me. I asked him directly on that day why he invited me to dinner, and he answered with a flattering smile: "Because you're the artist I like!" His words made me feel so comfortable that I no longer had an aversion to him.

He began to send me gifts after we had a few meals together – all kinds of gifts like cosmetics, clothes, jewellery, shoes and handbags. And I had to admit he was a very generous man. The more gifts I accepted from him, the more ashamed I would feel to reject his requests. For example, he would invite me to his company to sing for his employees during festivals, or to banquets to sing for his business associates.

After we spent more time with each other and became more familiar, he put forward another request. Of course, he mentioned it quite indirectly. He said he wanted me to accompany him to Beijing for a few days. I knew what he meant. I smiled and asked him what he planned to do there.

He responded brazenly: "Honestly, since I saw you on the stage for the first time, I've had a crush on you. I've totally fallen for you! You know, there has never been a woman who could fascinate me like you do. I love everything about you – your eyebrows, your eyes, your cheeks, your hair, your neck, your shoulders, your breasts, your legs and your feet. All of the simplest acts you make – laughs and sighs – have pulled my heartstrings. I swear to myself that I'll make you my woman. Now it's time. Let's go to Beijing, you and me. We can book a big suite in a five-star hotel and have some fun! You can decide everything! I'll give you 200,000 yuan daily in Beijing."

I told him straightforwardly on that day that I didn't want to go to Beijing with him – not because he didn't give me enough money, or because I didn't like him, but because there was someone else in my heart already, and when I managed to drive that man away I would go with him.

He was surprised and asked: "Who is the man? Will you let me help you to drive him away?" I smiled and didn't reply.

Nowadays, there's a view in society that we actors, news anchors and directors are sexually promiscuous and find it difficult to control our emotions. I think this is a lazy generalisation that's based on prejudice. In fact, many of us take relationships very seriously and never play around. That goes for me. At the very beginning, I just felt a bit grateful to Mayor Wantong. But after he expressed his affection for me, it was so hard for me to forget him.

It was more than a month after I rejected Jian Qianyan that he asked me out again. I remember we met in a private room in a restaurant. The moment he saw me he said: "I know who the man is that lives in your heart!"

Curling my lips, I said to myself: "Who do you think you are? Go on bragging! How could you find my secret?"

"Don't curl your lips!" he said solemnly as he took out an article from *Tianquan Daily*. Pointing at a photo of Ouyang Wantong inspecting a factory, he asked: "It's him, right?"

I was shocked that he could be so damn right! The only person who knew about the intimate contact between Ouyang Wantong and me was his secretary. All of my other encounters with Ouyang Wantong were work-related, and no one could find fault with those. And since my last intimate contact with him, I had never seen him again. How could Jian Qianyan guess it right?

"I'm right, aren't I? You might know very little about my abilities. In Tianquan or in the provincial capital or even throughout the whole province, I can get any information I want. I can do anything I want!"

"Where did you hear that?" At that time, I hadn't learned how to cover things up or say no in front of the truth. My question was an admission that he was right.

"It's a secret!" he smiled slyly. "There is a rule for all the intelligence agencies in this world – the source of the intelligence must be kept secret because it involves the security of the informant."

"So you know about it. What's the big deal?"

"Since I know who he is, I can help you drive him out of your heart!" He spoke with a serious tone.

"Go on bragging!" I smiled disdainfully. "I'm the only person who can drive him out of my heart!"

"I can be a very good helper! Come on – drink up." He poured me a glass of French Lafite from his own collection and handed it to me. I clinked his glass without any emotion.

After that day I put everything Jian Qianyan said behind me. I was occupied with my rehearsing and acting and at the same time was hopeful that maybe one day Mayor Wantong would want to see me and call me back. I couldn't forget his warm embrace and burning words that night, and I didn't believe he would completely forget me. I was confident that my youth and beauty would be irresistible for him. But the phone call never came. Instead, I received an express mail from Jian Qianyan. Inside the envelope was a photo of Ouyang Wantong and me. We were both naked, and he was holding me in his arms. At first, I was shocked, but then I came to understand it was a computer-generated photo with our heads superimposed! I was so angry that I wanted to call him immediately to swear at him, but then I worried that he might put it online if I annoyed him. That would be big news, and even if I could clarify it later, it would still go viral, and people would think there was no smoke without fire. Who would listen to my explanation then?

It was also impossible for me to explain to everyone!

It would indeed ruin Ouyang Wantong's future.

As long as the photo was online, no one would believe there was nothing between Ouyang Wantong and me. You know, this is an age when people have no belief in the innocence between men and women.

What should I do?

This fake photo paralysed me with shock and fear. Sitting in my room, I began to realise that Jian Qianyan was not an honest businessman but a scoundrel who operated like a triad. For such a person, it's necessary to use unconventional methods.

I came up with a plan. Before I carried it out, I couldn't hold back my tears, and I didn't know why or for whom. I just burst into tears. It was on that tearful night that Jian Qianyan came to knock on the door of my room by invitation. As usual, he brought me a lot of gifts. I watched him silently as he put all the gifts in place. When he came over and greeted me, I threw myself into his arms. He didn't say anything at first but just held me tightly. Then he said with complacency: "I finally defeated Ouyang Wantong!"

I allowed him to stroke my back and move his hands to the other parts of my body. I let him pick me up, walk into the bedroom, place me on the bed and untie my clothes. Just when he couldn't wait to do what he had long wanted to do, I suddenly pushed his hands away and asked him with a smile: "Tell me, are you a real businessman?"

He froze for a moment and asked: "Why do you ask me this?"

I said: "Before I dedicate myself to a man, I at least should know his true identity."

He smiled: "It's a very difficult question. What if I don't want to answer it?"

"You may go on having me, but all you'll have is a lifeless woman!"

"Well, since we're facing each other naked and you insist on knowing it, I'll tell you. I was originally an official, a minor one, a staff member of the County Finance Bureau. Once, I lost money playing mah-jong – about 70,000 yuan. The winner pressed me to give him the money. I had no choice but to secretly borrow some from public funds. Unfortunately, the higher authorities came to audit and discovered what I had done. Well, you tell me – was it really such a big deal? But they forced me out of office! I was outraged at that time! That was a fucking severe punishment! Too much! Those who often gave tens of thousands of public funds as gifts still worked in their office comfortably while I had been singled out and treated so ruthlessly. Why would they do this to me? I repeatedly made appeals to the higher authority, but no one paid any attention to me. Feeling hurt and in despair, I told myself that I would never believe in any government in this world. Damn it! I would depend on myself. I would establish a new society step by step. I would set up my own government where my words would be the sacred decree, and no one would dare to gossip or criticise, let alone punish me! Thank God, I met a man – an official in the current government – who was very capable and powerful. With his help, I soon had my own world established, an empire so to speak. There are a few companies under my name, but I don't want to be a mere businessman. You know, it's very tiring to be a businessman because you have too many things to worry about and there's no easy money. Now I can guarantee that I have enough strength to protect you. My strength is a combination of power, wealth and force. No matter what happens to you in the future, I can help you settle everything and ensure your safety and peace, and give you a wealthy and wonderful life! Do you understand?"

I answered him: "I understand. Now you have a finger in every pie!"

He smiled in triumph, then fingered my nipples and asked: "Beauty, may I start right now?"

I watched him coldly as he was busy working on my body!

He trembled all over with ecstasy!

Jian Qianyan stayed in my room that night. The next morning when he woke up, his eyes were full of contentedness. He watched me staring at the ceiling silently. "I finally drove Ouyang Wantong out of your heart!" he said.

I smiled faintly. "You've succeeded. You may leave now."

He continued with satisfaction and confidence: "Your body is so beautiful! You know, I'm experienced and knowledgeable, but I've never seen such an amazing body. Each part of it accords with a man's desire. It's perfect! It's to die for!! And you've given me such a big surprise. I never thought an actress like you could still be so conservative and save your virgin body for me! I'm so surprised, and I'm so fucking blessed. I must repay you. I'll buy you a large house so that we can be with each other regularly. From now on, you can perform in any play you choose, and I'll take care of the money issue. I'll make you happy every day. Good things will happen to you."

I listened to him calmly and smiled a little. Once he had finished, I said: "You may go now."

He left my room with much reluctance.

That very afternoon, I sent a text message to Jian Qianyan's mobile phone, telling him: "I've recorded everything that happened last night, you and me in bed and the talk between us. You're an agent of someone from the Provincial People's Congress, aren't you? How dare you make evil statements about Ouyang Wantong and me. Some of my friends will hand over the video and recordings to the Standing Committee of the Provincial People's Congress, the Provincial Public Security Department, the Ministry of Supervision and the Standing Committee of the National People's Congress. And at the same time, they'll put it online. You might as well send someone to kill me, but I can still ruin you completely after I die."

I moved on that day and withdrew from the Yu opera troupe too. I didn't perform on the stage any more. I first went to do some odd jobs in a drama school, and then I was transferred to the Provincial Theatre Research Insitute to do some administrative work. I've never seen that scoundrel Jian Qianyan again.

My aunt knew the first half of my story, but I didn't tell her what had happened next, mainly because I didn't want her to worry about me again.

After that incident, I said goodbye to my virgin life, and I would say I'm growing maturely.

That's all I can tell you. I have no children, and my present husband is understanding of my past, so I have the courage to speak out. As for how to write it into your book, you decide. But I have a small requirement – don't use my real name. After all, I still have to live on.

21

RUI LI

THE VICE PRESIDENT OF EURASIA INVESTMENT COMPANY AND THE FORMER CHIEF EDITOR OF NEO-ENLIGHTENMENT

YOU WANT me to say something about Ouyang Wantong? Well, that's intriguing! Who has asked you to do this? All right, no more on this question. To begin with, you need to know I didn't meet him very often. I didn't know much about him, and it's unlikely that I'll be able to tell you anything useful for your biography. Next, I should say he was different from the other officials I've ever met, and I kind of liked him.

When he was the secretary of the Provincial Party, I had a real encounter with him for the first time. At that time, I was still a student at Qinghe University. Young and passionate, a group of my classmates and I felt we still needed an Enlightenment in today's society, so we were determined to publish a school magazine named *Neo-Enlightenment.* We wanted to make it a place where we could share our observations and reflections, as well as enlighten our fellow students and ordinary people who should read our magazine.

I remember we published a lead article in our inaugural issue titled 'On Public Servants: Should Citizens Serve the Government or the Government Serve Citizens?' We invited a professor, who has been a visiting scholar in Europe for many years, to write this article.

He wrote that office buildings of foreign governments were all very ordinary. Most of their officials drove to work themselves. Citizens could go to government offices for consultations whenever they had any problem. Mayors in foreign countries could go to meet citizens and solve their problems without any attendants coming along. Government officials were not allowed to have any type of income aside from their salaries. Foreign officials would go back to their original work when their time in office ended.

In China, however, government buildings were competing to be the most luxurious. Officials at prefecture-levels or deputy-division-head levels all had government cars and chauffeurs. Citizens in China had to go through formalities with fear before they entered government buildings, and would most probably be scorned by the staff. Mayors in China acted like celebrities whenever they went out, surrounded by secretaries, office directors and many other subordinates, and sometimes even with police cars to clear the way. As for Chinese officials, salary was only a part of their income because most of them had grey income. Gifts from their subordinates and junior officials were very common. Chinese officials would often fix their children and relatives up with jobs before they retired and they would also enjoy lifelong benefits after retirement.

Government officials in foreign countries, administrators as they were, had to serve citizens carefully for fear that the slightest disappointment meant they would not vote for them again. Chinese officials, in contrast, were in fact masters or lords. Citizens had to serve them meticulously, and at the slightest displeasure, they would fly into a rage, yell at or even attack citizens. The purpose of forming a society and choosing government officials is to let them manage public affairs, maintain its proper function and ensure people's normal life. No one wants to elect a master or a lord to oppress him and make him a slave! Chinese officials should either choose to be honest civil servants working for the people according to the law or openly call themselves lords, no longer meekly proclaiming themselves to be civil servants.

The inaugural issue of the magazine created a great sensation when it was published. The students quickly circulated it, and it spread to the wider society after many copied versions were made. We discovered afterwards that within three days, the inaugural issue was placed on the desk of Secretary Ouyang Wantong with a note saying: "It's recommended that students stop the magazine because it's an illegal publication." Secretary Ouyang Wantong read our magazine carefully and then uttered three words to his secretary: "Wait and see."

In the second issue of *Neo-Enlightenment,* we published a long article titled 'On Citizens: Corruption and Mutual Betrayal'. In this article we listed cases of corruption in every walk of life. In the field of healthcare, there was a conspiracy among deans, doctors, nurses and pharmaceutical manufacturers to cheat patients and our country for money. In the educational field, principals and staff members, together with professors and teachers, took advantage of every means to ask for money from students and their parents. In the field of entertainment, actors, directors and agents worked together to get money from audiences and organisers. In the field of mining development, mine owners were obsessed with exploiting mineral resources crazily just for money, regardless of the safety of miners and the pollution of the environment. In the field of food production, manufacturers abused fertilisers and pesticides to increase output, while sellers mis-labelled stale food, with vegetables and fruits being coated with chemical preservatives and sold to consumers, without any consideration for people's health! As for cooked food production, the manufacturers sold meat from diseased pigs and chickens, expired braised meat marinated with bright and fresh broth, or expired steamed buns ground and then reprocessed, totally ignoring the health of the consumers! As for powdered milk, some businesses would add melamine! Did anyone care about the health of those infants who consumed milk powder every day? In the military field, training had become a show for the leaders to watch. Military exercises were just performances in which the two sides knew clearly who was going to win and who was going to lose! No one ever thought about what would happen if a real war should break out! In the academic field, fake papers and plagiarism still existed despite repeated prohibitions. Many papers without any creative ideas had been published in order to secure a professional post with no benefit for society. Even parking lot attendants would ask drivers whether they needed an invoice – if not, they could charge 10 yuan less, and create their own little income on the side.

In these circumstances, you're depraved, I'm depraved, and we're all hurting each other! We do have a lot of corrupt officials, but in fact ordinary citizens are greedy too. If we promote a hundred ordinary people to become officials, at least ninety of them will become corrupt unless the current system changes! Besides GDP, what else do we have at the moment?

When this issue of the magazine came out, it led to a heated debate on the campus. Opinions varied, with supporters saying we had sharp ideas, but opponents claiming we had taken a part for the whole. Because of this debate, people rushed to buy our magazine, and we had to do another print run. Later, we got the news that on the day after its publication, the magazine had again been placed on the desk of Secretary Ouyang Wantong with a note saying: "It is recommended this magazine be banned because it might cause adverse effects in society." It was said that Secretary Wantong fell silent for quite a long time after he read through this issue, and then he said to his secretary again: "Wait and see."

In our third issue, we published a long article titled 'On Fair Play: When Will We Stop Competing for Jobs Based on Our Family Backgrounds?' This article depicted situations in which young Chinese people were competing for employment. Children of cadres at or above the provincial level didn't have to worry because their parents had already arranged everything for them. If working in officialdom, they at least could be officials at bureau-director level, and if in business, they would either be leaders of state-owned enterprises or have their own companies, usually with the support of foreign investment. As for officials at the bureau-director level, their children didn't need to find their jobs either. Working in government offices, they could at least be cadres at the division-head level, while in business, they all could establish their own companies with the support of state-owned and private companies. For children of cadres at division-head level, they were guaranteed jobs at section-head level of officialdom. If in business, it wouldn't be a problem for them to make money with the help of their fathers' friends in the political field. Children of ordinary civil servants and ordinary people had to pass various exams to compete for posts using their skills. Among those people, if the father was a headmaster, the child would most likely become a teacher, if the father was a police officer, the child would probably end up the same, and this rule applied to almost all walks of life – judges, procurators, doctors and lawyers. Only a small number of good jobs were left for the children of ordinary families to compete for – that is to say, there was in fact no real difference between feudal hereditary and today's employment. Fairness had never been realised at all.

Later, we heard that Secretary Wantong paced up and down in his office for quite a long time after he finished reading this long article. He still made no comment.

In the fourth issue, we published a long interview with an agricultural scientist titled 'On Public Risk: Food Crisis in China'. In this, we made this scientist's deep concerns known to the public. He said China was facing many crises in relation to areas such as faith, economics and territory, but as long as we could maintain the stability of the military and our people could have food to eat, we would always find ways to overcome them. However, the food crisis was an exception. If people had nothing to eat, there was a real danger that nationwide disorder would ensue!

He said rice, flour and oil were all available in Chinese supermarkets in China, giving the impression of affluence, but in fact our food self-sufficiency rate was only 80 per cent, with the rest depending on imports. Eighty per cent of our oil was processed with imported raw materials, and in some years the import of soybeans could reach 60 million tons, which equated to more than a hundred pounds per person. We didn't set aside grain reserves, and everyone was eating fresh grains. The national grain depot had about one year's stock, but the grain production cycle is one year, so if war broke out, would we have the ability to cope? Would foreign countries sell to us on time? The US National Intelligence Council has predicted that China will have a serious food shortage by the year 2030.

The scientist also said that farmers used to select and save grain seed themselves, which was quite safe for the next year's crop. Nowadays, however, seed companies sold seeds to farmers, which could only be planted for one season and couldn't be saved for the next year! What if the seeds provided by the seed company failed to grow in a certain year? What would we do? That was not impossible because more than half of our seed companies are controlled by foreign capital. The biggest issue was that farmers' enthusiasm for growing crops was gone. Honest farming didn't make them rich. Some of them even found it difficult to survive. The price of one kilogram of rice was one yuan and twenty cents to one yuan and forty cents, plus the expenditure on fertiliser, pesticide, seeds and the hire of agricultural machinery. What could an acre of land provide for a farmer after a year of his hard work? Farmers were subjected to exploitation by everyone. So who wanted to be a farmer then? Also, there was a growing problem of water shortage. At that time, there were about 4.05 million hectares of land in China that had been irrigated with wastewater, and this had a huge impact on the output and quality of crops.

The fifth issue of *Neo-Enlightenment* contained an article about mass demonstrations in China. It was titled 'On Public Resentment: How Can We Express Our Protests?'

The next morning after this issue came out, I was told to go to the office of the Propaganda Department of the School Party Committee where someone wanted to have a talk with me about our magazine. Some of my fellow editors predicted that they were going to take action on *Neo-Enlightenment* and that they were probably going to ban it. They advised me to reason with them! If that didn't work, we would resort to street protests. I then marched towards the Propaganda Department.

Full of anger, I entered the office and saw a middle-aged man sitting at the table, drinking tea, alone. I wasn't facing a house of accusers, nor did I see that arrogant propaganda minister. It was far from what I had expected! The middle-aged man saw me in, smiled and said: "You must be Rui Li, the chief editor. Sit down please."

I sat down with a sense of urgency and waited for him to speak. You know, I didn't recognise him at that time because I was focused on formulating the right words to refute him. If he started criticising our magazine, I would fight back immediately. To my surprise, he handed me a cup of tea and then said with a smile: "Your magazine is very good!"

I froze there, not knowing what to say.

"Young as you are, you have the ability to look at the issues from a very sharp and accurate perspective! I like it very much."

All of the words I had prepared to refute him were useless. I could only fake a cough at that moment.

"I have a suggestion, and I don't know whether you're willing to accept," he said with a smile.

"What is it?" I answered automatically.

"Your editorial department works for the Municipal Party Committee as a think tank!"

"A think tank of the Municipal Party Committee? How could you have the right to do this? Who are you? You want to write a beautiful blank check for us?"

"I'm the secretary of the Municipal Party Committee, Ouyang Wantong. I have the power."

"What?" I stood up in surprise. I had never imagined the man who was talking with me was the most senior governor of this city.

"Though we do have a few think tanks now, we're short of young people, and we need youthful passion. If you agree, *Neo-Enlightenment* will be the internal reference for the Municipal Party Committee so that I can read your magazine at any time."

"Wait a minute. You mean you want to buy us?"

"Don't use the word 'buy'! It fails to describe the actual relationship between us. You and I both want to make the government and society better. We're like-minded people on the same road. Of course, my proposal might be too abrupt, and I should give you enough time to think about it. How about giving me your reply within three days?"

I could only nod my head. This conversation was completely beyond our expectations, and I was in a somewhat passive situation.

After I went back to the editorial department and told everyone about the conversation between Secretary Wantong and me, the whole room fell into silence – probably because it was such a complete surprise. We discussed it in our spare time after class the following two days, and eventually we reached an agreement after repeated debates on the two points. First, the purpose of *Neo-Enlightenment* was not to incite people to make trouble but to focus on the improvement of social management and people's quality of life. Therefore, it wasn't important whether we circulated our magazine on the campus or inside the Municipal Party Committee – what really mattered was whether we could achieve our goal. Second, enlightening government officials was consistent with the purpose of our magazine because they in turn would help the general public understand how society should develop. If *Neo-Enlightenment* should become the internal reference of the Municipal Party Committee, we could more effectively achieve our desire to enlighten government officials.

We finally made our decision that the editorial department of *Neo-Enlightenment* would become the think tank and internal reference of the Municipal Party Committee. I was later elected as the representative to go to see Ouyang Wantong.

I remember it was on a morning I went to the Municipal Party Committee with the newly published sixth issue of *Neo-Enlightenment*. Ouyang Wantong was waiting for me in the small conference room as we had arranged. I told him we agreed to make *Neo-Enlightenment* an internal reference of the Municipal Party Committee, and the editorial department was willing to be its think tank.

He smiled after I finished and said: "Thank you, Rui Li. When I see you, I think of my college days. At that time, I was hot-blooded like you, and I wanted to change society and the world. It's truly good to be young, full of aspiration and ambition, with no worries or burdens."

On that day, he also said: "I discovered something delightful from your series of articles – that is, young as you are, dissatisfied with reality as you are, and passionate and ambitious to reform society as you are, you don't promote radical extreme practices. I really appreciate that. Nowadays, radicalism has emerged in many regions and countries. Its believers advocate the use of extreme means to put their ideas of reforming society into practice. Whoever disagrees will be eliminated. Believers of this radicalism not only suppress their opponents mentally but also destroy them physically. They will eventually travel on the road of terrorism and be abandoned by their former followers and the whole society. We all want to reform our society by political means to make it more suitable for human beings to live in and to enable it to bring benefits to mankind. But at the same time, we should keep in mind that compromise is needed in politics. Any radical politics without any compromise can never reform a society. Instead, it often does damage to the society."

I thought there was some truth in his words.

When I bid farewell to him on that day, he said: "The Municipal Party Committee will fund *Neo-Enlightenment* 30,000 yuan for each issue starting from the next one. You don't need to worry about the budget anymore, so you can expend all your energy on the content and make it the best it can be."

I was full of joy when I left his office. I thought I had done a great thing for me, my classmates and my peers. To my great surprise, on that very night, news spread on the campus that I had been bought by the government, and the next day some students called me "Song Jiang", implying that I had accepted an amnesty offered by the government! I was so angry that I didn't eat anything for a whole day and my enthusiasm for the publication of *Neo-Enlightenment* waned. Turning it over in my mind, I decided to quit the editorial department of *Neo-Enlightenment* to show my innocence. As for how the magazine would cooperate with the government, I no longer cared. Though the editorial department continually asked me to go back, I had been deeply hurt by those who had misunderstood me. From then on, I didn't join them in any editing work of *Neo-Enlightenment,* and there was nothing between that magazine and me after that. To prove that I had not been bought by anyone, I didn't work as an official in any provincial or municipal department after graduation. Instead, I set up my own company.

After I entered the business world, I thought I wouldn't cross paths with Ouyang Wantong again because the world we were living in was so big and my social circle was so small. I could never have expected that I would get to know his stepdaughter Chang Xiaoxiao and have a romantic relationship with her later.

I met her totally by chance. One day, I went to visit Professor Ren Yiming at Qinghe University to ask him about some investment issues. After I finished talking with Professor Ren and left his house, a very beautiful and elegant girl came towards me, asking whether Professor Ren lived in this building. I nodded and turned to point at Professor Ren's unit and floor. She thanked me with a brilliant smile and walked into the building while I just couldn't move. Her beauty impressed me so deeply that my heart was seized by it suddenly. I couldn't move my eyes from her as she walked into the building and entered the elevator. Then I turned around to look for my car. Sitting in my car, I didn't start it at once. I sort of lost my mind. All that I could see was her smiling face, and her beauty hit me like a flash of lightning. To be honest, when I was in college and when I went into business later, I saw many beautiful women, but it was the first time for me to meet such a pure and pretty girl. My heartbeat lost its rhythm, and I had a feeling of attraction that I had never had before. My instinct told me she was the woman I had been looking for.

Opportunities can be lost in the blink of an eye, can't they?

I couldn't let her disappear. I had to do something.

I decided to wait for her in the car. I would just wait until she came out. I had to speak with her to find out who she was and where she lived. I would try to get her contact information. I couldn't let myself regret. You can't hesitate when you're chasing after a woman you love. You know, too many men in this world are better than you and more competitive than you, but you should never let them take her away from you.

I had been waiting for almost an hour and a half when that gorgeous girl came out. Seeing her coming out of the elevator and walking to my side, I quickly started my car and drove to meet her. I asked: "Did Professor Ren come downstairs?"

When she recognised it was me who had just shown her the way, she gave me another brilliant smile: "No."

"Oh," I pretended to talk to myself, "it seems he has cancelled today's lecture. Okay, I'm leaving since he doesn't need the car." I pretended to put the car into the drive gear and then asked her: "Where are you going? Would you like a ride?"

She shook her head: "No, thanks. I'm going to Changda Street. You couldn't be going the same way, could you?"

I smiled: "What a coincidence! It's on my way! If you don't mind sitting in my cheap car, please get in."

She smiled gracefully, stretched out to pull the door open and got in. "I can't refuse a free ride! Thank you!"

After the car started, I began to explore ways to find out her name and her career. "You must be a performance major at the Art Department in Qinghe University."

She looked down at her clothes in surprise and replied: "You think I'm a student of performance?"

"Such a beautiful girl like you! Wouldn't it be a waste if you didn't study performance?"

She smiled shyly: "Thank you for your compliment! I study finance, and I just graduated this year."

"Really? Then I need to have a word with my friend, the vice president of the Provincial People's Bank and ask him to hire you immediately. Otherwise, the other foreign banks are sure to poach you and my friend will have a formidable opponent!"

She giggled: "You're funny! I've already been hired by the Provincial Industrial and Commercial Bank, but thank you for your kindness!"

"Have you?" I laughed as well. Now I knew where she worked. The next thing was her name.

"Do you want to guess what I do for a living?"

"That's too hard. I give up." She shook her head.

"I have an investment company. You know, I often go to your bank, and it's so good for me to know you. From now on, whenever I go there, I won't behave like a headless chicken. I can consult you directly about anything I don't understand. I finally have an acquaintance there!"

"You're very welcome! I'm willing to help you whenever I can," she said with her hands raised.

"Great! Could I have your contact information?"

She gave a slight hesitation and then agreed.

My heart immediately sang with joy. Fearing she might change her mind, I hurriedly pull over my car on the side road, took out a pen and a piece of paper and handed it to her. Then I knew she was called Chang Xiaoxiao. But at that time I didn't identify her with Ouyang Wantong. I didn't know she was the stepdaughter of our governor!

After that, I began to pursue her tirelessly. In the beginning, I invited her for a cup of tea under the excuse of consulting on investment. Then I asked her out for dinner to thank her for her advice. Then I invited her to travel to inspect the environment of an investment site. And then I found any excuse to send her flowers, clothes and jewellery until she fell for me and threw herself into my arms voluntarily.

You don't have a problem with what I just said, do you? You won't mistake me for a playboy?

After we dated for nearly a year or so, she at last invited me to meet her parents. You know, she never talked about her family in the past, and I didn't ask her either. I had thought her parents might be university professors, so I was quite surprised when I went to her family and found she lived in the provincial residential area.

I teased her, saying: "You're not going to make me a son-in-law of an official, are you?"

She smiled and said: "I can't tell yet."

When I entered the house and saw Governor Ouyang Wantong, I was shocked. He recognised me as well and shouted in surprise: "Hey, I never thought you were going to be our son-in-law! What a coincidence!"

I was shocked speechless for a moment.

My goodness! Who did this? Is it the will of God?

The next day after I met her parents, I asked Xiaoxiao what they thought about me, and she told me they were both very satisfied. She added that her father wanted her to explain one thing to me in particular – that is, the current situation her family was in probably wouldn't last long, so I had to be mentally prepared for it.

I didn't understand what he meant at that time. I remember I asked her what her father was trying to say but she shook her head and said: "I don't know either. He just wanted me to tell you this."

Two months later, I had a wedding ceremony with Xiaoxiao. According to the wishes of Governor Ouyang Wantong, we didn't invite any guests except her parents and mine, including Xiaoxiao's biological father, who sat on the other side of her mother.

Her biological father worked as a cleaner in a factory after having been released from prison. He was not in a good physical or mental state. He coughed all the time, drank wine continuously and smoked cigarettes one after another. I saw the embarrassment of Xiaoxiao and her mother. Governor Ouyang Wantong kept on talking to animate the wedding ceremony, and he carefully took care of that biological father.

On the third day after the wedding, according to custom, I brought Xiaoxiao back to her home to her mother and Governor Wantong. Governor Wantong took me to his study and said to me solemnly: "Rui Li, Xiaoxiao's mother and I are both very happy to have you as our son-in-law, and we believe you've chosen to be with each other because of true love. Before Xiaoxiao married you, her mother and I were protecting her, and now we hope you can take the responsibility for us. At the moment, our family is covered with some kind of aura, but I know it won't last long and will fade away someday, perhaps very fast. I hope you will treat Xiaoxiao the same as you did in the past after we lose that aura and turn into an ordinary family."

I didn't quite understand what he meant at that time. Was he worried that I had been attracted not by their daughter but by her family background?

A few more months passed. When I heard the news of Governor Ouyang Wantong's resignation, I suddenly understood why he had asked Xiaoxiao to tell me those words and what he truly wanted to let me know in his study.

I realised he had long been mentally prepared for his resignation. As for why he put an end to his official career himself, and why he voluntarily gave up a senior government post that everyone dreamed of, I'm not quite clear, and I'm afraid you'll have to ask someone else.

Fortunately, his resignation wasn't approved, and he remained in his post until he retired.

How did we get on with him after we married? I should say we got along very well. Xiaoxiao and I lived in the house I bought, and we usually went to visit them at the weekends – you know, family gatherings and having dinner together. When I was with him, I found he was truly busy, taking phone calls one after another and being given documents to read. He often had to stop talking with us and go back to his study to handle these matters. I could sense the pressure he was under, which was quite apparent from his voice when he answered the phone and his frowning brows when he walked out of his study. But once he sat down and chatted with us, his expression relaxed as if he had pushed all these pressures away, and he laughed very loudly too. He never criticised Xiaoxiao, let alone criticised me. Perhaps it was because he wasn't Xiaoxiao's biological father and he thought he didn't have the right to do that, or perhaps it was because he had lost the love of his own son and he intentionally changed his parenting style.

In short, Xiaoxiao and I were both quite relaxed in front of him. He talked with Xiaoxiao mostly about the financial world. With me, he talked about the business world. He told me that speaking with us was a kind of research for him.

Once, Xiaoxiao said it was an open secret in some banks that many large deposits hadn't been transferred into the bank's books. They in fact were directly loaned to developers by the bank manager, and the interest on the loan would go to the bank, which meant the country got nothing. Governor Ouyang Wantong was shocked by this. He immediately sent people to carry out an in-depth investigation and found it was true. He hurriedly reported this to some relevant departments in Beijing and got the situation under control.

On another occasion, he asked me what the current business environment was like. I told him that whenever holidays came, I had to arrange for my staff to buy a bunch of gift cards worth a thousand yuan each and then send them to the Industry and Commerce Administrative Bureau, the Local Taxation Bureau and a few local police stations. All of their staff who could exercise administrative power over my company would receive one card each – not very much, but I had to do that. I called it lubricant, without which they would find any excuse to find fault with my company and make it hard for me to do business. He was lost in silence after he listened to me. He called the General Office to conduct a special investigation on the business environment, and then issued a document to rectify the problem of civil servants taking advantage of their positions and power to set up barriers for businessmen and extort benefits from them.

I could feel he had given all his fatherly love to Xiaoxiao, the love that he was unable to let go of in his heart. In the autumn of the year we got married, Xiaoxiao became pregnant. This was not in our plan, so we agreed on an abortion. On the night before the abortion, we just couldn't resist having sex again. I know you might laugh at this, but we were young, and we couldn't control ourselves. You were young once, so you can understand, can't you? The problem at that time was that neither of us knew how to do it safely during pregnancy period. We still had wild sex as we usually did, and disaster occurred as a result. Xiaoxiao was bleeding badly after we finished! I panicked and called my mother-in-law for help with a crying voice. Surprisingly, my mother-in-law had never experienced this before and was so scared by the news that she passed out! It was Governor Ouyang Wantong who rushed to help. He called the ambulance on his way to our place and directed me to carry the unconscious Xiaoxiao downstairs. He even helped me cover the bloodstained bed with a sheet. When we arrived at the hospital, he sat in the corridor until Xiaoxiao's operation was finished and she was out of danger. He then escorted Xiaoxiao to the ward with me and didn't go back until Xiaoxiao woke up and took some egg drop soup! Dawn was breaking at that time.

In my heart, he was my true father-in-law!

22

CHANG XIAOXIAO

THE STEPDAUGHTER

I HEARD you've interviewed a lot of people. That's good! Listen to both sides, and you'll be enlightened. Heed only one side, and you'll be in the dark. It's not easy to understand the whole life of a person. You know, I'm not Ouyang Wantong's birth daughter, but I've always called him Dad, and I'm willing to regard him as my family and my real father, both psychologically and emotionally.

When I began to live with him, I was about four and a half. At that age, you can't be sure whether a man is your birth father or not, but you can intuitively know whether he is good to you or not, you can distinguish whether he loves you or not, and you can feel whether he is worthy of your closeness.

The earliest thing I can remember about him was related to some trouble I had made. I accidentally knocked down a Jun porcelain vase he had placed on the table when I was playing in the living room. The vase made a loud bang and broke into pieces the moment it fell to the floor. Frightened by the sound and the consequences, I cried out. He and my mother ran from the other room almost at the same time. My mother uttered a cry when she saw the vase pieces on the floor: "My goodness! That was precious!" As she finished, she lifted her palm ready to strike me. Seeing her angry face and hearing the rushing wind brought by her arm, I knew she meant to beat me, so I closed my eyes in terror. Unexpectedly, I felt I was being picked up by someone at that time, and when I opened my eyes, I found I was lying in my father's arms. I heard him say: "She didn't do it on purpose! The vase is broken, so what's the point of beating her?" As he said those words, he caressed my trembling body and comforted me: "Xiaoxiao, don't cry! Daddy has long wanted to get rid of that vase. Now we can have a new one!" At that moment, I felt how warm his arms were and how attached I was to them!

Probably because similar incidents occurred quite often, I gradually felt it was him who was most likely to protect me, and because of this he became the one I would turn to for help first whenever I did something wrong or I failed to get good scores in my exams. With his protection, I would then tell my mother. Even after I knew I had a birth father, my attachment to him was no less. When I was in high school, I received a love letter from a male classmate, which made me very nervous and panicked. You know, it was the first time I had a letter like that. What should I do? The first person who came to my mind was him. I remember that evening when I went back home restlessly, I grabbed his hand, pulled him into his study, took out the note and handed it to him, face flushed with shyness. He smiled happily after reading it and said: "Hey, my Xiaoxiao can win the admiration of boys! You've become a big girl now! Good! This proves our Xiaoxiao is attractive. Your mother and I are very proud of you! But right now, it's not the time for you to begin a relationship with a boy because you're not ready, physically or spiritually. The most important task for you at present is to complete your education. My suggestion is you write back to tell him you appreciate his admiration very much, but at the moment both of you should focus on study, and when you're both in college in the future, you can think about this matter!"

I followed his suggestion and wrote a letter to that boy, who was deeply moved by my respect and promised to express his love for me formally after we both entered a good college. I didn't tear up the note but kept it as a memento. However, I didn't expect my mother would find it when she did the laundry. She thought it had just happened, and she shouted and screamed with overwhelming alarm, forcing me to tell her the truth with a threat to punish me severely. This made me firmly believe that if I had told her first, things would never have turned out so well.

My father was very concerned about the disharmony between him and his son – my elder brother Ouyang Qianzi – and he was very sad about it too. He told me more than once that he was in fact a loser as a father. He said that his son needed his company and wanted to play with him when he was a child, but at that time he was obsessed with his struggles in officialdom and was busy with his work. He said he seldom cared about his son and spent little time with him. And when he could spare some time later and wanted to make up for it, brother Qianzai wasn't interested.

He had a few long talks with me during his lifetime. They were all delivered to me when I was trapped in great difficulties, and they made a great impression on me. The first one took place after I had failed my college entrance exam for the first time. Proud and ambitious, I was not prepared to accept it. I was stunned by the result and too ashamed to face anyone. I locked myself in my room and slept for two days without eating and drinking, no matter how hard my mother tried to get me out of bed. Then he came, sat beside my bed and said: "More than five hundred and ten years ago, there was a young man in Wuzhou, Hubei province who followed his father's order to take part in the Imperial Examination in Wuchang for three successive years. Unfortunately, he failed each time. Greatly frustrated by his failure, he felt he owed his parents too much, so he climbed onto a cliff and wanted to kill himself by jumping off. At that moment, a man who was gathering herbs in the mountain saw him and laughed, 'Has that man gone to the cliff to kill himself? Good for him – we'll have one less coward in this world!' Hearing that, the young man was ashamed of himself and eventually changed his mind. He went back home and learned Chinese herbal medicine diligently from his father. He later put on his sandals, travelled into the wilderness, visited famous doctors and experienced scholars, searched for well-established folk prescriptions, collected herb samples and finally finished a masterpiece *Compendium of Materia Medica*. He was Li Shizhen, admired by future generations, while those who passed the Imperial Examination in Wuchang and became administrators were not remembered by anyone. Xiaoxiao, why did you take part in the college entrance examination? You're trying to further your education and learn a skill to make a living in the future. Of course, a girl can find someone to depend on through marriage, but it's not very safe to do that. If you have the ability to support yourself, you can take the initiative and be in control of your life. Suppose a girl marries the wrong man – she could leave him at any time without stooping to compromise for the sake of living on. However, you should remember that colleges aren't the only places where you can master a skill to make a living. So, it's good if you pass the examination, but it's totally unnecessary for you to try to end your life if you fail to do so. In society, opportunities for you to learn something and places where you can master a skill are all around you. What's more, you can take the examination again next year. You know, you did fail the examination this year, but perhaps fate wants to create another opportunity that's more suitable for you. Just one year late to go to college!" His words relieved me at once.

The next time was when I fell in love during my second year at college. It was with a boy in my class, and I took the initiative to confess my love for him. He responded enthusiastically. For a while, we were deeply in love, as if we were glued together, but later another girl came between us, and he began to behave coldly towards me. Eventually, he turned his back on me. I was inconsolable for the loss of my love. Again, my father sat beside my bed when all my mother's words were of no use. He said: "When people are trying to find their mates, they actually want to find partners with whom they can live together for a lifetime. If a man is in love with you for only a few months and then wants to leave you, it indicates he's not suitable to be your life partner. You should be grateful for his choice to leave you. Suppose he stayed with you for now and then left you when you're not young anymore. You would suffer even more. We know mutual physical attraction and passion between men and women is short-lived. However attractive a couple are, they'll lose interest in each other's bodies with the passage of time. So what should they do next? The major links to maintain the relationship between men and women are mutual responsibility and kindness. So, when you're finding your mate, don't believe in love only, because it won't last forever for any couple. Love will eventually turn into family connection, a kind of emotional attachment like blood relations, closely linked. Of course, this change is conditional, and both sides must have a sense of responsibility and kindness. So, what you need to pay more attention to is to notice whether that man is responsible and whether he's kind to other people."

His words greatly reduced the pain in my heart.

There's another story. When I was doing sports, I accidentally fell down and scratched my right ear. The doctor told me that the rim of my right ear would not return to its original appearance. I was shocked by this, and the fear of being disfigured made me again feel that I didn't want to live in this world. My father once again sat by me and said: "Don't tell me that you don't want to live just because you're missing a bit of your ear! What a minor defect! What about those disabled people? There are so many of them in this world! What should those people who have lost their arms, legs and feet do? Should they all give up their lives? After the Creator gives us life and we have all experienced the joy of youth, He gradually takes back everything He gave to us at the very beginning, including beauty, eyesight, hearing, athletic ability and life itself. Now you want to end your own life simply because of such a minor defect on your right ear. What will you do when the Creator begins to take back more important things from you? What if He makes you suffer from a stroke, and you end up paralysed on your face and one side of your body? What will you do then?"

His words calmed me down, and I began to accept this little change in my body.

As for why he suddenly put forward his resignation, I don't know the reason clearly. I just remember for a period of time he began to tell me his ideas about power.

He once asked me: "Xiaoxiao, do you think power is a good thing?"

I nodded and said, "Yes, everyone, including college students, wants to have power. You know, some of the college students would even get involved in a battle over the chance to be cadres in the student union."

He said slowly: "Seen from afar, power is indeed good. It brings material pleasures and spiritual happiness to those who have its glory. But seen up close, it is in fact very dangerous, a demon with a gorgeous cloak. If not careful enough, those who have it or deal with it would be so hurt by it and tortured that they would rather die than live. Those who are far away from it cannot see this, and that is the reason why people rush towards it, wave after wave, generation after generation."

I remember I laughed at that time. I asked: "Are you saying that because you're afraid someone will take your power away?"

He sighed and said: "I'm simply reminding you that in your future life, you should never regard power as your only goal! That's my advice to you. As for power, if it has been pushed into your hand, then seize it, but it can't be forced. Like forced marriage, power gained by force will bring bitter fruit."

Later, he asked me how I felt living in this family. I said: "I'm very happy. You and my mother love me, and you're tolerant, which allows me to visit my birth father quite often. With the care of so many uncles and aunts in the provincial government offices, I need not worry about many things at all. Everything can be fixed up very quickly. I have nothing to worry about. Honestly, I'm glad that my mother has brought me to this family."

He smiled faintly and said: "Yes, it's indeed convenient for our family right now to do anything, but it's not because your mother and I have any special skills. It's power that's at work. Power has brought us many conveniences, but this kind of life can't last forever. I'm afraid you'll have to be mentally prepared to live your life like an ordinary citizen without the shelter of power."

As I recall this now, he perhaps was thinking about proposing his resignation at that time.

Sometime later, I saw that he had brought home a few painting brushes and a suona. Out of curiosity, I asked him what they were for?

He smiled and said: "To prepare for my retired life! I use the brushes to practice painting, while the suona will help to drive away my loneliness."

My mother, standing beside, cut in: "There's plenty of time before your retirement! Why are you lazing around all day long!"

I didn't know he could draw, and I didn't expect the door god he painted would be so similar to the New Year paintings of Zhuxian town. The unicorns he painted resembled patterns I had seen on the eaves of rural houses. He could also paint dreams. Once he asked what I recently dreamed about. I said: "In my dream, a boy followed me closely." He therefore painted a young mother followed by a chubby child, whose sweet smiles made everyone happy. I liked it very much and hurriedly put it up on the wall of my bedroom. He told me if it had not been for his grandfather's intervention, he would have become an expert painter in the countryside.

When he picked up the suona in front of me for the first time, I didn't believe he could play it at all. Making fun of him as he was testing the sound, I said: "Stop pretending! Not everyone can play this!"

He smiled, "It will disturb our neighbours if I play it at home. What about going with me to the park after dinner? I could play you a piece of music there, and if it's unpleasant to your ear, I won't play it again."

It was probably out of curiosity that I took his suona and dragged him to the park after dinner that evening. When we arrived at the park, he led me into a small forest and began playing his suona. The first sound he made surprised me. It was so professional! The music he played was *A Hundred Birds Worshipping the Phoenix*. You know, I often heard him play this piece at home, so I was sort of familiar with it. Even though I was an amateur, I could tell he was very good at it, quite skilful! In the middle of his performance, many people strolling in the park gathered around him, standing there listening to him in high spirits. After he finished the music, they all clapped and shouted, and many of them went over to talk to him. Luckily, it was dark at that time, and the people thought he was just a suona hobbyist. If they had known he was the current governor, more spectators would have been attracted.

There is one more thing. I don't know whether I should tell you or not. Do you promise to keep it a secret? You should never tell this to anyone in this world, nor should you write it down! It has nothing to do with politics. It's about family. The reason I want to tell you this is because I've been suffocated by it. It's too painful! Can you promise? All right, now please turn off your recorder.

23

FENG RUNYUN

THE FASHION MODEL

MY CASE HAS ALREADY BEEN TRIED in public. The crime was money laundering. You must already know it had nothing to do with the deceased Governor Ouyang Wantong, right? I don't know why you've come to me if you're going to write a biography of him? There was something between Jian Qianyan and him? Are you sure? All right, I'll tell you something about it. Honestly, I've never had any contact with Governor Ouyang Wantong. Everything I know about him is from TV and newspapers. If it were not for Jian Qianyan, who always mentioned his name in front of me and asked me to pass on some documents about him several times, I wouldn't even remember who he was! Think about it – how could a person like me, who has never worked as an official in a government office, have any interest in a governor? Do you think I'm crazy?

How did I get to know Jian Qianyan? It was a complete accident! One year, Sunflower Clothing was recruiting models, and I went to attend an interview. I had never expected there would be so many girls competing for the job – all pretty girls crowding together as if it were a fair. Since then, I've heard that the two places where you can find the most pretty girls are model recruitment events and film academies.

At first, I felt discouraged seeing so many pretty girls in beautiful dresses competing with me. How could the daughter of an electrician win? So I decided to quit. Unexpectedly, the moment I walked out of the crowd, a middle-aged man came towards me and said: "Hey, miss, why are you leaving? The interview hasn't started yet."

I put on a bitter smile and said: "I'm not qualified! It's better that I quit."

He looked at me and said in a solemn manner: "I think you're in good shape and you have real class, so you meet the standards of being a model. Stay and have a try. What if you win?"

His words rekindled my confidence, and I changed my mind. Once the interview began, I was surprised to find the man who just spoke with me was sitting on the interviewing panel! You know, I worked as the host of a college party, and I also worked twice as the news anchor at a provincial TV station during my internship. Now, with the so-called acquaintance sitting opposite me, I answered the interviewers' questions in an unhurried manner. My interview went very well! Hardly had I finished my interview when I heard him speak first: "This girl is good! She passes!" Hearing that, the other interviewers didn't argue, so that's how I got my chance. Later, I discovered that man was Jian Qianyan, the boss of Sunflower Clothing.

After hearing I had been accepted, I was deeply moved and decided to go to thank Jian Qianyan. Before I went to his place, I wanted to buy him a gift. You know, without his help, it would have been very hard for me to get the job, and I wanted to show my gratitude. With the 200 yuan my father gave to me, I bought him a tie, which was the most valuable gift I could afford.

On my first day at work, I took the gift to his office and said: "Thank you, President Jian. If it were not for your help, I, a junior college student, might still be at home doing nothing. This is a small gift – an expression of my gratitude."

He smiled, took the tie, looked at it carefully and said: "Runyun, we share similar taste! The colour of this tie is exactly my style. Thank you! Try your best to learn some skills in the model team, and make contributions to the development of our company."

I nodded immediately and said: "President Jian, you may rest assured. Since you have valued me so much, I'll do my utmost for our company, and I'll do my work to your satisfaction."

After I entered the model team and began my training, I came to understand that in addition to displaying the clothes designed and manufactured by the company at shows and fairs, fashion models also have to take care of the company's public relations. Because of this, we were all required to learn two skills – the ability to dress and pose on a catwalk and the social skills to deal with people. Luckily, there was no need to learn maths, physics or chemistry to acquire these skills. I was not afraid of learning anything else, and I was full of enthusiasm. I was a fast learner, so very soon I knew how to walk on a catwalk and how to deal with public relations. Three months later at the provincial fashion exhibition, I officially walked on the catwalk. It might have been because I posed very meticulously, or because my parents had given me a pretty face, or because people wanted to see a new model, but my debut was a huge success. Large colour photos of me were published in the provincial newspapers, and the clothes I wore on the catwalk received a lot of orders.

Jian Qianyan was very happy and called me to his office. He presented me with a large bouquet of flowers and congratulated me. He then announced: "From today, you're the captain of our company's model team and the manager of our public relations department, with a monthly salary of 18,000 yuan."

Seized by the sudden joy, I almost fainted. My goodness! 18,000 yuan a month! That was indeed an astronomical figure for me! I held his hands and said gratefully: "Thank you, President Jian! Runyun won't forget your kindness in this life!"

He smiled and said, "Don't mention it! Tonight, I'm holding a celebration banquet at the Guibin Restaurant. Please be sure to attend!"

As I walked to the Guibin Restaurant, I was expecting there to be a lot of people at the celebration banquet, but when I entered the private room, I found there were only two people – Jian Qianyan and me. I was puzzled for a second and then felt very uneasy. I had never eaten alone with a president!

Sitting at the table, Jian Qianyan said: "I thought about inviting all the girls in our model team tonight, but then I suddenly remembered I have a task for you only, so here we are." I was happy when I heard this. You know, I was just thinking about how to repay him with my performance. I asked him what my task was but he waved his hand and said: "We'll talk about your task later. Let's drink first. Cheers for your successful debut and your promotion!"

I had learned to drink when I was training in the public relations department, but I was not good at it, and my cheeks would flame after a couple of swallows. The red wine Jian Qianyan ordered that night was Lafite, which I knew was a product of the Lafite Winery, one of the five famous Bordeaux wineries in France. It had a floral and fruity aroma, and it tasted pure, fragrant and mellow. It was very elegant – the queen of the wine kingdom. Jian Qianyan raised his glass and said: "You need to learn how to drink this wine because the task you're going to accomplish is related to it." I listened with more interest. What kind of task would have something to do with drinking Lafite?

After we clinked glasses three times, Jian Qianyan told me about my task: "Your mission is to go to Beijing, get in touch with an important business partner of our company and try to win his support for the business development of our company. Drinking Lafite is this man's indulgence."

I sighed and thought people who liked to drink this kind of wine must be very rich – otherwise, how could they afford it? But I was still very happy to have a chance to work in Beijing. You know, I had never been to Beijing, the capital of our country! It was a great opportunity for me to broaden my horizons!

A few glasses of wine later, Jian Qianyan told me seriously: "Runyun, your mission in Beijing is very important to our company, so I want you to have a physical examination done tomorrow, is that all right?"

I didn't think too much of it at that time, and I felt there was no harm in doing a physical examination, so I agreed immediately.

The next day after I arrived at the hospital, I found the physical examination Jian Qianyan required was nothing but a venous blood collection and a gynaecological examination, including a check on whether I was a virgin or not! Honestly, I was a bit annoyed about this. What was the connection between carrying out a public relations task and a virginity test? How ridiculous!

The third day after the physical examination was a Friday. Very early in the morning, Jian Qianyan asked his secretary to inform me that I would be flying to Beijing with him. When I received the phone call, I was so happy. You know, it was after all my first time to take an aeroplane and my first time to go to Beijing! I didn't expect that my two wishes could be realised on the same day!

The moment I walked into the cabin, I was filled with joy, observing the facilities, and the manners of the other passengers, and having no idea that what was waiting for me in Beijing was going to be life-changing.

When I got off the plane at Beijing Capital Airport, a middle-aged man came to pick us up. I had thought we were going to the downtown area and I could get a glimpse of the beauty of Beijing, but the car unexpectedly took us to a suburban area, and we eventually parked in the courtyard of a villa in a high-grade private community. Jian Qianyan told me our company bought it and made it the Beijing office. From now on, it was at my disposal, and I was the owner. A chef, a driver and a cleaner had been hired to work for me too, and I was their boss. Standing in the luxuriously decorated hall with great surprise, staring at the large landscapes on the wall and beautifully shaped crystal chandeliers, I felt as if I were in a fairyland.

Jian Qianyan showed me around all the rooms in the villa, letting me know how to use each of them. The chef, the driver and the cleaner all lived in the bungalow beside the villa.

That afternoon, he also told me he was going to entertain that important business partner he had mentioned to me, a famous young master in Beijing who had a huge influence within both officialdom and business circles. He asked me to put on a new dress, do my make-up and apply a little perfume in readiness for the reception. Meanwhile, he handed me a bank card, saying there was one million yuan on it and my date of birth was the password. As long as I served that important man to his satisfaction, the one million would be mine. I was taken aback! How could I accept such a great amount of money? I handed it back to him in a hurry and stated clearly: "President Jian, you may rest assured that I'll try my best to receive our guest!" But Jian Qianyan stuffed the card back into my pocket. I thought perhaps I would need some money when I took this guest to the downtown area, and then I could submit my expenses to the company when I returned. Anyway, I intended to be very careful with the money.

In the late afternoon, a car stopped in front of the villa, and the driver inside the car was the same man who had picked us up at the airport. A man in his late thirties stepped out of the car. He was fat and fair-skinned and wore a pair of black-rimmed glasses. He looked like an elegant gentleman. Jian Qianyan hurriedly ran to greet him with his hands clasped before his face and shouted: "How are you, Brother Tong? It's been quite a while since I last saw you. I have truly missed you!"

The man addressed as Brother Tong smiled lightly and said: "Jian Qianyan, you're a tycoon who has made a huge fortune. With so many people gathered around you, how could you possibly remember layabouts like us!"

"How dare I!" Jian Qianyan smiled and meticulously escorted this Brother Tong into the villa. Seeing that, I hurriedly came over to him and helped him up the steps, as I had learned in the public relations department.

"And who is this beauty?" he asked as he looked at me.

"The captain of our company's model team and the manager of our public relations department! The number one beauty in Qinghe, absolutely pure and innocent. She's in charge of taking care of you," said Jian Qianyan with a big grin on his face. Who could imagine such a man who used to be so bossy and arrogant in the company would act with such servility in front of a man younger than him.

When the dinner was ready, I seated them and gave them with hot towels to wipe their hands and faces. As I was about to help serve the dishes, Jian Qianyan asked me to sit with them, saying: "Runyun, you don't need to serve the dishes. Sit here and drink with your Brother Tong." I sat down nervously and found the glass in front of me had already been filled with Lafite. Throughout the dinner, I noticed Brother Tong had his eyes on me all the time, which panicked me a bit, as I was worried that I might make a mistake and my service would disappoint him. After all, we were in Beijing, the capital!

After a few glasses of wine, I felt extraordinarily hot, and I thought the Lafite was a little bit different from what I had in Qinghe. It was strong, and it made me feel so hot all over my body that I wanted to take off my clothes. My face must have been burning!

That Brother Tong looked at me and smiled: "Now Miss Runyun's cheeks are pink, and she can perform on the stage without any make-up."

I heard Jian Qianyan reply: "She'll perform for you in a minute."

I didn't know what he meant by that, and I just tried my best to preserve my grace and solemn manner and to control the urge to take off my clothes.

"Runyun, you should propose another toast to your Brother Tong!" Jian Qianyan filled my glass again and signalled me to stand up and make a toast. My head had already spun, but I dare not refuse his order. I rose unsteadily to my feet, feeling so limp as if I were stepping on cotton wool and about to collapse at any time. The moment I walked up to this Brother Tong, my legs gave way, and I leaned forward towards him. He seemed to be waiting for this and took me into his arms at once. Jian Qianyan smiled, and his words came into my ears at that time: "The show begins! Act one. Since the beauty has thrown herself into your arms, you should carry her into the bedroom."

I knew he had an ulterior motive by saying this. How could I allow a man I just met to hold me like this? It was not decent at all! Unfortunately, though my mind stayed awake, I felt groggy all over and didn't even have the strength to open my mouth and say no. I wanted to break away from his arms but I was powerless to stop him carrying me upstairs into the main bedroom! I was in a panic. Jian Qianyan had told me this room was for the guests, so how could he carry me there? Watching him put me down on the king-size bed, I tried to roll down to the floor, but I didn't even have the strength to do that. He went to close the door, and by then I knew something was wrong. I wanted to shout and scream but I myself couldn't even hear what I was saying. I knew that Lafite did not have this effect. You know, I drank it before, and it didn't make me end up like that. It must have been drugs. Yes, they must have drugged me. What kind of drug? Who did it? This bastard Tong or damned Jian Qianyan? After that bastard Tong placed me on the bed, he went to the bathroom. I made another attempt to run away, but I just couldn't move my body! He came out of the bathroom, stood beside the bed and smiled at me for a second. Then he began to strip my clothes. Horrified, I tried to avoid his hands, but I didn't have the strength. My body was not mine at all. I could feel him unbuttoning my clothes one by one and then taking off my bra. I begged him with my eyes but he simply ignored me. His eyes were gleaming with joy as my body was slowly laid bare. When I was at last naked in front of him, he lowered his head and took my nipple into his mouth. I closed my eyes in agony. I hated this bastard! It was the first time I had been naked in front of a man! I wanted to grab a brick to smash his head, but I could do nothing. I could only watch him suckle my left nipple and then the right, licking my breasts crazily like a dog. The drug probably made my body hot at first, but now all his licking and biting were making me very uncomfortable. I bit my tongue hard, hoping the pain could suppress my discomfort. The bastard then started to kiss my lower abdomen! Desperately, I thought about knocking my head on the bedside table. Yes, better to kill myself than to be insulted by him. However, I wasn't even able to do this, and once again I could do nothing but watch him licking my belly here and there, his eyes scanning me, and his hands like cold snakes crawling over every part of my lower body. Hopeless and humiliated, I closed my eyes. I knew the worst was yet to come. About ten minutes later, he removed his clothes and climbed onto the bed. Wearing a leering grin, he grabbed me and pried my legs wide open.

I shed tears silently as he raped me. The bastard smiled and kissed my eyes when he saw me crying. He even licked my tears away! There was nothing I could do but accept what he did to me.

At that moment I came to realise the real intention of Jian Qianyan when he made me the captain of the model team and the manager of the public relations department! How full of regrets I was! I had stepped into a trap he had long set up for me! How stupid I was!

I didn't know at what time I fell asleep in piercing pain. When I opened my eyes again, it was already daybreak. That Tong was still sleeping naked beside me. I tried to move my hands and feet. They had regained their function. The first thing I did was raise my hand and punch his face heavily. What a pity! Probably because the drug was still in effect, my punch was so weak that it simply woke him up instead. He opened his eyes and saw it was me. My eyes flamed, but he didn't care about my anger at all. He rolled over, enfolded me in his arms and said: "Hey, little Yunyun, I didn't expect that you would be a real virgin! From now on, you're my sweet little baby!" As he said this, he snatched the covers off us, showing me the red mark on the sheet. I rammed him suddenly and fiercely, hoping to knock him dead, but I only managed to touch his chest. He was not mad at me, but laughed and held me tightly in his arms instead. I fought against him. We rolled over in bed and eventually my restored strength was drained. He pinned my body between his and the bed and once again forcefully entered me. All that I could do was to bite him hard on the shoulder, and I didn't let go. He shouted in pain, but he didn't stop – he just pounded me harder! Although I was full of hatred for him, his thrusts made me feel a sense of strange pleasure that I never experienced before. I couldn't explain it. I felt ashamed and began to hate myself, and I didn't know at what time I stopped biting him and let go of his shoulder.

When he released me again, he said: "Little Yunyun, I really like you. Now there are two roads in front of you. The first one is this. From now on, you stay with me happily. Though I couldn't marry you and make you my wife, I promise you'll have the best life in this world, and your parents will receive the best care. The other one is to go and cry in front of your President Jian, complain about what happened last night, then go back to the community where your parents live and make a little money by doing some part-time jobs, living the same hard life as your parents. You're not the original you, and your body is not the one it used to be anymore! The decision is yours. If you agree to be with me, get up, wash, dress yourself and put on your make-up, then go downstairs with me to meet President Jian for breakfast, pretending that nothing has happened."

His words calmed me down. I lay there motionless, brooding on the two roads he proposed. Go on crying like this? Jian Qianyan would be mad at me. Now I knew it was he who had planned everything. If I undermined the relationship between him and that Tong, he would definitely be angry with me. It was quite possible that he might fire me immediately, which meant I would be out of work! The second consequence was that this Tong would deny what he had done to me. You know, in such a remote villa, how could I possibly take the evidence away? Even if I requested a medical examination, it would become the talk of the town, and I doubted that Tong would be punished. Even a powerful man like Jian Qianyan was afraid of him, so he must be quite influential. Besides, it was no use crying over my lost virginity. There was nothing I could do to make up for my loss. I myself was to blame for trusting Jian Qianyan and for being so blind as not to see what he really was. Well, I had no choice but to clench my teeth, swallow my tears and suffer in silence.

In the end, I ground my teeth and sat up. I put on the clothes that had been stripped off by that Tong and went to wash in the bathroom. Seeing what I did, that Tong took me into his arms after I came out of the bathroom and said happily: "Yunyun is really a smart girl! From now on, you're my girl, and I'll be responsible for you!" I resisted my resentment and forced a smile at him, choking back my hatred towards him.

When Tong and I arrived in the dining room on that morning, Jian Qianyan greeted us happily and set up the chairs for us, as if I had become a new person. They had a happy breakfast, chatting and laughing while I tried to wear a smile on my face though my heart was bleeding.

After breakfast, Jian Qianyan whispered to me when Tong went to the bathroom. He said: "You've truly earned my trust! The one million in the card I gave to you last night now belongs to you. You must hold on to him and let him fall for you so that he can't live without you! Your future will get better and better. I'll go back to Qinghe today. You just stay here serving him whenever he comes. Remember, ten or fifteen days later, show him this document when he's in his best mood. Tell him some employees in our company entrusted it to you before you came to Beijing. Make sure he reads it!" With these words, he put an envelope into my handbag.

Tong couldn't wait to take me upstairs after Jian Qianyan left. In the bedroom, he first put his arms around me and rocked my body, then he threw me onto the bed and took off my clothes hurriedly, doing the same thing that he had done to me the previous night. Last time, I had been too weak to resist but this time I just gave up. I felt like weeping but had no tears, letting him go wild like an animal.

He slept like a log after having sex with me. I took out the letter Jian Qianyan had given to me and read it. It was a report with the title 'Governor Ouyang Wantong is mediocre and greedy, and nearly 100 million people in Qinghe are suffering untold misery and hardship'. It was signed by a dozen employees of our clothing company, most of whom I knew. They usually had no interest in politics. How could there be any conflict between them and Ouyang Wantong, who was miles apart from them? Why did they jointly sign this report about Governor Ouyang Wantong? Jian Qianyan must have faked it! I was not in the right mood to read the material carefully, nor was I interested in anything about Ouyang Wantong. I simply wanted to find a chance to give this material to that Tong and accomplish the task Jian Qianyan had given to me.

On Monday morning, Tong's driver took him back to the city. Upon his leaving, he asked me to stay there, take good care of myself and wait for him to come to see me again. He then instructed the chef and the cleaner to take care of me. He told them that if something should go wrong, he would be sure to take action against them.

Just three days later, he called his driver again to bring him to my place. Of course, I knew what he came for. On that night, when he was so impatiently unbuttoning my clothes, I pushed his hands away and said: "Wait a minute! I want you to do me a favour. Before I came to Beijing, a group of my colleagues asked me to hand over a report to some relevant leaders. How could I know any leader here in Beijing? I'm wondering whether you could do this for me?"

He was so eager to have my body that he said hurriedly: "Bring it to me, quickly!" I took the letter out of my handbag and gave it to him. He flipped through it for a while and said: "You've found the right person! I promise to report all the bad conduct of Ouyang Wantong to the relevant leaders. You know, I don't have a good opinion of him either. Once one of my buddies asked him to help with some tenders for the construction of a highway. He paid lip service to my friend while playing tricks on him behind his back! Think about it – how could he be an honest man when he dares to play with my buddy? Tell your colleagues who wrote the report not to worry. I'll take care of this, and I promise this Ouyang Wantong will end up having bitten off more than he can chew!"

The next day, I reported this to Jian Qianyan. He was very happy to hear the news and praised me for my excellent work. He also said he would come to Beijing in a few days and speak with Tong about Ouyang Wantong.

I would say that Tong treated me pretty well since we were in a relationship. He kept buying me jewellery, clothes and supplies, and my room in the villa was soon filled with various brand-name products, ranging from things to wear, to use, to play with, to eat and to drink. Good things that I had never heard of in the past were sent to me ceaselessly by Tong. I could tell his love for me was true, so my hatred for him faded away. Without resentment, I gradually developed some love for him since I hadn't really loved a man in the past. With this little love for him, I treated him with more tenderness. I could clearly feel my little tenderness for him made him more satisfied and fascinated with me. Once, after we had sex, he murmured to me: "Yunyun, to be honest, I've slept with many women, but I've never met one as pure and warm as you. You're the first woman who has given me her first night, and I'll treasure you."

It was indeed from then on that I began to treat him sincerely and called him Brother Tong.

Did I have another choice? What else could I do?

On the day when I was tried, I heard some women curse me in a low voice. I wondered why they didn't think about what else I could have done in that situation!

It was almost a month later that Jian Qianyan came to the villa again. On the night of his arrival, Brother Tong came at his invitation. I asked the chef to prepare a table of dishes, and I myself served as they were drinking and chatting. For a while, I felt I was a bit like the hostess of this villa.

At the table, I heard Jian Qianyan say: "Brother Tong, I should take the liberty of reporting this to you. Ouyang Wantong, the governor of Qinghe, is indeed a person who likes trapping people. He's always ready to send the Commission for Discipline Inspection to investigate this person or that person, making a lot of officials and entrepreneurs feel like they would rather die than live. He doesn't care about other people's life and death at all! If he should have more power, he'll definitely be a curse to our province and our country!"

Brother Tong chuckled and said: "It seems Brother Qianyan is concerned about our country and our people! Not long ago, Yunyun also gave me some material prepared by a dozen employees of your company, reporting various problems about Ouyang Wantong. Some of my friends have told me that Ouyang Wantong is untrustworthy and unreliable. Don't worry. Though I don't have an official position, I'll definitely let the senior leaders hear your voice of justice! What use is he anyway? Will it matter if we remove him from office?"

Before leaving, Jian Qianyan told me secretly that our company planned to build a golf course in the suburbs of Qinghe province, with fifty villas and a five-star hotel. He had already finished the plans, but Governor Ouyang Wantong firmly refused to approve it. He asked me to give the report to Brother Tong when he was in a good mood, and urge him to help settle the matter in Beijing. If he should succeed, he shouldn't worry about how much reward he would get. Jian Qianyan said I could explain to Brother Tong directly that he – Jian Qianyan – was never an ungrateful person. If Brother Tong wanted to have some shares in the company, one fifth would be given to him. If he wasn't interested in owning some shares and wanted to have cash instead, 50 million could be transferred to him at once. As he finished his words, he slipped the report to me.

I had no idea how difficult it would be to settle this, nor did I know whether Brother Tong could help. But since Jian Qianyan had given me one million and since he had made me the leader of his public relations department, I had to give this report to Brother Tong. So, when Brother Tong came to the villa the next weekend, I stopped his hands when he was eager to unfasten my belt, and I said: "President Jian mailed a report to me and he wanted you to take a look."

He urged me impatiently as usual: "Go and get it for me, quick!" After I handed him the report, he flipped through it and murmured: "It's very difficult! Jian Qianyan has given me a tough task!" Hearing that, I told him what Jian Qianyan would like to do for him in return. When Brother Tong heard it, his frowning brow slowly spread out, and he said: "Well, as he has given me the best woman in this world, I'll help carry out his wish." With that, he pulled me into his arms.

About twenty days later, Brother Tong told me that he had got things done and asked me to call Jian Qianyan to come to see him. I was very surprised. How could he do it in such a short period of time? Jian Qianyan was also shocked when he received the good news from me. "Great! It's all thanks to you, Runyun! I'll remember this forever."

Jian Qianyan arrived in the evening the next day. He gave a deep bow to Brother Tong first as he entered the villa, and then he thanked him again and again: "Brother Tong, thank you so much! You've saved my life, and I'll never forget your grace! You know, that bastard Ouyang Wantong has been withholding his approval of my project, saying that I'm invading arable land! I didn't expect that you would save it! A million thanks!"

As he was talking on and on, Brother Tong just sat on the sofa, listening, not even bothering to stand up. After Jian Qianyan finished, he said with a brief smile: "I don't need any of your shares. I only need some cash to feed myself in the future."

Jian Qianyan smiled as he listened to this. "I have brought the money with me." He then took out two bank cards from his pocket. "There's 25 million yuan on each of the two ICBC credit cards, a total of 50 million. Your date of birth is the password. You can withdraw or transfer the money at the bank tomorrow."

Brother Tong uttered a sigh: "Well, you've helped me with my problem, and I don't need to worry about where to get my food. That's good! But Yunyun's situation is a bit pitiful. She has been living in your house, and I'm wondering whether you could help her as well?"

I cut in hurriedly as I heard this: "I don't need it. It's totally fine for me to live here." You know, I didn't want to leave an impression on Jian Qianyan that I was using Brother Tong to force him to pay me.

Unexpectedly, Jian Qianyan smiled again and said: "That's easy. I've been thinking about how to deal with this villa lately. Will it be okay to transfer the ownership of the villa to Runyun? It's the place where you two spent your honeymoon, so it's the best place for you to stay! I'll do the property transfer with Runyun tomorrow morning!"

I was shocked at that moment. How could such a great villa be given to me like this?

The next morning, Jian Qianyan came to ask me to go downtown with him for the property transfer. I had no idea what he really thought about it. Dare I go with him? As I was trying to decline, Brother Tong said: "Yunyun, do you know how many billions your dear President Jian will make from the project I've settled for him? What he offers to you is just a drop in the ocean, so you don't need to be overly polite! Go with him."

At his insistence, I agreed. In the car, Jian Qianyan said to me: "You deserve this villa! You've helped me with my big project, so how could I not repay you? Remember, hold on to this Tong! You know, there are still a lot of things we're unable to do without him. He's our god of wealth!"

When I got the property certificate of the villa and looked at my name on it, my hatred towards Jian Qianyan disappeared completely. You know, I'm just a daughter of an ordinary working family, and it's indeed good enough for me to have such a large villa in Beijing, to have a million in my savings account and to have such a high salary! Sure, I've paid for it, and it's Jian Qianyan who forced me to pay, but in this world, is there anything you can get without paying?

I was content.

That very night, Brother Tong didn't give the official approval document to Jian Qianyan until he saw my property certificate. Brother Tong said to Jian: "You could earn at least 10 billion from this project, kid. If it had not been for Yunyun, I wouldn't have given it to you."

After that, Jian Qianyan asked Brother Tong to do him a lot of favours via me. I still feel that Brother Tong is a lech, but he's also kind, helpful and trustworthy. He has his problems of course. He's extravagant, a man of pleasure, too casual about making friends and unable to distinguish people who are around him. But I know he's true to me, and he loves me for sure. He did have quite a lot of women in the past. I could tell that from all the phone calls, but since we were in a relationship, he gradually broke off relations with them. He later asked me to set up a company with the 50 million yuan Jian Qianyan had given to him.

The company is called Yunmei Communications. Brother Tong named it with one of the characters in my name. He said his little Yunyun – that's me – was pretty, so the company should be named Yunmei. I, however, was worried and said to him: "I have no experience of running a company, let alone a communications company. I have no idea about how to manage it at all!"

Brother Tong comforted me and asked me to take it easy. He told me there was nothing for me to take care of as far as the establishment and operation of this company was concerned except that I needed to go to my office there for a while every week. He made some phone calls after telling me this. A week later, he took me to an office building in the East Third Ring Road in Beijing. On the twenty-eighth floor, I saw a row of five office rooms whose doors were all emblazoned with the name 'Yunmei Communications' in red characters. He pointed at the biggest one in the middle and said: "That is your office."

I walked into the office and was pleasantly surprised. There was a sofa, a large desk, a telephone and a computer. A woman in her fifties was sitting at a small table in the corner. Brother Tong introduced her to me as my secretary, Sister Chen, who was responsible for the daily work of the company. He told Sister Chen that I was Feng Runyun, the president of this company and I was very busy and could only be there once a week.

Think about it, what else could I express about Brother Tong except for my gratitude?

As for Jian Qianyan, I would say he's very scheming, a back-stabber indeed. I don't know whether you've ever met him, but if you do, be aware that he might scheme against you. Think about it. Brother Tong has treated him so well. He did so many things for him, solved so many problems for him and got rid of so many of his rivals. But what did he do in return? He placed a surveillance camera in the villa and recorded every action of Brother Tong, including the times when Brother Tong was with me on the bed. Videos of us naked! What a bastard! We never expected that he would have mini hidden cameras in every part of the villa and that our driver would control the recording device! After Brother Tong was reported and arrested, that Jian provided all the surveillance videos to prove he was being blackmailed by Brother Tong. He claimed it was Brother Tong who asked him for a bribe and that he himself was innocent! Now, Brother Tong and I are in prison, but he has got away with it, continuing a life of luxury and pleasure. That's definitely unfair!"

Brother Tong and I later heard that when Jian Qianyan was relying on Brother Tong, he also had some other important people behind him!

You're a writer – could you appeal for my Brother Tong and me? We've been wronged!

How unjust it is!

24

GONG HEXIAN

THE CEO OF KANGREN FOOD GROUP

I WAS ALREADY familiar with Governor Ouyang Wantong when he became the deputy secretary of the Provincial Party Committee. In that year, my company was on the verge of bankruptcy because of cashflow problems. All of the banks had closed their doors to me, refusing to loan me a penny. In the end, he was the one who helped and saved my life. You know, at that time, I asked for help here and there, trying every means to find a way out, but not a single bank was willing to give me a loan. I came to realise at that time that bankers are the most snobbish people in this world. They come to you with smiles when you are rich for fear that you don't want to borrow from their bank, but they'll stay as far away from you as possible when you're in trouble for fear that you'll turn to them for help, that you'll fail to return the loan and increase their bad debts.

Facing the reality that the factory was closing and the creditors were demanding to be paid, I was in despair and made a careful plan to kill myself. My daughter, who was at college, heard about the situation and came back home at that time. I didn't know whether she had noticed some symptom of my suicide plan or not, but she took the initiative to come and say to me: "Dad, I'm studying finance. I know the president of the Bank of Fushang from when he came to give lectures to us in college. Let me go to his bank and have a try." You know, she didn't usually like to meet with strangers. I forced out a bitter smile, wondering how could I expect a young girl like her to go out and get a loan. But she insisted on doing that. I was not hopeful at all, still busy with all the things I had to deal with before I ended my life.

Quite unexpectedly, she came back home before lunch and said to me: "Dad, the president of Fushang Bank has agreed to lend us some money and he asked me to get the approval document this afternoon." Shocked and happy, I felt I had made a right choice to send my daughter to study finance, but at the same time I was wondering how she managed to persuade that president of Fushang Bank, who had a heart of stone. I remember when I went to him and begged for help, he didn't pay any attention to me. When I almost knelt down in front of him, he just said: "No. I can't have any more dead loans. I can't put my position in danger."

After lunch, my daughter went out to get the approval document while I was becoming suspicious of the whole thing, feeling that the president, who was not kind at all, couldn't change so fast. I therefore got in my car and followed my daughter to see what would happen. It turned out that my daughter didn't go to the office building of Fushang Bank. Instead, she went into a building in a residential community. I was more suspicious. Eventually, my daughter stopped in front of a door on the sixth floor. She knocked and out came the damned president of the bank who dragged her inside with excitement. I suddenly understood everything and flew into a rage, eyes turning red. When I went upstairs and banged on the door, that bastard bank manager was stripping off my daughter's clothes. I shouted and furiously lunged at him, brought him to the floor and beat him fiercely until he screamed like a pig being slaughtered.

After I beat him up, I went back to my office and began to write a farewell letter to my daughter. I wanted to tell her that her father loved her and understood her painstaking efforts to save the company. I hoped she could go on, and take care of herself and her mother.

On the afternoon when I was writing my farewell letter in the office, Deputy Secretary Ouyang Wantong came to inspect the industrial park where my company was located, by arrangement of some relevant department. In fact, my company was not in the inspection list because we were going bankrupt, but when he passed by our Kangren Company and heard that it was a private enterprise that was about to close down, he asked his driver to stop the car and went straight in. When my office director told me that the deputy secretary of the Provincial Party Committee had come, I finished the farewell letter, folded it, put it into my pocket and went downstairs to greet him calmly. I thought I would kill myself anyway, and it made no difference whether I did it right then or a few minutes later. After I spoke with the deputy secretary for a few minutes and saw him off, it would not be too late for me to jump off the building.

To my great surprise, after Deputy Secretary Wantong learned of my situation, he turned to the president of the Provincial Industrial and Commercial Bank who came to inspect with him and said: "This private company handles food processing. As a province that mainly depends on grain production, we should give special support to a company like this. The reason it's in trouble is not because of insufficient raw materials nor a lack of a market – it's down to fast expansion and excessive eagerness for quick success. So, what about giving them a helping hand? Spare them something from the loan you've planned to approve to the real estate company? Our province can't rely solely on real estate to develop the economy. If you need any guarantee, let the Provincial Finance Department take care of it, all right?"

When the bank manager heard this, he hurriedly replied: "No problem. We'll do it right away!" I was overjoyed at that time. Thank goodness! He was my saviour! I immediately gave up the idea to kill myself. I would go on living and fight! I must try my best to rise to my feet again!

Only one year after that, my company came back from the brink of death. Three years later, we've made huge progress. To put it bluntly, among all the food enterprises in Qinghe, I'm currently the leader, earning quite a lot of money every day. In addition to supplying the domestic market, our products are also exported to many countries in Europe, America and Africa. Without Ouyang Wantong's rescue and support, neither I nor my company would exist. Did you see that photo frame on the wall? Inside is the farewell letter I wrote at that time. I hang it there to help me remember the lessons of my past experience of management and remember who my saviour was.

For this reason, I have a special feeling for Governor Ouyang. If it hadn't been for his inspection, how could there be a Kangren Group today? How could I be talking with you right now? When he was still alive, I often went to visit him. Every time I went there, I would bring some gifts to express my gratitude, but he had a rule that the price of my gifts should not exceed 500 yuan. Think about it, what good stuff can you buy with 500 yuan nowadays! I had no choice but to bring him some new products of our company whenever I went to his place, such as wheat flour biscuits, snacks made with coarse grains, xylitol made with corn, yellow wine made with millet, sunflower oil and so on. He would always invite me to stay for dinner at his place, and his nanny would prepare a table of dishes, which sometimes cost more than the gifts I brought to him.

I was very anxious about not having a chance to express my gratitude. So, one Spring Festival, following what the other bosses usually did, I placed a pair of deer made of a thousand grams of pure gold inside a large biscuit tin and sent it to him. You know, the old saying goes that deer bring good luck and this would represent my best wishes for him. To my surprise, on the morning of New Year's Day, he asked his driver to take the biscuit tin and the gold deer back. His driver reported to me what he said: "It's not because I don't want it – it's because I dare not. One of my family members has been in jail. You don't want to send me there, do you?" I was greatly embarrassed by his words, and from then on, I never dared to send him any expensive gifts.

One afternoon just half a year before he retired, he called me out of the blue, saying: "Hexian, I urgently need your help!"

I was very happy when I heard that. You know, I finally had a chance to repay him. I said: "No problem. Tell me what you want me to do."

He said: "We have a key project that requires one million. Please lend me the money, and I'll give you an IOU for it."

I said: "Don't worry about that. I'm sending the money to you right now."

Putting down the receiver, I immediately asked my finance department to get a card with a deposit of one million yuan ready and then went to the provincial government by car. You know, we usually made appointments via his secretary, but it was the first time he had called me personally. I knew it must be something very urgent. Secretary Zheng greeted me downstairs. The first thing I saw when I entered his office was that he had thrown down the receiver in a fury.

He stood up with an angry expression on his face.

I dared not speak.

He walked back and forth behind his table twice as if to cool his anger down.

After a while, he turned to me and said: "Hexian, thanks for coming.

We don't need the money now. We'll never give in, and we'll never associate with those bastards. I don't believe this country will become theirs."

I didn't know who those bastards were!

Nor did I know why he was so angry.

I just felt amazed that a governor would lose his temper and swear like that!

I took the card back.

That was the only time he turned to me for help, but he cancelled it midway! From then until the day he died, I never had a chance to do something for him in return.

I felt miserable in my heart.

25

LAI CHUANDONG

THE ASSEMBLY LINE WORKER AT QINGHE AUTOMOBILE FACTORY

You want to know about the incident when I stopped the car? Yes, I did stop the car of Governor Ouyang Wantong. You haven't come to find someone to blame, have you? No? Good. If you have, I'm ready to argue it with you. I'm not fucking afraid of you guys. I'm a damned ordinary worker. Are you going to kill me just because I stopped the car of the governor once? Do you know why I did it? Because my son couldn't get into any middle school in the provincial capital! I've been living here for six years, working at an automobile manufacturing plant for four years, but you still call me a migrant worker who only has a temporary residence permit, and whose children are still not accepted by your schools here. We farmers have always been looked down upon by you. We are at the bottom of the social ladder you've established. Where's the justice? Going back to ten generations, how many of you damned people lived in the city? Aren't you all farmers? Just because you moved to the cities a few generations earlier, you despise us like this? Stop acting like assholes!"

Of course, I wrote letters of complaint, but no one knew where those letters went. There was no response at all. I tried appealing, and I visited the Bureau of Letters and Calls, but there are police and government people from each city guarding there, and after they found out where you came from, they would drag you into a car and take you back, claiming that you're doing harm to social stability. They never listen to your complaints. Did I have another choice? No! I had to stop the governor's car. Otherwise, should I have done nothing but accept the fact that my son had no school to go to?

My son finished elementary education in a school that was established and funded by us migrant workers. We had thought things would change when our kids needed to go to middle school. We never expected it would remain the same. Our country expressively stipulates that all children have the right to nine years of compulsory education, so why can't our children go to study in a middle school? Is it fair? Ask a favour of someone? How do you know I didn't? Dozens of us went to various places and people for help, from the Municipal Education Committee, to the District Education Committee, to leaders of the community, to principals of middle schools. None of them were any fucking help at all. Those people were horribly arrogant, explaining all kinds of rules to us. They all wanted us to understand one thing – migrant workers have no right to study in the city! Send money? Of course I thought of that! I wrapped 20,000 yuan in a piece of newspaper. Do you know what 20,000 yuan meant to me? It meant my four months' hard work was for nothing. It meant my family had to say goodbye to fruits and vegetables that year, eating pickles only!

One day, I took the money to the middle school that was closest to my rented place. I went into the office of the vice president who was in charge of admissions, and I told him about my work and my child. I begged him to accept my kid. As I told him this, I placed the money beside his hand, but he pushed it back to me. I had thought he was just being polite, so according to the custom in my farming community, I forcibly opened the door of the cabinet in his writing desk, with the intention to place the money inside. To my great surprise, the moment I pulled the door open, I found the cabinet was filled with cash – stacks and bundles of it! I came to understand my 20,000 yuan was nothing in his eyes.

That vice president was very angry when he saw me open the cabinet door without his permission. He yelled at me: "What do you think you're doing?"

I knew I had intruded upon his most secret place. I closed the door at once and said: "Sorry! I'm so sorry!"

After I left his office, I knew my son would never have the chance to study at this school! It happened to be at that time that I heard Governor Ouyang Wantong would be coming to inspect our plant. Damn it! I was thinking it might be an opportunity. I had to do everything in my power to give my son a chance to go to school. I tried every means and found out the governor's schedule.

On that day, I hung around the gate of our factory, waiting for the governor. When I saw three cars drive towards the gate, I guessed the governor would be in the middle car. Regardless of the consequences, I rushed to the car and climbed onto the hood, shouting: "Governor, you need to teach those people in the Education Bureau a lesson! They never think about helping us migrant workers!" The governor's driver was quick to react and hit the brakes immediately. The car stopped with a jerk, almost throwing me off the hood to the ground. Some policemen, perhaps thinking I wanted to do something bad to the governor, rushed up and held me down on the hood. I shouted: "I want to see the governor about my child's education. I will not hurt anyone! You can't arrest me!"

Probably my shout worked. I heard the door open, and Governor Wantong got out of the car. I had seen him on the TV and in the newspapers so I knew it was him. He came to the front of the car and waved at the policemen to let go of me. He then came to my side, held one of my arms and asked: "Tell me, what do you want to see me about?"

With tears in my eyes, I told him that my son had no school to go to. I knew he had a lot of things to deal with and time was precious for him, so I dare not go into detail. I just got straight to the point. After I finished, I asked: "Governor, please tell me whether children of us migrant workers can go to school or not?"

With his hands on my shoulder, he said: "Definitely, they can! I'll ask my people to handle this. It's my fault that you've been forced to report this to me in this way. I'm very sorry. What's your name? Lai Chuandong? Good, I'll remember it. You're working in this factory? Good! You can trust me. Go to work. I'll take care of the rest."

Never did I imagine that he could be so sincere and honest. I bowed to him and left.

Three days later, I received a notice from the District Education Bureau asking me to take my son to a middle school and fill all the admission forms. On the fifth day, the provincial newspaper published an article announcing all the children of migrant workers in the province could attend nearby elementary and middle schools in the cities where their parents work.

I was so happy! Some of my fellow migrant workers at the factory tossed me into the air when they heard the news. They were happy too.

I achieved my goal, but the leaders of our factory and the local police still lecture me from time to time. They say I'm a daring and bold guy and they're worried I'll get them into trouble sooner or later. That's why I thought you're here today to find fault with me...

After the incident, I questioned why I needed to resort to that method to find the governor for such a small thing. Why can't it be written into the law that all children must have access to a school? If there was a law, it would be illegal to deprive children of their right to go to school. Then we could go to court and sue anyone who dares to do that. Wouldn't that be simple?

26

QIN CHENGKANG

THE FORMER DEPUTY SECRETARY OF THE QINGHE PROVINCIAL PARTY COMMITTEE

My secretary told me you've been pestering him all the time and you even went to the General Office of the Provincial Party Committee to repeatedly request a meeting with me. Why won't you take no for an answer? Why do you behave so unreasonably? Is it because you're a writer? Because you want to write a biography for Ouyang Wantong? I've met a lot of writers. Who do you think you are! How many people actually read your books and articles? You think too much of yourself! I've never read any of that stuff. Novels, essays, poems – it's all a load of nonsense. Do I need to read all that to be able to govern this province? Life goes on without writers! Also, don't writers come under the Provincial Federation of Literature and Art? Let me tell you, the Qinghe branch of that organisation is under my governance. If you were in Qinghe, I dare say if I asked you to go eastward, you would dare not go westward. Do you believe me? Well, you're right to believe me. Tell me, what kind of good words about Ouyang Wantong do you want to hear from me? You don't want that? Well, what do you want from me then?

I can tell you clearly that I never had a good opinion of Ouyang Wantong. Yes, it's not very kind of me to say that since he's already dead, but I don't want to hide my views anymore. What's more, he never treated me kindly when he was alive! Now that we're getting into talking about this, I would like to let you know how he treated me in those years. It will be a way for me to let my anger out.

At that time, we were young and both worked in the Organisation Department of the Tianquan Municipal Committee. He was the section chief, and I was the deputy section chief. Later, a beautiful girl came to work in our department. She happened to be in the same office as me, so we naturally had more contact and usually talked with each other more casually. The girl's boyfriend, therefore, became jealous. He rushed into the office, swore at me and hit me too. Honestly speaking, as the section chief, he should have handled this and backed me up, but he didn't. He asked me to pay attention to unfavourable influence and separated the girl and me, making us work independently, which made people in the department feel there was indeed something between me and her. Didn't he set me up? He got promoted later. Wouldn't it have been common sense for the vacant position of the section chief to be given to me? I had worked with him for the previous few years as deputy section chief, and even if I didn't have any prominent achievements, I still made some contributions. But when he was asked for his opinion, he recommended another person instead of me! Don't you think he lacked the human touch?

When he became the deputy mayor of Tianquan city, I was the secretary of the County Party Committee. Once, he came to inspect the county where I worked. You know what, he didn't pay any attention to what we had achieved, but instead found fault with us. I tried my best to attract some foreign capital to build a paper mill, but he firmly opposed it, claiming the water discharged from the factory would pollute the land. As a result, the entrepreneur who was going to invest a large amount was scared away!

When he became the mayor of Tianquan, I was the secretary-general of the Municipal Party Committee. Once, the nephew of the secretary of the Provincial Party Committee came to Tianquan with his wife, looking for a piece of land to do real estate development. I arranged for the secretary of the Municipal Party Committee and Ouyang Wantong to have dinner with the young couple. You know what, he was unhappy, pulling a long face all the time and refusing to give any response to the young couple from the beginning to the end, which made me very embarrassed. After the meal, I asked him why he behaved so impolitely, and he said those people were not real developers and their purpose was just to sell approvals! He made me so mad that I just wanted to give him a good bawling out! Hadn't I done that for the future development of Tianquan? Who did he think he was!

After his wife went to jail, he behaved himself for a while. But after he came back, especially after he began to work in the provincial capital, he started to find fault with entrepreneurs. This entrepreneur was polluting the water or that entrepreneur was paying bribes or another one was associated with a triad, as if there were no good people in the business world. How could he behave like this? How could the region become rich under his governance if he refused to develop enterprises? I think he was somewhat bigoted, with some kind of personality disorder!

Who are you asking about? Jian Qianyan? I'm not familiar with him. So many businessmen in our province! It's not possible for me to know all of them.

After dealing with entrepreneurs, he targeted civil servants, claiming that this bureau director was corrupt or that department director-general received bribes or a mayor was dishonest. He approved documents that meant so-and-so would be interrogated. He issued an order to investigate this person, deprived that person of office and transferred so-and-so to another position. In short, there were no good people in Hongdong county. Anyone who dared to accept a box of mooncakes would receive an administrative punishment. Anyone who dared to hold a banquet with public funds would face the circulation of a notice of criticism. Anyone who dared to use a government car would probably be dismissed from his post! One after another, officials were overturned. One after another, officials were scared to death. Everyone in officialdom felt insecure and spent their days in terror like a swarm of ants on a hot oven. Some suffered from depression and were unable to sleep at night. Some were so scared that they ran to other provinces or even foreign countries, out of contact forever. Some ended up hanging themselves, jumping off high buildings or taking poison.

What a miserable condition we officials were in! Being an official used to mean a comfortable life, but now it has become a drudgery that demands sacrifice without any reward! If things go on like this, who would want to be an official? In a society, if no one wants to be an official, who is going to govern it? Wouldn't it be in chaos? An anarchic society!

This has ruined the civil service in our province!

This has created anarchy!

It's playing to the gallery!

If, as a governor, you've made your subordinates afraid and unwilling to do things, can we say you have the skills to be a senior official? In the end, Ouyang Wantong wanted to be famous for being an honest and upright official who spared no efforts on anti-corruption. He wanted to create an impression that the period when he was in power was a new era for Qinghe, the Administration of Wantong, a flourishing age in Qinghe history, his name in history as a hero. It's a pity that he was not an emperor, but merely a governor. No matter how much he messed about or how fancy his efforts appeared, not a single history book would record his deeds. The only result was that officials complained and no one would say a good word about him! Whose words carry the most weight anyway? Officials at all levels! When officials can't say a good word about you or they even gnash their teeth out of hatred, where can you go then? The power of word of mouth is huge! I dare say after his death he'll be a pile of dog shit in the history of Qinghe within a few years! Don't you believe it? Let's wait and see.

A pile of dog shit!

Do I have some personal grudge against him? Well, if I say no, that means no. We just have different approaches to governance. He wanted to make everyone feel insecure while I prefer harmony. He wanted a simple and austere life while I prefer to share the benefits. He enjoyed chaos while I prefer peace and serenity. If I say yes, it means yes. My son-in-law, a very promising young man who had already been promoted and worked as the deputy director of the Provincial Bureau of Finance, was arrested and put into prison under the charge of accepting bribes and procuring women because of Ouyang Wantong! My poor little granddaughter, who is only seven years old, couldn't see her father and cried all day long for him. I heard afterwards that my son-in-law had been accused of procuring women in his uncle's apartment! That was very unreasonable! No man would go to his uncle's apartment to have sex with a prostitute. Wouldn't that be asking for trouble? Obviously, Ouyang Wantong framed him!

My daughter was also a director in the provincial government. She spent her days in tears. But Ouyang Wantong still wasn't satisfied. He said they found a large cardboard box in my daughter's storage room. Inside the box was 800,000 in cash. They concluded that my daughter accepted bribes too. My daughter explained to them repeatedly that when the box had been sent to her, she was told it was iron yam, so she accepted it. But after that, she was so busy that she forgot to open the box to check. Ouyang Wantong didn't listen to her explanation and personally approved the interrogation of my daughter before he retired. Just for a box of cash under the camouflage of iron yam! My daughter didn't use that money, and she wasn't corrupt! He was so ruthless!

Those who like to ruin people won't end up in a good place. This is a truth that has been repeatedly proved by history. Things didn't end well for him, did they? Nowadays, men usually live to eighty while he only lived to sixty-six. God has seen him do evil things in this world, so He took him away in advance! We can't allow people like him to live longer! The Lord has eyes!

It serves him right!

You want to hear me say something good about him? Something about his great deeds, some hymns and eulogies? I can tell you directly – there is nothing! That's all I can tell you. Unsatisfied, disappointed and angry you must be, but I have no choice. You asked for it!

Secretary Zhong, see the guest out!

27

CHANG XIAOWEN

THE WIFE (SECOND INTERVIEW)

I HEARD you've interviewed a lot of people and collected a lot of materials. Thank you for your hard work. If you think you're ready to write the biography, just do it. I wonder what you want to see me about today. Feel free to tell me directly. You want to know whether I have something else to say? Well, there's nothing. I've told you everything I could say to you last time. About emotion? What do you mean? About what emotion? You should not have asked this. You want to know? Should I tell you simply because you want to know? All right, all right, you don't need to do this. Please take the deposit back. I don't want you to quit. I believe you can write a good biography for him. We don't want to look for another person to do it. If you insist on finding out the truth about the relationship between Ouyang Wantong and me, I can tell you. What's the point of hiding it now?

Allow me to be straightforward. It was not because of love that I married Ouyang Wantong. I've never loved him. Even today, it's not because of love that I paid you to write a biography for him. It's just out of sympathy. You're not surprised to hear that, are you? Well, perhaps you've worked it out after so many interviews. Or perhaps someone has told you something?

In the beginning, it was likely that he truly loved me and wanted to marry me. You know, I was young and sort of pretty, and I didn't want to be an official, which met his requirements for a wife. So, he revealed his love for me and expressed his hope to marry me. For me, the reason I accepted his love and his proposal was that I had made one important thing clear in my life – in China, the only criteria to evaluate a man was the seniority of his official position. This comes from the long-term influence of the Chinese official culture. In China, officials are in charge of the use and distribution of all of the resources of life, so it was in fact very difficult or even impossible for a woman to find a man who doesn't want to be an official. If I should remarry and happen to find a man who still hopes to be an official, I would have to go through everything, worrying about his promotion and suchlike. It would therefore be much better for me to marry a senior official than to be stressed about promotions. What's more, I would stand on top of the food chain and have nothing to worry about as far as the distribution of the resources of life were concerned.

That's why I agreed to marry Ouyang Wantong even though I didn't love him. Since you want to know the truth, I'm just giving it to you straight.

The truth always hurts.

Did he know this? Well, he didn't. I never let him feel that I didn't love him. I gave him everything he wanted from a wife.

What's more, for a woman like me who had experienced the failure of marriage, it's a luxury to talk about love. I've seen the true nature of men, and it's very difficult for me to have any feelings for them after gaining that insight. And in China, how many marriages aren't based on calculation and interests but on love?

After I married him, I found it was the best choice I had ever made. Being a wife of an official had so many advantages.

First, you didn't need to worry about your work. When things went wrong, it would have nothing to do with you, while you would always have a share when good things happened, like an increase in wages, distribution of bonuses and goods, holidays, visiting abroad, excellent worker awards, promotions and so on. The leaders in your workplace would take care of everything. They were afraid of annoying you and were willing to make friends with you – leaders in all working units.

Second, you didn't need to worry about domestic chores. The secretary would take care of anything you ate, drank and used. You had a nanny to cook for you. You had a driver to take you shopping. And you had a servant to clean the house for you. You only had to think about buying clothes, finding a match for jewellery and going to the beauty salon. To sum up, all you needed to do was enjoy your life.

Third, your family would receive the best care. The local officials would spare no efforts to help you, ranging from housing of your parents, job transfers and promotions for your siblings, to education and employment for your nephews and nieces. Sometimes they would do it for you even if you didn't ask for it and you were usually the last one to know it after someone had helped you. At that time, all you needed to do was say a few words of thanks to their faces.

I didn't realise until I got married that Wantong's ex-wife was stupid enough to want to be an official herself. She could have everything without being an official. Why did she trouble herself to become one? What was the point of worrying about things as an official and getting herself into trouble? Was it not stupid for her to do that?

I never wanted to be an official, and I was very satisfied with my status as a wife and my situation. I never asked for any work transfers – any adjustments were made by the authorities. Wantong didn't intervene either! The authorities said everything was done according to convention.

Sure, being a wife of an official has some inconveniences too. Too many people's eyes are on you, and they pay attention to everything you do. You can never go to some places, like pedicure shops or massage parlours. You can never speak playfully with men or dine with them, let alone flirt with them.

Yes, I did have some regrets in my life after I married him. There was a big age difference, and sometimes it was difficult for us to agree on things, such as what was the best style and colour of clothes, what kind of handbags and jewellery suited me better, what kind of hairstyles and make-up were fit for me, what food was good for our bodies and at what time was it proper for us to go to sleep. We found it hard to agree. The good thing was that these issues were not a big deal, and there was no need to force each other to reach an agreement. Then there was our sex life. Like most May-December marriages, it was impossible for us to have harmonious sex. I had been prepared for this from the very beginning. You know, I've never had a strong sexual desire. What's more, things couldn't be perfect, could they? You can't make an omelette without breaking eggs.

Living together with Wantong in those years, the aura of power around him disappeared naturally in my eyes. In front of me, he was just a man holding power. Without becoming distant, I found it was so difficult for a senior official to stay out of trouble.

The first pressure you're going to face is from your relatives, friends and classmates, who all want to get something from you, whether it be power or benefits. In their eyes, you're a power wholesaler and a golden goose. If you don't give them what they want, they'll get annoyed and might even curse you behind your back. You're a piece of braised pork, and all your relatives, friends and classmates want to have a share. On one occasion, one of his cousins named Ouyang Wansheng came to visit him and demanded that Wantong assign his son, who had just graduated from college, to work in the Provincial Personnel Department. Wantong told him that those who wanted to be civil servants must take an exam, without which no one had a chance to join the provincial government. But his cousin said: "Is there anyone who doesn't know how much power a governor has in his hand? You just need to say one word to appoint a director or an official at prefectural level, so wouldn't it be a piece of cake for you to get your nephew a job in the Provincial Personnel Department? It just depends on whether you want to help me or not for my sake, your old brother." Wantong had no choice but to explain again and again the reasons why he couldn't do this for him. This cousin, however, was mad and roared at him: "Do you still remember the time when you went swimming with me at the age of eight? You were seized with cramp and almost drowning. It was me who risked my own life to dive to the bottom of the river and pull you out. I was only eleven years old at that time. Where's your conscience, talking like a bureaucrat in front of your saviour? That's all. You're the great governor, and I'm one of the ordinary people. Since you look down upon us, I won't ask a damned favour of you. From now on, we're strangers!" With those words, he shoved the door open and left. I ran towards him, trying to pull him back, but failed. After that cousin left, Wantong sat on the sofa with his head in his hands for more than an hour, feeling so miserable that he didn't want to eat anything for supper.

The second pressure comes from your leaders whose requests you have to satisfy. Some of them believe that since they've voted for you and put you in your position, you should do something for them. If you fail to satisfy them, their faces will darken, and they begin to talk about you behind your back, wanting to drive you away from your position. There was a leader in Beijing who called Wantong from time to time, asking him to promote so-and-so. Who is that leader? Well, I'd better keep it a secret. When he recommended the first person, Wantong asked the Organisation Department to investigate, and it turned out this man was okay. Wantong did it for him that time. Before long, he called again to recommend another person. The Organisation Department reported that this man was doing poorly in his work. Wantong felt he couldn't do this, so gave the excuse that the Organisation Department needed more time to do the assessment on that person and declined that leader for the time being. After some time, the leader called again and urged him to promote another person. Wantong felt it improper and looked for all kinds of excuses to postpone doing it. The leader in Beijing probably had received gifts or money from that person, and he urged Wantong to do it quickly. It was impossible for Wantong to avoid talking about this issue anymore. He told the leader that he couldn't make the final decision and it had to be referred to the Party Committee. The leader was annoyed and scolded Wantong loudly over the phone, "Do I need you to tell me the procedure of promoting an official? Are you trying to talk to me like a bureaucrat? Damn it! I won't call you anymore!" After he had finished lecturing Wantong, he smashed the phone down! Standing nearby, I heard it very clearly. On that day, Wantong was so angry that he sat beside the phone motionless, his face red with anger. He later went to work without eating.

The third pressure comes from officials at the same level who want to exchange benefits. They think mutual help is natural since everyone has struggled to get where they are. It won't cost you anything to help me, and you can ask me for a favour in the future. If you decline, they'll definitely pay you back at a certain time and place, finding fault with you and trying their best to edge you out. A leader of a neighbouring province called him one day and said his younger brother, who ran an auto parts manufacturing company, wanted to become a supplier for an auto manufacturer in Qinghe province. He wanted Wantong to act as a go-between. Wantong told him he never dealt with things like the purchase of auto parts, and he wouldn't be able to help. Hearing that, the leader changed his tone immediately and sneered: "Great! Governor Wantong doesn't intervene in the business world! We should all learn from this!" After he finished, he slammed down the receiver. Later, the issue of the distribution of Jinfeng river resources were put on the agenda. Qinghe province went to negotiate with the province at the river's upper reaches, but the leader of that province created all sorts of obstacles, and they couldn't come to an agreement. Wantong called him personally but that leader asked his secretary to turn him down. Wantong exploded with rage, pacing around in the room and smashing three cups.

The fourth pressure comes from the bosses who have intimate contact with you. You have to be cautious. Some of them just want to use your power to help them make money, while you happen to possess the resources to make money on behalf of common people. So they find every means to get close to you and establish an intimate relationship. They send you gifts to make you feel comfortable, then they ask for a reward, something that will help them make money. If you reach out your hand and accept the gifts and money, you have to meet their demands or else they'll destroy you. Wantong's ex-wife is an example. If you decline their gifts and refuse to cooperate, some of them will slander you and try every means to get you out of your post.

The fifth pressure comes from your subordinates who are obsessed with the idea of becoming an official. These people are addicted. Their sole purpose of approaching you is to get an official post. To achieve their goals, they'll send you gifts on any occasion they can find – festivals, holidays, birthdays of your family members or celebration days. They will send you anything – money, gifts or even women. After you give them the official posts they want, they'll be seized with rapture first, but then they'll ask for more. If you don't give them what they want, they'll change their attitude towards you. They'll curse you, slander you and discredit your name. They can't wait to send you into hell!

Lastly, you have to be careful about those subversives in your team who like to calculate and scheme behind people's backs. It's impossible for everyone in your team to agree with you on the allocation of people and money and projects. It's impossible to make everyone in your team work together with one heart on supervision, auditing and punishment. Different professional opinions often turn into a battle or a game. Wantong never told me about this, but I could feel it from his look and mood. Whenever he turned on the stereo and played *A Hundred Birds Worshipping the Phoenix* while sitting on the sofa and drinking some tea, I knew he was not in conflict with others on that day. If he came back and sat on the sofa staring blankly, absent-mindedly listening to *A Hundred Birds Worshipping the Phoenix* after the nanny had put the music on, I knew he must have been involved in some dispute. Once, I saw him secretly wiping his tears while listening to the music. I asked him what had happened, but he didn't say anything. I asked his secretary who just responded with one word: "Betrayal!" Betray what? Who's been betrayed? Nobody told me the answer, and I felt it improper to go on seeking the truth.

What do you think? How could a man live a happy life if he lived in such an environment?

Gradually, I found that my daughter and I were living very well but he wasn't. His life was miserable.

I began to feel uneasy in my heart. I once advised him that since the general atmosphere and the common practice in officialdom had always been like this, he might as well just go with the flow. Everybody knew that when the water was too clear, there would be no fish. He sighed and said: "I could do that, but I wouldn't have a clear conscience. What's more, if I go with the flow, I'll end up the same as my ex-wife."

I was shocked by his words. I didn't want something to happen to him! He was the backbone of the family. Without him, would I have to marry again?

I therefore wanted to use my own strength to support him.

The first support I gave to him was to convert some small gifts I had secretly accepted from others into cash and pay back the people who had given the gifts. I had accepted some clothes, jewellery and make-up in the past and it was impossible to send them back, so I refunded those people according to the market price and asked them to write receipts.

The second support was that I would never accept any new gifts. It wasn't because I was noble or that I didn't want to accept them, but because I was afraid to do so. I knew as long as I should accept gifts, sooner or later others would find an excuse to beat him down one day.

The third support I gave to him was that I would never secretly seek profits for my parents' family via his secretary or anybody else – either in the form of official positions or projects. It was not because my family members didn't need this, but because if I should do it, Wantong would become embroiled sooner or later.

The fourth support was I would keep a low profile. I would never attend events and banquets as his wife. I would never make casual remarks about things outside my job, and I would never wear designer clothes or luxury accessories. It was not because I didn't want to be in the spotlight and make others jealous, but because I was afraid that my ostentation would get him into trouble.

I didn't love him, but I had sympathy for him, and I wanted to protect him.

I couldn't live without him, and I didn't want my life broken again. I couldn't withstand the violent storms and waves of life anymore.

Can you understand this?

You still have one more question? Go ahead. You can ask ten questions if you want. What? Do I know a man surnamed Ruan? How come you have so many questions? Which Ruan? Ruan Ruo? Where did you hear about him? You should collect more materials about Ouyang Wantong and find more good things to say about him. You shouldn't be interested in anyone else. All right, all right, please take the deposit back. I don't want you to quit. I'm just a bit annoyed. You know, I never thought you would ask me this question. Well, since you've raised it, I'll tell you without any reservation.

Sure, I know Ruan Ruo because he was my biological father. My surname should be Ruan instead of Chang, which is actually the surname of my foster father. After my parents committed suicide, a couple of my father's classmates who lived in another county adopted me. In order to let me grow psychologically healthy, my foster parents didn't tell me the truth, and I was kept in the dark.

It wasn't until I was graduating from college that my foster parents told me who I really was and took me to visit my parents' graves.

I had no knowledge of the story between Ouyang Wantong and my family before I married him, and he had no idea I was the daughter of Ruan Ruo. When did I discover this? Well, it was after we had been married for a long time and I brought my mother – my foster mother – to live with us.

My foster mother had been confined to bed for a long time following a stroke. She refused to move to the provincial capital to live with me for fear that she would become a burden on me. After my foster father passed away, I was determined to move her to my place to repay her for her love and care.

I remember that day clearly. It was at lunchtime when I took my foster mother to the provincial capital. Wantong had cancelled an appointment so that he could meet my mother and have lunch with her. Before that day, they had never seen each other. I had never told my foster mother the name of my new husband, and she had never asked me either. I just told her I married a man who had a senior official position. Everything went all right when my foster mother met Wantong, but after I told her his name, she looked quite strange, which of course aroused my curiosity. After Wantong left to go to work, I kept asking her what happened. She eventually told me that the criminal who had violated my biological mother was protected by Ouyang Wantong, who worked as the county mayor at that time.

I was totally stunned by the truth. What a cruel arrangement fate had made for us.

I should hate him.

But my life was already entwined with his.

What should I do?

My emotions told me he deserved to pay for it and I should take revenge on him. Reason told me it was water under the bridge, a mistake he made when he applied his power. He was not the criminal!

Should I have left him for the honour of my deceased parents?

But then the peaceful life would disappear completely for my daughter and me.

Before I made my decision, I tried to hide my pain in front of Wantong, who quickly realised there was something wrong with me. He asked me whether I was sick, and I had to pretend that I was not feeling well. My foster mother understood my dilemma and comforted me. She said: "He later restored and upheld justice and punished the criminal. What's more, it has been so many years since it happened..."

I eventually made my final decision – I would leave him. Short-term pain is better than a lifetime of regrets. If I continued to live with him, my parents' suicide would eat away at me, and my life would just get harder.

On the night I decided to leave him, I wanted to have a long talk with him. I questioned him directly at the very beginning of our conversation: "Since you became an official, have you ever done anything that has made you feel the tug of your conscience?"

He froze for a second, lowered his head to think for a while and said: "As an official, I have to make decisions every day, and more decisions mean more chances to make mistakes – it's inevitable. Naturally, there are a lot of things I feel sorry for. On reflection, there are two things in particular that have disturbed me. The first one is Qiangwei's imprisonment. No matter how many mistakes she has made, the root of her tragedy is me. I never really helped her step on the brake, and this eventually led to her destruction. The other one happened when I worked as a county mayor. My selfishness to protect a cadre I had appointed led to the suicide of a couple. I still remember the husband's name – Ruan Ruo. I feel I owe them, and I've been looking for their daughter all the time. I want to do something for the kid as a compensation for my sin, but I haven't found her yet. Compared with other professions, an official is more likely to have some regrets that he cannot make up for in his life. I've been feeling guilty about Ruan Ruo's daughter all these years."

It was his last line that moved me. It shook my decision to leave him and gradually melted the ice between us.

He never discovered the truth. I didn't want to give him a mental shock. You know, it was at that time I began to realise that he lived a hard life the same as I did.

Well, I have nothing to withhold from you now. What else do you want to know?

PERSONAL SAFE DEPOSIT ITEMS OF OUYANG WANTONG

The following three items are stored in the personal safe of Ouyang Wantong, vault number 03175 at Qinghe Bank of Communications.

Item one: a painting. It has turned yellow with age. In addition to trees and clouds, a goose is flying in the sky. At the lower left side of the painting is a signature: Ouyang Wantong.

Item two: some sheet music. It's for a solo suona performance of *A Hundred Birds Worshipping the Phoenix*. The paper is yellow and crisp after being folded many times. On the upper right corner of the sheet are some words written in pen: "When you play the suona, show the joy of the hundred birds as they worship the phoenix." The words have blurred.

Item three: a letter. The content is as follows:

Governor Ouyang Wantong,

We actually have many ways to express what we want to tell you. We have chosen to write you a letter so you can digest the following points at your convenience. Of course, a letter is also more dignified. Acting on instructions, I hereby tell you with the utmost seriousness: you can't stop us!

Nowadays, power can be bought and sold. You may use the power that the government gives you to restrict us, while we can use the power we have bought to restrict you as well. Perhaps you have already realised that our power sometimes overwhelms yours. We must solemnly remind you that you shouldn't bite off more than you can chew.

You could have had a better life or moved forward in your political career and reached a glorious position, but you have voluntarily chosen another path, wanting to leave your name in history. Have you taken the trouble to count how many names of provincial officials have been left in the thick book of Chinese history? What's more, isn't history written by human beings? If so, money can change history. Because my colleagues and I are younger than you, we can assure you that someone will write a biography for you after you die; a biography you might not be very satisfied with. No one can be prevented from writing a biography for you.

Enjoy your retired life then! We just want you to know that we can do anything we want by ourselves. And we need to explain one more thing to you: though we do want to see you step down from your position, we are not the only ones.

This province is not yours.

It is very likely to be ours. It belongs to all of the people in the province in name only.

You should live a little longer so you can watch the show we have co-directed.

Since you know who I am, there is no need for me to write my signature here.

QINGHE EVENING NEWS

REPORT ON OUYANG WANTONG'S FAREWELL CEREMONY

From our reporters – At 9.00am on the morning of 17 February 2015, the farewell ceremony of Ouyang Wantong, the former governor of Qinghe province, was held at the Yinshan Funeral Parlour in Chengzhou.

The leaders of the provincial government, the Provincial Party Committee, the Provincial People's Congress and the Provincial CPPCC and relatives of Ouyang Wantong went to the funeral parlour to bid farewell to him. Tens of thousands of people spontaneously gathered outside the funeral parlour to pay their last respects.

According to the wishes of the deceased, instead of funeral hymns, the suona solo *A Hundred Birds Worshipping the Phoenix* was played. The deceased enjoyed this piece during his lifetime, and the cheerful suona music filled the farewell hall for a long time.

When the music ended for the last time, Chang Xiaowen, the deceased's widow, threw herself at the body of Ouyang Wantong and burst out crying.

Outside the funeral parlour, there was a group of men and women wearing sunglasses and masks. Some of them were beating drums, and some of them were carrying a huge red banner which read: "Warmly send the cruel Ouyang Wantong to hell!"

The police lined up in front of the gate of the funeral parlour to prevent them from rushing inside.

Completed on 9 January 2015

ABOUT THE AUTHOR

Born in Dengzhou, north-central China in 1952, Zhou Daxin is a novelist, short-story writer and essayist whose realist fiction mostly focuses on ordinary people in his home province of Henan. He made his literary debut in 1979 and has published nine novels, thirty-three novellas and more than seventy short stories, as well as essays and plays. In 2016, People's Literature Publishing House published *Selected Works by Zhou Daxin*, a twenty-volume collection of novels, novellas, short stories, essays and a screenplay. Zhou has received numerous awards, including the National Outstanding Short Story Award, the Feng Mu Literature Prize, the People's Literature Award, the Mao Dun Literature Prize, and the Lao She Prose Essay Award. His works have been translated into a dozen languages including English, French, German, Japanese, Arabic, Spanish and Greek. He currently resides in Beijing.

CPSIA information can be obtained
at www.ICGtesting.com
Printed in the USA
BVHW072212030919
557523BV00001B/75/P